THE BEST **HORROR**
OF THE YEAR VOLUME SIXTEEN

Also Edited by Ellen Datlow

THE BEST **HORROR** OF THE YEAR

VOLUME SIXTEEN

EDITED BY **ELLEN DATLOW**

NIGHT SHADE BOOKS

NEW YORK

The Best Horror of the Year Volume Sixteen © 2024 by Ellen Datlow
The Best Horror of the Year Volume Sixteen © 2024 by Night Shade Books,
an imprint of Skyhorse Publishing, Inc.

Night Shade books may be purchased in bulk at special discounts for sales
promotion, corporate gifts, fund-raising, or educational purposes. Special
editions can also be created to specifications. For details, contact the Special
Sales Department, Night Shade Books, 307 West 36th Street, 11th Floor,
New York, NY 10018 or info@skyhorsepublishing.com.

Night Shade Books™ is a trademark of Skyhorse Publishing, Inc.®,
a Delaware corporation.

Visit our website at www.nightshadebooks.com.

10 9 8 7 6 5 4 3 2 1

Library of Congress Cataloging-in-Publication Data is available on file.

Cover illustration by Asya Yordanova
Cover design by David Ter-Avanesyan

Print ISBN: 978-1-949102-73-4

Printed in the United States of America

ACKNOWLEDGMENTS

Stefan Dziemianowicz for his recommendations and
for providing printouts.

Thanks to the Nightfire blog for keeping me informed as to the horror
novels published in 2023.

A big thanks to Tegan Moore and Theresa DeLucci for helping me
in my reading.

And a special thank you to my patient and supportive in-house editor,
Jason Katzman.

TABLE OF CONTENTS

SUMMATION 2023

Here are 2023's numbers: There are nineteen stories total in this volume and the story lengths range from 2,400 words to 10,600 words. There are seven stories by women and twelve stories by men. Ten stories are by contributors living in the United States, two in Scotland, one in Wales, and six in Great Britain. Five of the contributors have never before been published in any volume of my *Best Horror of the Year* series.

Awards

The Horror Writers Association announced the 2022 Bram Stoker Awards® winners at a banquet in The Sheraton Pittsburgh Hotel at Station Square, Saturday, June 17, 2023.

The 2022 Bram Stoker Awards® went to:

Superior Achievement in a Novel: Gabino Iglesias, *The Devil Takes You Home* (Mulholland Press); Superior Achievement in a First Novel: Christi Nogle: *Beulah* (Cemetery Gates Media); Superior Achievement in a Young Adult Novel: Robert P. Ottone, *The Triangle* (Raven Tale Publishing); Superior Achievement in a Middle Grade Novel: Daniel Kraus, *They Stole Our Hearts* (Henry Holt, and Company); Superior Achievement in a Graphic Novel: James Aquilone, editor, *Kolchak: The Night Stalker:* Fiftieth Anniversary (Moonstone Books); Superior Achievement in Long

Fiction: Alma Katsu, *The Wehrwolf* (Amazon Original Stories); Superior Achievement in Short Fiction: Mercedes M. Yardley, "Fracture" (*Mother: Tales of Love and Terror*) (Weird Little Worlds); Superior Achievement in a Fiction Collection: Cassandra Khaw, *Breakable Things* (Undertow Publications); Superior Achievement in a Screenplay (tie): Scott Derrickson and C. Robert Cargill, *The Black Phone* (Blumhouse Productions, Crooked Highway, Universal Pictures) and the Duffer Brothers, *Stranger Things: Episode 04.01* "Chapter One: The Hellfire Club" (21 Laps Entertainment, Monkey Massacre, Netflix, Upside Down Pictures); Superior Achievement in an Anthology: Ellen Datlow, *Screams From the Dark: 29 Tales of Monsters and the Monstrous* (Tor Nightfire); Superior Achievement in Non-Fiction: Tim Waggoner, *Writing in the Dark: The Workbook* (Guide Dog Books); Superior Achievement in Short Non-Fiction: Lee Murray, *I Don't Read Horror (& Other Weird Tales)* (Interstellar Flight Magazine) (Interstellar Flight Press; Superior Achievement in a Poetry Collection: Cynthia Pelayo, *Crime Scene* (Raw Dog Screaming Press).

HWA Lifetime Achievement Awards were given to Elizabeth Massie, Nuzo Onoh, and John Saul.

The Specialty Press Award was given to Undertow Publications.

The Richard H. Laymon President's Award was given to Meghan Arcuri.

The Silver Hammer Award for service was given to Karen Lansdale.

The Mentor of the Year Award was given to Dave Jeffery.

The Eighth Annual FINAL FRAME Horror Short Competition winners are:

Grand Prize: Michael Rich for *The Queue*

Best Writing in a Short Film: Michael Rich for *The Queue*

1st Runner-Up to Grand Prize: Øyvind Willumsen for *The Weaver*

Second Runner-Up to Grand Prize: Rosalee Yagihara for *Gnaw*

The 2023 Shirley Jackson Awards were presented July 15, in the Boston Marriott Quincy, at Readercon. The winners of the 2022 Shirley Jackson Awards are:

Novel-tie: *The Devil Takes You Home* by Gabino Iglesias (Mulholland Books) and *Where I End* by Sophie White (Tramp Press); Novella: *The Bone Lantern* by Angela Slatter (PS Publishing); Novelette: *What the Dead Know* by Nghi Vo (Amazon Original Stories); Short Fiction: "Pre-Simulation

Consultation XF007867" by Kim Fu (*Lesser Known Monsters of the 21st Century*); Single Author Collection: *We Are Here to Hurt Each Other* by Paula D. Ashe (Nictitating Books); Edited Anthology: *The Hideous Book of Hidden Horrors*, edited by Doug Murano (Bad Hand Books).

The 2022 World Fantasy Awards were given out at the 49th World Fantasy Convention banquet at the Sheraton Crown Center, Kansas City, Missouri, October 26-29, 2023

The Life Achievement Awards, presented annually to individuals who have demonstrated outstanding service to the fantasy field, went to Peter Crowther and John Douglas.

The World Fantasy Awards winners are:

Best Novel: *Saint Death's Daughter*, C.S.E. Cooney (Solaris); Best Novella: *Pomegranates*, Priya Sharma (Absinthe); Best Short Fiction: "Incident at Bear Creek Lodge," Tananarive Due (*Other Terrors: An Inclusive Anthology*); Best Anthology: *Africa Risen: A New Era of Speculative Fiction*, Sheree Renée Thomas, Oghenechovwe Donald Ekpeki, Zelda Knight, eds. (Tordotcom); Best Collection: *All Nightmare Long*, Tim Lebbon (PS Publishing): Best Artist: Kinuko Y. Craft; Special Award—Professional: Matt Ottley, for *The Tree of Ecstasy and Unbearable Sadness* (Dirt Lane); Special Award—Non-Professional: Michael Kelly, for Undertow Publications

This year's judges were Dale Bailey, Kelly Robson, Ginny Smith, A.C. Wise, and Ian Whates.

NOTABLE NOVELS OF 2023

Don't Fear the Reaper by Stephen Graham Jones (S&S/Saga Press) brings his hero Jade Daniels back to Prufrock, Idaho, four years after the massacre that traumatized her and the entire town. She hopes to put the past behind her, but as she returns during the storm of the century, an infamous serial killer escapes nearby, restarting a cycle of vicious, grisly murders. An excellent middle book of what is becoming the Indian Lake trilogy.

Maeve Fly by CJ Leede (Nightfire) is a banger of a novel about a lovable psychopath (well, *I* love her)—harrowing/funny/gross/tragic. Maeve Fly has always known there's something different about herself. She lives and takes care of her grandmother, a famous aged and dying movie star—the only person in the world who seems to understand her. Maeve works at a brand name amusement park as a princess, a job she loves. Her best (and only) friend who works with her is aspiring actress Kate, who is on the cusp of her big break.

A Haunting on the Hill by Elizabeth Hand (Mulholland Books) is a terrific homage to Shirley Jackson's *The Haunting of Hill House*. An intriguing cast of characters is slowly seduced by a house—with a bad history—in upstate New York. A struggling playwright believes she's found the perfect spot to pull together *Witching Night*, the play she's been working on for several years. She persuades her girlfriend and two actors to accompany her. As one would guess, things go terribly wrong.

Camp Damascus by Chuck Tingle (Nightfire) is about a young woman who comes to realize that the memories of her recent past and her so-called (by the religious cult she and her family belong to) deviant desires have been totally wiped at a local camp conducting extreme conversion therapy. Riveting, terrifying, and moving.

In *Silver Nitrate* by Silvia Moreno-Garcia (Del Rey), a talented but under-appreciated sound editor in 1990s Mexico City is introduced to her best friend's neighbor, a cult horror director who claims that his final film—never quite finished—was imbued with magical qualities that could bestow great power on those in the know. A Nazi occultist tried to harness that power but failed, dying in the process. Now several of his followers want to get their hands on the film to bring him back. A nicely rendered dark fantasy with horror elements.

The Reformatory by Tananarive Due (Gallery Books/Saga Press) is a suspenseful, harrowing ghost story which attains much of its power from the true life, historically accurate horrors it depicts. In 1950 Jim Crow south, a young boy is sentenced to six months at the Gracetown School for Boys, dubbed the Reformatory. Rumor has it that dozens of boys were killed there over the years, in addition to the twenty-five who died in a fire thirty years earlier.

The Insatiable Volt Sisters by Rachel Eve Moulton (MCD/Farrar, Straus and Giroux) is an excellent novel about two half-sisters and the island on which they grew up, where there is a history of rumors about missing women. Separated as teenagers by their divorced parents, one left for the mainland, but she and her mother return when the father dies. What begins as a family drama evolves into a terrifying story of monsters.

Lone Women by Victor LaValle (One World) takes place in 1915 as a woman leaves her family's blood-soaked home in California for Montana with a few possessions, a steamer trunk, and a secret. The book takes a too-often neglected look at the women and people of color who homesteaded the American west. The story is absorbing, powerful, and horrifying, and one of the best horror novels of the year.

Whalefall by Daniel Kraus (Entertainment Books) is a remarkable achievement. A young man, estranged from his family and bitter about his troubled relationship with his father, is swallowed by a sperm whale. Although the premise sounds unbelievable, this tale of memory, reconciliation, and survival is pretty amazing. Is it horror? Only on the verge, with its blood and guts (whale and human), but it's a read you won't regret nor forget.

All Hallows by Christopher Golden (St. Martin's Press) opens with multiple domestic dramas unfolding in a suburban Massachusetts neighborhood on Halloween eve. As the townspeople ready themselves for a fun night of trick or treating, four unknown children roam and beg the neighborhood children to hide them from the Cunning Man. This is a good, slow burn of novel with its increasing suspense and terror.

What Kind of Mother by Clay McLeod Chapman (Quirk Books) is an intense story of parenthood and grief and the power of imagination. A single mother returns to her hometown and encounters an old flame drowning in grief from the death of his wife and disappearance of their child.

All the Sinners Bleed by S. A. Crosby (Flatiron Books) is a powerful crime novel about the repercussions of the murder of a beloved schoolteacher and the suicide-by-cop of the man who killed him. The first Black sheriff of the county of Charon, Virginia, is faced with the always-present racism of the area as he digs into the two deaths and finds corruption and evil so horrible that it's difficult to comprehend.

The Spite House by Johnny Compton (Nightfire) is an excellent Black gothic about a father and his two daughters on the run from something that happened back in Maryland. Desperate for money and paranoid about being found, he takes a lucrative caretaker's job in the Spite House, so dubbed by the townspeople of Degener, Texas. The house was built out of spite and hatred, and is weird looking. It also has a reputation for people disappearing into it and for driving others crazy. It's refreshing to see a group of horror characters with agency with regard to their fates.

Where the Dead Wait by Ally Wilkes (Emily Bestler Books/Atria Books) is about a disgraced arctic explorer in the late nineteenth century whose failed expedition haunts him. Thirteen years later, when his former second-in-command has disappeared in the same part of the arctic, he embarks on a rescue. The book is complex, moving back and forth from describing the first expedition and the second, with many characters. Murder and cannibalism always excused by the refrain by some that survival is all. Grisly, ghostly, with some wonderfully powerful scenes.

ALSO NOTED

At the End of Every Day by Arianna Reiche (Atria Books) is a debut novel about a large, famous amusement park (*not* Disneyland) whose long-time employee is tasked with closing the park down after several staff disappearances and the death of a celebrity guest. *The Strange* by Nathan Ballingrud (Saga Press) is the author's novel debut and it's a science fantasy/western about a young girl living with her father in an American community on Mars. The colonists have lost all communication with Earth, and there's something in the mines where many of them work that is affecting/infecting and changing them. Think Bradbury and monsters—not really horror, but has some very dark moments. *Frost Bite* by Angela Sylvaine (Dark Matter Ink) is a coming-of-age story about two teens in a North Dakota town that's been invaded by an alien worm. The worm is infecting prairie dogs, creating chaos and memory loss. Only the teens can save the town's human inhabitants. *Organ Meats* by K-Ming Chang (One World) is another coming-of-age story, this one of body horror about two girls of dog heritage who decide to transform into dogs (not unknown in this book's world) binding themselves with red string to demonstrate their mutual loyalty. They become separated and things go downhill from there. *The Paleontologist* by Luke Dumas (Atria Books) is about a curator of paleontology who returns to his hometown and its Museum of Natural History for the first time since his little sister was abducted from the museum years before. *Graveyard of Lost Children* by Katrina Monroe (Poisoned Pen) is about a woman whose mother tried to murder her as a baby, and the trauma, fear, and paranoia that knowledge generates when the woman herself becomes mother to a newborn. *The Intruders* by Brian Pinkerton (Flame Tree Press) is about strange happenings in an Indiana town, beginning with the buzzing of insects from the sky and the disappearance of residents. *The Cthulhu Helix* by Umehara Katsufumi, translated by Jim Hubbert (Kurodahan Press), was originally published in Japanese in 1993—it's sf/horror about genetic research unlocking something that threatens the human race. *Smoke, in Crimson* by Greg F. Gifune (Cemetery Dance Publications) is about a man drawn back to the beach town where he grew up and had been engaged in a mutually destructive relationship with a woman who has now disappeared. *Bad Cree* by Jessica Johns (Doubleday) is a debut supernatural novel about a young Cree woman whose dreams come to haunt her waking life as she tries to make sense of the sudden death of her sister. *Vial Thoughts* by Van Essler (Raw Dog Screaming Press) is a steampunk/mystery debut with some horrific/body horror aspects about a woman who inherits her father's estate, a plague of insanity, and a horrific circus. *The Vampire* by Froylán Turcios, translated by Shawn Garrett (Strange Ports Press), is the first English translation of this Honduran novel titled *El Vampiro*, originally published in 1910. An evil priest disrupts the idyllic home of a boy, his mother, and his cousin. *Natural Beauty* by Ling Ling Huang (Dutton) is about a young woman who goes to work in a high-end beauty and wellness salon that uses unorthodox products and procedures. She loves the job, but things start going wrong as she's offered new products to try. *Charwood* by Josh Schlossberg (Madness Heart Press) is a combination of eco-horror and Jewish mysticism. A woman joins a group of supposed environmentalists living in the woods and it turns out they're up to no good. *The Dead Pennies* by Robert Ford (Cemetery Dance Publications) is both a supernatural and psychological horror novel about a woman who left an abusive relationship who becomes caretaker to a newly renovated building that originally housed infirm and unwanted children. *The Black Magician* by Paul Madsack, translated by Shawn Garrett (Strange Ports Press), is the first English translation of this German novel of the occult, originally published in 1924. *Episode 13* by Craig DiLouie (Redhook

Books) is about a ghost hunting team that dares to investigate a derelict mansion that was the center of the Paranormal Research Foundation. What they find may not be what they hope for. *The Vein* by Steph Nelson (Dark Matter Ink) is about a former detective returning to her childhood home in Idaho to sell it after her grandmother has disappeared. While there, a corpse of a man is discovered in one of the silver mines in the area and the woman is asked to help investigate. *Let Him In* by William Friend (Poisoned Pen Press) is about a widower with twin daughters who are seemingly visited by an imaginary friend that encroaches on their lives with more menace every day. *Only Monsters Remain* by William J. Donahue (JournalStone) is a post-apocalypse novel about tentacled monsters from the sky that destroy most of civilization, retreat, but leave something behind. *Apparitions* by Adam Pottle (Dark Matter Ink) is about a deaf teenager who escapes from his captivity by his father only to end up in an isolated psychiatric facility where he's preyed upon by a resident who initially seems to be his savior only to reveal more malevolent motives. *The Still Place* by Greg F. Gifune and Sandy DeLuca (JournalStone) is about a troubled artist awarded what appears to be a dream residency with an artists' collective. But the group's combination of art and spiritualism becomes worrisome. *Extended Stay* by Juan Martinez (University of Arizona Press) is about two siblings, who in escaping the hell of their home in Colombia, reach Las Vegas in the United States and end up in a hotel that may be no better than where their journey began. *Sister, Maiden, Monster* by Lucy A. Snyder (Nightfire), inspired by the author's award-winning story "Magdala Amygdala" (chosen for *The Best Horror of the Year, Volume Five*), is cosmic horror about the aftermath of a world-wide virus and the effect the virus has had on three surviving women. *Cruel Angels Past Sundown* by Hailey Piper (Death's Head Press) is an historical horror western about what happens after a naked, pregnant stranger arrives at a ranch with a cavalry sabre and death in her eyes. *Bad Moon Rising* by Luisa Colon (Cemetery Dance Publications) is a debut novel about two damaged young people who live miles away from each other but are linked by a dark, mystical past. *Our Love Will Devour Us* by R. L. Meza (Dark Matter Ink) is about a couple whose shaky marriage is overshadowed when their two children go missing in a snowstorm, and the traumas and evils of the past impinge on them all in the present. *The Sphinx* by Coelho Neto, translated by Shawn Garrett (Strange Ports Press), is the first English translation of this 1908 Brazilian occult novel about a group of people living in a boarding house who are obsessed with the strange Englishman living there. *Those We Drown* by Amy Goldsmith (Delacorte Press) is about a young woman offered a scholarship to a semester-long study program aboard a luxury ocean liner. Initially exciting, things start getting weird and dark pretty quickly. *Gris-Gris Gumbo* by Rick Koster (JournalStone) is about a guy in his mid-twenties living in New Orleans and working in a voodoo shop popular with tourists. He's not a believer, but a delivery he makes to a mortuary changes things. *Neverest* by T. L Bodine (Ghost Orchid Press) is about the widow of a mountaineer who disappeared while climbing Mount Everest. She instigates an expedition to search for his body, encountering supernatural forces. *Red Rabbit* by Alex Grecian (Nightfire) is a western about a posse stalking a witch, and the demons and ghosts they encounter on their journey. *The Vile Thing We Created* by Robert Ottone (Hydra Publications) is about a couple who, upon deciding to have a baby, discover that pregnancy and parenthood may not be all it's cracked up to be. *The Militia House* by John Milas (Henry Holt) takes place during the war in Afghanistan, as a unit of Americans are assigned to a base near an old Soviet barracks called the Militia House. Although they've been warned that the building is haunted, they check it out anyway. *Burn the Negative* by Josh Winning (G. P. Putnam's Sons) is about a journalist assigned to cover a new streaming horror series—a remake of the cursed movie she starred in as a child, during which a large percentage of cast and crew died horribly. *Ragman* by JG Flaherty (Flame Tree Press) is about the descendants of a murderous, tomb-robbing group of British soldiers plagued by a mummy's curse more than a century later. *The Haunting of Alejandra* by V. Castro (Del Rey Books) is about a woman whose family has been haunted by La Llorona, the creature of Mexican folklore, and how she must learn to fight back to save herself and her children from this soul-sucking demon. *Plastic Space House* by John F. D. Taff (Trepidatio Publishing) is an sf/horror novel taking place in the far future, when humans, ready to colonize space, hit a snag. Something out there really doesn't want us out there. *That Night in the Woods* by Kristopher Triana (Cemetery Dance Publications) is about a group of high school friends who experienced trauma in a place known as Suicide Woods and finally meet again decades later. *Wasps in the Ice Cream* by Tim McGregor (Raw Dog Screaming Press) is a coming-of-age story in a small town in which a teen experiences first love with a girl who practices folk magic and who his friends hate. His friends find out and decide to punish the witch who "stole" their friend. *The September House* by Carissa Orlando (Berkley) is a debut about a couple moving into a haunted house that bleeds from the walls every September, where former inhabitants appear, and something's in the basement that should not be. *The Others of Edenwell* by Verity M. Holloway (Titan Books) is a dark, historical novel in which a young man, rejected by the army in 1917, instead lives and works with his father in a hydrotherapy retreat surrounded by haunted woodlands in Norfolk, England. Another young man comes to the spa, there's a murder . . . and a monster. *Edenville* by Sam Rebelein (William Morrow) is about a novelist who, after his first novel flops, joins Edenville College as writer-in-residence. His girlfriend, who grew up nearby, isn't so eager to return to the area . . . with good reason. *My Darling Girl* by Jennifer McMahon (Scout Press) is about a woman forced to return with her husband and children to her dying, malignant mother's bedside, and what happens once they get there. *Jump Cut* by Helen Grant (Fledgling Press) is about a lost movie, its last surviving cast member, and a film enthusiast who yearns to discover what happened during the making of the movie. *Piñata* by Leopoldo Gout (Nightfire) is about a woman who takes her daughters to Mexico while she works on the renovation of an ancient abbey there. Disaster occurs and when the three return to the US, something follows, possessing one of the girls. *Vampires of El Norte* by Isabel Cañas (Berkley) is an historical gothic about the nineteenth-century conflict between Mexicans and their northern (US) neighbors, plus vampires and romance. *The Once Yellow House* by Gemma Amor (Cemetery Gates Media) is about a journalist's investigation into a massacre that took place in 2020 during which 347 members of a cult were slaughtered. *Mothered* by Zoje Stage (Thomas and Mercer) is about a woman forced to take in her newly widowed mother, despite their problematic relationship. Nothing good ensues. *The Shoemaker's Magician* by Cynthia Pelayo (Agora) is a supernatural crime novel about an obsessive search for an old TV horror host who might have something to do with a series of gruesome murders. *Hangtown* by Michael Bailey (Written Backwards) is a western based on the true story of hangings that took place in the mid-nineteenth century in Placerville, California. *Everything the Darkness Eats: Hymns for a Decaying God* by Eric LaRocca (Clash) is about a seemingly idyllic small town with terrible secrets. *How to Sell a Haunted House* by Grady Hendrix (Berkley) is about a woman forced to return to the home she grew up in to get it ready for sale now that her parents are dead. But the house has some ideas of its own about this. *Crow Face, Doll Face* by Carly Holmes (Honno) is about a woman who takes her two youngest daughters with her when she leaves a miserable marriage. A dark depiction of motherhood and dysfunctional families. *The Destroyer of Worlds: A Return to Lovecraft Country* by Matt Ruff (Harper Perennial) is a follow-up to Ruff's magnificent *Lovecraft Country*, bringing back some of the same characters dealing with evil, both supernatural and human. *Looking Glass Sound* by Catriona Ward (Nightfire) is about a novelist who, while writing about horrific events in his youth, dredges up bad memories that might or might not be accurate. *Our Share of Night* by Mariana Enriquez (Hogarth) takes place in two different places: Argentina during its brutal military dictatorship, and the London of the swinging sixties. A woman dies, and a grieving father and son flee the family's matriarch who heads a cult that wants to use the boy. *Holly* by Stephen King (Scribner) brings back a recurring character in King's work, who currently runs a detective agency. She's asked to find a missing person and is drawn to a couple of evil professors who might have something to do with the disappearance. *The Daughters of Block Island* by Christa Carmen (Amazon Publishing) is a gothic novel about two sisters, one murdered upon arriving on an island off New England in search of her birth mother. *Black River Orchard* by Chuck Wendig (Del Rey Books) is about what happens in a small town when several strange trees in their local orchard bear a new type of apple.

Magazines, Webzines, and Journals

It's important to recognize the work of the talented artists working in the field of fantastic fiction, both dark and light. The following created dark art I thought especially noteworthy in 2023: Dan Verkys, Lenka Simeckova, Asya Yordanova, Laurel Hausler, Lumitar, João Antunes, Jr., Jean Pierre

Arboleda, Mikio Murakami, Kim Jacobsson, Ben Baldwin, Richard Wagner, Greg Chapman, Dave Senecal, Vincent Sammy, Pat R. Steiner, Julie Hamel, Vince Haig, Jason Van Hollander, Zoë Van Dijk, K. L Turner, Lynne Hansen, Jesse Peper, Brian Thummler, Reiko Murakami, Jeffrey Kam, Stephen Jung, David Tibet, Elizabeth Leggett, Caniglia, øjeRum, Daniele Serra, John Coulthart, Welder Wings, Dave McKean, Glenn Chadbourne, João Ruas, Ifan Bates, and Jim Burns.

BFS Journal is a nonfiction perk of being a member of the British Fantasy Society, but there were no issues in 2023. Plans are for the journal to be revived with a new editor in 2024. *BFS Horizons* edited by Pete Sutton is the fiction companion to *BFS Journal*. I received #15, the first of their twice-annual journals, but did not receive the second, apparently published in September. There were notable dark stories and poetry by Verity Holloway, Sadie Maskery, Natalie Orr, and Thomas Booker. I always look forward to reading both journals, so hope they get back on track in 2024.

The Green Book: Writings on Irish Gothic, Supernatural, and Fantastic Literature edited by Brian J. Showers is an excellent resource for discovering underappreciated Irish writers. Two issues were published in 2023. Issue 21 focused on three Irish women: B. M. Croker, Althea Gyles, and Mary Frances McHugh, and included several stories and poems by each, plus essays by Simon Cooke and Jim Rockhill. Issue 22 is all about Bram Stoker, including a 2011 appreciation of "The Judge's House" by graphic novelist Mike Mignola, several essays, and four of Stoker's stories.

Rue Morgue edited by Andrea Subissati is a reliable, entertaining Canadian non-fiction magazine for horror movie aficionados, with up-to-date information on most of the horror films being released. The magazine also includes interviews, articles, and movie stills—many of them gory—along with regular columns on books, horror music, video games, and graphic novels.

Dead Reckonings: A Review of Horror and the Weird in the Arts edited by Alex Houstoun and Michael U. Abolafia published two issues in 2023. Both issues included book and movie reviews plus interviews. Issue #33 had an interview with writer Curtis M. Lawson and Issue #34 has an interview with me. There were also pieces about Del Toro's *Cabinet of Curiosities* series for Netflix, horror conventions, and Ramsey Campbell's regular column.

The Lovecraft Annual edited by S. T. Joshi is a must for those interested in Lovecraftian studies. The 2023 issue has around 240 pages of essays revolving around H. P. Lovecraft—interpretations of and the influence of his work on other writers, artists, and culture in general.

Ghosts & Scholars, the long-running journal celebrating the works of M. R. James, brought out two issues in 2023, the first edited by Benjamin Harris and the second by Katherine Haynes. In addition to the articles and reviews there were notable stories by Katherine Haynes and Marion Pitman.

Black Static 82/83 edited by Andy Cox is the magazine's final issue. Cox has published excellent horror just short of thirty years, first in his quarterly, mixed-genre magazine *The Third Alternative*. As *TTA* began to add more horror to its mix, I started to acquire some of their stories for the horror half of *The Year's Best Fantasy and Horror* in 2003. With Cox's takeover of *Interzone* in 2004, *TTA* gravitated toward being more horror focused. There were no issues published in 2006, but in 2007 the magazine, renamed *Black Static*, went fully horror with two issues. In 2008, the magazine published six issues and started its run as the best regularly published horror magazine (in my opinion). Almost every year since, at least one story from the magazine was reprinted by me in one of my annual Bests of the Year. Its demise is a major blow to the field of horror. In its last (large) issue it published notable stories by Sarah Lamparelli, Steve Rasnic Tem, Andrew Hook, Ray Cluley, Rhonda Pressley Veit, Neil Williamson, Tim Lees, and Aliya Whiteley. The Williamson, Hook, and Tem are reprinted herein.

Nightmare Abbey is a semi-annual magazine edited by Tom English and illustrated throughout by Allen Koszinski. Each issue included fourteen stories and essays, most of them new. There was notable original fiction by Steve Rasnic Tem, Rhys Hughes, Steve Duffy, Helen Grant, Ian Rogers, and Ray Cluley. The Cluley is reprinted herein.

Weird Horror edited by Michael Kelly published two issues in 2023, with columns by Simon Strantzas and Orrin Grey, book and movie reviews, and fiction. There was notable dark fiction by Tim Cooke, Nelly Geraldine García-Rosas, Alexander James, Spencer Harrington, Alexander Glass, Kay Chronister, Spencer Nitkey, Kristiana Willsey, Neil Williamson, and E. M. Linden.

Supernatural Tales edited by David Longhorn is a reliable venue for good short supernatural fiction and is published three times a year. In 2023, there was notable fiction by Helen Grant, Sam Dawson, Michael Chislett, Christopher Harman, Steve Duffy, Tim Jeffreys, Tina Rath, and Victoria Day. The Grant is reprinted herein.

Chthonic Matter Quarterly edited by C. M. Muller is a new print magazine of horror, dark, and weird fiction. It takes the place of Muller's *Nightscript*, with the only difference (according to the publisher) being its quarterly nature and name. In 2023, there were notable stories by Jonathan Lewis Duckworth, Gail Pinto, Santiago Eximeno, Gordon Brown, David Surface, Stephen McQuiggan, K. Wallace King, Tim Major, Zachary Rosenberg, Christie Nogle, Timothy Granville, Patricia Lillie, Erica Ruppert, Eli Wennstrom, Perry Ruhland, and Shawn Phelps.

Dracula Beyond Stoker edited by Tucker Christine is a print journal of fiction devoted to new and reprinted stories featuring characters from Bram Stoker's *Dracula*. There were four issues in 2023, one spotlighting the Bloofer Lady, another Renfield, and two one-story chapbooks. There were notable stories by Grace Athanasiou, JF Faherty, and Mark Oxbrow.

The Horror Zine edited by Jeanne Rector continues to publish reprint and original fiction on its website, and collects all the stories into three print and ezine editions annually.

Cemetery Dance #78, the magazine's first issue in four years, finally appeared in 2023, with reviews, columns, and interviews published way past their "sell by" date. However, the issue included nine new pieces of fiction, with notable work by James Chambers, Tina Callaghan, Richard Thomas, and Charles Kaiden.

Cosmic Horror Monthly edited by Charles Tyra began its run in 2020, but I only became aware of it around mid-2021. In 2023, the quality of its fiction has become more consistent. There were notable stories by Alan Baxter, Matthew M. Bartlett, K. M. Carmien, Megan M. Davies-Ostrow, Sarah Day, Jennifer Derkitt, Jason Kahler, Nicholas Kaufmann, RSL, S. P. Miskowski, Mob, Jacob Steven Mohr, Sarah Pauling, and Rachel Searcy.

Phantasmagoria is a chunky magazine of horror, science fiction, and fantasy edited by Trevor Kennedy, who is based in Belfast, Ireland. It publishes three issues a year covering past and current material, and publishes one special issue a year, usually focusing on a specific writer. Its 8th special issue focused on "Women in Horror" (I'm interviewed). It includes mostly reprint fiction with the occasional original story, plus columns, reviews, and art. One notable original story was by Jessica Stevens.

MIXED-GENRE MAGAZINES AND WEBZINES

Not One of Us edited by John Benson is one of the longest-running small press magazines regularly publishing horror. It's a quarterly, containing weird, dark fantasy, and horror fiction and poetry. There were notable stories and poetry in 2023 by Gretchen Tessmer, Rodney K. Sloan, Mackenzie Hurlbert, Jennifer Crow, Sonya Taaffe, and a collaboration by Brad Munson and Bruce McAllister. *Weird Tales*, now edited by Jonathan Maberry, brought out Issue #367, with a theme of cosmic horror but also including several stories and poems of dark fantasy. There were notable horror stories by Carol Gyzander and Caitlín R. Kiernan, and articles by F. Paul Wilson and Nicholas Diak. *Bourbon Penn* edited by Erik Secker always has enjoyable stories, often horror. The strongest dark stories in 2023 were by Corey Farrenkopf, Shane Inman, E. Catherine Tobler, Camilla Grudova, Naomi J. Williams, and Josh Rountree. The Tobler is reprinted herein. *The Magazine of Fantasy and Science Fiction* edited by Sheree Renée Thomas has been publishing consistently good science fiction, fantasy, and horror for seventy-five years. During 2023, there was notable horror fiction and poetry by Nuzo Onoh, Jill McMillan, Nick Thomas, Jennifer Hudak, Faith Merino, Fawaz Al-Matrouk, K. S. Walker, Rob Cameron, Dane Kuttler, Max Firehammer, Getty Hesse, Jenny Kiefer, Charlie Hughes, Lisa M. Bradley, and A Humphrey Lanham. *Underland Arcana* edited by Mark Teppo is a mixed bag of mostly weird fiction. During 2023, three issues were published and there was strong dark fiction by Jason Washer, J. P. Oakes, Frances Lu-Pai Ippolito, Phillip E. Dixon, Anthony J. Hartley, J. V. Gachs, Daniel Dagris, Michelle Knudsen, and an excellent fantasy by Kiya Nicoll. *Interzone Digital* edited by Gareth Jelley is an offshoot of the print version of *Interzone*, publishing fiction and nonfiction. The magazine was taken over from Andy Cox, who published it and *Black Static* (and occasionally *Crimewave*). *Interzone* still mostly publishes science fiction, with the occasional dark piece of fiction. During 2023, there were notable darker stories by Neil Williamson, Steve Toase, and Hesper Leveret. *Vastarien: A Literary Journal* edited by Jon Padgett Volume 6, Issue 1 was jam-packed with weird fiction, much of it dark. The more notable dark stories were by Corey Farrenkopf, Simon Lee-Price, Nadia Shammas, Shenoa Carroll-Bradd, and Brian Evenson. Also included is one piece of non-fiction by Dejan Ognjanović, delving into the works of H. P. Lovecraft and Thomas Ligotti. Tor.com (now called Reactor) regularly publishes short science fiction, fantasy, and horror acquired and edited by multiple in-house and consulting editors (I'm one of the latter). There was notable horror published by A. C. Wise, Jeffrey Ford, and Lyndsie Manusos. *Uncanny* edited by Lynn M. Thomas and Michael Damien Thomas is a monthly webzine publishing fantasy, speculative, weird fiction, and the occasional horror story. It also includes poetry, podcasts, interviews, essays, and art. In 2023, there were notable dark stories by Sarah Monette, Grace P. Fong, and Eugenia Triantafyllou. *The Dark* edited by Sean Wallace is a monthly webzine that publishes dark fantasy and horror. In 2023, there was notable dark fiction by Ai Jiang, Libby Cudmore, Françoise Harvey, Sam J. Miller, Leah Ning, Shari Paul, and Steve Rasnic Tem. *Penumbra: A Journal of Weird Fiction and Criticism* edited by S. T. Joshi published its fourth issue in 2023, with thirteen new stories, one classic reprint, twelve poems, and ten non-fiction pieces. *The Deadlands: A Journal of Endings and Beginnings* published by Sean Markey, with Editor-in-Chief E. Catherine Tobler is a monthly online speculative journal publishing fiction, poetry, and non-fiction about death. During 2023, there was notable horror work by Makena Onjerika, Betsy Aoki, and Angel Leal. *On Spec*, a Canadian magazine published by the Copper Pig Writers' Society published two good horror stories in 2023 by Cale Plett and KT Wagner.

There was also the occasional notable horror story published by *Kaleidotrope, Crow & Cross Keys,* and *Conjunctions.*

COLLECTIONS

A Curious Cartography by Alison Littlewood (Black Shuck Books) is this talented author's third collection and features nineteen excellent stories, one published for the first time.

Tell Me When I Disappear: Vanishing Stories by Glen Hirshberg (Cemetery Dance Publications) is the fabulous fifth collection by a versatile writer of all kinds of horror. The seven stories (three published for the first time) demonstrate a variety of settings that seem to have been created effortlessly. The title story is reprinted herein.

Monsters and Things by Robert Silverberg (Drugstore Indian Press) is an unusual treat—Silverberg is much better known today as a science fiction writer, but back in the late 1950s, in addition to writing science fiction, he started churning out men's adventures, mysteries, crime stories, porn, and horror. This volume contains twenty-six of his horror stories from that period of his life.

Only the Living are Lost by Simon Strantzas (Hippocampus Press) is the sixth collection by the Canadian horror writer, and it's a very good one. Two of the eleven stories are new, including a strong novella.

Fearful Implications by Ramsey Campbell (PS Publishing) is another excellent collection by this master of horror. It features twenty recent stories, including one published in English for the first time.

The Wishing Pool and Other Stories by Tananarive Due (Akashic Books) is Due's strong second collection of short fiction. Twelve of the stories—some horror, some science fiction—were originally published in magazines and anthologies, and two of them are new.

The Whispering Mummy and Others by Sax Rohmer, edited by S. T. Joshi (Hippocampus Press) features fifteen of Rohmer's best tales of horror and the weird, taken from his story collections from the 1910s and 1920s.

Not Buried Deep Enough by Gary Robbe (Denver Horror Collective) has thirteen stories, most published in various small press magazines and webzines, one appearing for the first time.

Dark Is Better by Gemma Files (Trepidatio Publishing) is one of two collections of Files's short stories. *Blood From the Air* by Gemma Files (Grimscribe Press) is the second. There are no new stories in either collection, but also no overlap, so if you haven't yet read the author's earlier collections, here's your opportunity to catch up with a very fine horror writer.

Such Pretty Confusion: Nightmares From a Damaged Mind by Peter N. Dudar (Trepidatio Publishing) contains twenty stories published since 2000, five of them appearing for the first time.

No Happily Ever After by Phil Sloman (Northern Republic) is the author's second collection and has seven stories, three published for the first time. Story notes are included.

The Measure of Sorrow by J. Ashley-Smith (Meerkat Press) is an impressive debut collection by a British-Australian writer. It includes nine stories, three new, and one excellent new novella.

Unshod, Cackling, and Naked by Tamika Thompson (Unnerving Books), the author's second collection, contains thirteen stories, four published for the first time.

Brian Evenson had two collections out in 2023: *Black Bark*, part of the Black Shuck Shadows series of mini-collections, contains six stories, all but one reprints. The second was *None of You Shall Be Spared* (Gallows Whisper/ Weird House), the author's tenth collection, with twenty-one stories, four published for the first time. Individual story notes are included. One story is reprinted herein.

Darker Than Weird by John R. Fultz (Jackanapes Press) is a strong collection of fourteen horror stories originally published in such venues as *Weirdbook*, *Fungi, Space & Time*, and other magazines and anthologies. With a foreword by Don Webb and cover art and illustrations throughout by Dan Sauer.

The Porches of My Ears by Norman Prentiss (Cemetery Dance Publications) is the author's fine third collection of sixteen stories and a novella. One story is new. The title story won the Bram 2009 Stoker Award for short story and was reprinted in The *Best Horror of the Year Volume Two*.

Jackal Jackal: Tales of the Dark and Fantastic by Tobi Ogundiran (Undertow Publications) is a fine debut collection of horror and dark fantasy by this Nigerian writer. Two of the eighteen stories were published for the first time, the rest appeared in venues ranging from *The Dark, F&SF, Fiyah*, and *Beneath Ceaseless Skies*. Story notes are included for each story.

Every Woman Knows This by Laurel Hightower (Death Knell Press) is a debut collection with twenty stories and vignettes, most of them dark fantasy and horror, fifteen published since 2020. Five of them appear for the first time.

Skin Thief by Suzan Palumbo (Neon Hemlock Press) is the debut collection by a writer of dark fantasy and horror. It features twelve stories, one new. With an introduction by A. C. Wise.

Have You Seen the Moon Tonight? & Other Rumors by Jonathan Louis Duckworth (JournalStone) is the author's debut collection, with sixteen stories, three of them new. Gabino Iglesias has written an introduction.

Gordon B. White is creating Haunting Weird Horror(s) by Gordon B. White (Trepidatio Publishing) is the author's second collection, with fifteen stories, two of them new.

No One Dies from Love: Dark Tales of Loss and Longing by Robert Levy (Word Horde) is a very good debut collection featuring twelve stories, including one new tale. One of the stories appeared in my *The Best Horror of the Year Volume Nine*. There is an introduction by Paul Tremblay.

The Devil Snar'd: Novels, Appreciations, and Appendices by Marjorie Bowen, selected by John C. Tibbetts (Hippocampus Press) is a follow-up to the editor's 2021 volume about the author and her fiction. This volume includes novel excerpts, a complete novel, various recollections about Bowen, and critical analyses of her work.

Linghun by Ai Jiang (Dark Matter) is a mini-collection containing an unusual novella about ghost houses and two short stories, one of the stories a reprint.

The Children of Chorazin and other Strange Denizens by Darrell Schweitzer (Hippocampus Press) is a strong new collection of twenty-six stories, mostly Lovecraftian inspired, with some of them taking place in an imaginary village in rural Pennsylvania. The four new stories are very good.

A Bright and Beautiful Eternal World by James Chambers (Weird House) is the author's third collection and features twelve effectively creepy stories taking place in the fictional town of Knicksport, Long Island, a place rich in cosmic horror and monstrosities. Most of the stories are published for the first time.

The Beast You Are by Paul Tremblay (William Morrow) is the author's second collection. Although better known for his novels, the fourteen stories—and one peculiar new novella written in free verse—beautifully demonstrate Tremblay's range. Two of the stories were originally published in anthologies edited by me.

The Inconsolables by Michael Wehunt (Bad Hand Books) is the author's second collection, with ten stories of weird and dark fiction, two of them new. There is an introduction by John Langan, and story notes by the author.

Now It's Dark by Lynda E. Rucker (The Swan River Press) is the strong, third collection by the author, and contains ten stories, one new. With an introduction by Robert Shearman and story notes for each piece.

Something Blue and other colorful deaths by L. L. Soares (Trepidatio Publishing) has seventeen stories, two published for the first time, and an introduction by Ray Garton.

Where Rivers Go to Die by Dilman Dila (Rosarium Publishing) is this Ugandan writer and film director's second collection of short stories, most of them dark, and based on his country's folk tales and myths. One of the eight stories is new.

The Ecstasy of Agony by Wrath James White (Clash) features seventeen stories and poems by one of the best current practitioners of extreme horror. His work is often cruel, sexually explicit, and violent, but compulsively readable. Nine of the stories and poems are new. Edward Lee provides the introduction.

Suburban Monsters by Christopher Hawkins (Coronis Publishing) is the author's debut collection, with thirteen stories set in the suburbs, three of them new.

Atomic Horrors by Tim Curran (Weird House) is a collection of sixteen linked stories about the survivors of a detonation of an atomic bomb. Demons, monsters, mutants, evil humans—this book has them all. All but two of the stories are new. With an afterword by the author and cover and interior art by K. L. Turner.

The Devil's in the Flaws and Other Dark Truths by David Niall Wilson (Macabre Ink/Crossroad Press) features nineteen stories, nine of them new—plus a very good new novella.

Ending in Ashes by Rebecca Jones-Howe (Quill & Crow) is the author's second collection and includes eleven gothic tales, some quite disturbing. Two of the stories are new.

Riding the Nightmare by Lisa Tuttle (Valancourt Books) reprints eleven stories and one novella published between 1986 and 2018. With an introduction by Neil Gaiman.

Thirteen Plus 1: Lovecraftian Narratives by Nancy Kilpatrick (NK Publishing) features fourteen stories focusing on cosmic horror, one of them new. With a foreword by S. T. Joshi.

Illusions of Isolation by Brennan LaFaro (French Press) is the author's debut collection and contains thirteen stories, nine of them published for the first time. With an introduction by Jonathan Janz.

Blood Wood and Other Stories by Christopher Harman (Sarob Press) is a retrospective of the author's work between 1994 and 2014, featuring eleven stories (not seen by me).

Devil Kin by Stephanie Ellis is a self-published collection of nineteen horror and sf/horror stories by this Welsh writer. Thirteen of the stories are new.

A Blackness Absolute by Caitlin Marceau (Ghost Orchid Press) is a collection of eight stories by this Canadian writer, all published for the first time.

Nightfall and Other Dangers by Jacob Steven Mohr (JournalStone) has fifteen stories, three of them new. One of the stories was reprinted in my anthology *The Best Horror of the Year, Volume Fifteen.*

Wrapped in Plastic and Other Sweet Nothings by Robert P. Ottone (JournalStone) has seventeen stories, six of them new.

White Trash and Recycled Nightmares by Rebecca Rowland (Dead Sky Publishing) has twenty-two stories of supernatural and psychological horror, six of them new.

Cold, Black & Infinite by Todd Keisling (Cemetery Dance Publications) has sixteen horror stories, three of them new. With a foreword by John Langan.

Midnight Masquerade by Greg Chapman (IFWG) has nine stories, four of them new. With an introduction by Lisa Morton.

Down in the Deep Dark Places by Jason Parent (Gallows Whisper/Weird House Press) includes nineteen stories, six of them new. With a foreword by Curtis M. Lawson.

Haunted Victorian America by Joshua Rex (Rotary) is a nicely done collection of seventeen new ghost stories taking place during the reign of Queen Victoria.

Midnight Self by Adrian Van Young (Black Lawrence Press) is a powerful second collection of ten dark stories, one published for the first time.

Pre-Approved for Haunting and Other Stories by Patrick Barb (Keylight Books) is this promising writer's first collection, featuring eighteen stories published since 2019, five of them appearing for the first time.

Hell, Delaware: One Town's History of Horrific Happenings by Kenneth W. Cain (Cemetery Gates Media) is a collection of stories all taking place in one town. All but four of the seventeen stories are new.

MIXED-GENRE COLLECTIONS

This Island Earth: 8 Features from the Drive-In by Dale Bailey (PS Publishing) contains eight stories—all with titles taken from 1950s monster movies— some of the stories are horror, one of them published for the first time. The stories were published since 2013 and appeared in *Nightmare, Clarkesworld, Asimov's Science Fiction, Lightspeed,* and *Tor.com. The Were-Wolf and Others: The Weird Writings of Clemence Houseman* edited by S. T. Joshi (Hippocampus Press) presents several weird works by the feminist sister of the poet A. E. Houseman and novelist Laurence Houseman. Included are *The Were-Wolf,* a novella originally published in a magazine in 1890 and reprinted in book form several years later; *The Unknown Sea,* a weird novel about a mermaid; and a short story. *Dream Fox and Other Strange Stories* by Rosalie Parker (Tartarus Press) is the author's fifth collection of stories. There are eighteen brief stories (several new), plus a book within the book, titled *May Belgrove's Book of Unusual Experiences,* which has nine more brief pieces. Not for the horror purist, but for those who enjoy strange stories. *The Fortunate Isles* by Lisa L. Hannett (Egaeus Press) is a gorgeous, lyrical new collection of dark fantasy tinged with horror by this Canadian-Australian writer. It includes fourteen stories, half of them new, several with overlapping characters and taking place in the same harbor village. Kirstyn McDermott provides an introduction. Aside from the marvelous contents, the physical object is stunning. *The Faces at Your Shoulder* by Steve Duffy (Sarob Press) is this British author's sixth collection and it's more of a mixed bag than his earlier ones. There's some science fiction and dark fantasy among the six stories. Three are new. One story is in *The Best Horror of the Year, Volume Two.* Dust jacket and frontispiece art are by Paul Lowe. *Nineteen Claws and a Black Bird* by Argentinian Agustina Bazterrica, translated by Sarah Moses (Scribner), is the debut collection by the author of the powerful, provocative novel *Tender is the Flesh.* Although the twenty very brief stories are usually weird and occasionally dark, unfortunately none of them evoke the horror of the novel. *Human Sacrifices* by María Fernanda Ampuero, translated from the Spanish by Frances Riddle (The Feminist Press), is the excellent second collection by an Ecuadorian writer. Most of the brief tales are psychological horror. *Voice of the Stranger* by Eric Schaller (Lethe Press) is the second collection by this talented, versatile author of weird, sometimes dark fiction. There are fourteen stories, one of them new. *Monstrous Alterations* by Christopher Barzak (Lethe Press) features ten broad retellings of myths, legends, and fairy tales, some dark. The one new tale is inspired by characters in several of Franz Kafka's works. *Root Rot & Other Grim Tales* by Sarah Read (Bad Hand Books) is the author's second collection, featuring eighteen strong science fiction, dark fantasy, and horror stories, four of them new. *Night Side of the River* by Jeanette Winterson (Grove Atlantic) is a collection of fourteen ghost stories, interspersed with the literary author's own ghostly encounters. *The Best of Our Past, the Worst of Our Future* by Christi Nogle (Flame Tree Press) is the debut collection of seventeen weird and often dark stories, two of them published for the first time. *The Privilege of the Happy Ending: Small, Medium, and Large Stories* by Kij Johnson (Small Beer Press), the author's second collection, features thirteen sf/f/h stories and one novella, with two of the stories published for the first time. *These Were the Angels* by Ralph Robert Moore (self-published) is the author's eighth collection and contains eighteen stories, most of them new. *Impulses of a Necrotic Heart and Other Afflictions* by Red Lagoe (Death Knell Press) include fifteen stories of sf, dark fantasy, and horror. Six are published for the first time. *Treatises on Dust* by Timothy J. Jarvis (The Swan River Press) is an excellent collection of fourteen weird, often dark fiction stories and vignettes, six published for the first time. *Time of Passing: Tales of Twilight and Borderlands* by John Gaskin (Tartarus Press) features thirteen weird and uncanny stories, nine of them new. *The Good Unknown and Other Ghost Stories* by Stephen Volk (Tartarus Press) is the author's sixth collection and includes ten ghost stories and a novella. The novella and two stories are new. Volk's work is always interesting and unsettling, and usually (but not always) horror. *Death Goes To the Dogs* by Anna Tambour (Oddness) is the author's fourth collection of very strange fictions—several of the seventeen stories are about death, but they're so . . . odd, often even whimsical, that the reader can't help but laugh. With great black and white illustrations by Mike Dubisch to complement the fiction. Six of the stories are published for the first time. *The Secret Life of Insects* by Bernardo Esquinca (Valancourt Books) is translated by James D. Jenkins and has an introduction by Mariana Enríquez. Eight of the fourteen dark fantasy, weird, and horror stories by this Mexican writer appear in English for the first time. *Lost Places* by Sarah Pinsker (Small Beer Press) is this talented author's second collection. It contains twelve stories and novelettes of science fiction, fantasy, weird fiction, and horror—with one new novelette. One of the stories was reprinted in *The Best Horror of the Year, Volume Thirteen*. *The House on the Moon* by Georgina Bruce (Black Shuck Shadows #33) is darkish sf/fantasy featuring seven original stories related to the discovery of a house on the moon. *Waterlore* by Teika Marija Smits (Black Shuck) has seven dark fantasy and horror stories, three of them reprints. *No One Will Come Back For Us* by Premee Mohamed (Undertow Publications) is the author's debut collection and is filled with seventeen strong science fiction, dark fantasy, and horror tales. One story is new. *Precarious Waters and Other Dark Tales* by Pamela Jeffs (Four Ink Press) presents nine stories of science fiction, dark fantasy, and horror. Three stories are published for the first time. *The Secret of Ventriloquism* by Jon Padgett, revised and expanded (self-published), has three new stories of the weird. *One or Several Desserts* by Carter St. Hogan (11:11 Press) is a fascinating mini-collection by a trans writer musician and educator. Included are eight stories focused on the body, with three of them new. *Imago and Other Transformations* by Erica Ruppert (Trepidatio Publishing) has twenty-one mostly dark fantasy stories, with a few horror. Four of the dark fantasies are new. *The Gold Leaf Executions* by Helen Marshall (Unsung Stories) has sixteen stories of fantasy, dark fantasy, and horror. One is published for the first time. *Spin a Black Yarn: Novellas* by Josh Malerman (Del Rey Books) has five new novellas of sf, crime, and horror. *Constellations of Ruin* by Andrew Fuller (Trepidatio Publishing) is the author's debut, with twenty-six weird, dark, sometimes sf, occasionally horrific stories. Eight of the stories are published for the first time. *Fleshpots* by R. L. Summerling (self-published) is an interesting mini-collection of prose and poetry with a misleading title. Five of the fourteen pieces are new. *Caged Ocean Dub* by Dare Segun Falowo (Tartarus) is an intriguing collection of eighteen Nigerian stories and vignettes: fantasy, weird fiction, a bit of science fiction, and a tiny bit of horror. More than half are new. *Malignant Stories* by Clemente Palma, translated by Shawn Garrett (Strange Ports Press), is a collection of seventeen decadent stories and a novella originally published in 1920 by the Peruvian author. *Malevolent Tales* by the same author contains an additional nineteen stories. *A Flash of Darkness* by M. M. De Voe (Borda Books) collects eighteen mainstream, sf, dark fantasy, and horror stories, six of them published for the first time. *Agents of Oblivion* by Iain Sinclair (The Swan River Press) is a collection of four original stories, perfectly illustrated by Dave McKean. *White Cat, Black Dog* by Kelly Link (Random House) presents seven delectable, imaginative, occasionally dark reinvented fairy tales, one of them new.

ANTHOLOGIES

Dark Matter Presents Monstrous Futures edited by Alex Woodroe (Dark Matter Ink) has twenty-nine stories of future dystopias, several dark enough to veer into horror. There's notable work by Koji A. Dai, M. H. Ayinde, Rich Larson, J. A. W. McCarthy, Avra Margariti, Simo Srinivas, and D. A. Jobe.

Zero Dark Thirty edited by Rob Carroll (Dark Matter Ink) presents thirty of the darkest stories published in *Dark Matter Magazine* 2021–2022.

Killer Creatures Down Under: Horror Stories with a Bite edited by Deborah Sheldon (IFWG) has eighteen stories about some of the things that might kill you in Australia. Two are reprints. There are notable new stories by Claret Fox Hill, Tim Borella, Keith Williams, Ben Matthews, and Anthony Ferguson.

This World Belongs to Us: An Anthology of Horror About Bugs edited by Michael W. Phillips Jr. (From Beyond Press) has nineteen stories, all but three of them new. The most interesting were by Gwen C. Katz, David Simmons, Bitter Karella, R. M. Kidd, Kealan Patrick Burke, Paula D. Ashe, J. A. Prentice, and Rowan Hill.

Bound in Flesh: An Anthology of Trans Body Horror edited by Lor Gislason (Ghoulish Books) has thirteen new stories of body horror by trans and nonbinary writers, with a few that some readers might find pretty raw and over the top. The strongest and most interesting stories are by Hailey Piper, Theo Hendrie, Charles-Elizabeth Boyles, Joe Koch, and Amanda Blake.

American Cannibal edited by Rebecca Rowland (Maenad Press) features twenty new tales of humans eating other humans over the centuries—in desperation, for revenge, for the hell of it. There are notable stories by Owl Goingback, Clint Smith, Elizabeth Massie, Douglas Ford, Gwendolyn Kiste, Jeffrey Ford, Clay McLeod Chapman, Ronald Malfi, and Jeff Strand.

The Horror Library Volume 8 edited by Eric J. Guignard (Dark Moon Press) is an annual, unthemed anthology series. This year's volume featured thirty-one stories—some quite brief—and several pages of work by guest artist Jana Heidersdorf. There were notable stories by Eric Del Carlo, R. A. Busby, Don Raymond, Bentley Little, Eric Nash, Frances Ogamba, Colin Leonard, Charlie Hughes, Thersa Matsuura, and Jo Kaplan.

Aseptic and Faintly Sadistic: An Anthology of Hysteria Fiction edited by Jolie Toomajan (Cosmic Horror Monthly) features twenty-six new stories focused on women and their justifiable anger. There are notable stories by Christi Nogle, Erin Keating, Diane Callahan, Sarah Pauling, J. Z. Kelley, Hailey Piper, Tanya Chen, Marisca Pichette, Joe Koch, and Kelsea Yu.

A Darker Side of Noir edited by Joyce Carol Oates (Akashic Books) has fifteen stories, all but one new. While all are dark, several of them aren't all that horrific in tone or content. There are notable stories by Tananarive Due, Elizabeth Hand, Sheila Kohler, Yumi Dineen Shiroma, Cassandra Khaw, Megan Abbott, Lisa Tuttle, Joyce Carol Oates, and Aimee Labrie.

October Screams edited by Kenneth W. Cain (Kangas Kahn Publishing) is a hefty all-original anthology of twenty-seven stories taking place around Halloween. There's notable work by Clay McLeod Chapman, Brennan Fredricks, Ronald Malfi, Gwendolyn Kiste, Gregory L. Norris, Frank Oreto, Gemma Amor, T. J. Cimfel, Rebecca Rowland, Kealan Patrick Burke, Cassandra Daucus, and a collaboration by Brian Keene and Richard Chizmar.

What Draws Us Near edited by Keith Cadieux & Adam Petrash (Little Ghosts Books) contains fifteen original stories written around the theme of people pursuing/becoming involved in things they know they should not be doing. It includes notable stories by David Demchuk, Premee Mohamed, Susie Moloney, Suzan Palumbo, A. C. Wise, and Hailey Piper.

Baptisms of Horror & Ecstasy: Supernatural Stories of the Great God Pan edited by William P. Simmons (Shadow House Publishing) is an anthology of twenty classic story and poetry reprints honoring the Great God Pan.

Never Whistle at Night: An Indigenous Horror Anthology edited by Shane Hawk and Theodore C. Van Alst Jr. (Vintage Books) contains twenty-six new stories. The best are by Tommy Orange, Darcie Little Badger, Shane Hawk, Amber Blaeser-Wardzala, Cherie Dimaline, Mathilda Zeller, David Heska Wanbli Weiden, Royce K. Young Wolf, and Marcie R. Rendon.

No Trouble at All edited by Alexis DuBon and Eric Raglin (Cursed Morsels Press) is a very good anthology featuring fifteen new stories about the consequences of compliance/politeness. With notable stories by Shenoa Carroll-Bradd, Matthew D. Urban, J. Rohr, Simone le Roux, Nadia Bulkin, Angela Sylvaine, Gordon B. White, and Gwendolyn Kiste.

Hot Iron and Cold Blood: An Anthology of the Weird West edited by Patrick McDonough (Death's Head Press) contains sixteen stories, three of them reprints. The best of the originals are by Drew E. Huff, Kenzie Jennings, Jeff Strand, and Vivian Kasley. With a foreword by R. J. Joseph.

Unspeakable Horror 3: Dark Rainbow Rising edited by Vince A. Liaguno (Crystal Lake Publishing) is the third volume of LGBTQIA horror stories. Of the twenty-six new stories, the strongest are by Sara Tantlinger, Amanda M. Blake, Paul Tremblay, Craig Brownlie, Lucy A. Snyder, Craig Laurence Gidney, Hailey Piper, and Michael Thomas Ford.

In the Cold, Cold Ground edited by Ed Kurtz (Cemetery Dance Publications) presents six horror novellas by William D. Carl, Kristin Dearborn, Ed Kurtz, Errick Nunnally, Kyle Rader, and Morgan Sylvia, each set in a state in New England.

Wicked Sick: An Anthology of New England Horror Writers edited by Kristi Petersen Schoonover and Scott T. Goudsward (Wicked Creative) is an all-original anthology of sixteen stories and poems about the impact of illness. There are notable stories by Catherine Grant, Mike Deady, L. L. Soares, Meg Smith, Gevera Bert Piedmont, and K.H. Vaughn.

A Night of Screams edited by Richard Z. Santos (Arte Publica Press) features eighteen all-new stories and four poems of Latino horror, many focusing on cartel violence, immigration, and bigotry. There is notable work by Richie Narvaez, Ruben Quesada, Flor Salcedo, Sydney Macias, Ann Dávila Cardinal, Adrian Ernesto Cepeda, Pedro Iniguez, Marcos Damián León, and Toni Margarita Plummer.

Shadows Out of Time edited by Darrell Schweitzer (Drugstore Indian Press) is an all-original anthology of Lovecraftian-inspired stories focused on conflicts in time. The strongest are by James Chambers, Frederic S. Durbin, Robert Guffey, Adrian Cole, Will Murray, and Nicholas Kaufmann.

The Canterbury Nightmares edited by David Niall Wilson (Macabre Ink) is intended as a dark homage to Chaucer's *Canterbury Tales*, using the conceit of eleven travelers enroute to the Grand Canyon after COVID has taken a toll on them or their loved ones. There are notable stories by Michael Boatman, S. A. Cosby, Anna Tambour, and an especially good one by Eric LaRocca, having nothing to do with COVID nor the Grand Canyon.

Remains to be Told: Dark Tales of Aotearoa edited by Lee Murray (Clandestine Press) is a very good anthology of twenty horror stories (all but three new) and poems by New Zealanders (or those who have lived there) using the country's myth and terrain in fascinating ways. There is notable original work by Paul Mannering, Denver Grenell, Tracie McBride, Jacqui Greaves, Gina Cole, Dan Rabarts, William Cook, Kirstin McKenzie, Helena Claudia, and Marty Young.

Literally Dead: Tales of Holiday Hauntings edited by Gaby Triana (Alienhead Press) features nineteen new winter ghost stories, not all of them dark. It includes notable horror by Ramsey Campbell, Brooke MacKenzie, Clay McLeod Chapman, Douglas Ford, and Chet Williamson.

The Drive-In Multiplex: An Anthology with Blood and Popcorn edited by Christopher Golden and Brian Keene (Thunderstorm Books/Pandi Press) is an excellent homage to Joe R. Lansdale's 1988 novel *The Drive-In*, which combined science fiction with east Texas horror resulting in bloody mayhem. Twenty-two writers splash their guts on the pages to great effect. All the stories are very good. With an introduction by the co-editors about how the novel influenced them and so many other horror writers.

Darkness Beckons edited by Mark Morris (Flame Tree Press) is an excellent entry in this annual unthemed anthology series. It includes sixteen stories, with notable ones by J. S. Breukelaar, Lucie McKnight Hardy, H. V. Patterson, Ally Wilkes, Reggie Oliver, Peter Atkins, Carly Holmes, Brian Evenson, Alyssa C. Greene, Sarah Read, Stephen Volk, and Angela Slatter. The Holmes and the Patterson are reprinted herein.

McSweeney's 71: Horror Stories guest-edited by Brian Evenson features sixteen stories from an array of talent. There's a satisfying variety of quirky, weird, and dark fiction within and while all the stories are good reads, there's notable dark work by Stephen Graham Jones, Natanya Ann Pulley, Erika T. Wurth, Nicholas Russell, Gabino Iglesias, Kristine Ong Muslim, Nick Antosca, Senaa Ahmad, Atilla Veres, and M. T. Anderson. Also includes a note about the production and design. I adore *McSweeney's* because each issue is a work of art, and this volume is no exception. The book itself is in a box within a box, with a gorgeous slipcase, attractive endpapers, and an interior that, while difficult to read (my one caveat), is very handsome. The Jones story is reprinted herein.

Terror Tales of the Mediterranean edited by Paul Finch (Telos) continues this series of regional horror, but for the first time ventures outside the United Kingdom. In this volume there are fourteen stories, four of them reprints. The interstitial material is by Paul Finch. All the stories are very good, with standouts by Jasper Bark and Carly Holmes.

Come October is an anthology of autumnal horror edited by C. M. Muller (Chthonic Matter), with eighteen new stories. There are notable stories by Patrick Barb, Tara Laskowski, David Peak, James Pate, Robert Helfst, Kurt Newton, C. W. Blackwell, and Mark Howard Jones. The Barb is reprinted herein.

Deathrealm Spirits edited by Stephen Mark Rainey (Shortwave Publishing) is an unthemed anthology of twenty new stories and poems inspired by the editor's small press magazine *Deathrealm*, published between 1987 and 1997. There are notable stories and poems by Linda D. Addison, Meghan Arcuri, Eric LaRocca, Brian Keene, and Maurice Broaddus.

Novus Monstrum edited by Douglas Gwilym and Ken MacGregor (Dragon's Roost Press) is an anthology of twenty-two new stories about monsters. It includes notable stories by Ramsey Campbell, Marco Cultrera, R. A. Busby, Jamie Lackey, Gemma Files, Joe R. Lansdale, and Jonathan Maberry. The Campbell is reprinted herein.

Black Wings VII: Tales of Lovecraftian Horror edited by S. T. Joshi (Drugstore Indian Press) features sixteen new stories and a poem, with notable work by David Hambling, Stephen Woodworth, Ann K. Schwader, Steve Rasnic Tem, and Mark Howard Jones.

Brute: Stories of Dark Desire edited by Steve Berman (Lethe Press) features nineteen stories full of masculine kink, violence, and sometimes supernatural encounters. Seven of the stories are new.

All These Sunken Souls: A Black Horror Anthology edited by Circe Moskowitz (Amberjack Publishing) is an unthemed anthology with ten new pieces of fiction. The most notable stories are by Donyae Coles and Ryan Douglas.

Shadows Over Main Street Volume Three edited by Doug Murano and D. Alexander Ward (Bleeding Edge Books) is the third and final volume of Lovecraftian tales taking place in small town America, and includes seventeen new stories and one reprint. There's notable work by John Langan, Laird Barron, Clay McLeod Chapman, Kristi DeMeester, Laurel Hightower, S. A. Cosby, Ramsey Campbell, Ao-Hui Lin, and Andy Davidson.

Morbidologies edited by John F. D. Taff and Shane D. Keene (Bleeding Edge Books) is a loosely themed anthology of people obsessed with unsavory and disturbing objects. Included are twelve new stories and one poem. There's notable work by Shane D. Keene, Gwendolyn Kiste, and Craig Wallwork.

Out There Screaming: An Anthology of New Black Horror edited by Jordan Peele and John Joseph Adams (Random House) presents nineteen new stories, with notable work by P. Djèlí Clark, Terence Taylor, Tananarive Due, Nicole D. Sconiers, Lesley Nneka Arimah, Maurice Broaddus, Rebecca Roanhorse, Nalo Hopkinson, Cadwell Turnbull, and Ezra Claytan Daniels.

Shakespeare Unleashed edited by James Aquilone (Monstrous Books) has an interesting concept as its theme—forty-two new horror stories and sonnets inspired by some of William Shakespeare's most famous works. There's notable work by Philip Fracassi, Steve Rasnic Tem, Gwendolyn Kiste, Hailey Piper, Jonathan Maberry, Marisca Pichette, Stephanie Ellis, Maxwell I. Gold, Geneve Flynn, Stephanie M. Wytovich, Simon Bestwick, and a collaboration by Kasey Lansdale and Joe R. Lansdale. It includes an introduction by the late Weston Ochse.

Azathoth: Ordo ab Chao edited by J. Aaron French (JournalStone) contains seventeen new stories and one new poem about the effects on humankind of Azathoth, the Lovecraftian God of Chaos. There are notable stories by Matthew Cheney, R. B. Payne, Richard Thomas, Samuel Marzioli, and Adam L. G. Nevill. Each story has a black and white introductory illustration.

Collage Macabre: An Exhibition of Art Horror (no editor) (Future Dead Collective) has eighteen stories focusing on different artistic disciplines. With an introduction by Gemma Amor. There are notable stories by Timothy Lanz and Ryan Marie Ketterer.

Blackened Roots: An Anthology of the Undead edited by Nicole Givens Kurtz and Tonia R. Ransom (Mocha Memoirs Press) features ten new Afrocentric zombie stories. There's notable work by Steven Van Patten, Erick Nunnally, and Eden Royce.

Christmas and Other Horrors edited by Ellen Datlow (Titan Books) is an all-original anthology of eighteen horror stories revolving around the solstice. The stories by Tananarive Due and Christopher Golden are reprinted herein.

Mystery, Murder, Madness, Mythos edited by Glynn Owen Barras and Brian M. Sammons (Drugstore Indian Press) is a good, all-original anthology of twelve murder mysteries tied to Lovecraft's mythos stories. There is notable work by John Langan, Nick Mamatas, David Conyers, Lucy A. Snyder, Thana Niveau, William Meikle, and a collaboration by Peter Rawlik and Sal Ciano.

Lonely Hollows edited by Cliff Biggers and Charles R. Rutledge (Pavane Press) contains fifteen stories of folk horror. The strongest are by John Linwood Grant and Amanda DeWees.

The Winter Spirits: Ghostly Tales for Frost Nights edited by Rosanna Forte (Sphere) is a British, all-original anthology of twelve stories revolving around Christmas and Advent. The best are by Andrew Michael Hurley, Imogen Hermes Gowar, Natasha Pulley, Catriona Ward, and Elizabeth McNeal.

A Darkness Visible: Explorations of Horror in the Postmodern edited by G. M. Miller, Ewan Moor, Lara Taffer, Justin A. Burnett (Ontology Books) features seventeen new stories that are described in the introduction as "postmodern horror." The introduction itself may be off-putting to some readers, with an academic slant that doesn't add anything to the reading experience. Better for readers to consider the anthology unthemed and just enjoy the stories, many of which are weird, some dark. There's notable fiction by Daniel Braum, Michael Harris Cohen, Gemma Files, Tyler Jones, and Jo Kaplan.

A Tale that is Told edited by Julia Kruk, Tracy Lee, and Maria Weidmann (The Dracula Society) is a celebration of the fiftieth anniversary of the Dracula Society, with sixteen tales and poems inspired by Stoker's *Dracula*.

Dead Letters: Episodes of Epistolary Horror edited by Jacob Steven Mohr (Crystal Lake Publishing) has twenty-one new stories told via letters, emails, podcast transcripts, police reports, and other means of communication. Reading a book filled with these kinds of stories is unexpectedly exhausting, but there is notable work by J. Rohr, Colin Leonard, Gemma Files, Zach Rosenberg, Jacob Steven Mohr, Gregg Stewart, and Justin Allec.

Night's Black Agents: An Anthology of Vampire Fiction edited by Daniel Corrick (Snugly Books) has thirteen reprints written between the early nineteenth century and the early twentieth century, including stories by Alexander Dumas, Leopold von Sacher-Masoch, Toni Schwabe, and others—most of them unfamiliar names.

The Fiends in the Furrows III: Final Harvest edited by David T. Neal & Christine M. Scott (Nosetouch Press) is an excellent original anthology of folk horror, with nineteen stories. There's notable work by Tracy Fahey, Dan Coxon, Timothy Granville, Fox Claret Hill, Rae Knowles, Thersa Matsuura, Richard Thomas, and Charlie Hughes. The Hughes is reprinted herein.

Seasons of Severance edited by Brhel & Sullivan (Cemetery Gates Media) features four authors each with four stories of dark fantasy and horror, most of the work new. The authors are Sara Tantlinger, Corey Farrenkopf, Jessie Ann York, and Red Lagoe. There was notable horror by Jessie Ann York.

Table for 3 by Douglas Ford, Holly Rae Garcia, Rebecca Rowland edited by Holly Rae Garcia (Easton Falls) is a charity anthology created to provide funds for a Texas Food Bank. The three novellas all deal with horrific visions of hunger.

Mixed-genre Anthologies

In Trouble edited by E. F. Schraeder and Elaine Schleiffer (Omnium Gatherum) presents twenty stories about unwelcome births/arrivals, three of them new. *The King Must Fall* edited by Adrian Collins, Mike Myers, and Sarah Chorn (*Grimdark* magazine) is a large reprint anthology representing nineteen dark fantasy stories originally published in the Australian Quarterly. *Underland Arcana Deck Three* edited by Mark Teppo (Underland Press) reprints all the stories published in the *Underland Arcana* magazine in 2023. *Joe Ledger: Unbreakable* edited by Jonathan Maberry and Bryan Thomas Schmidt (JournalStone) is an entertaining anthology of fifteen new stories (and one reprint) starring Maberry's iconic hero. All the stories are suspenseful, and some are horror. There are notable stories by Dana Fredsti, Scott Sigler, and Jonathan Maberry. *The Other Side of Never* edited by Marie O'Regan and Paul Kane (Titan Books) is an original anthology of eighteen dark stories about Peter and Wendy and Neverland. There are notable stories by Robert Shearman, Claire North, Muriel Gray, Edward Cox, and Paul Finch. *Lush and Other Tales of Boozy Mayhem* by Duane Swierczynski (Cimarron Street Books) is the first collection by a talented writer of science fiction, crime, and horror. The seventeen stories (all but one reprints) showcase a selection of his work over twenty-five years. Alas, my favorite of his stories, "Tender as Teeth"—a zombie tale co-written with Stephanie Crawford and which I've reprinted more than once—is not included. *Qualia Nous Volume 2* edited by Michael Bailey (Written Backwards) is an intriguing mix of science fiction and horror, as was the first volume, published in 2014. The forty-two stories and poems in the new volume are mostly new, except for three pieces. There's notable horror by Michael Paul Anderson, Geneve Flynn, Mark Grainger, Maxwell I. Gold, Eric LaRocca, Cynthia Pelayo, Eugen Bacon, Jeff Oliver, Gary A. Braunbeck, L. Marie Wood, Iglesias Gabino, Kaaron Warren, Josh Malerman, and a collaboration by Richard Thomas and Repo Kempt. *Uncertainties VI* edited by Brian J. Showers (The Swan River Press) is a regular series of anthologies of new weird, often dark fiction. There are eleven stories in this volume, with notable dark ones by A. K. Benedict, Méabh De Brún, Naben Ruthnum, James Everington, Ruth Barber, and Alison Moore. *Three-Lobed Burning Eye Volume IX* edited by Andrew S. Fuller (Legion Press) reprints twenty-five stories of fantasy and horror published on the website between 2021–2022. *Unquiet Grove* edited by Mark Beech (Egaeus Press) is an impressive all-original anthology of weird, uncanny, and dark fiction about Great Britain's forests and trees. It includes notable stories by Charles Wilkinson, Adam L. G. Nevill, Alys Hobbs, and Colin Insole. The Nevill is reprinted herein. *Swords in the Shadows: A Sword and Sorcery Anthology* edited by Cullen Bunn (Outland Entertainment) has twenty-one stories of mostly dark fantasy. The most interesting work is by Rena Mason, Mary SanGiovanni, Stephen Graham Jones, and Jonathan Janz. *Back 2 Omnipark* edited by Ben Thomas and Alicia Hilton (House Blackwood) features fifteen more new weird and/or dark stories about a very weird theme park. There's notable work by Gwendolyn Kiste, Jonathan Maberry, Brian Evenson, Kristi DeMeester, and Laird Barron. *Great British Horror 8: Something Peculiar* edited by Steve J. Shaw (Black Shuck Books) is an annual anthology series of new stories, all but one of the eleven by Britons, and one by a foreign writer. Only some of the stories in 2023 were horrific, but there was notable dark work by Stephen Gallagher, Steve Toase, Reggie Oliver, and Shona Kinsella. *Twice Cursed* edited by Marie O'Regan and Paul Kane (Titan Books) is a follow-up to the editors' earlier volume of dark fantasy (with some horror) about curses. There are sixteen stories in this one, with five of them reprints. The strongest originals are by Angela Slatter, Mark Chadbourne, and M. C. Carey. *Wilted Pages: An Anthology of Dark Academia* edited by Ai Jiang & Christie Nogle (Shortwave Publishing) has nineteen stories of dark fantasy and horror. There's notable horror by Simo Srinivas, John Langan, Steve Rasnic Tem, Brian Evenson, Ayida Shonibar, and Premee Mohamed. There was a second anthology on the same theme published in 2023: *In These Hallowed Halls* edited by Marie O'Regan and Paul Kane (Titan Books), with twelve stories of crime, dark fantasy, and horror. The best of the horror was by Kelly Andrew, David Bell, Helen Grant, and Tori Bovalino. *Open All Night* edited by Eirek Gumeny (Atomic Carnival Books) contains seventeen stories themed around the graveyard shift in retail. There's weirdness and there's horror. Notable horror stories by Amanda Cecilia Lang, Elena Greer, and Zachery Rosenberg,

Mooncalves: An Anthology of Strange Stories edited by John WM Thompson (NO Press) features twenty-three weird stories, some of them horror. The strongest horror stories are by Brian Evenson, Adam Golaski, Christi Nogle, Lisa Tuttle, Jeff Wood, L. Marie Wood, Meghan Lamb, and Glen Hirshberg. *The Dusk: Tales for Twilight* edited by John Hirschhorn-Smith (Side Real Press) is an intriguing anthology of twenty-one stories taking place during the time of day that the sun is going down. A mixed bag, filled with weird and sometimes dark stories. There is notable horror by Peter Bell, Colin Insole,

Steve Duffy, Katherine Haynes, David Surface, Victoria Day, and Kevin Patrick McCann. *At the Lighthouse* edited by Sophie Essex (Eibonvale) has seventeen stories about lighthouses, some of which are horror. The notable darker ones are by Tom Johnstone, Pete Sillett, and Tim Lees. *Obsolescence* edited by Alan Lastufka and Kristina Horner (Shortwave Publishing) is an anthology of twenty-seven new stories about tech gone wrong, with some horror. There are notable stories by Hailey Piper, Rob Hart, Katie Young, Emma R. Murray, Kealan Patrick Burke, and Clay McLeod Chapman. *African Ghost Short Stories* edited by Chinelo Onwualu (Flame Tree Press) contains a large selection of new and classic tales (not seen by me). *Scotland the Strange: Weird Tales from Storied Lands* edited by Johnny Mains (The British Library) is a good-looking treat that reprints eighteen tales originally published between 1818 and 1976. *Fantasmagoriana Deluxe: Fantasmagoriana and Tales of the Dead* edited by Eric J. Guignard and Leslie S. Klinger (Dark Moon Books) is a beautiful showcase reprinting and combining two ghost story anthologies. One, containing eight stories, was translated from German into French and originally published in 1812. The second was partially translated into English as *Tales of the Dead*, excluding two stories and adding one new one in 1813. With an extensive introduction by Lisa Morton.

CHAPBOOKS AND NOVELLAS

Nightjar Press, run by Nicholas Royle, continued to publish its series of short story chapbooks. Alas, only a few are dark these days, although of the ten published, the chapbooks by Cliff McNish, Tim Cook, Charlotte Turnbull, Robert Stone, Jean Sprackland, Amanda Huggins, and Cynan Jones might satisfy the dedicated horror reader. *The Salt Grows Heavy* by Cassandra Khaw (Nightfire) is a gorgeously written, grisly fairy tale in which a carnivorous mermaid joins a strange doctor on an eerie journey through a myth-haunted taiga (acquired and edited by me). *Bitters* by Kaaron Warren (Cemetery Dance Publications) is a brutal, dystopian tale about a huge metal man that is the receptacle for all the dead bodies in a town, creating "bitters," a drink that keeps the town prosperous and healthy—and addicted. *Sleep Alone* by J. A. W. McCarthy (Off Limits Press) is a powerful and engaging novella about a lonely succubus who has turned a rock and roll band into creatures like herself, although they start suffering from a mysterious illness. *Despatches* by Lee Murray (Absinthe Books/PS Publishing) is a beautifully rendered piece of historical horror about a battle during WWI that takes an emotional toll on its combatants and grows darker as the story introduces cosmic horror to the mix. *Slow Progress* by Sharon Gosling (Withnail Books) is a brief, disturbing post-apocalyptic horror story. *A House with Good Bones* by T. Kingfisher (Nightfire) is a southern gothic about a woman who returns to the family home in South Carolina to help her mother, whose personality has changed . . . is she losing her mind, or is she being haunted? The snarky tone of the protagonist and the eccentricities of those who live in the town are the perfect counterpoint to the creepiness of the plot. *8:59:29* by Polly Schattel (Trepidatio Publishing) is a clever tale about what happens when a faculty member plots revenge on her hated department head. The tale sits firmly in the sub-genre of film horror, creating a film that will influence and/or kill when viewed. *The Black Tree on the Hill* by Karla Yvette (Clash Books) is a gothic, alternate world western in which only one person—a witch—notices a tree that did not exist the day before and decides to investigate. *Bleak Houses* by Kate Maruyama (Raw Dog Screaming Press) collects two stories about familial dysfunction, one a reprint and one new. *Coffin Shadows* by Mark Steensland and Glen Krisch (Cemetery Dance Publications) is a gothic about a woman whose infant child died mysteriously and is now haunted by the appearance of a boy twelve years later. *Shooting Star* by Joe Lansdale (Pandi Press) is about what happens when two guys are going fishing and a flying saucer hits the train they're on. What emerges threatens the human race. *Horror Movie Marathon* by Kevin Lucia (Bleeding Edge Books) is a story of found footage, this time in a strange home movie that's part of a collection of tapes willed to a horror fan by the deceased owner of the last retail video store in upstate New York. *Split Scream Volume Three* features two horror novelettes in one book: one by Patrick Barb and one by J. A. W. McCarthy (Dread Stone Press). *The Bonny Swans* by P. L. Watts (My Dark Library) is a gothic novella taking place in 1789 France about a woman with amnesia, who is taken on as governess to the daughter of a rich merchant. *The Leaves Forget* by Alan Baxter (Absinthe Books) is about what happens when the brother of a missing woman receives a pack of her letters written a few days after her disappearance. *Mosaic* by Catherine McCarthy (Dark Hart Books) is about a glazier hired to restore the stained-glass window of a thirteenth-century church. But as she repairs the window, an ancient cosmic horror begins to emerge. *Corporate Body* by R. A. Busby (My Dark Library #6) is about a scientific experiment that becomes a body horror nightmare for its unwitting test subject. *They Shut Me Up* by Tracy Fahey (Absinthe Books/PS Publishing) is about a librarian who, in researching the true story behind the myth of a monster, discovers her own voice. *The Scourge Between Stars* by Nessa Brown (Nightfire) is an sf horror novella about a mysterious killer on a spaceship. *The Shadow Dancers of Brixton Hill* by Nicole Willson (Cemetery Gates Media) takes place in the mid-1930s and is about a woman who, while scouting for new acts to join her father's circus, is introduced to three young girls who can make their shadows dance independently of their bodies. *Vandal: Stories of Damage* by Kaaron Warren, Aaron Dries, and J. S. Breukelaar (Dark Tide Book 6) features three powerful, exceedingly dark novellas by Australian writers at the top of their game. Warren's is about a pack of cards commemorating death scenes and a woman obsessed (as her family was) with the places where these deaths took place; the Dries is about an estranged couple in Samoa trying to survive a tidal wave—but that's not the worst thing they have to survive. The Breukelaar is a dark fairy tale about a deal with a demon made by an artist in Poland and how his descendants attempt to break the curse he invoked with the deal. *The Wind Began to Howl* by Laird Barron (Bad Hand Books) is a new installment in Barron's dark crime series about P. I. Isaiah Coleridge. In this one, Coleridge becomes involved in a search for two brother musicians that strays into weird territory.

NON-FICTION

Night Mother: A Personal and Cultural History of The Exorcist by Marlena Williams (The Ohio State University Press) is a creative nonfiction collection of essays by the author—who was told by her mother to not watch *The Exorcist* but did anyway. Williams examines and analyzes the film with regard to its cultural influences, what it said about American girlhood, and its influence on herself and her mother. *When the Stars Are*

Right: H.P. Lovecraft and Astronomy by Edward Guimont and Horace A. Smith (Hippocampus Press) is a treatise about Lovecraft's lifelong interest and appreciation of astronomy and its influence on his nonfiction and fiction. *H. P. Lovecraft Letters to Hyman Bradofsky and Others* edited by David E. Schultz and S. T. Joshi (Hippocampus Press) introduces several people involved in amateur journalism who corresponded with Lovecraft while he was involved in the same. There are letters to others and some poetry (not by Lovecraft). This volume is pretty esoteric. *Modern Occultism: History, Theory, and Practice* by Mitch Horowitz (G&D Media) is a large, in-depth look at various aspects of the occult through history from astrology to witchcraft. *Frightfest Guide: Mad Doctor Movies* by John Llewellyn Probert (FAB Press) is a detailed history of the mad doctor archetype in horror movies, with an overview and more than two hundred reviews. *Middle Eastern Gothics: Literature, Spectral Modernities and the Restless Past* edited by Karen Grumberg (University of Wales Press) is the first scholarly volume on Gothic literature from the Middle East and North Africa. Its nine chapters cover material written in Arabic, Hebrew, Turkish, and Persian. *Literary Hauntings: A Gazetteer of Literary Ghost Stories from Britain and Ireland* edited by R. B. Russell, Rosalie Parker, and Mark Valentine (Tartarus Press) has 267 entries identifying and describing real-life places that have inspired the best fictional ghost stories in Britain and Ireland. *Corman/Poe: Interviews and Essays Exploring the Making of Roger Corman's Edgar Allan Poe Films, 1960-1964* by Chris Alexander (Headpress) covers each of the eight films Corman made of Poe's works. With a foreword by Corman and copious black and white and color illustrations and photographs. *Cornish Gothic: 1830-1912* by Joan Passey (University of Wales Press) is a literary history of Cornwall in the gothic imagination and its evolution from the perception of Cornwall as a foreign nation on the border of England to an actual part of the United Kingdom as a result of the Victorian expansion of the railway. The book covers writers such as Alfred Tennyson, Thomas Hardy, Wilkie Collins, Mary Elizabeth Braddon, and others. *A Critical Companion to Wes Craven* edited by Fernando Gabriel Pagnoni Berns and John Darowski (Lexington Books) is an academic study with seventeen essays of the director's work, most accessible to the layperson. The volume covers Craven's porn and television work, in addition to his horror movies. *The Routledge Companion to Folk Horror* edited by Robert Edgar and Wayne Johnson (Routledge) is divided into five parts and includes forty papers covering the history of folk horror from medieval texts to the present day. *The Black Guy Dies First: Black Horror Cinema from Fodder to Oscar* by Robin R. Means Coleman and Mark H. Harris (Gallery Books/Saga Press) is an excellent historical overview of Black actors' roles in horror movies from the very beginning of film when their presence was used for comic relief, with stereotypical reactions to scary or unsettling events through being villains in inaccurate/insulting depictions of Black centered religions, to being used as sacrifices to save the white hero or playing second fiddle to the white hero, and finally (at least sometimes) having the agency and ability to be heroes themselves. Entertaining, fascinating, and a refreshing tsunami of relevance to the issue of racism in US culture. It's an important addition to film history. *The Spark of Modernism: Twenty Speculative Stories and Writings that Defined an Era, 1886-1939* edited by William Gillard, James Reitter, and Robert Stauffer (McFarland) brings together science fiction and horror stories written during a period of cultural and technological transformation, plus essays that put the fiction into context. Horror fiction by Arthur Machen, M. R. James, H. P. Lovecraft, and Mary E. Wilkins Freeman is included. *Novels by Aliens: Weird Tales and the Twenty-First Century* by Kate Marshall (The University of Chicago Press) is an academic collection of essays examining the non-human and weird in recent fiction, particularly fiction from non-human perspectives. *Plague-Busters: Medicine's Battles with History's Deadliest Diseases* by Lindsey Fitzharris and Adrian Teal (Bloomsbury) is an entertaining and informative illustrated history of six diseases that were eventually conquered by medical discoveries. The book is intended for a younger audience, but its sassy treatment of the subject should make it just as attractive to adults. *101 Books to Read Before You're Murdered* by Sadie "Mother Horror" Hartmann (Page Street) is Hartmann's personal guide to her favorite horror books published since 2000. While she might not include all of *your* favorites, there's plenty in here for every horror reader to enjoy, mull over, and argue about. Informative, thoughtful, and most important—it's a fun overview of the field. *Unquiet Spirits: Essays by Asian Women in Horror* edited by Lee Murray and Angela Yuriko Smith

(Black Spot) is a powerful collection of personal essays by Asian women horror writers about the stories and traditions that have influenced—and at times—hindered their work. *160 Black Women in Horror* by Sumiko Saulson (Iconoclast Publications) is a useful reference work, with brief biographies of each writer included. *A Vindication of Monsters: Essays on Mary Wollstonecraft and Mary Shelley* edited by Claire Fitzgerald (IFWG) features sixteen writers who delve deeply into the lives of this mother and daughter, and how their circumstances and the time they lived in, in turn influenced their writing, particularly Shelley's masterpiece *Frankenstein; Or, The Modern Prometheus.*

POETRY

Spectral Realms edited by S. T. Joshi (Hippocampus Press), is a showcase for weird and dark poetry. Two issues were published in 2023. In addition to original poems there's a section with classic reprints and a review column. During the year, there was notable poetry by Adam Bolivar, Oliver Smith, Steve Withrow, Patricia Dompieri, Ngo Binh Anh Khoa, Lori R. Lopez, Lee Clark Zumpe, Christian Dickinson, Benjamin Blake, and Carl E. Reed.

Star*Line is the official quarterly journal of the Science Fiction Poetry Association. During 2023, it was edited by Jean-Paul Garnier. It regularly publishes members' science fiction and fantasy poetry—and occasionally horror. It also publishes reviews of other poetry magazines, collections, and anthologies plus a market report. In 2023, the journal published notable dark poetry by Brian Hugenbruch, Ai Jiang, Shelly Jones, Marisca Pichette, Devan Barlow, Melissa Ridley Elmes, and Jessica Peter.

Dwarf Stars 2023 edited by David C. Kopaska-Merkel & Miguel O. Mitchell (Science Fiction and Fantasy Poetry Association) collects the best very short speculative poems published in 2022. The poems are ten lines or fewer and the prose poems one hundred words or fewer.

The 2023 Rhysling Anthology edited by Maxwell I. Gold and selected by the Science Fiction Poetry Association (Science Fiction and Fantasy Poetry Association) is used by members to vote for the best short and long poems of the year, and can be considered an annual report on the state of speculative poetry. This year's volume, covering the year 2022, is a bit over 150 pages, and is divided into Short and Long Poems. It's an excellent resource for checking out the poetic side of speculative and horror fiction. The volume includes a history of past winners.

The Nothing Box & Other Poems by Steven Withrow (Mind's Eye Publications) presents fifty dark poems, most of them published for the first time.

Beautiful Malady by Ennis Rook Bashe (Interstellar Flight Press) is a short but powerful collection of thirty poems using fairy tales and folklore to put a gleaming spotlight on disability, pain, and death.

Bleeding Rainbows and Other Broken Spectrums by Maxwell I. Gold (Hex Publishers) is an audacious collection of poetry about monsters, lust, and sex. The language is crisp and concise.

A Shadow of Your Former Self by Amy Grech (Alien Buddha Press) contains poems and very brief stories written in the midst of the most virulent period of the COVID pandemic, about its horrors and New York horrors.

Rivers in Your Skin, Sirens in Your Hair by Marisca Pichette (Android Press) presents fifty fantasy and dark fantasy poems, often using myth and folklore as touchstones.

Paper Houses by Thomas Tilton (self-published) is an excellent collection of horror haikus—having a surprising impact for such a specialized form.

Numinous Stones by Holly Lyn Walrath (Aqueduct Press/Conversation Pieces) is an excellent collection of poetry, much of it about grief. Each poem is written in the form of the pantoum, derived from the Malay verse *pantun berkait*, which is comprised of interwoven quatrains (four lines) of alternating lines. When done well, this creates an almost hypnotic rhythm, which initially (to me) was annoying, but by the end of the book won me over completely.

The Subject of Blackberries by Stephanie M. Wytovich (Raw Dog Screaming Press) is a strong collection inspired by the author's personal hardships and anxiety, some of it triggered by postpartum depression.

The Patient Routine by Luna Rey Hall (Brigids Gate Press) is an ambitious book-length impressionist narrative poem about being trapped in a hospital (for health, and other reasons), sickness, and body horror.

A Wheel of Ravens by Adam Bolivar (Jackanapes Press) is a lovely collection of dark fantasy alliterative verse in "Olde English style"—an ancient poetic form outlawed by the Normans upon their conquest of England in 1066. The poems themselves are influenced by Germanic and Nordic mythic sagas.

The Price of a Small Hot Fire by E. F. Schraeder (Raw Dog Screaming Press) is a powerful collection of poetry about grief, survival, and the mother-daughter relationship.

Hemlock and Hellfire: Poems About Witches and Woodlands by Morgan Sylvia (self-published) is an excellent collection of mostly new poems.

Darkest Days and Haunted Ways by Ashley Dioses (Jackanapes Press) is a collection of dark poems, some originally written when the poet was a teenager and since then polished upon maturity. Most of the poems are new.

What the Night Brings by Frank Coffman (Mind's Eye Publications), with illustrations by Mutartis Boswell, is the poet's fourth collection of speculative poetry, including science fiction, dark and weird fantasy, and horror in several different poetic forms.

For the Outsider: Poems Inspired by H. P. Lovecraft edited by S. T. Joshi (Hippocampus Press) is a good-sized anthology of poetry written to, or inspired by, H. P. Lovecraft. Although most of the poems are reprints, many appear for the first time. There are notable new dark poems by Maxwell I. Gold, Leigh Blackmore, and Frank Coffman.

Poetry Showcase Volume X edited by Angela Yuriko Smith (Horror Writers Association) is an annual anthology of some of the best poetry that the members of HWA have to offer. Always excellent, there were standouts by Sarah Tantlinger, Emily Ruth Verona, Saba Syed Razvi, Pauline Yates, Corey Niles, Grace R. Reynolds, Janine Cross, and Jacqueline West.

Pictures of Apocalypse by Thomas Ligotti (Chiroptera Press) is a collection of twenty poems about the end of the world, with illustrations throughout by Jonathan Dennison.

Odds and Ends

Infinite Black: Tales From the Abyss by Jeff Oliver and Dan Verkys (self-published) is a gorgeous/terrifying collaboration of black and white art and science fiction horror poetry about the encroachment of machines into human flesh.

The Stephen King Catalog 2023 Annual (Overlook Connection Press) is a charming oddity (emphatically *not* a catalog) I haven't seen before. Produced by Dave Hinchberger, who has been putting this out for years. This one is full color for the first time and dedicated to King's *Creepshow*. With cover and interior art by Glenn Chadbourne. Includes art, calendar, bits and pieces and articles about *Creepshow*. Hinchberger has decided to take the word "catalog" out of the title from now on. It's a worthy collectible for King fans/readers.

THE IMPORTANCE
OF A TIDY HOME

CHRISTOPHER GOLDEN

f anyone had told Freddy he would one day be elbow deep in a garbage bin behind a third-rate restaurant in Salzburg, searching for a late dinner, he would have scoffed at them. Haughtily, of course, the way professors are meant to scoff. That had been his occupation—both vocation and avocation—until 1957, when addiction to morphine had led first to petty crimes and then to a psychiatric hospital. This was before Austria had begun to approach drug addiction as a problem requiring treatment instead of punishment, and so there had been a bit of time in prison as well.

Prison had helped.

Freddy knew that wasn't the case for many who had been in his position, but for him, prison had been a time of clarity. Without drugs, without alcohol, without distraction. He had learned that the mania he had always experienced, the way his skull felt like a hive of agitated bees, could be survived. And if that meant he sometimes saw things that weren't there or said things that others interpreted as either a bit mad or wildly inappropriate, well, that was the eccentricity of a professor.

Of course, once he had been released, no one wanted him as a professor anymore.

Or anything else, for that matter.

By that night, the fifth of January, 1973, he had been living without a home for nine years, during which time he had never diluted his brain with a single ounce of alcohol, nor the use of any illegal substance. But since the polite society of his city had finished with him, Freddy had finished with it. He lived in its parks and haunted its alleys, he accepted the offerings of strangers but never met their eyes, he forged a life from their castoffs, from food and clothing discarded and forgotten just as he had been.

The first time he saw the Schnabelperchten walking the streets in their black robes, with their gleaming shears, and with their enormous, bone-like beaks protruding from beneath their hoods, it did not surprise him that they passed him by. Their duties could not bring them to his doorstep, because of course he had none. No threshold, no door, no visitors, nowhere to mark the start of a new year, only the continued existence of life invisible, a creature unseen. Quiet, even when loud.

The Schnabelperchten were even quieter.

Tonight, he and his friend Bern were out together in search of food, and Freddy had forgotten the date until he spotted the creatures. It was the fourth January 5th he had seen them, and each time they had ignored him. He presumed they appeared every year and that he had slept through their arrival in the years he had missed them.

He watched as they crept along the streets, leaving no trace of their passage through the lightly falling snow. They were delicate creatures, some with their brooms and others with shears, and no door was ever locked to them. Every home opened, no matter how tightly it had been shut up for the evening.

"Chi chi chi," they whispered in the hush of falling snow, and they went about their business.

Freddy climbed down from the side of the garbage bin, holding the bag of leftovers he had known he would find there. The kitchen staff always wrapped the food being discarded and placed it in a single bag along with the uneaten bread. The restaurant manager frowned upon this practice and had shouted at his employees for encouraging nightly visits from the homeless, but they were kind and waited until he was out of the kitchen before putting out the bag. This place was no Gablerbräu, but the staff there had never been so kind, and even if they had been, Freddy did not like roving around that part of the city late at night. It felt more empty, more open, as if anything could happen. Here, there were more homes, lived in by people who desired quiet evenings, away from the downtown.

A clang of metal echoed along the alley.

Bern had let the garbage bin's cover come crashing down. Freddy glanced anxiously around, afraid they would draw unwanted attention. If they created any nuisance, their lives would become more difficult. Sometimes he grew frustrated with Bern for his clumsiness, though never for his addiction. Alcoholism made Bern a fool, but it was the engine that drove him, as much a part of him as his left leg.

"Hush," Freddy said in German, more a plea than an admonition. "Don't be a fool."

Bern did not so much as look at him. Thin and gray, unshaven and unkempt, in an ill-fitting suit that did nothing to disguise the state of his dissolution, he staggered from beside the bin to stand next to Freddy.

"Don't you see them?" he whispered. They were both Austrian, speaking German.

Freddy glanced from the alley into the street again. The Schnabelperchten were still passing by, spread out like a hunting party, perhaps twenty feet separating each from the next, some on one side of the street and some on the other. The most fascinating thing about them was the size of those beaks, at least eighteen inches in length, but wide enough that if one could draw back their hoods, the creatures would not have any face at all, or so it seemed. Only beak, the gray-white of bone. The first year he had seen them, nine years ago, Freddy had been reminded of old photos of plague doctors, but these were not masks, nor did they have anything like goggles to resemble eyes.

They glided along the road. Even as he looked, he saw one approach a door that led to a stairwell, rising to the apartment above the flower shop across the street. Silently, Freddy hoped the owners of that shop kept a tidy home.

"Freddy," Bern rasped, shaking him by the shoulder. "Don't you see them?"

"Hush. Of course I see them."

"Are they ghosts?" Bern whispered. "They don't look like ghosts—they seem solid enough. Are they demons?"

Freddy pondered that. "Honestly, I'm not really sure what they are, though they are certainly not people. They are Schnabelperchten."

The word caused Bern screw up his face in a way that made him look like a toddler given an unfamiliar vegetable for the first time.

"I don't understand. You've just said they're not people, not human. Aren't you frightened?"

Acid burned in Freddy's gut. His laugh was bitter. "Of the Schnabelperchten? Certainly not. You and I have nothing to fear."

"But what *are* they?" Bern prodded.

Freddy gazed at him, trying not to let his friend see the flicker of distaste that passed through him. "I forget, sometimes, that you are not from Salzburg—"

"What has that got to do with anything?"

"If you were a child here, you would know the story," Freddy replied. He patted Bern's back. "Come with me."

His friend hesitated, but when Freddy began to walk along the alley, Bern followed. Most of the Schnabelperchten had already passed by, but there were a few stragglers who had gone into the homes along the street and only now emerged. Without eyes, it was difficult to know for certain whether the Schnabelperchten noticed them, but they showed no interest. They might as well have been dust motes in the air or dry leaves that skittered along the road.

"Do they not see us?" Bern asked.

"They are like most of the people in this city. We are invisible to them," he replied.

One of the Schnabelperchten passed by, and in the light of a streetlamp they could see blood on the blades of his shears, dripping onto the street. When Bern saw that blood he looked as if he might be sick.

"Come," Freddy said. "Those two."

He pointed at a pair of the creatures further up the block. They approached the door of a two-story home. Bern followed anxiously as Freddy crept up behind the two beaked Inspectors.

One of them extended a skinny hand with long fingers like the legs of spiders and turned the doorknob. It ought to have been locked, and Freddy believed that if he or Bern had tried the knob it would not have turned. But for the Inspectors, no door was ever locked. They opened the door and stepped across the threshold. Freddy caught the door before the Schnabelperchten could close it. He heard Bern suck in a terrified breath behind him, but the Inspector who had tried to shut the door just left it and began to move through the house.

"I've followed them before," Freddy whispered, worried more about disturbing the family living in the home than drawing the attention of the creatures.

Inside, the Inspectors began to move about the place, spidery fingers gliding along tabletops in search of dust, beaks lowering to discover if the floors had been swept or vacuumed.

"Chi chi chi," they said quietly, without mouths.

One in the kitchen brought his head down close to the stove and seemed to study its surface for much too long, perhaps deliberating on its relative cleanliness.

Freddy leaned over to whisper into Bern's ear. His friend was trembling.

"It is the Epiphany," he said. "Christmas ends tonight. January first begins the calendar year, but tonight is truly the beginning of the New Year. The Schnabelperchten bring happiness and blessings for the coming year, but only to those who are properly prepared for this new beginning, who have set their houses in order."

"What happens if they enter a home that has not been tidied in anticipation of the new year?" Bern whispered.

Bern watched intently as one of the Inspectors went up the stairs, shears hung at his side. Freddy understood his fear, even found it somewhat delicious, but Bern was his friend and he knew there was cruelty in allowing him to continue in ignorance.

"Something horrible," Freddy said. He took his friend by the wrist and shook it, forcing Bern to look at him. "But we have no home. They are not here for us. Do you see?"

At last, Bern seemed to exhale.

Moments later, the Inspector who had gone to the second floor returned, his shears still clean. It joined its fellow Schnabelperchten and the creatures walked right past Freddy and Bern and out the door. This time it was Bern who led the pursuit of them.

Out on the street again, the breeze was chilly enough to remind them they were alive. Snow fell gently, a hush that felt like it made some sound just beyond the limit of their hearing, though it was only silence.

In morbid fascination, they followed the two creatures while other Schnabelperchten drifted along the street around them, wordless and intent. Moving amongst them, ignored as if invisible, long after midnight and in the quiet hush of gently falling snow, they might as well have been wandering the street inside some Christmas snow globe.

"What *are* they?" Bern wondered aloud.

"Spirits," Freddy replied. It was the only word that felt acceptable. He had so many questions but no real answers. The Schnabelperchten came out one night a year, which meant every other night they were somewhere else. If he could ask them anything, it would be about that.

Schnabelperchten glided silently from building to building. Up along the road, he saw others crawling on the outside of several taller buildings, cloaks billowing in the breeze as they slid open windows that should have been locked. One perched at the edge of a rooftop, scuttled to a domed skylight, opened it and vanished within, his beak leading the way.

Somewhere Freddy heard a baby crying. The infant's wail pierced the oh-so-silent night, and then abruptly ceased. He pressed his eyes tightly shut, forcing himself not to imagine the things his darker fears wanted him to imagine.

They reached the house where the two Schnabelperchten they had followed had gone inside. Bern turned the knob and the door opened. It had unlocked for the Inspectors and remained unlocked, at least until the creatures departed. Bern did not hesitate now—he stepped over the threshold as if he had forgotten Freddy entirely, too curious. Too eager.

Suddenly this felt too intimate. They were intruding on this quiet moment, this breath taken and held until sunrise, when the new year would really begin in earnest. He had a spot behind an old, crumbling school building where heat vented from inside created a small bubble of warmth near the dumpster. The roof's overhang kept the elements off his head except on the worst nights, and he wanted to go back there now, to his spot.

"Bern," he rasped, trying to grab his friend by the back of his coat.

But Bern had passed through the home's little entryway, where coats hung haphazardly on metal hooks—too many coats, too few hooks—and three pair of winter boots were arranged along the wall. Not impeccably neat but he thought they would pass inspection.

Then he followed Bern into the living room, and he froze.

Antlers hung from the wall above the fireplace. The room held an eclectic array of furniture, most of it threadbare and in mismatched floral patterns. A small black-and-white television stood on a tray table beside a fat armchair. Magazines were strewn across the coffee table and piled beside that armchair. An open box of biscuits sat amongst the magazines. A coffee cup and a plate of crumbs and grape stems had been abandoned there. The entire room needed to be straightened, vacuumed, dusted, but the worst of it was the stink of cat urine and the litter box in the far corner, in front of an overstuffed bookshelf that looked as if the books had been stacked and piled by an angry drunk.

Across the room, through an arched entryway that led into the hall, Freddy saw the two Schnabelperchten return from the kitchen and start up the stairs. Bern padded across the stained carpet to follow.

Freddy lunged to grab his arm. "Don't be a fool."

Bern turned to glare at him. "They can't see us."

"We should not intrude," Freddy said. When Bern ignored him, Freddy grabbed him again. "You don't want to see this."

Bern scowled, shook himself loose, and darted for the steps before Freddy could try to drag him from the house. Freddy cursed under his breath and followed. He reached for Bern's coat a third time, but the other man was younger, quicker, and reached the second floor before Freddy could catch up to him.

The top step might as well have been a brick wall. This was as far as Freddy was willing to go. On that last step, he watched as Bern slunk along the corridor and peered into one room, then moved on to the next. Before he reached that room, the noises began.

From the room at the end of the hall came a sound Freddy had heard once before in life, and far too often in nightmares. The sound of shears plunging into flesh—a wet, violent puncture—and then the hushed metal clack of the shears being used.

Bern reached the door from which the noises emanated.

Freddy had warned him, had as much as told him without telling him, but the fool had needed to see for himself. Grim fascination, perhaps, or pure sadism—Freddy didn't think it mattered which. In that bedroom doorway, Bern stood with his eyes widening and let out a scream of horror. Freddy knew he should run, but his feet moved him in the wrong direction, toward his friend instead of away.

He rushed up behind Bern and clamped a hand over his mouth. It muffled the scream, and a second later Bern went silent, perhaps realizing how foolish he'd been.

"Quickly," Freddy whispered in his ear. "Let's go."

Bern whimpered but did not move. Freddy nearly dragged him, but in glancing up at his friend, he had a view over Bern's shoulder and into the bedroom. One of the Schnabelperchten straddled the woman on the bed, using his shears to open her from groin to breastbone. The whole room was in disarray, clothes piled everywhere, plates and cups on the nightstands.

On the floor, the second Inspector knelt beside the corpse of the husband. His guts had been laid open by the shears of the Schnabelperchten and the creature had reached both hands into the dead man's torso and now slid intestines out from his steaming insides, hand over hand, arranging them around the body with a kind of artistry.

The Schnabelperchten disemboweling the man on the floor kept working, but the one on the bed had frozen in the midst of cutting, disrupted by Bern's scream. Shears in hand, it turned its eyeless, mouthless beak toward them and Freddy could feel the weight of its regard, knew that despite the lack of eyes, the creature studied them.

The dead woman's head lolled to one side. Perhaps she had not quite been dead, but now her sightless eyes seemed to gaze at the two men in her bedroom doorway as if accusing them. As if asking why they had not stopped this, why they did not step in, even now, to prevent the further evisceration and desecration that would unfold here.

Freddy held his breath, telling himself that none of this was his fault. These people had comforts that had been beyond his grasp for years. They had heat and running water and a roof over their heads. They had quiet nights in which they could pretend the rest of the world did not exist. They had food to eat and they'd had each other. He told himself they must not be from Salzburg, or they were jaded young people who did not believe in the old stories. He told himself perhaps they had been unpleasant people whose neighbors and friends did not care for them enough to warn them, to teach them the importance of a tidy home.

"Freddy," Bern whispered, his voice cracking.

The hooded Schnabelperchten tilted its head, its focus more intent.

"Chi chi chi," it whispered, with no mouth.

Freddy backed away from the bedroom doorway, tugging Bern with him. The moment they began to retreat, the Schnabelperchten on the bed returned to gutting the woman, no longer interested in the witnesses.

Hauling Bern behind him by the wrist, Freddy bustled down the stairs and out the front door. It clacked shut behind them, the noise like a whipcrack in the night. The snow fell thicker and heavier now and the creatures on the street moved like ghosts, their soft *chi chi chi* carried on the wind.

Instinct sent Freddy down a side street. A Schnabelperchten emerged alone from a doorway, gore dripping thick and red from its shears. Its beak did not turn toward them but it paused and stood in statuesque silence as they passed.

"Where are we going?" Bern whispered, voice cracking.

"My spot," Freddy said, as if it were the stupidest question in the world.

Bern twisted his wrist free and stopped, there in the quiet of Epiphany Night. "Too exposed. We need to hide."

For the first time, Freddy saw the tears in his eyes, the wetness of his cheeks, red from the cold. He wanted to tell Bern they had nothing to worry about, that they had no homes and therefore were in no danger, but he had not liked the way the creature inside that second house had noticed them. Looked at them, if it could be said to look at anything.

"Where, then?"

Bern wiped at his tears. He hesitated a moment as if making a decision, then waved for Freddy to follow. With Bern leading the way, they jogged along the street, then through a side alley, alongside an old stone wall, then behind an ugly, no-frills hotel. Through a gap in the fence behind the hotel, they emerged in the lot of a used car dealership and auto body shop. The pavement had cracks everywhere, weeds growing up between them.

Freddy looked back through the gap in the fence and felt a ripple of relief. There was no sign of the Schnabelperchten.

"I think we're okay," he said.

"This way," Bern replied.

He led Freddy to the other end of the car lot. There were junkers back here, probably only used for parts. Bern brought him to an ugly gray Auto Union station wagon from the late 1950s, tucked between the shells of cars in even worse condition. Rusted and dented, the windshield covered in snow, the wagon was otherwise intact. The tires sagged like an old man's belly.

Bern opened the driver's door, head low, and gestured for Freddy to get in on the passenger side. Aside from the wagon's rear hatch, those were the only two doors. Freddy glanced around, but he realized this wasn't the sort of place that would have a security guard. There were no brand-new vehicles here.

Inside the car, he tried to close the door as quietly as possible, gritting his teeth at the rusty squeal of its hinges. Bern shut his door, and then they were out of the wind and the snow. From inside, Freddy could see the windshield was spider-webbed with cracks and covered in grime under the coating of falling snow, and it was certainly cold in the car, but better than being outdoors tonight.

"The owner of the shop knows I sleep here," Bern said, his voice dull and hollow, as if all the life had been drained out of him. "We can hide until morning. They . . . those things will be gone by morning, right?"

Freddy nodded. It surprised him that Bern had brought him to this shelter. They had known each other for long enough that Freddy thought of Bern as his friend, but if the owner of the car lot really didn't mind Bern sleeping in this dead, rusty car, it was a secret he had taken a risk in sharing. If Freddy told others, soon there might be a dozen people trying to sleep in these cars, and surely that would lead to the owner having a change of heart.

"Thank you," Freddy said.

Bern understood. "I'm trusting you."

"I know."

That was it.

Freddy thought Bern would want to talk about what they had seen, but Bern only shivered and then climbed over the seat into the back of the wagon. There were blankets back there, dirty and musty, but warm. Freddy watched as his friend began to dig himself into a kind of nest of blankets and clothing. There were empty bottles and crushed cardboard boxes, and a squat wooden crate that seemed to be Bern's pantry, with a box of crackers, a jar of some sort of spread, and other things impossible to make out in the dark. In the front seat with Freddy were half a dozen dog-eared books and the debris of food cartons.

It wasn't much, but it was so much better than Freddy's spot. Safer, drier, warmer. He found his envy simmering and forced it away. If he played his cards right, and Bern really trusted him, maybe he could find a junker back here with intact windows and set up a similar berth without pissing off the car lot's owner. Wordlessly, he promised himself he would do nothing to jeopardize Bern's good luck.

"You have a spare blanket?" he asked.

Bern looked at him. With obvious reluctance, he peeled off one of his own blankets and pushed it over the seatback. Freddy knew words were not sufficient, so he tried to put the depth of his gratitude in his eyes and the nod of his head, and then he swaddled himself as best he could and lay down across the front seat.

He was sure adrenaline would keep him awake, that he would see the Schnabelperchten when he closed his eyes and be unable to sleep. But in the midst of such worries, he drifted off . . .

◄◦►

. . . And woke to someone screaming his name. A hand gripped his shoulder, shook him hard. Freddy twisted around in the seat and looked up to see wide eyes and a face etched with terror. Bern loomed over him from the back of the wagon, pointing, shouting.

Freddy finally got it, the words making sense.

"Start the car!" Bern screamed at him. "Start the fucking car!"

The words didn't make sense at all. The veil of sleep had finally been stripped away and Freddy knew where they were, in that stretch of junked cars at the back of the parking lot. How was he supposed to start this car?

"Get the keys, Freddy! Under the floormat!"

Bern started to drag himself over the seat.

Freddy grabbed his wrists and sat up, pushing him back. "Christ, Bern. Calm down. You've had a nightmare, that's all."

Bern tore his right hand free and punched him in the face. Screamed, spittle flying. "Get the fucking keys!"

Angry, Freddy nearly hit him back, but he still had Bern's blanket wrapped halfway round him and that reminded him that his friend had been hospitable enough to trust him with his secret spot, to get him warm and out of the snow.

Bern ripped his other hand free, but now he stared at Freddy from behind the front seat with pleading eyes. "Freddy, they're here."

He saw movement to his left. A dusting of snow clung to the passenger side window, but Freddy could see a figure just beyond the glass, and when he went still, trying to tell himself it was just some security guard, he heard a sound.

"Chi chi chi."

The bone-white beak, gray against the snow, leaned forward to peer eyelessly into the car. The creature tapped its bloody shears against the window, as if asking him to unlock the door.

This time, Bern whispered. "The keys are under the mat, Freddy. Start the car."

Freddy stared at the Schnabelperchten. It tilted its head, just as it had back in that house while it cut open the woman on the bed. He wondered if this might be the same one, but it didn't matter.

Another rapped at the glass of the hatch at the back of the station wagon. Freddy whipped his head around and could see the shadows of others beyond the snowy windows. They should not have been here. He had followed them in previous years and they had always treated him as invisible. Why would they follow him and Bern tonight? Why pay any attention to them at all?

"Freddy, please," Bern said, weeping in terror.

Then it struck him. The keys under the mat. He turned to stare at his terrified friend. "This is *your* car. You live in your car."

Bern smashed his hands against the back of the seat and screamed at him to get the keys. This time, Freddy acted. Shoved his hand under the mat, dug around, found the keys, chose the correct one for the ignition the first time out, jammed it home, twisted it . . . and the engine growled, trying to turn over. He wondered how often Bern started the car to keep the engine from becoming a block of useless metal and guessed the answer was not-often-enough, but still he tried. He let it rest, counted to three, turned the key again. The engine choked and snarled and tried its best, and Freddy let it rest again.

"You live in it," he said, mostly to himself. He glanced around at the debris of meals, of life—a dirty blanket, some dog-eared books, takeaway boxes stealthily donated by restaurant staff at the end of a night.

Bern lived in his car. It was his home. And it was an utter mess.

The rear hatch of the station wagon clicked and opened, letting in a gust of frigid air and a swirl of snow. It opened as if it had never been locked at all, just like the doors of each of the homes the Schnabelperchten had visited.

Freddy glanced in the rearview mirror as Bern screamed a different sort of scream. This one held as much sorrow as it did fear. One of the Schnabelperchten bent and thrust his arms and beak into the back of the wagon, grabbed Bern by the legs.

"Chi chi chi," it said.

Bern screamed and reached out, shrieked Freddy's name, cried for help, in the moment before the thing dragged him out into the snow. Perhaps Freddy could have caught his arms in time and given the Schnabelperchten a fight, but instead he turned the key in the ignition again.

Coughing. Growling. Not starting.

Freddy began to cry.

Out the window on his side of the car, another of the things leaned in close to peer at him through the snowy glass. On the passenger side, the first one he'd seen grew impatient and simply opened the door, the lock notwithstanding.

Freddy turned the key.

The engine roared to life.

The Schnabelperchten at the passenger door bent its head and reached across the seat toward him. "Chi chi chi."

Freddy ratcheted the gear shift into Drive and hit the gas. The car hitched once and then surged from its place amongst the junkers. The creature inside the car snagged his jacket, but then the open passenger door struck the rusted shell of an old Volkswagen. The door slammed on the Schnabelperchten.

Its cloak caught on the rusted, twisted bumper of that Volkswagen and the Schnabelperchten clawed at the front seat of Bern's car before it was dragged from the vehicle.

With the passenger door still hanging open, Freddy could hear Bern back amongst the junkers, screaming in the snow. He did not glance in the rearview mirror or try to look over his shoulder. The hatch at the back of the station wagon remained open and he might have seen what they were doing to his friend, might have seen those shears employed at their gory work.

Hands locked on the steering wheel, he drove through the snowy parking lot. The tires were so low they were nearly flat and he didn't know what that might mean, how far he could get in this weather on those tires. So he drove.

He clicked on the windshield wipers to scrape snow off the cracked windshield. They worked, but poorly, and not well enough to keep him from smashing into the front end of a used Mercedes proudly on display near the front of the used car lot. The Mercedes banged aside and Freddy kept going, shaken, headed for the front gate.

The impact shattered the windshield. Splinters showered around him as he raised one arm to shield his eyes. When he lowered that arm, face dotted with little specks of blood and glass, he was stunned to find the car still moving. His foot had come off the gas and now he floored it again, twisting the steering wheel, heading for the river. He needed to get away from Salzburg, away from the Schnabelperchten, but as he drove he saw them in the falling snow. They emerged from rowhouses and apartment buildings, some of them watching him go in silence, their heads swiveling to follow as he passed.

The car had been Bern's home. Did they consider it his, now? Bern was dead and the car was in his possession. What were the rules? Did they need to kill him because of what he had seen, or simply out of spite? Would they let him go?

The engine coughed. He wondered how far the car would get him, how much gas might be in the tank. If he could put the river between himself and this group, he thought he could escape the city before they caught him. How far would he have to go before he was beyond their reach?

One of the headlights had shattered when he hit the Mercedes. The other was weak. Snow and wind buffeted him through the broken windshield.

But he saw three Schnabelperchten in the street as he approached one of the bridges across the river Salzach. Which bridge was this? The Lehener, maybe? In the snow it was hard to tell. And were there figures drifting across the bridge in the snow, dark robed creatures with bone-white beaks?

Freddy thought there were.

The engine coughed again.

The car isn't mine, he wanted to scream through the broken windshield. *I don't own it. Never sheltered in it.* His only home was the city itself. Not only the city, but all of Austria. His home was the sky and the ground below. His home was the whole of the world. The world might be anything but tidy, it might be insane and brutal and unforgiving, with all the mess and ruin the human race produced, but he could not be to blame for that. He refused. The people responsible for the mess of the world had never done anything but take from him.

Freddy turned toward the river. The old car jumped the curb. The impact would have blown those half-flattened tires but the snow provided a cushion.

He popped open the driver's door. Its rusty hinges shrieked. He took his foot off the gas and let the car roll down the embankment.

Freddy hurled himself from the car, hit the snow and tumbled twenty feet. Heart thrumming, he struggled to rise to his feet, but once up he managed to remain standing. The old, rusted, dented Auto Union wagon plunged into the river, bobbed for a few seconds, and then the river poured through the broken windshield and the car began to drown. Bern's belongings, his blankets and clothes and the castoff debris of his life and home, floated up around the car and were quickly swept away by the river.

"Chi chi chi."

Freddy whipped around and saw them through the snow. Three of them, coming along the embankment toward him from where they had been standing in the road, near the foot of the bridge.

He faced them, cold and tired and bruised, not sure where he could run.

"Chi chi chi."

Too tired, in fact, to run. Angry, he walked toward them. Off to his left, the car vanished beneath the icy current of the river.

"It's not my mess," he said, staring at the one in the middle.

They kept walking, passing around him as if he weren't there at all.

He turned to watch them go. Back on the street, they split up, angling toward homes along the road, where they would leave coins for those whose homes were tidy in preparation for the new year, and where they would make a deadly ruin of those who could not be bothered to care about the state of their homes and lives.

From a distance, he heard the sound again, carried on the wind.

"Chi chi chi."

Freddy raised a trembling hand to cover his mouth, to muffle the sound of his sobbing.

Then he began the long, cold trudge back to his spot. He had to get the hell out of this city, as far away as possible. But not tonight.

Tonight he was tired and sad and broken, like the world.

Tomorrow he would start over, and one day he would be glad and warm and joyful again. He wished he could have said the same for Bern, and for the world. It was too late for Bern. For the world, he could not be sure. After all, he was just one man without a home or a family. What did he know?

DODGER

CARLY HOLMES

Lorna sat in the jagged shade of the church's ruined wall, legs stretched out before her and one hand slanted against her brow to keep the late afternoon sun from finding her eyes. The steady trample of passersby kicked up a dust that swirled and spurted from the heels of trainers, settled like ash on naked toes. She watched the march of strangers' feet from her quiet patch of grass and pulled long channels of smoke into her lungs, whistled it out through barely parted lips. Music crashed in the distance; children shrieked and galloped by, tugging on garish balloons.

Lorna glanced at her watch and guessed she had another five minutes before she'd need to stand up, insert herself into the crowd and find her husband. But there were at least three more drags left on the cigarette and she was going to idle here for now and savour every one.

The little boy wailed from the spiralling dust like a tiny stampeding bull and charged at her. His face was a crushed cherry from crying, the flesh from his peephole eyes down to his chin silted and slimy with mucus. His shadow flowed ahead of him, leapt the warm grass and pounced. Before she could move, raise a hand to ward it, him, off, he'd barrelled into her and knocked her backwards, pinning her to the ground. She lay there with the cigarette smouldering beside her, gazing up at a sky that was faded and unreachable, purest baby blue, while the child squirmed and bellowed against her chest. His soaked face oozed against her neck, sticking her skin to his and making her stomach clench with nausea. She tried to flip herself free but couldn't manage more than a weak convulsion. She was too winded to speak.

"Mummy," he sobbed.

The woman who'd been following him stood over them both, fists worrying at her hips. "Thank god," she snapped. "He was beside himself." She ground her trainer into the cigarette, taking her time to make sure it was out, then crouched and patted the boy's heaving shoulder. "All's well that ends well," she said in a high singsong. "I told you we'd find your mummy. You really need to keep a better eye on your child." The last sentence was sharp and just for Lorna, who nodded weakly, shook her head. She flailed onto her elbow and tried to say something, but the boy scrambled up her raised body and grabbed at her desperately, pushing his fingers into her mouth and twisting her bottom lip. He began to roar with relieved fury. Warmth flooded her thighs and she thought he must have wet himself.

"Goodbye, darling. Be a good boy for Mummy," the woman said. She gave Lorna another long, narrow look of disapproval and turned away. Beyond the retreating body, Lorna caught a glimpse of her husband Phil at the other side of the abbey grounds. He'd seen her, was running towards them with arms stiffly outstretched and mouth glossy and wide. He might have been laughing and she couldn't blame him. *Only you, Lorna darling, could get embroiled in such bizarre situations.* She tried to lift her arms in response, urge him on, but the boy had his legs wrapped around her, heels drumming painfully against her pinned wrists. She could taste salt, something bitter beneath it, and tried to spit his fingers out of her mouth.

When Phil reached her side and plucked the child from her lap she jackknifed onto her hip and retched, scrubbing at her cheeks with her palms. "God, thank you," she said hoarsely. "God. I have to wash my face." She reached out a hand to her husband, a mute gesture for him to help her up, but he wasn't looking at her. His expression was hidden, buried against the neck of the boy. His arms were tightly wrapped around the solid little body and his shoulders shook. The boy screamed and sobbed against his chest.

"Where did you find him?" he asked finally, raising his head. His gaze was blind and inverted, pupils flickering between unspooling nightmares. He dipped down again and again to kiss the boy wherever he could, pecking at an ear, a tip of nose, landing a smacking cheek kiss that was almost cannibalistic. "I looked everywhere. I had to check the pond . . . " His voice cracked and he sucked a deep breath in, held it, grinned shakily at her. "Shit, Lorna, that's the most scared I've ever been in my life, I can barely stand up. I need a sugar hit, like, now. Hey, let's go to Oscars and eat ice cream. What do you reckon, Dodger?" He held the boy out at arms' length, dangling from the armpits. "It's okay, Jack, Mummy found you safe and sound. You can stop crying now. What do you say to three whole scoops of ice cream, one for every year of your life?"

He set the child on the ground and finally reached for Lorna, wrapping her hands between his huge palms, hauling her upright. She tugged herself loose and stepped back, rocking on her feet, staring from him to the boy who was smiling now at the prospect of a treat, tugging at Phil's legs.

"I have to wash my face," she said, her voice shrill. "I want to go home."

Her husband leaned close, an arm heavy around her shoulders. "It's okay, darling," he whispered into her ear, "it wasn't your fault. Don't look so broken. You take your eye off them for a second and that's all it takes; nobody would blame you. Let's go straight home then, and you and Jack can clean up while I pop out and get something nice." He winked down at the boy. "I'm going to get *all* the ice cream, Dodger. Every flavour in the whole world. That's what we're having for dinner tonight."

They walked, the three of them, through the park, past the squeal of happy families and the detritus of the village fete, out through the gate. Phil held one of Lorna's hands and the boy took the other, swinging it with wild enthusiasm as he jogged beside her, grinding her arm back and forth in its socket. Every step jerked a startled moan from her, a swift grimace down at him. She smiled falteringly when they chattered to her, but she didn't speak. Beside them, their linked shadows clung and hobbled, indistinguishable one from the other.

❧

Lorna locked herself in the bathroom and stripped off her clothes, unpeeled the soaked jeans from her legs and kicked them towards the laundry basket. She turned the shower on and waited until steam lapped against her throat and the mirror clouded. She pushed the plug into the drainage hole, stepped into the bath and scrubbed herself with soap and flannel beneath the jet of scalding water. She used an exfoliating scrub on her face, a cleanser, the scrub again, opened her mouth and swilled fragrant gritty water until she gagged and gasped for air.

Something sharp snagged the side of her foot when she waded backwards to hook the shampoo from its rack, forcing a stumble that almost tipped her over. She bent and flailed a hand beneath the murky water, scooped up a red plastic fire engine. One of its wheels was missing and its roof was dented: a well-loved toy. She dropped it and watched it float for a moment, bobbing on its side valiantly and then flipping over onto its roof before it sank slowly through the fruity foam of her sloughed shower gel and down. It left a hole in its wake, a perfect rectangle that cut scarlet through the sludgy residue and didn't close even after she splashed it with her toes; it pressed like a wound against the bottom of the bath.

She hugged herself close and looked around. Scattered along the edge of the bath were a small tractor, a truck, several stout plastic figures in bright primary colours. A parade of yellow ducks, mould trimming their pursed beaks, were lined up beside the taps. She reached out to touch them, drew her hand back and pressed it against her stomach. Smooth flesh, taut. No creping of the skin below the bellybutton, no scar. She remembered the shock of seeing her mother's body when she was young, the sag of it, being told *she'd* done that. But this body she cradled now was unmarked, still hers. Her womb had never swollen and stretched to accommodate another life. She would have known if it had.

Beyond the door, Phil rattled the handle and called her name; the boy pounded with his fists and howled something unintelligible. Lorna held her breath and stood still, a hand over her mouth, waiting, but they didn't go. After only a few seconds' silence the banging started again, the name-calling, the outraged need for her. She turned the water off and towelled her body roughly, wrapped herself in a hooded dressing gown and released the lock, letting them into the room.

"Why did you lock it?" Phil swung the half-naked child past her briskly and planted him on the toilet, steadying him with a hand on his back as the boy slithered and then settled onto the misty seat with a dreamy frown of concentration, baggy shorts cascading from his bare feet. "I can't find the potty and he's been doing so well. We don't want an accident, do we? Do we, Jack? No, sir, we don't. Undo all the good work."

"He already had an accident, all over me." Lorna wrapped a towel around her hair and kicked a leg sharply towards the sodden clothes she'd discarded. She half turned away from the hunched figure of the grunting child, crouched squat and gnome-like on his throne of white porcelain. Her husband's body was folded in half and hidden from her as he attended to the boy. She felt a stab of wild, desperate rage and tied the dressing gown tighter around her waist. "I'll open the window."

There was no mistaking the dense, almost hollow thud of solid matter hitting the water in the toilet bowl, the sudden violent stench of other people's bodily waste. Lorna gagged again, flapped a hand in front of her and waved away the fistful of toilet paper Phil held out to her. "Your turn I think," he said with a smirk. She shook her head and backed out of the room, crossed the landing to their bedroom at a run and shut the door. Blood throbbed and knocked against her temples; her vision starting to clot and waver. Her migraine tablets were downstairs in the top cupboard in the kitchen, safely shut away high above the counter. She could picture them, too many steps away from where she was. She didn't know why they'd be secreted so carefully, so far from her, when she needed them now, here.

A cheer ricocheted from the bathroom, the sound of the toilet flushing and then the tap briefly running. Lorna scrambled into clean shorts and T-shirt and met her husband as he emerged, flushed and grinning. He gave her a double thumbs up and knocked a clenched fist against his heart. "First time on the grown-up toilet," he exclaimed. "What a pro!"

She smiled weakly, embarrassed for him, by him. The boy ran full tilt over the rug and tangled himself between her thighs, spun around and around her and crowed with pride. His hands were damp against her bare legs, hot and greasy. The fine hairs on her calves prickled as his fingertips scraped over them. She thought of fleas, spiders, the bedbugs that had infested her home when she was a child, and she had to force herself to stand still and not slap the imaginary creatures off.

"Right, I'd better go." Phil kissed her quickly and laid a hand on the boy's forehead. "I'll be as quick as I can. Be a good boy for your mummy, Jack, and hop in the bath without any fuss." He ran down the stairs and turned to wave. Lorna trailed after him, stopped halfway and lowered herself slowly onto a step. She bent her head forward and whispered into her lap. "Phil."

The word left her mouth as a soft purr, tentative and wispy as a dandelion clock. She swallowed hard and spoke again, louder. "Phil?"

He turned then, house keys in hand and bouncing on the soles of his feet. "What is it, darling?" He planted one foot on the bottom step, and she willed him up, willed him to come back to her and put his arms around her, laugh at the ludicrous joke he'd played on her, or just divine her unspoken question without questions of his own; without judgement.

As he waited for her to answer he tossed the jangle of keys from palm to palm, glancing around him at the front door, and then from behind her the child called out in a high gleeful shout and dropped something, or threw something, and she jerked around.

"Text me!" Phil said, turning away. "I've got to get there before they close." The door swung shut behind him and she heard the slap of his trainers on the tarmac as he started to jog away.

Lorna pulled herself upright, gripping the banister, using it to haul herself back to the landing, one careful step at a time. "You need a bath," she told the boy.

He led the way to the bathroom, strutting and blowing an imaginary trumpet. He lifted the toilet seat and slammed it down over and over while she ran water and squirted bubble bath, swept the plastic toys into a bright heap to join the ducks by the taps. She could do this, one simple chore at a time. *Test the water temperature, collect a large towel and a small one, lay them in a neatly folded pile on the side of the sink. Keep going, one foot in front of the other, and things will get back to the way they were.*

"In you get," she said, pointing. The child looked at her uncertainly for a moment, then tried to scramble over the side of the bath. His naked buttocks floated, creamy pale as mushroom caps, as he sprawled, caught on the rim, then wriggled free and heaved himself belly-down into the tub. Water surged over the side onto the mat as he rolled onto his back and sat up, spluttering.

"Good boy," Lorna murmured. She closed the lid of the toilet and perched on it, watching him as he busied himself with his toys, chattering to her and himself as he staged peril and then rescue with the firemen. She nodded and smiled, gasped when it seemed warranted, and all the time she searched his face, his frowning concentration and his quick, triumphant glances up at her from eyes as sludge-grey and heavy-lashed as her husband's.

"Have a proper wash please," she said. "Phil will be home soon." Could she run to the kitchen quickly and get her migraine tablets? She'd be there and back in under two minutes if she hurried. She stood up, edged towards the door.

The boy tugged the flannel from where he'd draped it on the top of his head and stretched a hand out to her. "Where are you going, Mummy?"

"Nowhere. You need to scrub harder than that if you're going to get rid of all the dirt." Lorna moved to his side and took the flannel in her fist, pummelled it with soap. "Lean forward." She watched her hand float through the steam—it could have been a stranger's hand—before she placed it firmly on his slippery neck, touching him of her own volition. She felt the bones there, delicate as quills, shift beneath her palm. She pushed down a little, just a little, and sensed his immediate resistance, the warmth and solidity of his existence as he reared back against her and craned his head away.

"Ow, Mummy," he said. "That hurt."

"Sorry. Lift your arms."

He was blotched a deep pink when she declared him clean and wrapped him in the larger towel, lifted him from the bath. *Pull the plug, sluice clean water around the tub, dry the sides off with the small towel, push the window wide to let the steam out. Just keep going for a little while longer.*

He rubbed his finger along his forearm and let out a short, rasping squeal that made her jump. "Squeaky clean and good as new," he announced, grinning at her expectantly. She groped for a response, the response he was looking for, and settled for nodding briskly and herding him towards the door. "Indeed. Yes, you are."

-‹o›-

Late that night Lorna slid out of bed and settled in the chair by the window. She opened the curtains just enough to let the streetlamps smudge the darkness in the room a faint orange. From her corner, tucked partly behind the chest of drawers, she looked across at Phil's curled body, the milky blur of his face on the pillow. She couldn't make out if his eyes were open or shut, didn't know if he was watching her. The more she stared at him the less like Phil he looked.

The room seemed different from this perspective, unfamiliar. Or it might have been she who felt skewed, adrift from the safe and knowable landscape of her home and her life. Every tiny sound beyond the bedroom door—the house ticking as the day's heat left it; the night-time creatures rustling in the garden hedge—drove a pin through her carefully controlled breaths and unstitched them; brought her stomach reeling sharply up to the level of her heart, her heart to the level of her mouth. She needed a cigarette. She needed a cigarette. She needed a cigarette.

She began to cry, covering her face with a cushion to keep the sound contained. She used to go and sit on the top stair when she needed to do this but she didn't dare risk going out there, rousing the child who now slept in the room across the landing. He'd taken an age to get off to sleep, three stories and any number of eye-spy games, though Phil had cheerfully taken charge of all that while she'd stood helplessly in the doorway and gaped at the sheer amount of *stuff* the room held. It would have been an impossibility to walk across to the bed or the window without treading on something, being forced to negotiate a way over or around it. Plastic toys lay heaped on the rug; teddies spilled from the cupboard. And the state of the walls. They were striped with thick crayon in every colour, the lovely green paintwork ruined.

"Lorna? What's wrong?" Phil was at her side now; she could feel his muggy breath on her scalp, his hands scrabbling to prise the cushion from her face. She shook her head, clung to it with fierce panic.

"Have I gone mad?"

He knelt between her legs and held her close, rocking her as he tried to soothe the rising sobs. "I knew you were upset about today; I knew it. Of course you're not mad, darling. It's okay, I promise you. It's going to be okay." He stroked the back of her neck. "You've been behaving a bit . . . oddly, recently, since you went back to work. A bit vague. Maybe it was too soon? Maybe you need more time off?"

She raised herself up in the chair, wiped her cheeks with the cushion, and pushed him away gently. "No, I'm fine. Really. I'm probably just overtired. I'm going to pop into the garden for a cigarette and then I'll come back to bed."

He sat back on his haunches and stared at her. "What?"

"What?" His tone made her instantly defensive, her voice now chilly as she stood up and walked past him to the door.

"Are you joking?" Phil asked. "You gave up smoking four years ago when we found out we were pregnant."

The door handle against her palm was sticky with humidity. She held onto it, squeezing until it hurt, concentrating on the dig of metal against her skin. "Oh, fuck off, Phil," she said softly, turning her head slightly to address the room behind her. "*We?* Why do you have to be so bloody priggish all the time?"

The cigarette smoke was silk in her mouth, the rush of poison to her head a beautiful, giddy pleasure. Lorna smoked two, lighting one from the butt of the other, standing directly beneath the bedroom window so that Phil would smell it and know what she was doing. She waited until the bedside lamp was switched off, and then she moved to the garden lounger and settled down on it and smoked another.

◄◦►

The boy refused to eat the cereal Lorna set in front of him the next morning, pushing his bowl away with an expression close to shock on his face. "Mummy!" he whined. "You know what day it is!"

Phil came into the kitchen, dressed in a suit. He gasped theatrically as he swept the bowl up. "It's Eggy Bread Monday!" he said. "That's what day it is. What a forgetful Mummy! Don't worry, Dodger, I'll take care of it." He bent and whispered something quickly into the child's ear, sliding a sly look at Lorna. They both laughed, the sound harsh and malicious, too loud in the white humming space, and then Phil straightened to look at her fully, clashing gazes. He leant in again and murmured something else and the boy clapped a hand over his mouth and nodded vigorously, crowing with delight, his eyes crinkles of mirth.

Lorna cupped her mug of coffee close to her chest and fumbled in her dressing gown pocket for her cigarettes. Not there. Had Phil found them earlier this morning, hidden them somewhere? Or had she left them beside the lounger?

She walked to the French door that opened onto the back garden and looked out, affecting interest in the scorched grass ringing the trampoline. Her neck was stiff with exhaustion, her eye sockets tender. The rage she felt towards Phil was a vicious thing, barely containable, and she was scared of what she might say, of what she might do. She could hear the spiky hiss and buzz of their whispers behind her, knew they were watching her, but when she turned sharply to confront them Phil was at the stove and the boy was scratching at the worn surface of the table with his spoon. Both figures seemed blurred, their outlines slightly out of focus, as if they'd been in the act of moving and had frozen in response to her sudden attention.

Phil glanced over. "Did you manage to get any sleep in the end?"

She shrugged, shook her head. "What were you saying about me?" she asked. "Just now, you were talking about me."

Her husband slid golden slices of fried eggy bread onto plates and carried them over to the table. "There you go, Jack. Ketchup on the way. I can't remember," he said to her, over his shoulder. "Just silliness." He sighed. "Oh, Lorna, do cheer up, please. Sit down and eat your breakfast."

"I've got to get ready for work," she said. "Maybe when I come home this afternoon you might have decided this—" she waved her hand vaguely around the room, pausing at the table with a flourish of the wrist and then sweeping on "—sick joke, this cruel trick, has gone on long enough."

She left the room as Phil started to say something, closed the kitchen door behind her with a brisk click that wasn't quite a slam and felt a spiteful pleasure in cutting him off mid-sentence, a smug sense of achievement in her own self-control. She was halfway up the stairs when he called to her from the hallway. "Do you have to go in today? Maybe you could take the day off. And you have remembered you've got to take Jack to nursery, haven't you? I haven't got the time."

Lorna stumbled, swivelled round to stare down at him. "Yes," she said. "I know. You don't have to keep going on about it."

◄◦►

The nursery at the end of their road was one Lorna always walked past on her way to and from work, edging nervously around the extravagant farewells and the tiny howls of anguish.

She hovered at the gate for a moment, hoping somebody would approach her and take charge of the situation, at the very least appear to recognise her so that she knew she was in the right place, but the parents were too preoccupied and the staff too busy counting children in through the door to notice her hesitation. It was as though her true self had become invisible: her sense of who she was, or who she had thought she was, hacked down to no more than a heap of splinters. They could re-form into the rough shape of a person, of *her*, if squeezed hard enough in a strong enough fist, but they were no longer the original thing.

She steered the boy in through the gate and stood in the busy yard, clasping his hand and grimacing hopefully at every adult who passed. The day's heat was already gathering itself, forcing sweat in a greasy rush through the thin cotton of her blouse. A man nudged into her as he passed, woebegone child dangling from the crook of his arm. He nodded a curt apology but didn't look at her. Lorna tugged her hand free and blotted it on the inside hem of her skirt, glanced at her watch. She needed to leave now if she was going to stop at the newsagents for cigarettes before she got to the office.

The boy pressed himself tighter against her side when she tried to step away, peeking shyly at the milling children. Lorna nudged him slightly towards a small girl who'd stopped to wave frantically at him—"Hi Jack!"—but he clung even closer and hooked an arm around her knee. His bottom lip trembled; his eyes narrowed to paper cuts. She knew he was going to start crying any second now and she couldn't bear it.

"There you are! Did you have a nice time at the fair yesterday?" A woman in the nursery staff uniform of yellow T-shirt and black shorts, smile radiant, stopped in front of them. Lorna let out a hollow laugh and was about to speak when she realised that the woman wasn't talking to her. She'd crouched in front of the boy and now applied herself to loosening his grip on Lorna's legs, chattering cheerfully about the fun they were going to have, gently transferring his attention to herself. "There we go, Jack!" she said, straightening up and beaming at Lorna. "We're going to have a lovely time! Say goodbye to Mummy before we go inside."

Lorna crouched beside the child and leaned slowly into him, watching his face swim closer to hers until he filled her entire world and panic seized her, a sour flood of saliva filling her mouth. She swallowed hard, forced it back down into her stomach to burn there.

"Have a lovely day, darling. Be good," she said. She leaned close as if to kiss his cheek, turned her head slightly at the last second and found his ear. She whispered, softly, "I hate you."

He jerked as if she'd slapped him, eyes huge and blank with brimming tears. "Pardon, Mummy? What did you say, Mummy?" He scrabbled towards her, but the nursery worker kept a tight hold of his hand and nodded at Lorna kindly. *Best you just go.* Lorna thought about saying it one more time, saying it louder this time, but didn't.

She straightened and smiled gratefully at the woman who was going to make this all go away for a few hours, then patted the boy's head quickly and turned her back on them both. She felt the air heave and resettle behind her as a small body clawed away from his carer and was pulled firmly into line. Her steps quickened as she neared the gate. She didn't look, but she could hear the rising wail, feel the child's throbbing need as a sharp, pinching knot between her shoulder blades that tried to tug her back.

It was only when she stepped out of the nursery's yard and onto the street, swung right briskly and strode away—the tobacconist at the corner of the main street her urgent objective—that the pain lessened and she was able to suck a breath in deeply, hold it in her lungs as a blessing and release it in a long whistle. Every step she took away from the boy, every step towards the office and the knowable mundane routines awaiting her there, returned her to herself. There, she would have a name. There, people would call her Lorna. And when they looked at her, they would *see* her.

She felt a pang, just briefly, when the hot breeze sailed over the suburban garden walls at the crossroads and brought with it a faint cry. Probably a gull. Or another child. Not something she need concern herself with.

◄○►

By the morning break Lorna wished she'd taken Phil's advice and stayed at home. It wasn't that she felt ill as such, just a bit *vague*. Hadn't he used that word, last night? She was sure he'd accused her of being vague. The sun drilled mercilessly in through the large windows and Polly had moved the only fan to her corner of the room, mantling over it with feral possessiveness.

Lorna's desk, which she was sure she had left neat and clean last Friday afternoon, was a clutter of screwed-up pieces of paper, lidless biros oozing ink in navy clots, and last week's coffee mugs. She knew some of the mugs weren't hers—she always washed up at the end of every day—but Polly shook her head impatiently when accused. She didn't even bother to look away from her computer screen. Watching her frown over her emails, tendrils of hair wafting merrily around in the cooling breeze of the fan, Lorna felt that vast rage crashing through her again. She imagined slapping the woman until her cheeks were purpled, tender and raw as mashed kidneys, then pushing through the building and out onto the street. Not walking towards home but away. The where didn't matter.

When her phone rang, she was checking the figures for the monthly report and chewing absently on a sandwich. She ignored it, ignored Polly's tutting, and then ignored her mobile when it started to trill in her handbag. Working on the columns of numbers had soothed her and she was almost cheerful, determined to hang onto that. Once she'd finished this task she was going to reward herself with a cigarette and catch up on the office gossip, always the spiciest and most up to date in smokers' corner.

She leaned back in her chair while she finished her lunch, strangely pleased with just how irritating the duet of landline and mobile phones were. They continued to ring, and she continued to chew and swallow, take another bite, chew and swallow. Polly got up and swept out, muttering. Lorna considered dashing over to her side of the room and stealing the fan back but couldn't summon the energy.

The framed photograph of her and Phil, taken on their honeymoon, was toppled over and dull with dust. She used a tissue to wipe the glass clean and righted it, looked for a moment at the young, happy faces. Her cheeks had been fuller back then, her eyes wider and her gaze steadier. Phil's grin was huge, infectious. She felt an urge, a sudden choked need, to see him and put her arms around him, try to dance them both back to that place and hold them safely there. When her mobile rang again and she saw the call was from him she dropped the apple she'd been gnawing on and answered it immediately, warmly. "Darling, hello!"

"I've been trying you for ages," he said. "Why didn't you pick up? You need to get Jack."

"Jack?" She stared at the computer screen with its calming rows of numbers, tried hard not to bridle at his tone.

"Yes. Jack. Your son." There was a long beat of silence, and then he said in a clipped, end-of-my-tether voice, "Jesus, Lorna, what the hell is going on with you? Jack's had a complete meltdown at nursery and you need to go and get him. Now. This is *your* department, we agreed that when he was a baby. Why are you suddenly making this so hard?"

She reached a hand out and moved the mouse, clicked it a couple of times and corrected a small error on the screen in front of her. There, done. Once she'd emailed it over to her manager she could nip out for a cigarette. "I'm busy right now," she said. "Can't it wait?"

"No. It can't fucking wait." He sounded close to hating her and that gave her a twisted, bitter satisfaction. The thrill was almost sexual. "Lorna. You need to leave right now and collect our child. Right. Now. He's been desperate for the last hour. Inconsolable. He needs his fucking mother."

She laughed then, high and hysterical, covered her mouth quickly to hide the sound. "Fine," she said. "I'll speak to Rob and leave in a minute. Okay? Happy?"

Phil sighed. "No, not happy. But thank you, Lorna. I'll let them know to expect you in the next half an hour, and I'll see you at home later."

◂◦▸

The walk back to the nursery was hotter, brighter, slower than the walk from it had been a few hours earlier. Lorna dawdled along the quiet streets, paused for a few moments in the deep shadow of a horse chestnut tree to smoke a cigarette. The late-summer sunshine blushed the drooping leaves of the tree a deep rose gold, its bristling conker cases glowing the fresh green of peridot.

Phil phoned her again while she was stubbing out her cigarette; added another message to the voicemail pileup. She didn't bother to listen to it, switched her mobile off and dropped it into her bag.

The gate leading into the nursery yard was locked. She had to press a button and speak into the intercom, wait while someone was sent to let her in. Faraway voices wailed and groaned tinnily through the little machine as she spoke to the faceless gatekeeper. It sounded like an entire village of ghostly children were queued up in the nursery corridors, all desperate to be let out.

A different woman from this morning emerged from the building and crossed the yard. She held the yelling boy against her chest, his small body writhing and bucking, making forward progress difficult. "Look, Jack, there's Mummy!" she exclaimed, pointing. He twisted round and saw Lorna, let out one long piercing scream, then half leapt, half fell out of the woman's hold and ran across the yard to the gate. He tried to climb it as the key was wrestled into the lock, clawed a frantic path over and dived into Lorna's arms. His teeth against her throat were sharp and hungry, nipping along her collar bone. He wanted to devour her.

She crouched to try and loosen his grip, heard the cotton of her blouse rip as he thrust his face against it, blindly lipping at her chest. The woman towered over them both. "He's been like this for a couple of hours," she said. "He hadn't seemed right since he arrived but then after their morning snack he got a lot worse." She bent to help Lorna, tugging the child back and hanging onto him. "Has anything happened to unsettle him over the last few days?" she asked.

Lorna stood and rebuttoned her chewed blouse. Apricot lace peeked through the torn cloth and she saw the woman glance at it, divined unspoken disapproval at the unmotherly choice of bra. "No," she said. "He's been fine."

She reached for the straining child and held him by the shoulders. "You need to calm down," she told him. "The longer you scream, the longer it will take us to leave here." She nodded at the woman. "Thank you for letting us know. I'm sorry he's being difficult."

The woman started to back away through the gate, relief plain on her face. "He's at that age," she said. "And probably just overtired and missed his mummy." She locked the gate quickly behind her. "He'll be right as rain after a nap."

Lorna nodded and watched her go. She wondered how on earth they did it, these people, day after day. The boy leaned against her leg, exhausted. His head jerked back and forth as sobs rattled through him, slower now.

His left thumb crept into his mouth and with his right hand he twisted the hem of Lorna's skirt into a ball, hobbling her. "Come on," she said. "I'd better carry you."

His weight in her arms, the loose swing of his leg against her waist, made the walk to the park harder in the afternoon heat. Lorna paused a couple of times to rest and catch her breath, hoisting the sleeping boy back up to her chest when he slithered down. His head nestled into her neck, his mouth a snuffling creature pressed against her skin. Something about his smell reminded her of Phil or reminded her of home. She kept her face turned away as much as possible, craning to see where she was going and breathing through her mouth.

The park was empty, the end of the school day still a couple of hours away. A man walked a small dog on a lead in the distance and a young couple dozed and kissed on a rug under a tree, but nobody paid any attention to Lorna as she crossed the hot grass towards the tucked-away shade of the ruined church wall. She lowered the boy gently down and sat beside him, resting a hand on the tight curl of his body so that he would sense her presence and not startle awake.

She smoked a cigarette and gazed out across the park. There were still patches of churned earth from the weekend's fete, a few wrappers tangling around the swing set. Against her back the wall stood cool and sharp, grounding her.

Phil shouldn't be back from work until 6pm, maybe even a little later if traffic was bad. If she left now she'd be home in ten minutes, have hours to herself. She could lie in a cool bath, tackle the weeding, read a novel. When she got home everything there would be just as it was, just as it should be.

She closed her eyes and saw herself standing in the driveway, opening the front door, stepping inside. Her home and her life returned to her and this terrible interlude, that had started right here, scrubbed out.

Lorna loosened the thin cotton belt from her skirt and slipped it free. She shuffled to kneel beside the boy and watched him for a moment. His eyelids shimmered, pearlescent as the inside of abalone shells; his sucking mouth crumpled around his thumb. She looped the strip of fabric around his ankles, looped it round and round and tied a knot. Tied another, and another. His socks bunched above and below the tether. She wouldn't be able to undo it now even if she wanted to.

He muttered something in his sleep, tried to kick out his legs. Lorna stroked his head and hushed him, settled him back into a dreaming state. She gathered her bag and edged away, got slowly to her feet.

When she reached the gate that led to the street, she knew that if she looked back now there would be nothing to see. The boy would be gone. Because the boy had never been.

She unlatched the gate and stepped through, pulled it carefully closed behind her, walked away. She didn't look back.

ROCK HOPPING

ADAM L. G. NEVILL

Here, on the rock, was not at all like being out there, on the sea, from where they had emerged. At first light, they'd paddled a seascape matching the hue of the vast grey battleships that had once rolled and lurched from the naval base, several kilometres to the north. The three paddlers appeared incongruous, as if they were later additions to an old photograph, or a drab oil painting depicting a bitter body of winter water. With no sight of land in any direction, the bright kayaks of red, yellow, and lime green had slowly toiled across the shifting surface. In the undulation of ashy swell, several corrections had been required during the five kilometre route, aimed at an indistinct horizon.

Jon had watched the conditions for the preceding five days. The wind falling, rising. Wind speed and gust, falling and rising along with his hopes for the paddle; a wild camping expedition out to the Great Saban Stone, by kayak. Every two hours, for the preceding three days, he'd checked the usual websites—YT, Windy, the Met Office—cross-referencing that information with the Beaufort Scale. Tide and tidal stream were forecast as optimum for the first leg of the paddle, near the coast. The wind, however, was not ideal. This introduced variables he couldn't predict. On open sea, a few kilometres offshore, he didn't know how the forecast westerly would affect the surface. Nor did he know how other atmospheric conditions, deep in the Atlantic, would already have been acting on the surface.

They'd already booked time off work, so it had to be then. They were all experienced in dynamic water, had good kit, were proficient at deep sea rescues and self rescues. This was one of those paddles when you pushed yourself to a new level. That's how he'd squared it with himself. Gemma and Archie were keen to go. They knew the score.

They'd launched onto a benign sea, catching a neap tide.

Chop appeared during the second kilometre. Bows slapped the surface hard. But that was nothing beyond their comfort zones or experience. Within the third kilometre, when the dwindling coastline was reduced to a few millimetres of dark matter, any chatter between the paddlers needed to be repeated. Gusts suppressed their voices to within a few centimetres of their own shouting mouths, or snatched away their words.

"Bumpy," Archie had said, in typical understated fashion. "Did you check the forecast?" he'd also asked Jon. A sarcasm the paddle leader was also familiar with.

"Remember Milton's paddle . . . Brixham . . . " Jon had replied, to identify that they'd seen far worse when they possessed less experience. Anecdotes followed in snatches, none fully heard.

". . . only time I've ever . . . terrified . . . " Gemma added.

"My old Stratos . . . through . . . miss that boat."

". . . as bad as the time me and Jon . . . Start Point . . . "

"Jesus . . . two deep sea rescues . . . "

When the misty opacity they had seen at the horizon swept closer, they'd stayed closer together, each leaning forwards and falling silent in the rags of fog. A whiteout followed, a purgatory with visibility dropping to a few metres. The swell picked up. Engulfed and blind, they were tossed about, sliding sideways down wave faces, lurching forwards when buffeted from behind. Muted by the first clenches of fear, they'd all shared the same thought. If you were to capsize here . . . Self rescue. The others wouldn't be able to see you. Re-entry and roll. Should he capsize, Jon had already visualised how he would get back inside his boat, before bailing it out and heading home, wet and cold.

They had paddle floats. Three radios. Flares.

Gonna be fine. Fine. Fine. Fine.

Inside the misty fret, the wind fought the tidal stream, confusing the sea. They were akin to aircraft bumped through clouds by turbulence, the compass mounted on Jon's bow their only guide to keep them heading southwest. All three VHF radios crackled inside pockets of their buoyancy vests, then fell silent. No one had the head-space to ponder why channel sixteen went dark. All the batteries were fully charged. They concentrated solely on the presence of each other, staying close and barely avoiding collisions. Panting from exertion, blinking in spray, all of them began to suspect they might have done something better that day.

Sweep strokes, lots of them. Stern rudders used in the salt and pepper coloured foams of relentless, buffeting waves. Skegs down and stomachs dropping away as the boats plunged, everyone wanting more keel, yet grateful for the food and camping gear stowed in their stern and bow holds, that weighed their touring boats down and embedded them in a shifting surface to prevent weather-cocking; a muscular yearning in the air and water determined to drag them due west and off course.

They'd been toiling for thirty minutes that felt like five, when the water abruptly boiled and the flow ran crossways at the bow.

Jon was leading. "Eddy line!" he cried out but inside incessant gusting the other two would never have heard. "Power strokes . . . " he yelled, then paddled forwards into what resembled a rain-bloated river, pouring from the moors but in the middle of the sea.

Jon caught a glimpse of Gemma, inside her yellow Virgo, edging straight behind his stern and giving the water less of her hull to catch. And then she was gone, quickly, taken by the eddy in whatever direction it ran. She was there; she was not there. The fret slipped her into the misted void.

No sign of Archie. No idea. Behind him when . . .

Every man for himself. It was that time.

Jon's mental clocks all stopped at once. Upright, torso and spine limber, he paddled hard and aimed straight ahead. Teeth clamped enough for him to sense a crack of crockery, a saucer chipping inside his mouth. There was only his bow now and his paddle blade flashing and dipping fast to drive him through the racing crosscurrent. No glances to either side could be risked. Tightrope balance through the feet, knees, buttocks, hips, all fused into the hull of his kayak. And he maintained the stroke and determination until he crossed the outer eddy line and found himself sat in a boat that glided across greenish bumps. Relief demanded he scream but concern for his companions, who were not beside him, sickened him white.

The fret fragmented into ghostly tendrils. The wind dropped. Or had never, uncannily, blown on the far side of the eddy. Warm sunlight yellowed the air and turned the surface a dull emerald. He might now have been paddling on a different sea, in another part of the world.

"You need to bin the Met Office. Forecasts are not fit for purpose." A voice, to his left. Archie.

Jon looked to his left. Nothing.

"Fucks sake." Behind him.

Jon turned one-eighty in his cockpit. His clenched core released tension stored during the episode of terror.

Archie wasn't smiling. He was shaken. Jon hadn't seen an expression and pallor like that since their first white water, eight years before.

"Gem?" he asked Archie, as he drew alongside his friend's kayak and rafted up. The gentler swell moved their boats up and down, softly bumping them together. Archie nodded across Jon's bows and Jon swivelled to face the opposite direction.

There she was, a good thirty metres away, edging and turning in their direction.

"Thank fuck."

"Never known the sea do that," Archie said.

Gemma was shouting something but Jon couldn't hear her. "What?"

Closer, she paddled closer with her tight rhythmic style, blades low. Her mouth moved. He finally heard her voice, then some of what she was saying. ". . . was interesting . . . seen it?"

"Radio's fucked," Archie said.

"Can't hear," Jon shouted at Gemma.

She was breathing hard and that depleted the strength of her high, thin voice. "We're here!" she managed. "Almost."

That Jon heard but frowned. "Come again?"

"Great Saban Stone."

"Navigation. Least you got that right," Archie said from beside him, while fiddling with his phone inside an Aquapac. "Checking conditions needs work."

Jon looked to where Gemma pointed. And he saw it too.

How could that only be classed as a rock?

Half a kilometre distant, the foreground obscured by dispersing shreds of the fret, the rock reared from the sea. Triangular but flat on top like a volcano. One long extinct and now greened with gorse and dry grasses. In places, small stunted trees gave the appearance of blackened people who were waving, or pointing south at where the rock disintegrated into a black reef. That foamed white as the distant swell struck ramparts sure to tear through any hull of wood, carbon fibre, or steel. Were the bent trees pointing out the rocks, Jon wondered, or directing you to smash yourself apart upon their teeth?

On the northern side of the rock, slate cliffs plunged into the sea.

The sky was clear. The water about the rock's hems slopped a tropical, syrupy green.

"Let's do it," Gemma said.

"Hang on. Catching my breath here. No phone signal either," Archie said. "Didn't expect one, to be honest."

Jon exhaled, whistled and said, "Fuck's sake. That eddy?"

"Went with it. No choice. Evasive action." Gemma was smiling. "Bit sudden. Bloody hell. Reef under here. Must stretch this far from the rock."

"No lighthouse?" Archie said, preoccupied with his phone. "Plenty of ships must have gone down here. I've no radio either. Check your channel sixteens."

"Nicely done," Jon said to Gemma and he felt his shoulders relax and droop for the first time since they'd hit swell. He'd planned the paddle. He was responsible. Paddle leader. Checking stats and websites was one thing but whenever he stood on the shore and looked out at the water that he was going to paddle into, gravity changed. He'd feel as buoyant as if already on water. Lighter on his feet, he'd stop breathing then take shallow breaths. Once on the water, twenty minutes usually elapsed before his boat stopped feeling tippy and memory filled his muscles with a sense of what they must do. They'd been paddling for a decade in all kinds of conditions. "On the return journey, we'll go back north, then correct northeast. Gonna be a bit longer but we'll avoid that eddy."

They'd be talking about this trip for years.

Ignoring the exchange and the rock, Archie prodded his phone screen. "Won't be able to check the forecast though. Unless we catch a smidgen of reception."

"I know the forecast for tomorrow."

"You knew the forecast for this morning, which resembled nothing of the actual conditions."

"It changed."

"Often does. Are your radios picking anything up?"

◄◦►

On myriad outcrops of stone around the eastern and southern base of the huge rock, the silhouettes of shags, cormorants, and gulls stirred then stilled to eye their approach. In the better light, the reds, greens, and purples of the slates glimmered up high like mould on ham. At the waterline, crevices in the lumpy hem of the cliffs vanished into darkness. Caves that Jon wanted to explore. They had time. Today until night fell and tomorrow morning before paddling home.

Lagoons festooned with rock pools and meadows of yellow, brown, and red weed yawned as they glided across the western side. A canyon the colour of pewter cut through the outcrop. On one side the steep side rose to a cliff edge of grass and bristling gorse. Deeper inside the gully lay a distant cove with a pebbled floor. More rocks, caves and pools surrounded the cove. Great slopping scarves of coloured weed had given the shallower water a scarlet hue at the mouth of the ravine. That gave way to a brownish pasture, before yellow weed consumed the shoreline.

Forming a natural barrier across the western side, great tilting pyramids of grey stone offered shelter from the constant wind. They leaned at the ocean. Vast sloping plates of slate eroded to astonishing angles and white-washed with bird droppings. Smaller rocks upon which seals basked, dotted the channels between the leaning triangles.

No one spoke for a while. Their expectations of the Great Saban Stone had been exceeded.

Completing a circuit, they paddled under the shadowy north side but all stopped paddling when Archie cried out, "There! See it!" He removed his phone from his buoyancy jacket to take a picture.

A house made from the slate of the rock. A building resembling a squat tower with a tiled cone for a roof, cut into a platform about twenty metres above them. A circular window akin to a large porthole stared from rounded walls, greened with lichen. A big pupil, unblinking, forever staring out. Perfectly camouflaged, the materials of the building's construction blended into the surrounding cliffs. About the stone cylinder, the branches of an emaciated hawthorn tree clawed.

"That where they lived?" Gemma asked.

Jon didn't know who built the house. Information about the rock was scant online. Scores of these large rocks littered the Devon coastline and this specimen was half enclosed by a hideous reef and too far out at sea to attract visitors. He, Archie, and Gemma had explored all of the other Mew Stones, Blackstones, Leadstones, and Orestones of South Devon. But Jon knew of no one who'd attempted a paddle out to the Great Saban, because of the five kilometre stretch of English channel prone to rough sea. Trespassing was also forbidden. But he'd learned that there had been several residents on the Great Saban Stone across three hundred years.

The first recorded inhabitants were a convict and his family. The Beedalls. Or so Jon had read on the Coastal Land Trust website. The Trust was the rock's current steward. Three private owners had passed the rock between themselves in the early 1900s, though they may never have lived on it. The last owner handed it over to the Coastal Land Trust after the second world war. Currently, the Great Saban was merely listed on charts as an area of conservation, closed to the public.

Other than that, the usual folklore existed. Rumour had it that the military had occupied the rock during the war and stored hazardous weapons. Rusting munitions were said to exist. Mariners considered the area bad luck, though they seemed to think that about everywhere. There had been some information online about the hazards of hidden rocks, warning pleasure craft to give the rock a wide berth.

Birds and seals were said to flourish but no one had made the rock the focus of a considered study, at least not one posted online. There were pictures of the grey mound taken from passing yachts, but Jon had found no pictures taken by anyone standing on the actual rock.

"That the witch dude's house?" Archie asked, while aiming his camera at the curious round building.

"Did he build it though?" Jon wondered out loud. "Horace Beedall."

Beedall, the first recorded occupant. Marooned here for theft, for laying curses, for smuggling. A Cunning Man, apparently. Loved by his neighbours and fishermen who regarded him as a folk saint. He'd eventually fallen foul of the church and local magistrate far too often for his own good. Or the good of his family. So all of them had been imprisoned out here; Horace, his daughter, Minnie, and husband, Albert. There was a child too, though the kid's name wasn't mentioned online. The Beedalls. And they never left. They'd lived on the rock for decades. Once their sentence had been served, they chose to remain.

Some years later, the rock was discovered to be deserted. The Beedall family had gone, or left. No one knew where to, or so the folk tale claimed.

There were only a couple of paragraphs about them on the Coastal Land Trust website. He hadn't searched any further but had decided that the rock would provide an excellent expedition, in nimble kayaks, able to hop effortlessly between rocks dangerous to larger vessels.

"Never seen so many birds." Gemma said. "Counted seven seals too. A colony!"

"Undisturbed by paddleboard wankers. And only twats would think about coming here in kayaks," Archie said.

They all laughed at that. It was good to laugh after the swell and eddy and fret and being apart for a period that had quickly filled their minds with premonitions of disaster.

"Even trees," Gemma said. "Just clinging on."

Jon nodded. "Beedall planted them. Apparently, he even had a vegetable patch. A few animals too."

The smattering of small, wind-bent trees mostly struggled around the rocky summit. A rough ring of trees, the tops all curving away from the prevailing wind. Skeletal miracles, surviving out here in salty air but barely upright.

As they drew closer, Jon imagined he was seeing grief-stricken women, starving and bent in despair. At the end of their tether they flung their arms and wild hair into the air. A few other spindly articles appeared to be crawling to the edges of cliffs, as if to hurl themselves off. Around the trees a barbed wire of holly crept, oily green and partially absorbed into hummocks of gorse. The remainder of the visible rock was engulfed by coarse grass and large eruptions of common gorse that sprinkled a golden blossom across the grey stone.

Though the sustained pitch of his anxiety from the rough crossing had wilted, the shaft of Jon's paddle continually banged the hull of his boat. Clumsiness and fatigue. Sweat cooled between his shoulder blades. His helmet rubbed above his ears and his lower back issued a constant thump of aches. "Let's get ashore. I saw a place to pull in. Other side. Cove at the end of the gully."

Protected from the west wind, by the great sloping pyramids of slate and the blackened outcrops bristling with sea birds, they were soon gliding through the silent chute again, the walls jagged with splintered slate, the air unmoving. This time they explored deeper, in search of the distant cove Jon had identified. Beneath their boats, the water became shallow and clear, revealing each pebble and shell on the seabed, Soon, their boats waded a tugging meadow of oarweed, spread like vast ribbons of shredded brown leather.

"Hear that?" Archie said, once they were probing inside the slate canyon. He swished by, overtaking Jon.

"Yeah. What is it?" Gemma asked.

"Can't hear any—" and then Jon did.

A faint voice. Even laughter. He was reminded of a child.

"Bird?" Jon offered.

Oarweed gave way to submerged rock pools and crops of sugar kelp, the stones to which the weed was moored were vivid purple. And then a forest of sea spaghetti engulfed the waters of the cove at the far end of the gulch. More than Jon had seen anywhere, choking every crevice and tributary with fronds as yellow as dandelions. The water between the countless strands of floating weed was black, sunless; a vast, discoloured scalp from which freakish hair extended.

Gemma and Archie soundlessly and elegantly edged around rocks, that humped the surface, to reach the cove. Jon hung back and fished out his camera. As his companions disappeared behind an outcrop, he dipped his hand into the cool water. Silky tubes of weed investigated his fingers and wrist. He took pictures of the astonishing pasture beneath his boat. When he withdrew his arm from the balm of seawater and checked the camera's viewfinder, his flash, against a background of lightless water, had turned the weed the colour of turmeric.

Ahead of his boat, the voices of his companions rang out and echoed through the gulley. Excitable voices turning uncertain. Gemma and Archie were concealed behind natural barriers of protruding stone. Jon had no idea what they were talking about. "Have you seen this weed. Incredible," he felt compelled to call out.

"So how the hell did it get here?" Archie asked Gemma, as Jon cruised to the shore of the cove and his hull crunched pebbles. He plucked his spray-deck free of the cockpit, released his legs and stepped out of the boat in one fluid motion, his feet selecting smooth stones on the ridges between the shadowy rock pools, each vivid with rainbow wrack.

"Or up there?" Gemma countered.

There was too much happening all at once. Too much to take in. Birds, seals, swaying forests of iridescent weed. Devon's PR was often lacking but whoever played custodian to this rock may have been remiss in not revealing this rock's natural bounty; the fecundity below the water and the solemn beauty that hung heavy about the rock. Or was the lack of information deliberate, to preserve its sanctity and leave it unspoiled? When their hulls scraped these rocks, they'd leave plastic in a delicate, undisturbed ecosystem.

Since the lockdowns, people had ventured out all over the local waters, in just about anything that floated. None of them were surprised at where they happened across random people on the water, most often with no safety equipment. But if he posted any pictures of the Great Saban online, others might come here too. Maybe they did already but kept the rock's secrets to themselves. His joy of sharing his discoveries would need tempering, not least for fear of prosecution for trespassing. The lifeboats wouldn't thank him either, for being responsible for encouraging scores of paddle-boarders and holidaymakers, in inflatable canoes, to venture so far out and into that eddy.

Jon rounded the obscuring rocks and found his companions. Archie and Gemma stood at the foot of the steep slate cliff that vaulted above the apex of a deep cave, forming the shape of a triangle. They were looking up, oblivious to his presence. Their boats lay on the shingle, side by side.

For several moments, Jon's thoughts stumbled, drunk with confusion. Until he too saw the sheep, a shorn ewe, standing above the cave, partially camouflaged by the lighter skeins in the stone. It bleated piteously. That's what they'd heard before, distorted along the sides of the gully. But the appearance of the sheep didn't sober him from confusion because there should be no animals on this rock, besides seals.

"How do we get it down?" Gemma asked them and herself.

"How can it be here?"

"They're pretty nimble," Jon said, frowning. "It must have fallen from up there." He pointed at the grass mopping the cliff edge above. "It was either brought here, or . . . "

"Or?" Gemma said. She turned and smiled. They were only friends and she liked girls but that smile and teasing cast to her eyes still made him shiver, exquisitely, and deep inside his abdomen. She knew he was sweet on her. Once when tipsy on cider, she'd said that back when she liked guys, he'd have been a catch.

"A survivor of past occupants who kept animals? Now wild sheep."

"It's shorn," Archie said. "There's a plastic tag in its ear."

Feeling tired and light-headed, even irritable at the sheep for such an unwelcome diversion, Jon changed tack. "Forget it for now. Let's unload the boats. Eat. Get something to drink. We gotta get up there yet." He nodded at the sides of the gorge that narrowed over the cove. His eyes began exploring steps and crevices that they could climb to get on top. It took no more than a few moments to spot a route upwards.

"We can't just leave it," Gemma said, admonishingly, as if to a child.

"I cannot see a way of climbing up to it. And how would you carry it down?"

"It's frightened."

"And if we panic it and it falls, it'll be injured too."

"It's been shitting on the pebbles," Archie said, looking about his feet. "So it's been down here, in the cove. Maybe it climbed up when the tide came in? And maybe it will figure out how to climb down. Cattle can swim between islands. Can sheep swim? Fell overboard possibly? Never seen a sheep on a boat, though. Have you?"

"We'll get a picture of its tag. When we get back, we'll let someone know. Come on, unload. I need blood sugar."

-◦-

Once clear of the shelter of the rocks at sea level, the wind blew incessantly, registering as a constant combing of the grasses and quivering of gorse about their knees.

After securing the boats above the tidal line in the cove, they'd recovered their packs and bivouac tents and made an easy climb from the cove, stepping from one ledge to another to reach overhanging clumps of grass. Once amongst the verdure, they'd followed a well worn track with a surface of grey slate. Jon had felt strangely grateful for the sign of past use, though hadn't articulated the feeling to his friends for fear of embarrassment. The sheep on the ledge had watched them go, calling as the sight of them dwindled. Gemma kept looking back at the animal until they passed from sight of it.

Jon wouldn't have liked being here alone. Already gripped with a mild vertigo and an unpleasant sense of exposure beneath the canopy of sky, his instincts suggested they camp lower on the rock, near the sea and not up so high.

The track led to the summit and to the copse of defiant, wind-blasted trees. Other narrower tracks branched off the one they'd used and led down, though it wasn't clear to where. A sheet of greyish cloud moved in from the west.

When they made highest point they stumbled around each other amidst the crooked branches and looked out. Took pictures. Around them, in every direction, the sea. There were no sails in sight. Not even a distant speck of another rock was visible. And no land Plymouth way either. Bumpy water threw spumes of foam over the outlying reef. Some kind of localised tidal current was more visible from so high up. They'd stayed shy of it while paddling so close to the rock's stony skirts. It ran from west to east and must flow into the eddy they'd crossed.

Just three of them now and the trees gathered about them like beggars, stooped from some awful penitence or abandonment, reaching for passers-by who'd made the mistake of stopping. Each tree was leafless. The curvature of the branches had been fashioned by perpetual wind into what now resembled old brooms, constructed from hawthorn twigs. Each of the longest branches appeared to have just released something into the massive expanse of thin air. Thrown something, up and away. The branches rattled.

"Ugly mother fuckers," Archie said.

"Survivors," Gemma said.

Jon already missed the rock pools and weed below. The cove was sheltered by the triangular outcroppings of the reef on the western side. He wanted to spend time in the ravine, that tranquil and colourful introduction to the edifice. He wondered how far the sea came in down there and if it was possible to camp in the cove. Being that close to the water would be cold and damp, though the prospect of sleeping closer to their boats offered the prospect of a protection that he felt the summit lacked.

"The witch house," Archie said. "Must be over that way." He pointed north and to the noise of the swell flopping against hidden cliffs. "That path leads down. Let's go."

◄◦►

"Jesus, they spent decades out here. With a kid. And they lived in that." Gemma voiced what they were all thinking about the intact but derelict building. She turned her attention to the sea. "Every day. The same rock, gorse. The sound of the wind. Constant. So few trees you can count them on three hands." They sat outside the house, close to the lightless cavity of the doorway and on the same sheltered ledge upon which the house had been built—a long, uneven, rocky ledge, tufted with coarse grass.

"I'm assuming this was the vegetable patch," Jon said, keen to change the subject. He patted a clump of the springy turf.

"Couldn't produce enough to feed four," Archie said. "Half the size of a tennis court? Maybe their diet was augmented by seals and fish. Shellfish."

Between them, the Jetboil stove hissed, the tiny roar of ignited gas like an agitated crowd of tiny people. The tiny blue flame cast a brighter halo between their legs as dusk seeped across the rock. Soon they would need head torches. "No. They must have been resupplied by the mainland." Jon supposed a boat could moor in the cove, after ferrying supplies to and from the island. "Or they'd have starved. Surely. Maybe they supplemented their provisions with the garden. They were convicts but not condemned to death."

At the north side of the lumpy paddock, slate cliffs plunged into restless water. Waves walloped through a cave far below. As the sea withdrew, the cave produced a choking sound as if a great throat struggled to clear itself of liquid.

"In a way they were condemned," Gemma added and shuddered to register her disapproval of the treatment of the Beedalls. "Don't forget fresh water. Or did they collect it? And what did they do here? Three adults and a child? You can cover the rock on foot in twenty minutes. They were here for decades."

Jon shrugged. "And never returned to the mainland, apparently. Wasn't much information online. I'll do some more mooching when I get back."

"They probably weren't allowed to have a boat," Archie added, pensive. "Maybe they got fed up and tried swimming for it. Bad storm might even have swept them off the rock. The kid first and the adults went in after it."

"Shut up! Archie. Please." Gemma frowned but her eyes were smiling as if she was trying not to laugh.

They ate the tinned chilli down to the last beans and followed it with chocolate and flapjacks. Brewed coffee followed before they traded swigs from Archie's flask until the spiced rum was gone.

When Gemma yawned, she triggered the other two who also yawned. They were all pleasantly fatigued. Jon had spent most of the afternoon exploring the rock, each cave, the outcrops and their seals, the fabulous pools of vivid weed. Archie had joined him initially, though they'd eventually separated to indulge their own enthusiasms, Archie preferring to catch waves out by the reef and to glide between the rocks. The reef had offered the most swell and biggest challenges. An unnecessary risk, Jon had thought, hopping rocks in swell this far out. But then, how many kayakers could resist that?

Gemma had spent her time trying to befriend the sheep. She'd harvested small plants and grass that she'd ferried down to the cove and deposited in the mouth of the arched cave. She'd also emptied one of her drinking bottles into a plastic cup and propped it up within a ring of stones. When he and Archie returned to the cove and had seen the result of her efforts, Jon had cooled with guilt. The animal had also managed to climb down and was skittering anxiously about the cove, ignoring Gemma's purred entreaties. It was still alone in the cove.

After they'd eaten almost everything they'd brought with them, a sensational night sky covered the rock. As Archie pointed out planets, Jon was distracted by a persistent unease. His vertigo worsened in darkness.

The idea of sleeping and being unconscious so close to the cliff edge the cause. Though he'd erected his bivouac tent, he'd decided to sleep inside the little house, snuggled inside his sleeping bag, an inflatable mat beneath the four-season bag. "I'm turning in," he said. "But I will avail myself of the existing accommodation. In there." He thumbed a hand at the house. "You two be all right out here?"

"Safer than in there," Archie said. "Witch guy's house. Who knows what evil shit went down in there."

"I'm going to check on the sheep," Gemma said. "See if she's touched the food and water. Then look at the stars for a bit."

"I see a tearful farewell tomorrow," Archie said. "Or a stowaway."

"Please, don't even think about it, Gem. Your boat will be unstable."

She didn't answer as she skipped off, up the path towards the summit. Light from her head torch bobbed about the dark grass and eventually struck the distant silhouettes of the wretched trees.

Beedall's house was damp and further chilled by the tang of the sea. Inside, the structure resembled a large igloo made from stone. One artfully constructed from slate stacked horizontally, curving neatly into a cylinder and a high roof. Despite the blackened hearth, no other signs of past habitation existed. The house was as bare and unadorned as a lime kiln, or robbed tomb.

Once his head torch was doused and the cocoon of his sleeping bag embraced him, Jon listened to the muted rustle of wind through gorse. The distant swell and retreat of the waves, reflecting off the northern cliffs, hushed a lullaby. His core muscles and upper body retained the memory of the day's near constant paddling and softly thumped as if with a pulse. Food lay heavy within his belly. The rotations of his thoughts effortlessly transformed into nonsensical imaginings, bits of memory, darkness, sleep.

And soon after, he thought, though without any true concept of time, he found himself in the cove, lit up by the sharp light of a steely dawn. He stood on the ledge above the cave, where they'd found the sheep, with his back pressed into wet slate. He found himself to be naked and shivering. Or rather, he experienced what a dream emulated as a physical sensation. Beneath the ledge, below his feet and the cliff-side that he was flattened against, a thrashing of many sticks commenced inside the arched cave. A whipping of the inner walls. Of what raked the stone down there, he saw nothing.

Archie appeared in the cove. He looked up at Jon and grinned. "You know, mate, it was in the Devonian period that the jaw evolved. That is when the breaking started. The splintering, the ripping, the tossing, the upturned eyes. They'd have everything out of each other. Clawed out, like sticky meat from bowls. All flopping wet on these old rocks. It's where the screams started. The screams that were never supposed to end. All the stones are full of old screams. Trees here, they know about the murdering and the eating." Archie tapped the side of his tousled head. "But there's more than jaws and teeth that can do the breaking. There's more to the hunting here. And a big gate to the North. It's open, mate. They go through it. In and out. They never wanted to leave, so they've been coming back. Pretty amazing if you think about it. Have you checked the forecast?" Archie's voice altered to that of an old man. Because he was just that, an old figure now, naked, sopping wet and shivering. "They'll have us afore the sun rises."

Jon snapped awake. Sat up. And tried to shake the horrid vision from himself, in the same way that he would shake seawater from his face. And was, at once, drawn to the sounds of a commotion outside the stone house. In bewilderment, he suspected that, impossibly, the rock had become crowded as he'd slept. Others must have come here, in the dark. Because these others, these intruders, they were responsible for the whistling and whispering. That came from nearby, not far from the door.

Reason seeped into the confused interior of his dark, half-dreaming mind. He didn't call out but felt an urge to get outside. When the zipper snagged on the lining of his sleeping bag, he lost his temper and kicked his legs free.

By the time Gemma was screaming, he was standing up, dressed in his bottom layer—thermal leggings and undershirt. Jon stepped forward, tripped over his rucksack and fell to his knees. He righted himself and pawed the ground of the black hut, seeking his head torch. He never found it.

He next heard the noise of a zipper. Archie's tent. Must be. A rustle of nylon and flexing of poles as his friend fought his way out of the tent. Abandoning his hopeless search for the torch, Jon stumbled into the thinner darkness of the rectangular doorway.

In which he met Archie, under the lintel and so quickly that their faces smacked against each other. Jon backed away, blinded by a streak lightning of pain that spread from his nose and threaded his skull. Archie pushed him aside and shouted, "They've got her!"

"What?" is all Jon managed. The whistling outside rose in intensity and within the cacophony, Gemma was crying. He told himself that he was hearing the cries of sea birds that he didn't recognise. He then assured himself that they were being raided and arrested for trespassing. Holding his painful nose and blinking at the tears flooding his eyes, he said, "Who are they?" Archie didn't answer as he rushed from the hut.

Outside, the outline of three tents. Pale glimmers from a heaving sea. The canopy of night pinpricked by stars. A carpet of black grass, growing in clumps. And the lumpy masses of rocks assuming the shapes of things other than rocks, looming around the paddock and house. All of this blurred through Jon's vision before his eyes were drawn to a white light on the ground. A head torch on the far side of the paddock but one not strapped around a head.

"Torch. Knife." Archie's voice squealed with panic. He was on all fours in the mouth of his shaking tent, scratching about and conducting a desperate search. A sudden, violent movement, partially illuminated by the discarded head torch, drew Jon's eyes to the other side of the rocky ledge. From there, a thin scream escaped a mouth, similar to the sound of air escaping burning wood, or gas squeezed through a valve. But the cry seemed to come out of the air, from above the rock.

He also assumed that he was seeing people over there. They had to be people, those forms that lurched and hobbled across the rocks at the far end of the ledge, opposite the hut and two tents. He was reminded of elderly women, hobbling on sticks. Whatever was wrapped about their heads, curved downward like torrents of stiff hair. In such bad light, the three figures appeared to be facing the ground. And between two of them, a heavy object was tossed again. That's all that he saw during the first toss, a lump airborne. When he stilled his eyes, the lump became a body. Those were legs and arms that wheeled and flopped as a body was hoisted across the night, to then be collected by another of the hobbling things. The catcher braced and shuddered as Gemma's body was received and suspended in a multitude of limbs no thicker than pencils.

Jon bent double, slipped his hands onto his knees. He felt that he might be sick. He thought he might faint.

Archie withdrew from his tent and concentrated on whatever he clutched within shaking hands. White light exploded about him and Jon. Now their tents and one side of the stone house, the stubbly ground, the rugged fields of rock and slate that rose to the summit, were lit up. The colours of the world nearby were stark white, contoured by black shadows.

Immediately, Archie directed the beam upon the frenzied commotion at the far end of the paddock. The glistening body of the sheep was revealed. A carcase in the middle of the paddock. The animal's neck was bent backwards. All four legs had been snapped like kindling.

When his torch light fell upon the tossing and catching game, that involved their companion and friend, Jon uselessly thought of a documentary that he'd once turned his eyes away from watching; a film that had featured footage of killer whales playing with a seal baby. In the sea, among themselves, they'd thrown the pup like a ball. But here the projectile was Gemma and not a seal.

Others had been drawn to the fray. In the skirts of where the torch light faded as powdery as pollen, before being swallowed by the shadows of the ancient rocks, new participants stumbled and swept about as if blind or drunk. At least four, he thought. They weren't involved in the tossing and catching, the tossing and the catching. Not yet but they appeared eager to join in. They issued the loudest whistles of pain, or despair, or sheer excitement, or maybe all three. It was hard to tell.

Gemma's body had been stripped naked and never fell lower than a few metres from the ground. Red and wet she glistened. Her eyes and mouth were open. She didn't scream again but gargled an inarticulate cry. Blood mired her mouth and cheeks in the places that her flyaway hair wasn't stuck to her skin. Her voice, when she tried to call again, was as muffled as if she had no tongue.

"Trees." Archie said. "The trees." But trees cannot scamper like drunken hens and nor can they hop, rustling, between the stones at the edge of the paddock. Though that is precisely what they were doing. "We gotta help her!" Archie shrieked and ran at where his friend, Gemma, flopped and grunted, as she was hurled again, again, again.

Jon snatched at Archie, to prevent him getting nearer but missed his friend's arm. He took two steps in pursuit and stopped. He couldn't breathe for his terror. His consciousness seemed intent on rolling backwards through his skull, before shrinking to a pea-sized sphere of incomprehension. He opened his mouth to speak but then found he wasn't sure how that was done. Not anymore. Not here. Not before this.

Between the swaying black trunks, Gemma was passed along the messy chain of sticks until, finally and perhaps mercifully, she was cast over the cliffs. A terrible thump below followed a terrible pause; silent moments that had no right to stretch themselves out for so long.

Jon felt his way towards the house. From the doorway, he peered back.

Both head torches were on the ground now, shooting their luminance at odd angles, upwards and to the side. But through the whitish glow, he established that several of the eager blackened things had seized Archie. They thrashed their wispy crowns of twigs, back and forth, whilst the lower appendages tugged at his friend's arms. Archie's legs peddled thin air. Six trees had reached the paddock and now milled and rustled. Others still made rickety descents down the slope from the summit. Spidery silhouettes with tufted hair, supported by a single hopping leg. Below, those awaiting the game to resume, threw desiccated limbs, bushels, and capillaries of twig, forwards then backwards, forwards then backwards. A kind of rustling dance had taken hold of the gathering; the same rhythm that had been achieved to cast and collect poor Gemma. A task they soon set about with an equal vigour, with Archie as their plaything.

Jon fell inside the hovel and scampered about on all fours, as fast as an animal, seeking his torch. He could only think of jawbones and screams inside stones. A sheep's neck bent the wrong way. Gemma's lovely face a scarlet mask, puffy with lumps. The pale star shape of her body as she went over the side of the rock. Archie, strung out, as if crucified, pulled back and forth like a recalcitrant ox. Jon vomited the bits of his evening meal that he hadn't yet digested.

Thin light defined the doorway, peripheral radiance from the two discarded torches outside. And the lintel and sides were soon eclipsed by the bustle and sway of a shape that pressed itself through the aperture and into the darkness where he crawled.

He saw little of what had pushed itself inside; the visitor blocked most of the light. But he heard the intruder rise and expand itself within the stone house. It was as if a tall man, festooned with an abundance of wiry hair, had just squeezed himself inside a Mason jar before enlarging to fill the confines. On the ceiling and over curving walls a scratching commenced. A multitude of twigs raking stone.

Cornered and reduced to the last of his wits, Jon made a desperate attempt to run around the outside of the interior. As he did so, he imagined himself running over the summit, then down the eastern face of the rock, to reach his kayak. The urge, or fantasy, seemed possible for about one second.

What seized his ankle felt similar to a hand. What gripped and squeezed possessed hinged joints that clenched, appendages as hard as bone and stripped of the upholstery of flesh. The second hand immediately groped around his head. He'd heard it approach his ears like a hedgehog's claws on cement, before a spiky extremity caged his face.

Along the stone floor he was dragged. To the door and out the door, to where the others hobbled arthritically and bustled. And together the trees whistled and whispered the songs of their endless vigil on a wind-flayed rock, and of their passages to the other places nearby. Jon's voice rose to join the infernal chorus, to add helpless confusion and outright terror to the already hysterical strains.

Pulled earthward to an accompaniment of creaking tomato canes, he briefly thought of a long bow pulled taut before the releasing of an arrow. Then he was airborne, flung through the cold night until gravity placed him within the bristling hands of another—one who was waiting for him to fall like a boy from a tree.

◄◦►

Wheezing under the weight of three collapsed tents and three rucksacks, the man who had come ashore in the dinghy made his way, haltingly, down the side of the gulley and into the cove. He threw the camping gear to the pebbles, before picking through the pile and dumping each article inside the dinghy.

In disbelief, he then inspected the kayaks again. "Good Christ." He dragged each of the sea kayaks to the water and pushed all three colourful boats away from shore until they bobbed in the weed. He waded out, pulling his dinghy behind him, then loosely tied each boat to the stern of the dinghy.

When he rowed to the squat fishing vessel, moored beyond the reef, the three sea kayaks jostled in the wake of his dinghy like tethered dogs. He was still shaking his head when he reached the boat. From the cabin of the fishing vessel, another man appeared. His default expression of surly disgruntlement gave way to shock. "Fuck's sake!"

"Aye. Old Beedall's been hopping."

"Hopping mad, I'd say. Had them all by the looks of things. Where are they? Usual?"

The man in the dinghy nodded his head back in the direction of the Great Saban Stone, as if to indicate a location known to them both, out there in the vast heaving expanse around the rock. "Over the cliffs. What's left of them."

"They'll be in a right state."

"Rocks was a mess by the edge. I ain't looking closer."

"Who were they?"

"Kayakers. Names, addresses, phone numbers are on labels inside the boats. One was a girl. Come from Plymouth way."

The fisherman nodded. "Bet they wish they hadn't. We'll push the boats out. Upside down. Stream will take them east."

"Their gear's all here too. Couple of tents. Bags."

"Got all of it?"

The rower nodded. "New shoots next Spring."

"Still planting his wood, old Beedall. The sheep?"

"Had that and all."

The captain of the boat pondered the situation. "We'll put all their gear over the side, past black rock. Accident. Twats in boats. Out of their depth. Not the first. I need a drink." The captain ducked down to seize the rope thrown up by the man in the dinghy. "Let's get packed up and piss off."

"But will he think, you know, that it was us lot? I mean, who gets the credit? Three no less? Does he even think in them terms now?"

"Don't work like that. And you can't ask for nothing neither. You keep up the drop-offs, regardless, and you hope your nets and your fields is full. That's a back door up there. That's how I think of it. Lets them Beedalls hop through, now and again, from where they is. With their mates, who I hope I never meet. You follow? My old man used to say that the more food you grow, folks don't keep eating the same amount and store the rest. They just eat more food. So amount don't matter. Thought that counts. They have to be kept sweet. And there is acknowledgement. You know me dad saw them up there once, harvesting what he give."

"Aye. I heard the story and I don't feel up to hearing it again. This ain't the time."

"Maybe. But keep in mind when all was losing their boats, me Dad had a dozen and his nets was always bulging. What's a few sheep? They get eaten anyway."

"This lot weren't bloody sheep."

"No. But did we tell them to come out here?"

"Give us hand with these bags."

And not for the first time, the man in the dinghy tossed up the bits and pieces that people had left on the rock to the captain of the boat.

THAT MADDENING HEAT

RAY CLULEY

There have been three particularly severe summers in Bowers during my lifetime, the entirety of which I have lived in this small town, and while I shall write to some extent of all three, it is the first that concerns these papers most. I was a child at the time, of that age where I was impatient to be considered otherwise, but Bowers has never been a town for rushing things, and my adolescence was no exception. We have always been a town where time runs a little slower than most other places. For example, it would be another five years after the summer I'm about to describe before I saw my first motorcar, though I had heard talk of them my whole young life. We've grown as a town since then, but not much, and as many people seem to move away as arrive. My mother left while I was too young to remember her, bored by the seclusion and simple living, and I was raised by a father who, though sometimes stern, raised me with love. When he passed away late last year, during the second of the three harsh summers, I inherited the store and its accounts (and its debts) along with a number of personal affects, among which were included the papers retrieved so many years previously from the home of Mrs. Winifred Dolores.

Mrs. Dolores, or Winnie as she had been less formally known to those who knew her better, had been one of our regular customers, and in that she was little different to most people, for our store was one of only two in town and of the two we had the fairest prices, if not the greatest range of goods. Mrs. Dolores lived on the outskirts of Bowers where the land begins to slope into a narrow wooded valley, a beautiful if isolated spot where she and her husband had raised goats for a number of years, but despite our willingness to deliver her groceries, she always came to the store to personally collect whatever it was she needed, as her husband had always done before her. She said it helped her feel connected to the community, and prevented her from becoming a recluse, the temptation of which grew stronger for each year that passed after her husband left. She was always very frank about his leaving, though rarely about the reasons why, seeming to accept her circumstances with admirable grace and fortitude. Of course, there was plenty of gossip to counter her reticence, and even as a child I heard some of this, for I was easily overlooked when the adults chose to talk and trade stories amongst themselves. As an adult myself now, I have very little interest in sharing the idle speculations the people of this town seem to enjoy and it is with some reluctance I tell this particular story now, except that it concerns events to which I was a witness, events that seem to have some influence on my life even now, so many years later, as I shuffle towards old age. Events that have had me dreading since boyhood a summer as hot as the one of which I write, and as hot as the one, now, in which I write of it.

My involvement in the affair begins at the end of that hot summer when Mrs. Dolores failed to come in for her usual provisions and I was sent to check on her welfare. Prior to this, my father made some rather discreet enquiries as to whether Mrs. Dolores was being supplied by our rivals in town (rivals being a term I use very loosely, and with some humor, for we had always been friendly with the McIntyres) and upon learning that she had not bought so much as a grain of salt from McIntyres Trading, and realizing that nearly two weeks had passed since her last visit to town, I was sent to her farm with instructions to both check upon her health (with polite subtlety) and to reiterate our willingness to deliver whatever goods she might need that we could provide. The most general of these I took with me, as if to prove the ease with which it could be done.

Her property was not a large one, and as such was easily maintained by husband and wife, if not quite by a wife alone. The house, I saw, did bear some minor signs of neglect, but these were easily addressed, and the opportunist in me made a mental list of the chores a young lad such as myself could help with, such as repainting the doors and sills or realigning fences that had fallen askew. I was, that summer, trying to save enough money for a handsome saddle I had seen displayed at Pearson & Haverston's, and never mind that I didn't yet have the horse for it. Thinking of this saddle, I noted there was some weeding that could be done in the small garden of the Dolores property, and closer to the house I noticed that perhaps the windows needed some attention as well for they were all of them open. As I have mentioned, it had been a particularly hot summer and so I could have understood a desire to air the whole house through perhaps a week or so ago, but the weather had turned since the worst of it and though we were yet to know rain again, the temperature had dropped enough that a woman of Mrs. Dolores's advancing years might feel the chill of it. With her age in mind, I wondered if perhaps the wood of the window sashes had warped to such a degree that closing them had become difficult. It would be no bother at all for me to do that for her, while I was here, free of charge!

I knocked on the front door and waited.

I knocked again, and called, "Mrs. Dolores?" and waited a few moments more.

My enquiries received no answer.

I went behind the house with the intention of repeating the procedure at the back door, but upon the first knock I discovered it to be open. Not wide open, like all of the windows, but as if it had been pushed to and failed to catch upon the latch.

"Mrs. Dolores?"

I opened the door with my foot so that I could enter with my arms full of groceries, an immediate visual explanation for my intrusion should Mrs. Dolores choose that moment to appear, but still she did not answer. I set the box down on the kitchen table.

"Mrs. Dolores? It's Pip, from the store. I've brought you some things."

There was no answer to my call, nor had I expected there to be. You're probably as familiar with the feeling as I am, knowing a house to be empty even before you've checked any of the rooms. There's a silence that settles on an empty place that's different from the silence of an occupied one, and I was certain the house in which I stood was empty.

There were some papers on the kitchen table which I shall come to. I did not read them at that time, as they seemed at a glance to be of a personal nature, but I looked up from where they had been written and saw directly into the yard at the back of the building, noticing then something I had not when coming around the house to knock.

The yard at the Dolores property was a wide area trodden down to dirt that separated the main building from the fenced pen where they once kept their goats. At the center of the yard was a well. All of this I had seen already. What I noticed now, however, standing at the kitchen table and looking into the yard through the open window, was a length of rope on the ground near the well, one end of which was tied to a toppled bucket. At a glance, it would have appeared that the bucket had been discarded after water had been drawn from the well, and that whatever slack that had gathered in the rope was coiled beside it, so perhaps I had noticed it and disregarded it as unimportant, but what I was in fact looking at, still tied to the bucket handle, was a short section of *cut* rope. The rest of it I could see hanging taut to the fullness of its remaining length, disappearing into the circle of stonework, down into the well.

I knew without looking why the rope hung taut, much as you have likely guessed the cause, but I had to look to be sure of it, and on my way across the yard made another discovery. A kitchen knife had been discarded next to the bucket. I gave it little thought at the time, presuming its purpose had been to cut the bucket from the rest of the rope, though I would amend my thinking of that before too long.

Foolishly, at the edge of the well, I called as I had at the door, "Mrs. Dolores?" though I'm sure I have no idea how I might have reacted to a reply. Finally, steeling myself against the certainty of what I would find, I peered into the dark of the well and confirmed what I already knew and feared, namely that Mrs. Winifred Dolores, Winnie to her friends, had hanged herself.

It was a shock to see, and when I went to fetch my father, I did it running, though there was nothing that could be done to warrant such urgency.

◄◦►

My father received the news solemnly. He asked me several times if I was all right, worried at the haste with which I tried to tell of what I'd found, and he put his hand to my forehead several times as if I might have caught a fever, though it seemed he was not satisfied by his own findings, because when he went for Dr. Crombley to tell him of poor Mrs. Dolores, he took me with him for the man to examine. Dr. Crombley was so certain of my health that when I volunteered to go back with them to the farm, he vouched that my returning might actually be mentally beneficial in processing the initial shock of my discovery, and though he would later come to regret the decision, my father was persuaded to agree.

Dr. Crombley had a cart which had served him more than once in the transportation of someone passed, and this we took with us to the farm. We no doubt inspired more than a little gossip, and several of those who saw us followed the cart a short distance so as their speculations in our absence might be better supported by our direction of travel.

"Half the town will know of her death before we even retrieve her body," Dr. Crombley said.

"And the other half by the time we return with it," my father agreed. After a moment, he added, "There'll be talk again of Gorman," meaning Mr. Gorman Dolores. "Rumors always return upon news of a death."

The doctor nodded. "Gorman, the goats, the whole mess of it."

We were a few hours yet from evening, but the afternoon sky had darkened somewhat with the promise of rain. A great deal of the heat of recent weeks had passed, but the humidity left in its wake was yet to break and we were still to know the relief of rain, so the clouds were very much welcomed.

"All her windows are open," I said as we neared the property. It was a detail I had forgotten previously, and unnecessary now when both men could see for themselves, but it was important to me upon seeing them again that we close the windows to prevent any rain from ruining the indoors, though of course, upon arrival, our priority was Mrs. Dolores.

She was in a sorry state of injury and decomposition, and I shall remember the horrors of it for the rest of my days. Or perhaps, as I should more accurately write, I shall remember it for the rest of my nights, for that is when I see her again most often. I never had the good fortune to marry, though I had been close to the occasion once, and at my age I don't dare hope it could still happen, but whenever I suffer those summertime nightmares I am glad to have no wife. Bad enough that I am tormented by remembered terrors without startling a wife awake with them, and embarrassing enough that I alone have to clean the sheets when fear regresses me to bedwetting. I record it here only inasmuch to provide as full and honest an account as I am able. There are nights when Mrs. Dolores speaks to me in dreams, and what she has to say scares me more than anything I have read in her papers, but these are the frightened fancies of an old man, and they have no place in this document.

We drew Mrs. Dolores from the dark of the well like we were drawing water, though she did not come up with the same ease. Death lends a greater heaviness to any weight and Mrs. Dolores was no exception, my father and the doctor heaving at the well handle and rope between them. My father told me to look away as the top of her head came towards us, but I have not always been an obedient child and he was too busy at his task to notice my morbid curiosity. Not until I gasped at the sight of her swollen face did he tell me again, sharp with reprimand this time, but by then I had seen her bulging eyes, wide as if with the horror of her demise. I had seen how her tongue protruded from a mouth made slack from gravity. I saw, as well, how her throat had bloated over the rope that wrapped it, as if to deny it was tied there. My attention was drawn to worse, though, when Dr. Crombley exclaimed a profanity so loaded with blasphemy I thought he'd have to confess it at church every following Sunday.

"What has she done?" he asked afterwards, though it seemed to me a rhetorical question, for the evidence was plain before us. A better question would have been to ask why she had done it, and to this day I have no satisfactory answer.

Closer to the lip of the well, where the light could reach more of her body, Mrs. Dolores was revealed to be without so much as a nightgown and wore only the grotesqueries of her death, namely a horrid wound that split her across the middle, just below the stomach. It sagged open like a spewing mouth, and she hung suspended in a state of partial disembowelment.

"Look away, son."

This time I did as I was told.

"Her neck's not broken," Dr. Crombley said, and I tried not to imagine his fingers feeling at the fullness of that bulging throat, "but with a wound like that, the drop would have sent her guts slopping out—"

"Doctor, *please*."

I was sprawled on the ground a short distance from the well, leaning aside in the expectation of being sick, but I knew the look that would have come with my father's words, and I could see enough of Dr. Crombley to know that when he said, "My apologies," he was giving the words to me. My father received the same by way of a nod.

"She either suffocated her way to death, or bled to it," the doctor said, and as he was a learned man of medicine it was no difficult task for us to take his reasoning as our own when he declared, "Self-murder, albeit of a most grisly kind."

Both my father and I have since decided otherwise, or at least considered the possibility of an alternative conclusion.

Between the two of them, my father and the doctor managed to bring the poor woman out of the well shaft and lay her to the ground. I no longer wanted to see anything of her, but a sharp intake of breath from my father and another profanity from the doctor drew my attention to how the wound beneath her stomach gaped so widely, either from the force of her fall or the state of her decomposition, that she was very nearly split in two and I wondered that they were able to retrieve more than just her upper body. What looked to be tangles of bloody rope around her waist were in fact loops of what she'd once held inside, and at the sight of them I was finally (and violently) sick, my lunch heaving from me with all the burning unpleasantness you have no doubt been unfortunate enough to experience for yourself, although I hope it was with less gruesome a cause. The noise of it had me imagining the splattering sound Mrs. Dolores would have made as the rope yanked her opened body to a stop and I heaved again until all of me was empty.

I felt my father's hand, cool on the back of my neck. When I was done, he helped me to my feet.

I was grateful to Dr. Crombley, too, who had stripped to his shirt sleeves to drape his fine coat over Mrs. Dolores, concealing the worst. We had sheets in the cart with which to wrap her, but she was such a ghastly sight that he'd felt it necessary to cover her even for the short time it would take to fetch them.

"You'll never see a sight like it again, lad," he told me, "perhaps you can take some solace in that, at least." He offered me a sympathetic look to which I replied with a nod.

"Shut those windows," my father told me. "The doctor and I will prepare Mrs. Dolores for her trip back to town."

I was glad of the distraction and left the men to their grim task.

To my surprise, the windows were shut very easily, so Mrs. Dolores must have kept them open for reasons of her own or had passed during the worst of the heat. Her house was situated where the land begins to rise into the valley, and it may be that such a location trapped a great deal of heat, in which case our recent summer spell must have been insufferable. Insufferable enough that one might end their own life to be free of it, though? I did not know, and I tried to put the thought of it from my mind.

To that purpose, there was plenty in the house to remind me more of her life than her death, and as I went from room to room I took some grief-tinged relief in seeing framed pictures of Mrs. Dolores and her husband, and other personal effects such as a hairbrush and comb set on a dressing table before a mirror, a nightdress cast across the bed, a glass half full of water in the kitchen. Things that spoke of living. What I mean to say is that it was easy to believe that Mrs. Dolores might return to her house momentarily, and that in closing her windows I was merely carrying out a favor for the woman in her absence.

I was in the kitchen, closing the last of the windows, when my father and Dr. Crombley entered the house. Dr. Crombley spent some time leaning against a countertop and staring out of the window at the well. My father returned the knife from the yard to its appropriate drawer. Presuming, now, that it had been used not only to cut rope but to make that awful mortal wound, I thought the return of the knife a somewhat macabre decision and wondered who might use it again on some future day without knowing the part it played in a woman's end.

At the kitchen table, my father took up a handful of the papers I'd left alone as something private. He read the first page, and then the second, but the third and fourth he read so quickly I thought he could have only skimmed the content, at which point he gathered up the rest and folded them into a pocket. He meant to do this discreetly, and I turned away before he could see me looking, but not before I saw how pale he had become. His face could have been carved from wax, such was its pallor, and the hand with which he tucked the papers away trembled so that he couldn't pocket them with his first attempt.

He took the papers for the sake of Mrs. Dolores' reputation, to protect her from any further scandal. He told me this twice, once directly while drunk on whiskey, and again a second time (which he probably thought the first) in an indirect fashion via the reading of his will. As I have mentioned, I inherited the papers along with the store, though why he did not destroy them shall remain a minor mystery to me. Perhaps they didn't feel enough like his to do so. I will summarize them here as I move towards concluding my story, though I'm not sure how much they might explain.

◄◦►

The papers begin like a letter written to her husband, Gorman Dolores, though before long she only writes to him in an abstract fashion, as if he is merely a useful means by which to discuss her personal concerns, and so the papers take the tone more suited to a diary, and it was with the same shameful sense of voyeurism one might feel reading another's private records that I first read them. I feel that way again now, reading them a final time so as to accurately record their details here in papers of my own.

As I say, Mrs. Dolores begins with *My dearest Gorman*, and what follows is a saddening account of the loneliness she has felt in the years of his absence. So deep is her sense of loss without him, that were I to have abandoned my reading after the first page, I would have presumed the letter a final farewell of the type often left behind by those who choose to end their own life. Come the end of the second page, however, and from the third onwards to the last, Mrs. Dolores addresses her absent husband only as one might a confidant when confessing a distressing tale. It seems in these pages that her mind takes a terrible turn towards madness, though I am no longer as certain of that as I once was. My father, too, had a change of mind in that regard.

After detailing the extent of her loneliness and expressing her wish that her husband were with her still, she writes of a mysterious figure who she claims visits the farm at night. She has seen it *creeping* about the yard, she says, sometimes bent at the back like someone keen to remain unseen, other times crawling on all fours as if tracking a scent across the muddy ground.

I must confess that my earliest reading of this was affected by the sadness I felt for how her mind had so badly turned, though even in presuming thus, I must also confess to the shiver of fear I felt in imagining such a visitor, and I did so while safely embedded in the heart of town. It must have been a thousandfold worse for a woman alone at that isolated farm.

It seems Mrs. Dolores coped initially, and rather desperately, by longing for this figure to be her husband, come back to her after all these years. Be him alive or a great deal more ghostly, she shares her hopes that the figure she sees by the light of the moon is her lost love, and declares how she can love him, still, however unsubstantial a form he might be forced to take, so long as he chooses to remain with her. Even when her strange visitor behaves like an animal, sly and snuffling, this good woman is still willing to believe it may be her husband and reminds him in her writing that were he now of unsound mind, she accepted him *in sickness and in health*. Alas, the figure is *not* her husband, as she realizes very quickly, is in fact something altogether very *different* to Mr. Dolores or indeed any other man, for she notes how it *proved beyond a doubt that it was not of heaven or of this earth, but elsewhere,* though how it proved this to her she does not reveal. Instead, and with a shaking hand, she writes *I fear not so much for my life as for my soul, for why else should such a thing appear if not to strike me damned?*

Content, at first, to limit its visit to exploring only the yard, there is yet an instance in which it looks at the house *with some awful intention* that troubles Mrs. Dolores, even as it seems to excite her. She writes that she has seen the figure several times but offers very little by way of specific detail, combining all but one of her sightings in a single line of writing, and it is in this line she notes of its new interest in the house. *I have seen it skulking in shadows, hunched in hiding,* she writes, *seen it creeping in circles, snorting at the ground like a beast with a scent, and once, to my awful wonder, it stood boldly by moonlight, staring at the house with some awful intention, the anticipation of which seems to please it.* She adds, *I wait for its return to see what such intentions, and my role in them, might be.*

I understand now, at least to some extent, the strange thrill she must have felt then, though she waited for its return in a braver state than I could ever manage. I, who write this with my doors locked and a bar across my shuttered windows, though in this heat I'd like to throw them wide for any coolness of air they might offer, despite the consequences.

◄○►

There is a moment in Mrs. Dolores's papers when she blames this skulking, creeping figure that visits for luring her husband away. In a brief interlude she remembers with some regret her accusations that he had been continuing some torrid affair with someone from town, though she never puts a name to this woman, and while it may seem an error on my part to presume it truth and not simply the creation of a jealous, abandoned wife, let me note here that I have learnt in subsequent years that Gorman Dolores was indeed rumored to be a man of questionable moral rectitude regarding his marriage vows. With that recorded, I should also note that it appears the affairs he allowed himself were few, and brief, and for the most part without consequence beyond the slow and silent breaking of poor Mrs. Dolores's heart over a period of years. I say for the most part because there was one incident that may be of some relevance regarding the events I write of now, and Mrs. Dolores herself alludes to it briefly.

As I have mentioned, Mr. and Mrs. Dolores used to keep a number of goats, selling the milk and cheese and sometimes the meat, until one year, over a short period of time—I believe it was no longer than a week—they were all slaughtered, down to the last. This was not an intended butchering for market, as they might carry out themselves, but a violent attack, or rather a sequence of attacks, that saw every animal gutted and crudely displayed. Do I need to write that the week had been a particularly hot one? That the animals had been slaughtered at the height of a terrible heatwave?

Upon the first awful occurrence, Mrs. Dolores and her husband suspected it to be the work of some savage predator, perhaps driven into ferocious frenzy by the severe heat, but with subsequent attacks Mrs. Dolores's thoughts went to her husband's suspected adulterous affairs, and she considered the possibility of someone who might bear them grievance, such as a scorned woman or a jealous partner, though it seems in her writing of it that she never put a voice to such suspicions. In each instance, they saved what they could of the meat, though none of it made the market price they could have normally expected and they were never able to replace any of the animals.

There were those in town (and are, still) who supposed it was this loss of livestock and livelihood that drove Mr. Gorman Dolores to abandon his wife, perhaps to seek work, perhaps because he saw the slaughtering of the goats as a threat to his own person, whereas others were (and are) of the opinion that he merely saw it as an opportunity to leave a woman he no longer loved, despite having sworn quite the opposite in till death do us part. Whatever his reasons, Mr. Dolores was soon gone, and Mrs. Dolores remained alone, resigned to never knowing why.

That said, and as I have mentioned already, there is a moment where she blames the figure in her yard for luring her husband away, admitting that even a married man might find himself lonely and seeming to forgive her husband for any previous indiscretions before turning her attention to one who might encourage them. It makes for distressing reading, the sudden shift in tone to a voice so angry and resentful that her handwriting becomes jaggedly erratic on the page, and it is at this point that she imagines a different reader for a short while, no longer addressing her husband or recording events in a diary-like fashion but rather speaking directly to the figure she claims to see in her yard. *You took him from me,* she writes. *You drew him to you with the coolness of one who has no want for what might come so easily, though you crept in the night with the manner of one intent on stealing.* While there is evidence of control in her word choices and syntax, nevertheless there is a vehemence to her script that nearly presses her pen through the paper.

She is far less aggressive when accusing the nocturnal visitor of driving Gorman Dolores away in fear. Indeed, she writes of this possibility with such calmness and clarity that it seems she harbors no regret at all that this was so and may even be relieved by such a prospect. I would go so far to suggest there is even some joy in how she writes of her realization that her strange visitor was in fact *mostly male,* an observation that allows her *to sleep at last, despite the maddening heat that keeps me fidgeting.* What she means by *mostly* is never disclosed, nor do I have the imagination for it.

The final pages of her account are filled with such woeful accounts of loneliness and rejection (and, as I understand it now, frustration) that reading them without pity is an impossible undertaking, all the more so because of how much her mind seems to have deteriorated by this time. How long must the poor woman have suffered so privately? There were more than a few people in town who could have offered companionship, had they only known.

It was a thought that troubled my father a great deal in the last years of his life, which was when he turned more frequently to the comfort of drink. Could it be that Mrs. Dolores came personally to the store not only to collect her groceries but to see my father, similarly abandoned by one he once loved? McIntyres Trading were, after all, better stocked. And had he, also, looked forward to her visits? I know, with certainty, that I did. She had no children herself but she had a motherly nature I appreciated, and I had always been fond of her; perhaps my father had been, as well. I remember finding him more than once, in his chair by the fire, quite melancholy with the thought that for each day that Winnie (as he still fondly called her) came into town to fetch her food and other supplies, she spent six more in isolation at her farm without so much as even a single goat for company, at which point, depending on his temperament, he might launch into a violent deconstruction of her husband's character. Come the morning he would always apologize for his recollections of Mrs. Dolores (or for his diatribe regarding her husband) as he knew the memory of her upset me, but the truth of the matter is I welcomed such drunken monologues, for they reminded me more of the woman herself than the state in which we found her, and I took some comfort in witnessing a more emotional side of my otherwise stoic father, for it helped me understand that my own occasional lapses into an unhappy mood were not unusual.

He was troubled, too, by another detail.

"How was the knife so clean?"

Though he talked of this less frequently when troubled, the knife he meant was the one found in the yard. The knife Mrs. Dolores likely used to cut the bucket from the rope for which she had a darker purpose. The knife which I'd presumed she'd used to commit awful violence upon herself so as to be certain of her death at the end of that rope. It was the knife my father had returned to the kitchen, because as he said, and as I remembered again at his prompting, it had been clean.

"Long knife like that, and such a wound, and no blood upon the blade? Not a single drop?" my father would ask. "There had been no rain for days. Not for *days*."

I have mentioned the lack of rain already, though it came the very night we brought Mrs. Dolores back to town. Prior to that, the week had been uncomfortably warm, the summer heat settling upon us like a hot, stifling blanket. Just as it does again now, as the curling of these sweat-damp pages upon which I write this evening testify. And so it is I am almost brought to the end of this tale.

For Mrs. Dolores, the tale ends at the end of a rope, the horrid details of which I have already provided, but her papers end with a few paragraphs more detailed and distressing than the others, which I reproduce here in full. It concerns the final sighting not included in the compression of one line like the previous visits, and Mrs. Dolores gives it an entire page of her writing.

Yesterday, I witnessed for the first time its arrival and later its departure. I had always supposed that it appeared as if by magic, prowling out from the dark like it was made of the same shadows or riding down on a moonbeam or some other such fanciful method, and no doubt you would blame the fiction I enjoy, Gorman, for having put such ideas in my mind, but having seen the truth of the matter I wish that there had been more substance to such imaginings. Instead, what I saw as I watched my visitor's arrival was how it climbed out from the very well from which I daily fetched my water. A graceless thing, it grasped at first with long-taloned hands the edge of the well wall and then hooked more with the thin crook of its elbow to pull itself out of the dark. There followed, then, a scant thigh and bony knee, and then a shin like a goat's rear cannon, before it fell into the yard. From there it crawled, low to the ground, not on its forearms and knees but upon its palms and feet. A bent-backed thing as thin as a reed, it shuffled as much sideways as forwards, its rump on proud display until the moon appeared and bathed its sickly skin with silver, at which point it stood without shame or modesty despite its obvious nudity, and I fully saw how wicked it was. Though in its eventual departure it returned to the well, yet was I glad to see it go, for the sight of it that moonlit night was almost too much for my mind to bear. Better that it should fold itself over that wall and descend, headfirst into the well, crawling spider-like down out of view, than remain a moment longer in the yard with every detail of its form exposed. And in that form, I had some idea of its intentions, and, oh, how foul a feeling that aroused in me.

Before it went—and this is the worst of it, dear Gorman—before it went, it said something I'd been keen to hear for many years. Its voice was like water, slow and trickling, and though in writing this I can no longer remember a single word it spoke to me, I understood its want and find I must give it what I can, and all I can, just as I understand, now, that I want too.

There is a declaration of love, a plea for forgiveness, and a signature, but those details aside, such is how the story of Mrs. Winifred Dolores comes to its end. With a hitherto unseen grammatical error that provides some ambiguity as to the meaning of her final sentiment.

My own end will come soon enough, and I fear that applies to more than my writing, for I, too, have seen this thing from the well these last few nights. Perhaps it comes to me from the old Dolores farm, but if it does then I wonder that there might be more than one, for the individual that visits me is far from *mostly male*. Indeed, were I inclined to provide a detailed description (which I am not) I would note there are prominent if ill-proportioned *female* attributes. It is yet to speak, and I am glad of that for now, though the silence in my house is beginning to feel like an empty one despite my occupation of it and I am concerned that I will soon long to hear whatever this visitor might choose to say. That I shall succumb to it as I have that maddening heat that had me, at last, opening all the windows.

I shall watch for it and write what more I can in the time that remains to me. There are some details yet to tell.

First, to conclude the mystery as to the whereabouts of Mr. Dolores, they found his body in the very same well, which is to say, they found bones enough to suggest a human skeleton, albeit with some minor deformities. The well was filled shortly after, though considering my own nocturnal visitor I find myself wondering how thoroughly.

I should, as well, offer some more detail regarding my father's passing. He suffered a fatal heart attack one night, collapsing in the store yard where he was discovered the next morning by one of our traders. The most likely explanation is that he had been investigating the possibility of an intruder (and perhaps had found one and been more startled than they upon the discovery) as he had confided with several customers, as well as myself, that he suspected someone was loitering in the yard in recent nights. Do I need to add that this was during the second of those bad Bowers summers? Perhaps the heat was why he had stripped himself down to only the most minimal of clothing when his heart so abruptly stopped.

Upon inheriting the store, I moved back into the rooms above the business and it is from the open window of one of these that I have the view of that same yard where my father died. I don't pretend that it is he who comes again now, while the nights are hottest, to crawl in the moonlight down there or to beckon me to follow, and I do not think I imagine the rank, stagnant smell of brackish water, though I do suppose that should I be visited again, and should the visitor speak, that smell will become at once cool, and welcoming, and impossible to resist on a night as stifling hot as this.

I have no one, and leave these papers to you, whoever shall find them. Please do not judge me too unkindly and know that though I am (and have been for some time) very lonely, I go to my new friend sound of mind.

I can see her now, shimmering in that maddening heat, and her voice, when she speaks, will be as welcome as the rain.

JACK O'DANDER

PRIYA SHARMA

The backdrop Graham uses for the Zoom meeting makes it look like he lives in a luxury apartment, which is highly unlikely because Graham is hanging on to life by his fingernails.

Of a group defined by absences, he's had it the hardest. His mum told him that she was going out for a loaf. She locked him in and told him to stay out of sight if anyone knocked. He was six. A neighbour called the police because they heard him screaming with hunger. *Saved by shoddy, paper-thin walls*, he told us with a rueful smile.

Her body was found later on an abandoned building site. She'd escaped the husband who'd broken her jaw only to meet someone more monstrous while trying to supplement her meagre income with sex work. A desperate woman, reduced even further by the tabloid headline "Prostitute Slain."

Very few of us here like the press.

Graham at sixty still bears all the scars of a childhood in care. His Zoom box bulges with pent-up pressure. His shoulders are up around his ears.

The thing about Zoom is that people can't tell who you're really looking at. In my case it's the man in the box adjacent to Fiona, our facilitator. She asks him to introduce himself when Graham finishes.

"Hi, I'm Dan." He clears his throat and rubs his forehead with the back of his right thumbnail. "I guess I'm here for the same reason everyone else is. My sister Caitlin went missing when she was fourteen. She's never been found."

Every face on the screen distorts in sympathy. The possibility of being reunited is torture. The lack of closure. As if losing someone is a door that can be shut.

Dan and I are a unique subset in this group that overlaps mother, father, son, sister, brother, the murdered, and the disappeared. Dan and I are the siblings of the missing.

◄◦►

Memory is malleable. I've been asked what happened, over and over. I'm worried that I've invented details to plug the gaps, or subconsciously drawn on my family's version of events or news reports.

Some things I know to be true.

The smell of the sunblock that made us slippery and pale-sheened. The holiday complex at the edge of the new part of town, stacks of tessellating white apartments, bright in the sun's glare. Air-conditioning units that looked stuck on, metal shutters and tiled floors for coolness. The kidney-shaped swimming pools and plastic loungers spread with bright towels. The tennis courts. Palm trees. The glint of the gold necklace around Aunty Samantha's neck that caused such a ruckus.

Don't go up into the hills, the company rep warned us. Her lipstick was orange. I couldn't stop staring at her mouth. *There are wild dogs up there.*

◄◦►

I visit Mum every month. She's still in the house that was once home to us all. She won't move, insisting Isobel won't be able to find her if she does. She's redecorated everywhere except Isobel's room. I loathe being here. You can't wallpaper over unhappiness.

"Why do you hate me, Mum?"

"I don't hate you."

Not even that, then. My cheeks burn. It was a mistake to ask her.

"What a strange thing to say. Why do you always have to be so dramatic?" She shakes her head. "Not everything is about you."

I want to reply, *No, nothing is* ever *about me,* but I don't because it won't help.

"You're going to spout some cod psychology that you've learnt in therapy, aren't you?" Her pitch rises in mockery. "*You hate me because Isobel was taken instead of me.*"

"It's true though, isn't it?"

"Don't you dare. You'd enjoy that, wouldn't you? Making me to blame for everything."

Mum likes absolutes and extremes: always, everything, never. And blame is a particular sore point. Or rather, her perception of it. Mum was the most vilified in the end, to be fair to her.

The search for Isobel led nowhere. Not to a child-snatching ring. Not to a body in a drain. Not to the wild dogs living in the hills. My private, distant mother was an easy target for both suspicion and speculation. More than my easy-going, affable father. She was singled out as a negligent mother at best, or guilty of infanticide at worst, be it accidental or deliberate.

We're here now, so I persist.

"You were different with me to Isobel, for as long as I can remember."

"Different? What do you mean different?"

"Like I was in the way."

"You're being ridiculous."

I want to cry. I don't know if they're tears of anger or shame at allowing myself to be bullied like this, even though I'm a grown woman.

"You acted like I annoyed you. Isobel was only a child. She took her cue on how to treat me from you."

It's a eureka moment. The truth has crystallised in trying to talk it through. I was so angry at Isobel, but she was only a child. It was all Mum. The truth only makes my guilt worse.

"Oh God, Natalie, I'm seeing Samantha later and I haven't got the energy for both of you in one day."

I should've brought an umbrella because it's raining revelations. The overwhelming fear of weeping has passed. I pick up my bag.

"I'm your daughter, not your sister. And I no longer have the energy for you, either."

◄◦►

Isobel disappeared while we were on holiday. Disappeared. That makes it sound like a magic trick, doesn't it?

Aunt Sam and her family were already at the resort when we arrived. Our apartment was at the very edge of the complex. Theirs was further down the wide walkway on the opposite side.

They came over to meet us. Aunt Sam looked loose-limbed. Happy.

"Kelly!"

"Let me just get the bags unpacked." Mum smiled but always found a way to be busy around Aunt Sam. She was an expert at constructing barriers, even then.

"We've brought you drinks."

Aunt Sam put down a glass for Mum, the same colour as the half-full one in her other hand. The contents were blood orange, with a wedge of pineapple jammed on the rim.

"Hey, come here, big man." Uncle James put down a pack of beer. A head shorter than Dad, he clapped Dad's back as they hugged.

I'm glad they're still close friends. I'm not sure Dad would've survived without him.

Ellen, my cousin, stood in the middle of the room and spun around. At ten she was the eldest of us. The frilly hem of her sundress swirled out. She always had such nice clothes. They were handed down to Isobel and then to me.

Our fathers flopped in chairs, beer cans in hands, and started talking immediately. Aunt Sam fussed over us, telling us we'd grown, then perched on a kitchen stool. She called to Mum, who moved between the two bedrooms, unpacking.

Isobel was drawn to Ellen. I followed. Ellen carried a beach bag filled with things to show us. She pulled out a mobile phone.

"Mum? Ellen has a phone. Can I have one too?" Isobel pulled at Mum's top.

Mum put a box of teabags and tubes of sunscreen on the kitchen counter. "No, darling, not until you're older."

"But Ellen has one. I'm only a year younger than she is."

"When you're older." Mum sounded gentle but resolute.

"Here, have your drink." Sam pushed the glass across the counter. "Go on. You're on your holiday now."

Mum picked up the glass and took a sip. "God, that's sweet."

Aunt Sam drained hers.

Isobel and Ellen piled into an armchair together. It was always like that when we cousins were together. I was six. Too babyish for them.

I could see a plastic panda in the beach bag full of treasure. I took the panda out. It was a pencil case. I unzipped it to reveal pens in neon and sparkly pastels. I pulled the cap off one.

"No," said Isobel loudly. "You'll break it."

"Natalie, put it down." Mum came over and pulled it from my hand. "Haven't I told you not to touch other people's things?"

"Oh, she's okay—" Aunt Sam started to say, but Mum stopped her with a raised hand.

◄◦►

I arrive at the café twenty minutes early. I wanted somewhere nice, even though it's not a date. A place with good coffee and homemade cakes.

After seeing Dan at online meetings for three months, I messaged him privately. Just a message of support. We kept in touch, soon talking every day. I wanted to meet him. I wanted to see if what I was feeling could survive out in the real world. I feel like I know him. I hope I'm not wrong in thinking he feels the same way too.

I stand up when I see him in the doorway. "How was the drive?"

"I got stuck outside Birmingham, but apart from that it was okay."

I hold out my hand as he opens his arms. We both laugh and then I nod in consent. He leans down and I am enfolded. Nobody has ever held me like that before.

"I would have come to you."

"No. The drive was good for me. I needed to be busy."

"What will you have? I'm buying."

I watch him as he studies the counter. He's grown a beard since that first Zoom meeting. It suits him. His hair is a lighter shade that's almost blond.

"A latte, please. And some chocolate cake. It's not too early for cake, is it?"

"Never."

We sit and wait for our order. The coffee machine splutters and hisses.

"Thanks for today, Natalie." I watch his lips as he says my name. "I didn't want to be alone."

"I understand."

"I know you do. That's why I wanted to spend it with you. After Dad died I'd meet up with friends on Caitlin's birthday, but I could tell they felt uncomfortable."

"The world carries on turning, while we're stuck. Waiting."

Without a body, we've not been given permission to grieve.

"Yes." He sounds grateful. "Someone I thought knew me really well once said, 'You've got to let her go.'"

I've noticed he does that thing of rubbing his forehead with the back of his thumbnail when he's nervous. I want to clasp his hand in mine.

I hold up my coffee instead. "Happy birthday, Caitlin."

"Happy birthday, sis."

We talk about our lives. Work. His love of music. My love of cinema. It sounds like small talk after what we've shared, but I want to piece Dan together until he is more than the sum of loss. He's earnest most of the time and when he laughs he stops himself as if we're not allowed to be happy.

◆

We were at one of the resort's swimming pools. Our parents were stretched out on loungers. Isobel and Ellen were splashing and shrieking. I put my head under the water and watched them swim to the pool's edge. Their legs scissored as they clutched the side. I surfaced. They were deep in conversation.

After we got out, our parents towelled us down. Ellen got something from her mum's wicker bag.

"Not near the pool with that, Ellen."

Isobel sat so close to Ellen that their upper arms looked welded together. Their wet ponytails stuck out at odd angles. I saw the phone in Ellen's hands. Ellen whispered in Isobel's ear, covering her mouth with her hand. She showed her something on the phone. They talked some more, voices hushed.

"Natalie, look at this."

It was the first time Isobel had spoken to me directly since Ellen had arrived.

"Come on." Ellen beckoned and moved aside to make space for me.

They showed me cat videos on the phone. Cats falling off kitchen counters. Cats in outfits. Cats staring at dogs. Cats chasing dogs. We had two cats at home. I wanted a dog but Mum said they were too much work.

Then they showed me another video.

It was taken from a bedroom, I think. There were Lego models on the windowsill. Someone was filming the street below. It must have been late autumn, from the light. It was already fading at a time when groups of children in school uniforms were on their way home.

There was a figure under the trees on the opposite verge. I couldn't see his face. He was wearing a dark suit and a black hat. His hands were in his pockets.

The schoolchildren hadn't noticed him.

"Who's that?" I pointed to the screen. He was turning: left then right, then left again. Watching each group of girls.

"She can see him. She can see Jack O'Dander." Ellen's nose was freckled and slightly upturned. She has grown into that promise of prettiness. Her facial tattoos and scars aren't armour. She's mortifying her own flesh. On the rare occasion that we meet, she can't look me in the face. I think she's suffered more than any of us.

"Who's Jack O'Dander?" I asked.

"If you can see him, it means he can see you. He'll come and find you."

I looked at my sister.

"It's true."

"Why would he come to find me?"

"To take you away. Then we'll never see you again."

"Can you see him?"

"No. Can you?" Ellen asked Isobel.

"No." My sister shook her head. I couldn't tell if she was joking or not.

When I glanced back at the phone, Jack O'Dander had stepped out from beneath the trees. He walked to the kerb and looked up. The streetlamp cast a shadow from the brim of his hat, hiding his face, but I could tell he was staring towards the window. In that moment, it looked like he was staring at *me*.

I snatched the phone from Ellen and threw it down. It landed on the tiled poolside. Ellen shrieked. Then she started to cry.

"It was Nat." Isobel drew up her legs and wrapped her arms around them.

Aunt Sam knelt down and put her arm around me. "What happened, sweetie? Was it an accident?"

"What have you done?" Mum stood over me.

"She did it on purpose." Isobel, my betrayer.

Uncle James picked up the phone and pressed the buttons. The screen was cracked. "It's dead." He sighed. "Told you she was too young for a mobile." He hauled Ellen onto his knee and hugged her. "It's okay."

"You apologise to Ellen right now." Mum gripped my arm. "Do you think we can afford to replace this?"

"It's okay. It's insured." Aunt Sam's voice was soft and soothing. "What happened, Natalie?"

I couldn't explain. I started to cry, too.

"Don't fret, sweetheart." Sam made a sad face. I wished she was my mum. "Let's not make a big thing of it, Kelly."

"Was it deliberate, Isobel?" Mum ignored Aunt Sam.

Isobel nodded.

"Right. Get your shoes."

Mum marched me back to the apartment. People stared at us, a sobbing child and a mother, thunder-faced at some unspeakable misdemeanour.

‹•›

Life after Isobel.

I came in after school and dumped my bag in the hall. I pulled a dirty bowl from the sink, rinsed it, and tipped in the last of the cereal. I ate it dry because the milk smelt off. It was early September, a yellow, buttery quality to the light.

It was just Mum and me by then. Dad told me: *You won't understand this now, but your mum and I can't help one another, not when we need the same thing.*

It was a shitty thing to say, because neither of them had considered what I might need.

After I finished, I opened the glass-panelled door to the lounge. The curtains were half drawn. Mum sat on the floor, her back against the sofa, phone clutched in both hands. I didn't need to see to know that she was watching a video of us as children. I could hear Isobel's voice. It sounded tinny and distant. She was singing. Mum didn't look up. She didn't see me. Not in the virtual world and not in the real one.

In fact, I knew the final time my mother had *really* seen me. It was the night she'd opened the door to our room and seen that Isobel's bed was empty. She pulled me from the bed, where I was pretending to sleep, huddled up to the wall. She shook my shoulders.

Where's your sister? Where is she?

I was mute with terror. She only let me go when Dad intervened.

Mum resented my every milestone. Puberty. My first day at high school. My first date. Graduating. Everything Isobel should have done before me.

Isobel was good at maths, wasn't she? Do you remember that poem she wrote? She could sing. Do you remember how she liked to paint? Isobel's potential eclipsed me. In the moment she was taken, a trajectory of possibilities were closed to me. She was a fragment of shrapnel that entered me, and I was remade around her.

◄o►

It seemed like hours before Dad returned to the apartment on the afternoon that I broke Ellen's phone.

The bedsheets smelt unfamiliar. The twin bed opposite mine had an indentation in it, as though someone had slept there while we'd been out. Apart from that, all the room contained was a small wardrobe, a floor lamp, and a long mirror. Dad had put one of the empty suitcases in the corner, stood on its end. It looked huge. It was open, just a fraction. I hadn't looked at it before we went out, so I couldn't say whether Dad had left it like that or not.

The room was full of afternoon sun. It reflected off the white walls and had faded the prints of the old town hanging there. It only made the suitcase's maw worse. It was an absolute black, without shade or nuance. What did it hold? Was it large enough to fit Jack O'Dander? I imagined his fingers sticking out, widening the gap. Then him stepping out: one long limb, then the other.

I pulled the sheet over my head. The flimsy cotton couldn't protect me. I needed a duvet or heavy blankets to shield me. Sweat gathered in my creases and ran down my back. Fear held me there. It stopped me from running to open the bedroom door and to Mum.

I thought I could hear Jack O'Dander breathing.

"Where's Isobel?" Mum's voice was loud.

"Playing with Ellen." It was Dad.

The door opened. I pulled the sheet down.

"Hey, kiddo." Dad's expression changed. He sat on the bed beside me. My face felt tight and swollen. Dad placed a hand on my forehead, checking for a fever. He smoothed down my hair.

"Are you feeling okay?"

I nodded. I could see Mum. She was on the sofa, reading a paperback. She didn't look at me.

"Come on, chicken." He pulled me onto his lap, arms around me.

"Natty, why did you break the phone? It's not like you." He was the only person to call me that.

I wish I could've found the words. He might have understood. It might have changed things.

I'm scared Ellen and Isobel are lying to me about not being able to see Jack O'Dander.

I'm scared of Jack O'Dander.

"You won't be in trouble if you tell me." He stroked my back. I felt comforted until Mum's shadow fell across the bed.

"Of course she's in trouble. She broke something expensive, although God knows why you'd give a phone like that to a child. Ellen's only ten."

"That's not really our business, is it? And yes, I know what you're saying, but look at Nat. She's in a right state." The strokes turned into a gentle pat. "You *are* sorry, aren't you?"

"Yes." It came out high-pitched and childish.

"And you'll say sorry to Ellen and to Aunt Sam and Uncle James."

I nodded because I didn't know what else to say.

"Good girl."

Mum sniffed.

◂◦▸

"Does this mean we'll be kicked out of the group?" I intertwine my fingers with Dan's.

His smile fades. I curse myself. I meant it as a joke, not a reminder.

"We thought we'd found Caitlin once. It was five years ago. Just before Dad died."

Such is our pillow talk. I'm lying in the crook of his arm, naked. It takes all my self-control not to get up and pull on some clothes, making an excuse about needing the loo.

"It wasn't her, though. I think the shock of it finished Dad off."

For an awful minute I think he might cry.

"I feel guilty all the time." He *is* crying now. My stomach tightens but I put my hand on his cheek. "If I'd walked back from school with her that day, like I normally did, she would've been safe. But I was with a girl. It was the first time. You know."

I want to comfort him, I really do. I put my arms around him, tight, and stroke his back so he can't see my face. The truth is that I don't want to know. Not about Caitlin or his loss of virginity. He wriggles out of my embrace to look at me.

"What do you remember about the night that Isobel went missing?"

Dan's never asked me this before. I tense up. If he notices, he doesn't say anything. So Isobel manages to even be here in bed with us, and Dan and I are knotted together by loss, not love.

Dan's tears for Caitlin have been the foreplay to this moment. I know what Dan wants. I never talk about the night itself. Not in group. Not to anyone. I told my mother I'd been asleep and have stuck to this lie in the face of every authority.

I once asked if Isobel was dead. Mum slapped my face. Dad let her.

Dan must know my story. Dad makes sure no one can forget. It's his reason for living. He fundraises and campaigns. *If only he'd shown that much gumption when we were married*, Mum once said. He visits the Archbishop of Canterbury and the Home Secretary on a regular basis. He is funded by millionaires. He thinks if he brings Isobel home, life will go back to how it was, even though it was awful. Or maybe it's just to expiate guilt. We're *all* guilty. Me more than anyone.

"What do I remember?"

Is it Dan's way of asking *Why her and not you? Were you awake? Did you see him? Why didn't you scream? Did you blank out the whole thing?*

"I'm not sure. It was a long time ago. I was only little."

"You must remember something. What about the video?"

I don't like this version of Dan. He's got no right to question me.

"It was going around lots of British schools. Ellen told the police it was a joke, but they had to check it out. It was just a stupid children's prank. It was of some bloke watching some schoolkids. If you could see him as you watched it, then he could see you too, and he was going to come and find you."

"You must have been terrified." He's watching me intently. "What was his name?"

"I don't remember." I pull on my T-shirt. "It was just a silly thing that kids did."

"You're lying."

"Why are you so annoyed?"

"I don't see how you could forget that. And I thought we trusted each other."

"Jack O'Dander." Saying his name aloud is like pushing a needle deep into my flesh. All the pain is located on a single point. "There. Are you happy now?"

I can't read Dan's expression. It's not unhappiness exactly, but something else that I can't identify.

⋅◇⋅

We went into the old town the day Isobel disappeared. Aunt Sam's apartment was across the path from ours, halfway down the block. We met in the resort's foyer that looked more like it belonged to a hotel. There was a marble counter and uniformed staff. They directed us to the coach. There was a queue. I think it was midmorning.

Isobel and Ellen rushed to sit together. Sam noticed my hurt look and held out her hand to me with a grin. "Will you keep me company?"

Dad followed James, but Mum pulled him into the seat beside her instead.

The bus was crowded so Sam pulled me onto her knee to give a seat to someone else. I liked it. Mum said I was too old for that. As we pulled off, I leant back against Aunt Sam. She kissed the top of my head. Her arms around me felt good. Safe. I looked out the window. The landscape was different to home. Drier. Paler. Flat-roofed houses, never more than two storeys. Chain-link fences. A collapsing shed in a field.

Isobel and Ellen, who had the seats in front of us, peered from the window to look at something. I turned to see it, too. We passed a figure on the road. The man wore a dark suit and a black fedora despite the rising heat of the day. He was thin and leggy, just like in the video. A trail of dust rose behind him.

"Did you see him?" I put my head through the gap between the seats.

Isobel twisted around to answer me. "Who? I didn't see anyone."

-◦-

My phone rings. I'm surprised to see it's Dad. We normally talk on a Sunday night. I answer.

I know what he's going to say. The certainty of it makes me feel like something cold is running down the inside of my chest.

"Natalie, we've found her."

I don't know how to answer.

"Natalie, are you there?"

"Yes. Is it really her?"

"Definitely. It's been confirmed by genetic testing."

"Testing? When did you find her?"

"A month ago."

"Oh." We've been talking all these weeks and he never said.

"Isobel needs time. She's been through so much."

"Where she's been?"

"She's not ready to talk about it yet. Not to us, but she's been talking to the police. All I know is that she was in Spain until her early teens and then lived on the streets in Algeria for a few years. The investigator found her living in a commune in Greece. God knows what she's been through."

"Where is she now?"

"At your mum's." I hadn't spoken to Mum for months. "Don't say anything to anyone yet. She needs her privacy."

"You've not told Aunt Sam either?"

"Not yet. Isobel wants to see you first."

The thought made me feel sick.

We got off the coach and walked through the old town's square. We took photos by the fountain, water gurgling down one side of the statue of a woman holding a baby in one arm and a fawn under the other. Interpol examined those photographs later, in search of evidence.

Mum and Aunt Sam walked together at a slow pace, both frightened of putting a foot wrong. They're the same even now. Advance and retreat. Frequent skirmishes followed by short-lived peace.

They stopped to look at shop window displays. At the street hawkers' handbags and sunglasses laid out on blankets, ready to be scooped up in a quick escape from the local police. I stood close to Aunt Sam while she looked at racks of postcards. Mum's stare made me step away.

Lunch was at a restaurant in a long stone barn. The waitress gave us menus in English before anyone had to ask, and then brought crayons and paper placemats to colour in while we were waiting. Mine was a picture of a unicorn. Isobel and Ellen both had fairy-tale castles.

Plates were put down in front of us. There was a bottle of wine, then another. I don't remember what the grown-ups were talking about. Their voices got louder. Combative. Even I could see the surreptitious glances from the other diners.

Then Mum leant over the table and pulled at the gold necklace around Sam's neck. She fished out the gold locket that hung beneath the neckline of Sam's sundress. It was engraved with an ornate scroll pattern. Sam had to lean forward, tethered by the chain.

"When did Mum give you that?" my mother asked.

Sam took it back, clutching the locket in her fist.

"Mum gave you Nan's diamond earrings," Mum persisted, "so I thought that I'd get her wedding ring and locket."

James glanced at Dad, who pushed a piece of fish around with his fork. I shoved the last of my chicken nuggets in my mouth, making my cheeks bulge.

"Here." Sam took off the necklace and dropped it on the table between them. "You just can't help it, can you? It always ends up like this, no matter what I do. I thought this holiday would be good for us all, but I can't keep trying. James, I want to go back to the hotel."

Uncle James held up both his hands in exasperation. Isobel and Ellen huddled closer together on the bench.

"Please. For me, love."

He got up. "Come on, Ellen."

"No, Daddy!"

"Ellen." His voice was low. I'd never heard him be so firm. "Now."

Isobel got up to go with Ellen, but sat back down when Mum shook her head at her.

I wanted to cry. Everyone was staring at us. I didn't want Sam to go. I didn't understand why, but it would be worse for me after she left.

Halfway to the door, Sam turned back. "Do you know why Mum gave it to me?"

"Because you're her favourite."

"No. Because she gave you twenty thousand pounds when you got into debt. I've never asked her for a penny. Not ever."

Mum was red in the face.

"There, Kelly. You thought I didn't know. Well, I do, and I kept my mouth shut because it's got nothing to do with me. And here you are getting all huffy about a necklace that you once called bloody ugly."

"You're so perfect, aren't you?" I thought Mum's head was about to blow off. I knew that look. She was moving past reason into fury. "You're so much better than me."

"Stop acting like a child. Yes, I am perfect in comparison to you." Sam had the last word. Mum hated that. The last word was always hers in our house.

When the door closed, it was Dad's turn to get it.

"Why do you always do that?"

"What did I do? I didn't do anything."

"Precisely. You're so pally with James. Why don't you and him go on holiday on your own?"

"I would if I could."

Mum blinked.

"Everyone thinks you're the happy one. You want to be everyone's friend. *Dave is so much fun.* You never back me up."

"I can't interfere with your family."

"*You're* meant to be my family."

"Yeah, I am until I disagree with you, and then you tell me to butt out."

"You're happy enough when it comes to asking them for money."

His gaze drifted upwards. He was biting his lower lip.

"Not now, Kelly. Not in front of the kids. I'm ashamed enough as it is." He took a deep breath. "When did you get so angry all the time? You never used to be like this."

I put my forefinger on the locket that lay on the table. How was it that it had caused so much trouble?

Mum turned in her seat to face me. She wore the same expression that she used for Aunt Sam.

"Don't. Touch. That."

I pulled my hand back as if I'd been burnt. Our waitress was watching us. She saw me flinch. After she cleared the table, she brought two bowls of ice cream. *For your beautiful girls, on the house*, she said. *Everybody likes chocolate ice cream.*

She winked at me. The kindness of strangers is staggering sometimes.

◄○►

Everything was shuttered after lunch. A postprandial hush settled on the town. Tourists were sluggish as they shuffled through hot streets.

Mum and Dad walked in a silence that was heavy on us all. She stopped to check the map she'd got at the resort, and then folded it up and slipped it in her bag.

"The church is up there," she said to no one in particular.

We followed her along the narrow streets until we reached the oldest part of town.

My abiding memories of that afternoon are the colours. Whitewashed houses, so bright in the sunshine that it hurt to look at them. Doors painted cerulean to match the sky. Blue to fill your eyes.

We'd entered a labyrinth. Bougainvillea spilled flowers in rich purple over walls. Pots of red gardenias graced doorsteps and windowsills. Passageways led to private courtyards, making us double back. I heard murmurs from open windows, a soft song drifting from a radio. Our own footfall. The distant revving of a motorbike. I thought we were trapped and would never escape.

We came to a set of cobbled steps that rose gradually above us. I lagged behind my family. A door was ajar, halfway up. A woman sat in a cane chair in the entrance hall. The floor was a monochrome chequered pattern. Her face was turned to the sun, flower-like. She hummed to herself, sounding younger than she looked.

Something wound itself around my legs and I tried to stifle a cry. The woman stopped humming, her head turning in my direction. I realised she was blind. The cat was soft and silky against my bare calves. I could feel its tiny bones beneath its fur. When I reached down to stroke it, it darted away. It pushed its length against the door and then froze, looking deep into the hall, beyond where the woman sat. Something moved.

The woman called out, but I didn't understand what she said. The cat flattened its ears and hissed before it turned and fled past me down the steps. Startled, I ran up towards my family. The pale tower of the church peeped out over the rooftops above us.

I was breathless when I reached my parents, but they didn't slow down for me. Isobel clung to Mum's hand. We climbed until we reached a plateau from which God looked down on the town.

The church doors were huge, with Bible scenes depicted in bronze relief. They were patinaed by time except where people had touched them in reverence, revealing the true colour of the metal. These accents of faith shone brightly. Mary's head as she shied away from Gabriel at the Annunciation. The baby Jesus in his crib. The feet of Jesus as he hung on the cross.

I looked at Dad, but he had turned his back on us. Mum and Isobel went into the church. I stood on the threshold, caught between them, but then followed Mum in. It was cold inside, rather than cool. The coloured glass in the window behind the modest altar stained the stone floor with elaborate patterns. Mum lit a candle and put it on a rack with the others. I wondered if she had to blow them all out for a wish to be granted.

I felt sick after all the ice cream and the climb. I went back outside and joined Dad at the railing at the edge of the terrace. We could see the rooftops, some covered with washing lines and others with canopies. The alleys were laid out below. Slanted shadows. It was midafternoon. A hush had settled. The world was dozing.

All except for one person, who flitted across the mouth of one alley and into the next, coming from the same direction as we had. Jack O'Dander was a thing of limbs, an arachnid of a man. The blackness of his suit and hat made him an absence of space. Like he was a cut hole in the world.

I watched his dark progress towards us. Sometimes he'd disappear from view, only to appear somewhere much closer, like he'd magically transported himself from one spot to another. He groped along a wall as if he could read who'd been there with his fingertips. He came to a junction of alleys and got down on all fours to sniff the cobbles, trying to catch the scent of something. Someone. Me.

My sister nudged me as she clutched the railing with both hands.

When I looked back, Jack O'Dander was scrambling up a wall.

"Can you see him?" I asked her.

"See who?"

I opened my mouth and screamed until I was sick.

◂◦▸

"Where are you?"

It's Mum. I'm parked around the corner from her house.

"I'll be a few minutes. I got delayed. Car issues. "

I hang up. I've been sat in the car for nearly twenty minutes. It doesn't occur to me to tell her the truth. That I'm nervous. That I'm frightened.

It's a shock when Mum opens the door. I've never seen her so bright-eyed. I don't recognise her clothes. They must be new. She's had her hair done.

"We've been waiting."

It's *we* versus *me* already.

"Go on then, don't just stand there. Go through."

Her giddiness is unsettling.

Dad and Isobel are at the kitchen table, mugs in their hands. They're laughing at something. Mum goes over to them. They have already learnt how to be together.

"Hi." I hover in the doorway. I'm the intruder here.

Isobel gets up, arms wide, waiting for me to go to her. She's in her rightful place.

"Isobel." It's all I can say.

"Natalie."

She has a Spanish accent. She's tanned. Sunburnt, even. She has a nose ring and henna tattoos on her palms. She's an exotic bird in English suburbia, but I don't need genetic analysis to know she's my sister. Isobel beckons me. Her hands are loaded with silver rings. I'm wood in her arms. She's so thin that it's painful.

"Hello, little sister."

The way she says it makes me think she knows what I did, but how would she?

⦿

On the evening of the argument, we were put to bed early. There was a knock at the apartment door. I rolled over in bed. Isobel was asleep. It was dark outside.

"What do you want?" That was Mum.

"We can't keep doing this. We need to sort this out, once and for all." Aunt Sam.

"You can't come in. The girls are asleep."

"Then come out here."

"What's there to talk about?"

Our door was ajar. I peeped through the gap. Whatever Sam said in reply was enough to make Mum join her outside. Dad slumped on the couch, the droop of his shoulders making him look more tired than he ever did after a day at work.

Their voices grew louder. More strident. Dad raised his head, listening. Then he got up suddenly, like something in him had snapped. He followed them out.

I tiptoed to the front door. It was a warm night. To my right, insects buzzed in the yellow halos of the lamps along the path. Some apartments were dark, others were awash with the light of televisions. Ours was at the end of the block, at the edge of the resort, so to my left there was only night falling on the service road, the hills, and the wild dogs. I heard them barking.

Sam walked backwards in the direction of her apartment. Mum went after her. At one point Dad grabbed her arm but she shook him off. Her face was contorted. Someone shouted from an open window above them and Sam held up a middle finger in response. That was so unlike her.

I went back to our room. Unhappiness rolled around in my stomach. Isobel was still asleep. Her head had slid off the pillow and she'd pushed the sheet off. A strand of hair lay across her face. I wanted to wake her but I didn't dare.

I climbed into bed and pulled the bedsheet up under my chin. I turned to face the wall to try and block it all out. The front door creaked. I waited for the fight to continue indoors, but Dad had returned alone. He sounded puffed out, like he'd been running.

I sat up. It wasn't Dad.

Was it Jack O'Dander? I was convinced of it, even though he wore a black sweatshirt and jogging pants, rather than his suit. His baseball cap was pulled low over his forehead, hiding his eyes. He'd come for me.

I cowered against the wall, clutching my pillow to me. A poor defence. I couldn't hear my parents or Sam. The room was an echo chamber, my own heartbeat repeating so quickly that it deafened me. Jack turned from me to Isobel and back again, as if surprised to see two of us.

I pointed to my sister. Jack nodded and gently eased her from the bed.

◄◦►

Dan is due at my place for dinner. I've cooked things I know he likes. Chicken roasted in herbs. Dauphinoise potatoes. Dark chocolate mousse.

All Dan can talk about now is Isobel. What happened to her. Where she might have been. Why she's taken so long to come home. He hasn't asked to meet her.

"You can talk about her, you know," he says when I refuse to join in with his speculation. "This must be strange for you."

"I don't know what I feel." I do know, but it's nothing I can share with him.

He's trying to wear me down. At first his concern was touching. Then I began to wonder if this is a vicarious experience, his longing for his own sister. He's insistent, though. Invasive. I don't like this Dan. He's not what I thought he was. Is this where all relationships end up? The real person leaks out eventually and it's too late by then.

"You're still in shock."

"Isobel's a stranger to me."

"You just need time."

No amount of time will help.

My door cam buzzes. It's not Dan. Isobel is miniscule in the small screen. The drizzle refracts the light around her head. She turns her face from the wind.

"Hi, Natalie. Can I come up?"

She says it like her popping over is a regular occurrence. Mum or Dad must have given her my address.

"I'm expecting someone."

"I've let the cab go. Can I come in while I wait for another?" She speaks with a cordial authority that makes me feel six years old again.

Time is tight. I want to get her out of here before Dan arrives.

"This is nice." She drops her wet coat on a chair and starts wandering about before I can stop her. "Very chic."

I can't tell if she's being sarcastic.

"You're expecting a man, aren't you? How long have you been seeing him?"

"Three months. You'd better call a cab now, in case there's a wait."

She nods but doesn't do it.

"What's your lover like?"

Lover. A more carnal word than *boyfriend.* I blush.

"Don't be coy, Natalie. Is he handsome?"

My smile is a taut line. None of this is right. We're not loving sisters who can share intimacies.

"Is he gentle? Or do you like to him to be rough? Does he hold a pillow over your face?"

I turn and walk away, feeling sick. Is that what happened to her? Isobel follows me into the kitchen. She peels back the foil covering the cooked chicken that I've left resting in the roasting pan until it's time to carve. She pulls off a leg with a deft twist and gnaws on it.

"Where have you been all this time?"

Isobel drops the bone on the countertop and wipes her greasy mouth with the back of her hand.

"I've told you already, but that's not what you're really asking, is it?"

"What am I asking?" I put the foil back on the chicken.

"How is it that I've survived?"

"And?"

"I'm alive because I made myself an ally to monsters." Isobel's enjoying this speech. She's had a long time to rehearse it. "I thrived under Jack's tutelage. If he was bad, I had to be worse to impress him enough to keep me alive. I was so pleased with myself, until the day he told me that you were a far better accomplice, even at the age of six."

Jack. I turn and look out the window. She knows. She knows. She knows. She knows because Jack told her.

"We're too old for children's games. The question you *should* be asking is why I'm here now."

Isobel comes up behind me and puts her arms around my waist, her chin resting on my shoulder. Her lips are close to my ear. I can smell the chicken on her breath.

We can see the road. Hawthorn trees line the bottom of the garden opposite. The movement of their boughs in the wind catches my eye, so I don't see him at first.

I gasp. Jack O'Dander leans against the garden wall, his face in shadow. Isobel's arms tighten around me.

He steps forward and pushes back the hood of his parka. It's Dan. He crosses the road and stops under the pool of the security light so that we can see each other clearly. He rubs his forehead with his thumbnail. The gesture is all Dan, but his expression isn't diffidence. It's outright mockery.

I know what I felt instinctively at six years old when the man wearing the baseball cap, who didn't look like Jack, came into our bedroom. Him, Dan—they're just costumes for Jack O'Dander.

"It's okay, Nat," says Isobel, "I can see him, too."

THE ASSEMBLED

RAMSEY CAMPBELL

E ach bite Justin took left the burger bun floppier. He used up a wad of paper napkins before he risked touching his phone to thumb Sandra's number. The only other customers in the motorway food court were a woman in a wheelchair and her equally wordless male companion, both apparently giving their paper cups of coffee ample time to grow lukewarm. In seconds he heard Sandra, but only in recorded form. No doubt she was asleep in bed by now. "Not even halfway yet," he said. "I'm going to the lorry park in case I can get another lift. I'll see you sometime tomorrow."

"Where are you going?"

He thought the woman was addressing her companion, who'd begun to stump his chair away from the table without standing up, until he saw she was gazing at him. Her face looked held firm by dogged determination, while the man's had grown flabby around a version of the same cramped set of features: small close eyes, token nose, mouth not much better than begrudged. Hers was barely able to contain her extravagantly uneven teeth. "Down to Bristol," Justin said.

"We can take you. Push me, son."

Her son towered over the wheelchair as he propelled it towards Justin. "What lovely long fingers you've got," the woman cried as she reached him. "Lovely eyes as well. Give me your hands."

Her painful effort to let go of the arms of the chair made him wince. He supposed arthritis was the problem, which had distorted her fingers so much they looked unmatched. When she turned up her palms he felt bound to lay his hands on them, as flat as her infirmities permitted. "You'd think I was going to tell your fortune," she said.

Her son's voice was a sluggish bray far larger than his mouth seemed likely to emit. "Go on then, ma."

"I didn't say I would." Justin thought she was sending him a wink until he saw her left set of eyelashes had fallen askew. "Why didn't you say I was coming unstuck?" she demanded of her son. "Do you want me looking even more of a sight?"

"He doesn't think you do, ma. He'd have said."

She snatched the lashes off her wrinkled drooping eyelid and dropped them on Justin's plate. "Ready for your ride?"

"Don't you want your coffee first?"

"I've got enough to keep me awake. Push me to the car then, son." Despite her gaze, he thought this wasn't aimed at him until she said "Show us how strong you are."

No doubt she meant to give her son a brief respite. Justin had to fight to steer the chair straight as he inched it effortfully to the exit. "Glad you're stronger than you look," the woman said.

Shadows outnumbered the infrequent vehicles in the floodlit car park. As Justin guided the chair down a concrete ramp the woman used a fist to indicate the car skewed across the nearest disabled space. "Don't judge by appearances," she said. "If I can keep going it can."

It was a decrepit saloon with a grimy cracked rear window above a deeply dented bumper. The absence of a hubcap displayed how rusty the left-hand back wheel was. "Just put me by the front," the woman said. "He'll do what we need."

Her son hauled the door wide with a screech of the hinges, rousing a dim light under the roof, and lifted her out of the chair as if she weighed no more than a hollow plastic doll. "Gently," she cried, though with the delight of a child sent high on a swing. "Save your strength for later."

While her son deposited her on the seat beside the driver's, Justin tried the left rear door. Was it locked? He was bruising his fingers under the handle when the man caught his wrist. His light grip hinted at considerable force. "I'll do it," he said. "We don't want you messing your hand up."

"That's my boy," the woman said. "Always caring."

Her son wrenched the door open, releasing a squeal. As soon as Justin sidled past him onto the rear seat he slammed the door so hard it shook the car. "Just seeing you don't go tumbling out," his mother said.

"I expect the belt should stop me."

"That's it, you see you keep it on. Make yourself the comfiest you can." Less maternally she said, "Somebody didn't. That's why the door's in such a state."

Justin strapped himself in behind her, since the rest of the rear seat was occupied by a suitcase with its muddy wheels turned towards him. "Don't you forget your belt either," she told her son as he clambered into the car and shook it with another slam. She dragged the belt across him and poked its tab into the slot between the seats, then groaned at flexing her fingers. "Let's go where we're going," she said.

Her son dug the key into the ignition, only to stare at it. "I know," he said as she took a breath like an inhalation of impatience. "Don't start telling me again."

"Turn it like the clock, not how we dance."

"I knew." As he gave the key a vicious twist the man stamped his foot, trampling a creak out of a pedal. "I said."

"Don't go getting yourself in one of your states. There's the way out where the arrow's pointing."

"I can see. I've got as many eyes as you."

Justin wondered why this should earn a giggle like a reminiscence of her girlhood. The depressed pedal had stalled the engine, and the driver screwed the key around so furiously Justin thought it might snap. The exhaust emitted a clogged splutter, and the car jerked forward. It was halfway across the car park before Justin felt compelled to say "Excuse me . . . "

The woman sent him an asymmetrical blink in the mirror. "Forgotten something, son?"

It made him feel too much like a child who'd neglected to visit the toilet. "I think you need to switch the headlights on."

"He can do that himself. Don't go thinking he's incapable."

"I wasn't saying that. I mean he needs to."

"He'll do it when we're past the lorries. He doesn't want to wake them up."

This sounded like a fancy meant for someone younger than the driver. The car coasted past the lorry park, where drivers dozed in their elevated cabins. Justin thought of asking to be let out of the car in the hope of hitching the kind of lift he'd planned to seek, but why should he assume anyone would take him? He ought to be grateful for the ride he had. The woman had taken pity on him, after all, however discomforting he found some of her dealings with her son. "What's the matter with the lorries?" he said.

"He doesn't like anything skulking behind him."

"I hope I don't seem to be."

"He can handle you," the woman said as the car gathered speed past a petrol station. "Put your lights on now like our new friend wants."

The car faltered while her son activated the headlamps. "Go faster now," she said. "Nothing's coming. You won't bump into anyone. Put your foot down like you do."

Each of her remarks left Justin feeling he should have chanced the lorry park. He was opening his mouth when the car raced onto the motorway, and he could only clamp his lips shut, hard enough to swell them into an ache. "Enough lights for you, son?" the woman said.

The driver flailed a hand at the oncoming beams across the motorway. "Don't want them."

"Not you, son. We know you don't like it much."

"So there won't be any more confusion," Justin said, "my name's Justin."

"We don't need to hear names," the woman said.

While he attempted not to feel dismissed, Justin was compelled to speak. "Do you mind if I ask if you have a licence?"

"I've got everything I need right now."

"I was asking your son."

"He's got me."

"It's only I don't know if you're supposed to take a learner on the motorway."

"Then it's a good job it's dark, isn't it? That's one good thing about it." She stared at him so fiercely he could feel it through the mirror. "Everybody's some use," she said. "What about you? Can you drive?"

"I'm only learning or I would."

"I wasn't asking you to. You wouldn't want him thinking he's no good to anyone. Better keep him occupied while you can." She gave her son a sidelong smile and then returned her scrutiny to Justin. "Let's see if I'm still good at guessing," she said. "I'll say you're another student."

Justin felt unable to avoid saying, "Like your son, you mean."

"He won't be any of you." Her laugh implied Justin hadn't made much if any of a joke. "He could use your brains," she said, "but you can keep them."

"Like who, then?"

"Like all the rest of you we've seen offering their thumbs."

"I wasn't thumbing, was I? I mean, thank you very much, but I didn't even ask for a lift."

"We aren't complaining, nothing like. All I'm saying is we've seen a lot of you about. You'd think you could get yourselves a bit more together. Safety in numbers, isn't that what they say?" Before Justin could decide on a response she said "So what are you learning besides how to drive?"

"I'm reading English."

This earned a grunt like the start of a laugh from the driver. "I can."

"Well, good. I mean, well done."

The suitcase beside Justin broke a silence with a muffled thumping as the car sped over some unevenness. He thought his listeners had found his comments patronising until the woman said, "He doesn't mean that, do you, son?"

"Sorry," Justin said without believing he had reason. "Who are you talking to now?"

"Only trying to make you feel part of the family. Tell me to shut my trap if it bothers you that much."

"I'd never be so rude." He felt bound to answer her first remark as well. "I do have people of my own, though."

"We heard her. She didn't have much to say for herself."

"If you mean my girlfriend, that was her answer message."

"I've got no time for all this electronic stuff. I hear there's even people putting bits of robots in themselves. I'll trust the old ways, thank you very much." As Justin tried to discern any relevance, the woman said, "Is she another one like you?"

"We're both reading English. Studying its history."

"And what's that going to do for us?"

"I'm not sure what you'd expect it to."

"Not just me and him, the world. It sounds less use than him."

"I thought you believed everyone's some use."

"You will be."

He took this to mean she regretted dismissing his prospects. "We hope we'll teach our subject when we've finished university."

"What use is that to anyone? I wouldn't call it any of a life."

"You're doing it again, ma. Telling people's futures like you say you always can."

Justin's anger overcame the politeness he was striving to maintain. "So," he challenged the woman, "what have you done with your life?"

"Lived. Still do." The dark glint of her eyes in the mirror might have been providing evidence. "I won't be put down for a while yet," she said, "not while there's any left of me."

"If you're saying that's enough—"

"It is for me and him." As if she was proposing some notion of indulgence she said, "Now it's time you helped."

The driver stared at her, allowing the car to veer sideways into the dark. "There's miles yet, ma."

"I just want something passed," she said and found Justin in the mirror. "Can you open my case?"

Even with the intermittent fleeting aid of distant upraised headlights, he could barely distinguish the suitcase. A defiant pair of beams stayed level long enough to let him find the tag of a zipper. As the beams abased themselves he tugged the tag along its track and felt the suitcase grit its metal teeth. The case began to gape as if its contents were eager to emerge. Its lid flopped open, releasing a smell that put Justin in mind of the refrigerator at his student lodgings—of the time they hadn't realised it had failed until they'd scented evidence. "Find the tin for me," the woman said.

The road had reverted to unhelpful darkness. Justin groped for his phone and shone the flashlight into the case. Black shapes swarmed away as if they were seeking to hide: shadows of some of the contents—a stained lumpy bag choked by a drawstring, the handless wrist of a ragged sweater raised in an empty gesture, a round tin illustrated with images of wrapped sweets scuffed to crumbling. He managed not to touch anything except the tin as he lifted it out of the case. "This one?"

"Don't go expecting any treats, will you? You'd only rot your teeth."

A muffled tinny clatter suggested objects smaller than the sweets pictured on the lid. Justin crouched forward to pass the tin between the front seats. "In my lap will do," the woman said.

By straining as far as the belt would allow and stretching his arm to its fullest extent he succeeded in planting the tin on her thigh. Her jagged nails scraped the back of his hand as she seized her prize—the tin, not him. Having scrabbled at the lid to prise it off, she stood the tin on it. "Let me have your light," she said.

Why should he feel wary of illuminating the contents of the tin? When he hunched forward to train the beam between the seats he couldn't see what he'd lit up. "Not like that," the woman complained. "Give it here."

He might have refused if the belt hadn't been bruising his chest. As soon as he brought the phone within her reach it was snatched from his hand. "Sit back now," she said more maternally than ever, and fumbled at the mirror to angle it towards her face. It found her garishly illuminated mouth stretched so wide the wrinkled lips quivered, framing a variety of sizes of skewed teeth set in greyish gums, beyond which a tongue writhed like a snail emerging from its shell. "What do I look like?" she complained. "Those won't do."

She began to rummage in the tin, which uttered clatters like a multiplication of dice. Justin heard her choose items only to drop them back in. "Why did I bother with these?" she muttered as she abandoned yet another selection. "I knew how big a mouth she had. It made enough noise till it stopped."

Justin was restraining a question if not several when the flashlight beam fluttered across the splintered dashboard while the lid of the tin clanged into place. "They'll have to do for now," the woman said. "I'll be getting better soon. Here, put it back."

She inched the tin between the seats, and Justin had to struggle against the seatbelt to retrieve it. As he returned it to the suitcase she said, "May as well leave that open."

Rather than ponder the reason he said, "Can I have my phone?"

"We don't say can I, do we, son?"

Justin was wondering how much this was addressed to him when the driver brayed "May."

"That's what we say, and just you remember."

Justin had to force the words out, feeling like a rebuked child. "May I have my phone."

"He didn't say it nicely, ma."

As Justin tried to bring himself to make that effort too, the woman appeared to relent. "Let's have the light off first."

"It's not time yet, is it, ma?"

More nervously than he cared to understand Justin said, "Why do you want it off?"

"We don't want you wasting your power, do we?"

He strained forward and thrust out his hand. "I'll do it, thanks."

"I can see how." In a moment the light was extinguished. "Here then, take it," the woman said, and Justin was reaching into the unproductive dark when he heard a thud. "Damn the wretched thing," she said. "Slipped out of my hand and no wonder."

"Can you find it?"

"You don't want me straining myself, do you? That's what's going to happen if you start me fumbling around."

"Can't your son?"

"Not unless you want us going off the road. Just try waiting till we've got some light and we can see what's what."

She must have seen the signboard ahead, proclaiming that the nearest services were a mile beyond it. Surely he could wait that long. The lit board sailed past, and the darkness closed in. How could he have been so thoughtless that he'd tried to distract the driver? The man was barely equal to his task as it was. The imminent halt began to feel not merely welcome but essential—an opportunity to bid goodbye to his hosts and find another ride, however long that might take.

Was it only a mile to the services, or had nervous eagerness caused him to misread the sign? He was quelling a compulsion to ask how much further, that most infantile of questions, by the time he saw the first marker beside the road. Three white stripes on the blue post signified that many hundred yards to salvation. The car sped past the sign, restoring the avid dark. "I think you're meant to indicate you're leaving the motorway," Justin said.

"Still learning, aren't you," the woman said.

"That's how I know what the rules are."

Her eyes glimmered with some emotion in the mirror she'd adjusted. "You'll learn."

Could he see her eyes because the car had grown a little less dim? The outlines of the front seats and the unkempt scalps that sprouted above them had taken on more detail, because headlights were catching up with the car. Suppose they belonged to one of the lorries the driver disliked having at his back? Perhaps it was best not to draw his attention to it, since Justin would be safe soon enough.

The car passed the second marker. Two hundred yards to go, but the driver wasn't indicating. A backwards glance showed Justin the approaching vehicle. It wasn't a lorry, it was a car, and not just any car. "I think you'd better put your indicator on," he said. "Here come the police."

"Don't worry about them," the woman said.

"I'm not, but maybe you should."

Her eyes glinted like knives in the mirror. "What do you think you know?"

"If they stop you they'll find out he doesn't have a licence."

"Nobody's going to give them a reason to stop us."

Was this a warning? Her son's grunt resembled one. If his negligence prompted the police to pull them over, that might be more welcome than Justin had let himself think. The possibility sustained him as far as the last marker. Even now the driver failed to indicate, but why should this alert the police? They couldn't know he meant to leave the motorway, if indeed he did. "We're coming off here, aren't we?" Justin urged.

"Why would we want to do that?" the woman said.

"So I can find my phone."

"What's the panic? Your lady friend must be well asleep. You don't want to go waking people up."

"They'll have got their eyes shut," the driver said, "them that's still got any."

"You said we'd stop where there was light," Justin told the woman as calmly as he could.

"There will be when we stop. You saw it come on in the car."

Though they were almost abreast of the entrance to the services, the car hadn't moved into the lane. "I could use the toilet while there's one," Justin pleaded.

"You all end up wanting that. You'll have your chance."

The car sped past the lane without slowing. Justin twisted against the restraint of the belt and began to thump the back window. "No call for that," the woman cried. "You know we don't want you spoiling your hands."

Had the police seen him? It seemed neither of them had. Their car veered into the entrance to the services without indicating even once. Justin slumped on the seat as the services receded, and then he caught sight of the police car along the lane that rejoined the motorway. They must have raced across the deserted service area, having observed his appeal for help after all. He was trying to relax so as not to tip off his captors when he saw the police had pulled in at a petrol station. In moments they were gone, and he was back in the dark. "Nearly there," the woman said.

She might have been placating a fretful child. Justin glimpsed the dim silhouette of the hand she raised to beckon to him. "Pass the strangle bag," she said.

He was nowhere near certain he wanted to learn. "The what?"

"That's what he calls it," she said with audible pride. "The bag with the string round its neck."

"I can't see where it is without my phone."

"Just stick your hand in. You'll find it soon enough."

His protest had been partly a ruse. He'd noticed the bag while he was lighting up the contents of the suitcase. Surely if he did as he was asked his captors would eventually let him go. He peered into the case and managed to distinguish an object like a heart on the way to losing its shape. When he risked touching the soft lumpy item, he encountered a veinous tendril—the drawstring. He pinched it between a finger and thumb to swing the bag between the seats, trailing the stale smell. "There you are," he heard himself beg.

He hoped the discontented noise the woman made wasn't aimed at him. As she dragged the bag open she came close to poking her son in the face with an outflung elbow. Ducking her head, she began to delve in the bag. Was she rubbing her fingers together, perhaps inadvertently? Some such activity appeared to be involved, though in the dimness Justin could have fancied they were excessively numerous. Her disgusted groan wasn't much of a surprise, given how pronounced the stale stench had become. "It's a good job we've got you," she said. "They're no more use to me. They've all gone off."

She lowered the window to shy the bag out of the car. It landed on the hard shoulder like a specimen of roadkill. "That'll give them something to think about," she said and giggled. "Don't worry, son, they'll never find us."

Justin doubted this was meant for him, and found he hoped none of her recent comments had been. Might the sign for the next exit represent any kind of promise? It appeared to name places he'd never heard of, though the jittering of the light that crowned the board left him uncertain. "Go on then, son, put your light on," the woman said. "Keep him happy while you can."

Justin succeeded in hoping she meant to search for his phone until the driver set off the left-hand indicator as they passed the signboard. Surely the car would have to slow down at some point, giving Justin a chance to escape. He let his hand fall beside him on the seat, uncomfortably close to the suitcase and whatever it contained, and then he inched his fingers to cover the clasp of the seatbelt. As the car passed the first marker for the exit from the motorway he began to press the catch.

How rusty was the mechanism? The button felt determined not to release the belt. He edged his other hand across his waist to add more pressure and hide what he was desperate to do. The second marker swept by, and still the catch refused to yield. Why wasn't the car losing speed? As it reached the final marker all too soon Justin felt the snagged tab spring loose of the slot. The belt began to whip across his chest, and he barely managed to recapture the tab. He was afraid the woman or her son might have noticed his flurried activity, but they seemed intent on the road. The car slowed at last as it climbed a ramp to an unlit roundabout, where the headlamps found a sign for Flinders Forest. "There's a bit of history of language for you," the woman said. "They named it for the likes of me."

Justin had no time to ponder this, because the car had halted at the top of the ramp while a lorry drove around the roundabout at length. He released the seatbelt, which fled into its housing with a clang of the tab as he threw himself against the door and levered at the handle with both hands. It gave as much as the door—not a fraction of an inch. "Don't bother trying that," the woman said as if speaking wearied her. "Nobody can open it but him. He'll do it for you soon enough."

Justin saw the taillights of the lorry vanish around a bend, too far away for him to shout after the driver. "Let me out here, then. This is fine."

"It's nothing like. No use to anyone."

"I can walk. I don't mind walking. I like to walk."

"That's why you were asking for a lift, was it?"

"I said before, I never asked."

"You've got one, so try being thankful. We are."

As he searched for some way to persuade her, the car sped around the roundabout onto the Flinders Forest road. It was narrow and devious, walled in by hedges whose vicious thorns the headlights seemed to rouse. Some of the spikes clawed at the door beside him as though mocking his bid to escape. "Better be getting myself ready," the woman said.

However much of a question this invited, Justin preferred not to open his mouth. As the car raced around yet another unmarked blind bend, the woman lowered her window again. "Not too cold there in the back, are you?" she scarcely asked. "You won't be too much longer."

Surely this meant they would let him out soon, and then he would be able to escape, whatever he might be eluding. He had to think he could move faster than her son. He was trying to prepare himself while he bided his time when the car swerved off the road at a constricted bend and bumped across a ditch. He thought the driver had lost control until he saw they'd swung onto a forest track, if progressively less of one. As lit trees reared up ahead of the car the woman started singing in a high uneven voice. The nursery rhyme might have been intended to amuse a child, or perhaps the driver. "This little piggy went to market . . . "

She hadn't found much of a tune. It was more a chant suggestive of a childish rite. While she uttered the line she bent forward over a task, and a harsh groan of protest followed her words. Her arms flew apart as though achieving her objective had freed them, and her elbow almost jabbed her son. As she tossed a thin object out of the window Justin glimpsed her right hand, which looked depleted in a way he was anxious not to comprehend. "Join in if you want to help," she said. "This little piggy stayed at home . . . "

Her son lowed along with the line, though not with her approximation of a melody. The headlight beam set trees dancing with their shadows to greet the car as it lurched and swayed along its route, which no longer resembled anything Justin would have called a track. While the woman gave another wounded moan before jettisoning a second item, he clung to a notion as if it might shield him from any further thoughts: the rhyme was meant to be about toes, only toes. "You'll have to do the other ones for me," she told her son. "I'm sick of all this lot. This little piggy had roast beef . . . "

Justin didn't know why he was bracing himself, clenching his fists as if to keep them safe, until he recalled the last line of the rhyme. It was indeed even more dismaying than its predecessors. "Wee wee wee," the driver screeched as the car staggered deeper into the prancing forest. "All the way home," his mother cried, and his continued porcine squeals covered up whatever sound she made while performing the last of her task. "Nearly there," she told whoever needed to be assured of it, and flourished her right hand in anticipation if not celebration, though Justin saw the hand no longer warranted the name. Far too soon to let him feel prepared, the car juddered to a halt and the driver switched the headlamps off. "Here's our dark," the woman said. "I don't like seeing what we have to do."

The driver sprang his door open, triggering the light under the roof. Despite its feebleness, it seemed to offer Justin the pitiful hope that it would fend off enough of the darkness to forestall whatever the woman had said she disliked, at least until he succeeded in making his escape. As the driver tramped to loom outside the passenger door he poised himself to leap out of the car. The man wrenched at the handle and hauled the door open, then stood back. He retreated no more than a couple of feet, stretching his arms wide to block any bid to escape. There was no way to avoid him, and Justin could only launch himself at the man in a desperate attempt to knock him down. He was about to try when a phone began to ring.

It was his, on the floor in front of the woman. The driver turned towards the sound and stepped away from the passenger door, and Justin darted through the gap. "Sand," the phone just had time to announce before the woman trampled it into fragments. The grab the driver made missed Justin, who dashed away from the car, slipping on leaves treacherous with rain and rot, almost sprawling headlong. "Fetch him back," the woman cried as though she felt robbed of a prize. While she sounded by no means sufficiently distant, the glow from the car was already so remote that Justin barely glimpsed the people who crowded into his path.

It wasn't a crowd, he realised as he dodged them. It was just a few people huddled together—not so much huddled as heaped. Nor had they moved to hinder him. If they were capable of moving they would certainly have sought to ease the discomfort of their position and of their incompleteness. Justin was floundering out of their way, not least to avoid distinguishing any more details, when an outstretched leg tripped him. Whoever it belonged to, it was unreasonably aloof from them. As he scrabbled at the leaves in a frantic attempt to shove himself to his feet, a weight pressed him helplessly into the mud. The driver had knelt on his back. "Wee wee wee," the man enthused, and set about chanting the rhyme as he bent to his task.

R IS FOR REMAINS

STEVE RASNIC TEM

The naked man stood in the doorway, eyes unblinking. A portion of the left side of his skull was gone, but there was no blood, no gore. Gene tried to outstare him, afraid to look away, and was about to give up from the pain of the attempt when the naked man began to disappear, first his chest, then his legs and dangling bits, his pale lips and whatever lay in the cavity beyond those lips, and finally those eyes, still rigidly, defiantly staring.

They'd been told it was a double suicide but knew few of the details. Gene heard the shriek of distant sirens, and close by the soft bubbling of writhing maggots. The bittersweet stench had been overpowering at the front door, but here, outside the clean zone, they wore respirators. The two bodies had been here undiscovered for weeks, long enough to liquify in a massive meltdown, and although they'd been removed, fat deposits still pooled along one of the baseboards. There were rat droppings. Perhaps the rats had eaten off the bodies. He didn't know.

Fluid had wicked up into the drywall. The floor had an eastward slant. Decomp had travelled into at least four rooms. The event began in this room, but the couple had moved around, panicked, or determined, coughing and bleeding. Alcohol, poison, knives, and a gun were involved. Bio contaminated much of the house.

"Did you see something?" It was the new employee, Ed something-or-other.

"What do you mean?" Even though Gene knew exactly what he meant.

"The others, they say you can see them sometimes. Ghosts, whatever."

"They're just hazing you. Ignore them."

"Ha! That's what I thought."

He hadn't yet decided if Ed was reliable or not. More than once, Gene had seen a new employee run out of a job. The work had a rapid burnout rate. Besides, Ed didn't radiate competence.

He could see Ed's red-rimmed eyes through the goggles. Maybe the fellow was taking drugs. Gene could have told him that only helps for so long.

Gene rarely got enough sleep, but he didn't use drugs, not sure what he might see as a result. What he saw on just a regular day was bad enough.

They both wore blood suits, boots, two pairs of gloves, goggles, respirators, but Gene could still tell the fellow was new on the job. A little too eager to prove he wasn't disgusted by the cleanup scene, moving nervously, clumsily, spreading biomaterial further than necessary. More than once, Gene had stopped him from tracking remains into clean areas. "Focus, Ed. That's the key. Just follow my lead."

Ed sprayed water over the floor, re-hydrating the blood to make it easier to clean. "At least they were together, right? This couple? At least they weren't alone."

Most of their cleanups were single bodies, the unattended dead, left alone to die. "I try not to think about what happened here. Our goal is to make the location look normal again, as much as possible. Sanitized and ready for repair. I want to know as little as possible about the families or the circumstances, Ed. I suggest you do the same. I know the others like to gossip, but I don't recommend it."

"So, it's just a job to you?"

"I didn't say that. It's a sad situation. But we can't feel their pain. All we can do is clean up after them. Somebody has to do it and that's what we've chosen to do. It's what we're paid for." Gene was talking too much. Sometimes he did that on a job.

The naked woman appeared behind Ed and to the left. She was probably beautiful once. She appeared to be running, screaming a silent alarm. Most of her hair was still by the couch, stuck to the floor. Her body was riddled with ragged holes. Gene could see through some of them to the shredded wallpaper behind her. The two of them, they must have clawed at the wallpaper in this room. He found a piece of fingernail embedded in the drywall. Much of the wallboard in this room was contaminated and would have to be removed.

"Are you married, Gene?" Ed used a long-handled scraper on the field of rust-colored human debris layering the floor. The decomp had pooled in places, travelled in rivulets down the hall, created additional pools in other rooms, spread under carpeting. There was contaminated tile and porous grout in the kitchen, and the floor in this room was soft pine not well sealed. The demo crew would have to remove a great deal. The couple's landlord was in for an enormous financial hit. "You got kids? Family? What do they say about what you do? I haven't figured out how much to tell mine. I just tell them the pay's good."

"I live alone now," Gene said. "No girlfriend. No prospects." Ed didn't reply. Gene picked up broken liquor bottles, a shattered lamp, a sticky hairbrush, and dropped them into red hazardous waste bags inside cardboard hazardous waste boxes. He sprayed and scooped dead maggots into a separate bag.

Gene didn't want to be found like this, people in hazmat suits cleaning up after him. But for now, he couldn't see how to avoid it. "We clean up life's unfortunate mishaps," was the way the company's owner put it, a man who no longer went out on jobs. He'd named the company "Bio Genies." Their logo was three identical genies with tornado bodies leaving sparkling stars in their wake. It was embarrassing.

"Why do you think they did it?" Ed asked, rolling in the extractor, a powerful bio-hazard vacuum.

"Ed, please. I don't—" But Ed had already started up the machine, apparently not interested in the answer. *Suicide* was a small word for everything this couple had done. They had committed *rage* here.

Flies were everywhere. At one point he turned around and was confronted by a cloud of flies in the vague outline of a man. He turned around and walked the other way. He checked all the corners where debris tends to gather. In one he found small chunks of jellied flesh like rotting fruit.

They found where a few footprints tracked through the blood. The cops said someone robbed the place afterwards, even with all this carnage spread through the house.

At the end of day one, they cleaned up their equipment in the clean zone and slipped out of their gear. Before leaving Gene switched on the ozone machine to purify the air overnight. He posted a warning on the door.

✦

After a day like this Gene was reluctant to spend a long evening alone in his apartment. He couldn't talk about what he did for a living. It repulsed most people.

He retreated into the library at the end of the street. Gene knew the neighborhood well. This was their fourth case on Alphabet Row in two years, a large number for such a limited area. With small brick bungalows built in the late twenties and early thirties, it was meant to be a cute, fairytale-like neighborhood with large letters on the houses to help teach the local children the alphabet. Maybe at one time it had been exactly that charming, but many of the homes were now in poor repair, and many of the letters which had given the neighborhood its name were missing or replaced with lettering of more modest size. But the current client's house still had its enormous R mounted on the outside by the door, painted a bright candy red.

Gene imagined these old bungalows were cheap enough, and small enough, they might seem the perfect places to house elderly relatives in their final years. But bad things can happen when you're left alone, when there's no one around to find you. But Gene wasn't the one to point out other folks' isolation.

The library appeared full. Gene found it calming to be around a large group of people. Of course, seeing several people wasn't the same as being *with* them. He didn't like to think of himself as a recluse, but he supposed he was. He'd lost the knack for talking to people.

Numerous chairs were placed in and around the checkout area and the stacks. They were famous here for never turning vagrants away. Like most libraries Gene patronized this one contained large numbers of the dead: lounging, sleeping, reading, and re-reading the same page. It always made him curious, what that single page might be, but he kept his distance out of respect, or maybe fear.

A few ranted silently to themselves. Several mimed dramatic scenes, a reprise of their final moments, played again and again.

Many of the dead were obvious about what they were. They wore their torn cheeks, empty eye sockets, and missing ears almost proudly, as if they were carefully selected ornamentations. Gene thought of these as the honest dead. Others were more challenging to distinguish, their scars and stains easily mistaken for the evidence of careless, difficult lives.

An elderly man whose multitude of facial wrinkles made him appear fractured had a newspaper over his lap. Gene wondered if he were hiding something there. He appeared unable to keep his tongue in his mouth.

A woman in an ill-fitting green sweater sat hunched forward, staring at her shoes, an unmatched pair. As Gene walked past her, he noticed the chunk missing from the back of her neck.

One fellow's ballcap was crushed and splitting at the seams. He turned around and stared at Gene with huge, bloodshot eyes. This one, apparently, was alive.

A few nudes were present as well, wandering the aisles. Sometimes they reached out and touched the ones who were seated. There were also people lying in the middle of the floor spreadeagle. Gene assumed all these folks were dead. Some were bodies he had helped remove or cleaned up after at various crime scenes. Some he recognized from bedside photographs at the sites of suicides.

He found his wife and his beautiful little girl in the children's section, reading together. He tried to ignore their obvious wounds, where the car he'd been driving had crushed or tore their bodies. At one point his daughter looked up at him, but with no signs on her face she recognized him, or even that she registered his presence. Instead of being traumatized, he was grateful for the reminders: how his wife tilted her head when reading, how his daughter folded her hands into her lap while listening.

He walked out to his van and drove to his apartment. He knew if he didn't do something soon, he'd one day become one of the unattended, lying undiscovered for days, for weeks, for months.

◄◦►

On the morning of day two Gene felt restless, anxious to begin. Their boss called a couple of times, wanting to know when one or both of them would be free. They had other jobs to go to, other human messes to clean up. But seeing the house with fresh eyes, Gene found hundreds of examples of further contamination, hundreds of spots requiring a thorough cleaning.

Gene wouldn't go on jobs in which dead children were involved. He was a good employee, so his boss made allowances for him, although not always happily. A two-person demolition crew arrived to remove flooring and chip away at the tile. His boss was trying to rush him, but there was much more cleaning required in those rooms before any demo could take place. Many spots were stubbornly resistant and might require hours, but Gene refused to walk away prematurely. His task, wherever possible, was to turn back the clock.

What he did here would not redeem him, but it was responsible work, and it filled the time. For him personally, he knew there would be no fix, no matter how much effort was applied. Remorse was too small a word for what he felt.

Ed worked with the radio tuned to a country station, the volume turned loud enough to grate on Gene's nerves. But he didn't complain.

He scrubbed one wall in stages, spending hours on it. He sprayed on industrial strength disinfectant, wiped off switch plates, door frames, any place they might have touched or coughed on while running through the house, dying. He climbed a ladder and cleaned the ceiling fan blades, top and bottom. He examined anywhere flies and other insects or rats might have carried the biological material. He sprayed blood indicator onto surfaces and followed the results throughout the house. He rubbed and scrubbed until no traces were left.

There were few pieces of furniture in the room they called location zero. A couple of old chairs, a small table, a floor lamp. They were contaminated by the decomp drawn up from underneath them and would have to be thrown away. There was also a sideboard sitting directly on the floor. That, and everything inside it, would also be thrown away.

The demo team cut the wall about halfway up and removed the bottom portion of drywall. They removed all the baseboards in the room. They began removing floorboards and subflooring. In spots the floor joists were exposed. The room appeared frozen in deconstruction, but at least it would be clean.

Ed continued to ramble on about sports, news, weather, arguments with his wife, how his kids misbehaved. Gene found those latter complaints particularly hard to take. But at least Ed kept working. Gene could tell he had a talent for the job. They both tried to be thorough. They took turns making rounds looking for things the other might have missed.

So, Gene was startled to discover a large spread of decomp in the middle of the bare bedroom floor. They'd been through this room dozens of times, sprayed and scraped and sprayed, but somehow this enormous stain had reappeared. He could see how the dying couple ran through the room, both trailing blood. Maybe one stumbled and fell and this was what he or she left behind.

But Gene cut the blood stain out of the carpet yesterday, as well as the portion where it leaked into the pad. He put those pieces into a biohazard bag and the rest of the carpet was disposed of as solid waste. The blood had not reached the floorboards underneath it. There had been no stain left on the floor.

Yet here it was, rusty red and crusted with human grit.

A hand rose out of the stain. This was not the first time Gene had witnessed such a thing. He struggled not to react. He had worked hard to regain some limited composure. Now he felt on the verge of relapse.

The hand did not go away. The fingers separated as it tilted in his direction. Unable to resist, Gene walked over and grasped the hand and pulled. He continued to pull until he'd pulled the woman out of her own remains.

She swept past him, and even though he wore a respirator he could still smell her.

⟶⟨⟩⟵

Gene waited in his van parked on the street until the others left. Ed was the last to leave, waving to him and shouting that he would see him in the morning. Tomorrow would be a full day. There was both a murder and a suicide on the schedule. Gene didn't expect they would have time for both. Gene and the boss would argue, and Gene would win.

He stepped out of his van and walked across the street. He could see the dead lying on the sidewalk in a variety of distressed poses. Bodies lay up and down the lane in differing degrees of brokenness, their fluids leaking into the gutters.

He didn't leave the house until the flames were well established and unlikely to stop by themselves. He'd stashed cleaning fluids in several closets, and when the flames reached them, they went up with a gasp.

This wasn't the first time he'd done such a thing. But he always made sure the homeowner had insurance. They needed insurance to pay the company what it charged for these extensive cleanings.

But sometimes despite everything they did, they couldn't get a house clean enough. He knew he'd get caught someday. He didn't care.

Gene waited to make sure the fire remained contained and until he heard the sirens. He watched the dead walking the streets as the house burned, a sloppily organized parade of regrets. A pale figure paused and stared at him through the windshield. It was like gazing into a mirror.

THE LOUDER I CALL, THE FASTER IT RUNS

E. CATHERINE TOBLER

In the predawn dark, Annie found herself in a bed, holding onto another hand beneath the cool weight of the pillow. Floral case, it was the trailer—her trailer—and slowly she came back to herself, to her body, and kissed the folded fingers beneath the pillow before claiming the ringing phone, dreadful thing. The voice on the other end was frantic, offering double pay because the cops needed her—needed her boat, a man had gone missing—Ricky had that charter, didn't she remember—it had to be her, there was no one else. Triple, she said. She lived plain, but there were always bills.

She dressed in the dark, phantom chill of the lake already clinging to her. Her skin pebbled everywhere and she was surprised when she pulled her hair back into its customary tail that it did not leak lake water across her shoulders.

It was twenty-four minutes from the RV park to the lake, not counting the time she spent hitching the boat trailer to the truck. Years ago they'd told her: don't stay hitched overnight, anyone could drive away with the whole shebang. She'd never seen it happen, but there was plenty she hadn't borne witness to that still was in the record of the world.

The sun stayed hidden the whole way there. The roads were barren and she liked them that way, listening to the even breath of tires over asphalt. Dry, smooth. The trailer had a wobble, a squeak, but it would wait until the afternoon—depending how long they kept her out. A man had gone missing.

It wasn't the first time and surely wouldn't be the last. She had helped the law before—it was a fine diversion, given how well she knew the lake, its surrounds. Usually people wanted to know where the fish were: rainbow trout, sockeye salmon. A man was many times larger than a fish, but the lake was larger still. Sometimes the lake won.

The police were gathered near the boat launch when she arrived. One of them thought he could guide her with a set of flashlights, like he was bringing in an aircraft; she said nothing, backing her trailer into the water and paying him no never mind. Men—policemen—meant well on the surface, but it was easy to slip below.

She met each one and shook each's hand, and no one asked her name. They were all the same: overly warm in the cool morning air, redolent with musk and salt. Would be nice, one said, to get this done ahead of sunrise. The lake would be open then—it didn't need saying. Summer profits were on the line, no one needed a missing tourist mucking up a perfectly good summer day on the lake. Whistling lines and reels, cold beers, shining ice to cradle any legal catch.

The lake would win that battle, though; she didn't have to tell them it was five hundred feet at its deepest. If their man was in there, it could take a while. She knew the currents—where might a body go, they asked her. Wherever the lake liked, she said. You make it sound alive, one of them said with a cigarette-rough laugh, and she didn't reply, because the idea that the lake wasn't a living creature as any of them was absurd.

They went slower than any of the men liked; the radar on board wasn't the best, needed an upgrade, but the men waved it off during conversation; she was the real radar, knowing the lake like no one else did. She'd worked it so long now—how old, the youngest asked with a gleam in his hazel eye, and she said softly fifty, because it was a good number, given how old he thought she was. Just a grandmother to him, silver hair tied back to show every line upon her face. When the sun began to rise, she somehow looked younger, like a girl the youngest wouldn't hesitate to ask out, a stroll along the lakeshore where no one could go missing.

The radar sweeps showed fish and more fish; twice, the youngest shouted excitement over a fallen log, but the third time he wised up and let it pass in silence. The one in charge radioed the shore; told them the lake was closed until further notice.

She supposed they had good cause to believe this man was in the lake, but asked about other leads. There were two other lakes—but that this was the only natural one hadn't escaped her notice. The man-made lakes were tamer. The men hemmed and hawed; she went back to driving the boat. It was what she did; it was what she knew.

Steve Miller, they said, was a father. Wouldn't just wander off and leave his family to wonder. Plenty of things weirder than that had happened in the world, but she didn't argue. When her radio chirped with a call from Ricky, she also didn't argue with him, but told him in the covert way she had before to keep his eyes open. He was on the largest of the three lakes that day; maybe he'd turn up a missing father who'd never leave his family to wonder.

They came back to the launch for lunch. A crowd had formed behind yellow police tape some ways up the road. The police headed toward the lodge, but she stayed with the boat, not liking to eat with an audience. Eileen, who had called her that morning, waved from the porch of the lodge.

They didn't find Steve Miller that afternoon; the chief called it, on account of how many men he was paying to look. He didn't say it that way, but she heard it underneath it all. The chief asked her to come back tomorrow (he was bringing half his men); she said triple, and he bit down on the toothpick that had been working his teeth all afternoon. He didn't say no, just gave her a curt nod and headed out.

The lake remained closed. She didn't drive home, but lingered at the lodge, listening to the people speculate. It's what people did best, spinning tales about affairs, thefts, lake monsters. From the lodge's height, the lake didn't look so monstrous, flat blue and empty under the cloudless sky. It was the perfect postcard photograph, framed by quaking aspens that circled the lodge porch.

Eileen brought her usual salty Lambrusco spritz with its olives, and asked her about the lake, about being out there with the police. Eileen always wanted a salacious story, but there wasn't one here, not yet. The chief, she said, was cash-strapped, but that news didn't surprise Eileen, who moved toward the lodge doors at the arrival of more local reporters.

Men wandered off; it was the easiest explanation. They got into their own heads so deep about life and the universe, they just dropped off the face of the earth—sometimes for a few weeks, sometimes forever, heads finding new pillows on which to sleep. Even family men.

She chewed green olives and pondered the lake, watching the empty water. Not empty, of course—running with life where they could not see. The fish and the reeds and the worms and the frogs and the dragonflies. The mosquitos, the water hyacinths, the long grasses she had not learned the names of. She craved the lake water in her mouth and needed for the day to end, so that she could accomplish that without anyone's supervision.

But Eileen kept the lodge open late—people were worried, wanted to mingle and speculate because there was safety in numbers, and what if the man reappeared? The lodge lights would welcome him. Trusting the lodge lights would also mask the night-dark lake from view, she left the lodge as quietly as she had come. Truck and boat were where she'd left them, and she let them sit, hiking to the lake via no discernible path whatsoever. The water called her.

It was ritual, but it was also life, the way she answered the water's call. At the lakeshore, she stripped out of hoodie, sneakers, and jeans. Underwear came last, all of it left in a heap in the summer-cool grasses she did not know the name of.

She walked into the water until the bottom came out from under her, then she sank and swam. She should have perhaps been blind in the dark water, but she was not. Every sense came alive in the lake in ways they did not on land.

Beneath the water she could search in ways that she could not above. She took mouthfuls of the fresh water into her nose and mouth, veils of bubbles gathering at her temple, her collarbone, her hips. She strained the water between teeth and tongue, and spat out what was of no use. She pushed deeper into the lake, and deeper still, finding the point where freshwater was occluded by salt. Where blood stained the water, she knew.

He still looked human, but even another twelve hours could change that. His eyes were open, but he saw nothing of his surroundings. He was dressed in a suit, his tie tangled around a log, holding what remained of him in place. To her relief, he possessed both hands, but his spine gleamed like pearl beyond where a monstrous mouth had taken most of his left side. The liver, she thought, the fatty, delicious liver.

Morning brought rain. The chief wore a plastic cap over his official hat, a camo rain poncho over his uniformed shoulders. He brought only two men with him this time, each also wrapped in plastic.

She took them out as she had yesterday, listening to them speculate about the man they sought. A real dirtbag, one offered up; Steve Miller looked like a family man, but harbored secrets the same way the lake did. In the wrong place at the wrong time, said the other; Steve Miller was a family man, but saw a thing he shouldn't have seen. Were others out looking elsewhere, she asked, and was given a sharp scowl for an answer. She wasn't in a hurry, given she was occupied with silent speculation all her own.

The lake had been her home—her world—for a while now. She would have to sit down and work out the years, because years meant something different to her than they did to these men. She could say she remembered the price of fuel for her boat had once been .50 cents, and was now $3.11, but that didn't tell her how much time had passed.

No matter how long she'd been here, she had been careful. What she required to live, the town and its surroundings gave her. She had never taken more than was necessary. There had been other deaths throughout the years of course, but this was unlike those—this was something akin to *her.*

It made her uneasy. She hadn't slept for the way the idea kept her thinking long into the night. There wasn't supposed to be another like her here—they kept their distances intentionally, so they could pass unseen, so they could live. Matings happened, offspring came, but they were taught solitary lives, so that no person would know the truth beneath their skins. It could have been a youngling, she thought, especially given how careless it all was. Someone known, a family man—she would never.

When the police began to grumble at her seeming ineptitude, she gave them another half hour of it, then maneuvered the boat closer to the submerged body. She drove slower and scanned more carefully; a school of fish fled the crime scene, darts shooting north.

Looks promising, she said, and showed them the logs and debris on the radar, all places where things might get stuck. Things like bodies, one man asked, and she gave no answer; he didn't want one. She slowed so the men could drop their underwater camera rig into the lake. The chief gave over controls to one of his men, seeming confused by the tech, or the responsibility that arrived with the body's discovery.

The monitor showed what she had seen last night, the logs and the trapped body. But the man was floating upside down now, more of the body missing. The sight sent a chill through her; the predator had returned?

The chief let out a hard breath when he saw the body; said it looked like a shark had been at it. She couldn't help but agree, even though they knew sharks didn't live in these waters.

The chief had enough speculation for the both of them; she cut the engine and dropped anchor while he blathered on. He called for the coroner to come out, which took long enough the men were verbally dreaming about lunch. The chief wondered how they could think about food at a time like this, but his own growling stomach gave him away.

The men paced the length of her boat as they waited for the coroner's team; the youngest smoked, even though he was asked not to. She didn't mind, thought it made him smell more interesting. Younglings were interesting, after all, for the way they didn't conform. The more she considered the body, the more she grew fixed on the idea that what had killed Steve Miller was young.

It wouldn't be a police matter, she thought as the coroner's boat arrived. The police would try—she had seen it before—but they wouldn't understand what they were looking at. In these mountains, it would probably be chalked up to a bear. It made the most sense, and most people wouldn't read the details—what was a bear doing in the lake, at that depth? Bears didn't feed like that, or hunt like that, even in desperation. But people didn't care; tell them a bear had killed a man, that was all they'd hear.

A bear wouldn't necessitate the closure of the lake; they would call the rangers, see what they might find—a mother wandering with her new cubs—and would work to relocate the offender. That would be that, unless the presumed youngling wasn't set on a new course.

She chewed the inside of her cheek until she tasted blood. That wouldn't be that unless she found the truth of the death. No bear, but her own kind, and she had never— Couldn't fathom how, but when the body came up, pale and bloated like something from another time altogether, she knew one way. The youngling had come back, perhaps thought its cache of meat was safe. The youngling *would* come back.

Camera shutters, calculations, conversations had by small huddles of smaller men. She had nothing to do but watch the men work. Two divers went down, bringing up things that had likely been in the man's suit pockets. A key for the lodge, a wallet, a wad of sodden paper.

The team spread these things upon a shaky folding table and photographed them one by one. She leaned in to see the wallet, spread open to show the drivers' license—to show this man was not Steve Miller, but someone else entirely. Wallace Crescent, from Oak Park, Illinois.

The chief bit out a curse and she leaned against the rail, looking into the waters. They moved slowly, reflecting the day's gray sky between lazy raindrops. Another body meant Steve Miller was still out there somewhere and maybe the youngling wouldn't come back.

When the chief felt the scene was secure, he sent the coroner on his way, and then turned to her at the rail. The chief wanted another sweep of the lake, as many as it took, to ascertain they hadn't missed their target. His eyes were unsettled; he had a considerable problem on his hands now and knew it.

She raised the anchor and they set back out, scanning, always scanning. The youngest officer stood beside her, asking where they were on the map. She pointed, showed him where the body had been, and he made marks on the lake map, checking off sections as they scanned through them. Sunken logs, tumbled boulders, the prow of another boat, a rack of mossy antlers looking like a melting candelabra as it peeked out of the lake. The moose she had taken a summer ago, she thought, but didn't see the skeleton as they passed by. A moose, the young officer guessed, and she nodded, idly.

He marked it on the map with a big M, and they continued on, no sign of their family man emerging from the lake by the time the chief's patience had worn through. At the boat launch, she kept out of his way, taking the warm Thermos Eileen offered her. It was filled with salty homemade chicken soup.

The chief ordered the lake closed one more day, but said he wouldn't need her services. She watched him walk away with his men, and radioed Ricky from her truck. Ricky hadn't turned up a blessed thing, and when she told him they'd found the wrong body, there was a strange pleasure in the whoop of laughter she heard over the channel. She supposed Ricky and Eileen were the closest she had to friends; their reactions provoked something similar in her.

For a second night, she didn't drive home. She sat in her truck and felt something she hadn't felt in a long while: utter confusion over what to do. She'd lived here long enough that the days had their own rhythm. Nothing untoward happened here. She lived off the land the way countless other animals did, and one path never interfered with another. One life kept clear of the other. Until now.

Beyond her windshield, the world darkened. Crickets made themselves known, but fireflies rarely roamed this far north so the woods remained unspangled. Only the sky put on its starry show and she watched the distant, dead light, pondering the potential youngling.

It wouldn't be unheard of—had surely happened before somewhere. In every culture, younglings went off, thinking they knew what they were about, believing they understood the world they inhabited. A wrong step didn't scare them because they believed themselves unbreakable if not immortal. Wounds would heal, so why not leap off every cliff presented to them?

She found the youngling on the lakeshore where she'd gone in the water the night before. It was no bear, but her own kind. Young, male, it added up. Males often got it into their heads more than females that they couldn't die or be killed. She thought it was the process of giving birth that did it—carrying another life, birthing it. The experience changed a body, a mind, enough to know how haphazardly life was bound into a physical shell. The slightest mishap could send it fleeing.

The youngling was naked and crouched on all fours, smelling the grass where she'd discarded her clothes. She watched him in silence as he took a mouthful of grass and chewed the taste of her out of it. Piss would have been more effective, but she hadn't had to mark territory since coming here.

Maybe he caught her scent when the wind shifted, maybe the long line of her shadow edged into the corner of his vision. Either way, he jumped backward at the discovery of her, feet sliding down the gentle bank and into the water; in his panic he vomited the grass he'd eaten, and pedaled backward into the lake.

She moved swiftly, pursuing him into the water. He made no sound but for the splash of water, mouth seemingly sealed against complaint. He dropped beneath the surface and she followed, lunging to take hold of his arms. He felt human, he looked human—they all did—but she knew he was not. As he knew she was something other, so she knew of him.

He also knew he wanted to get away—seemed to instinctively know that she understood his transgressions and had come to settle the matter with him. This territory was not his—he knew it wholly, the way one understands an arm is his own—and further, worse, mistakes had been made. Men had been taken.

She was old and perhaps wise, but he carried with him the luck of youth, the strength—the ability to surprise. She was solid, but he wedged an elbow into her again and again, and slipped from her hold in an explosion of bubbles and mud, and when she could at last clear her eyes, he had gone. She pulled herself from the water and onto the bank where the scent of him lingered, and she vomited water until she was empty. Shock rushed through her—that he was here at all—and she could not think what to do, and so she left. Got back to her boat and her truck and left, until she'd circled back to the RV park. She walked through the pulsing waves of crimson neon. NO VACANCY it flashed, and she wished the youngling understood the meaning.

That he had chased her from *her* lake was not lost upon her. In the trailer, she showered the muck from her body then lay on the cool floral sheets. She sought the hand beneath her pillow. It looked so small now, withered in death; the man whose hand it had been had not been small. She had taken her time with him and wouldn't need another meal for some time, but the youngling . . . He wouldn't understand the need for care.

She counted the ways on the hand before her—the ways she might help—and the idea of leaving was strongly at the top of her final list. Leave the lake to the youngling, go somewhere new, some place where she would not be noticed. But it was her lake—and she snarled at the idea of leaving it. The youngling would destroy the balance, would be found and—studied. She went cold at the word.

She studied the hand in her grip. It might have been Steve Miller—while she had destroyed the man's wallet, after extracting $12.76, she had not read his identification. She could recall no photographs, no anything to tie him to the missing Steve Miller. If it was Steve Miller, the police would never find him, deep in her belly.

She drove to the launch come morning, and there was Eileen with the chief. Arguing, she thought, and when Eileen slapped the chief, it was everyone in the vicinity who jerked in response. When she got to Eileen's side, the woman turned on her heel and vanished into the lodge.

Women, the chief muttered, then looked at the one who remained beside him. He made no apology, only lit a cigarette and took a long drag. He reminded her he didn't need her, that they'd cleared the lake, then he strode away, toward his men. She followed Eileen, taking a seat at the counter inside where the woman was crying.

"Sam's gone," Eileen sputtered. "Chief won't do a damn thing—says it's too soon and you know young men," she continued, imitating the chief, "they wander off, get drunk, and forget to call their mommas."

But Sam didn't, she thought. Sam was the responsible kind of offspring, helping his mother at every turn. He wanted to run the lodge someday. She gently touched Eileen's shaking hand, thinking about mothers and sons and how the youngling might've been taking other men down because he saw them as competition. There might have been no reason—she knew that too, because animals were animals and sometimes hunger had no source, only *was*—but she wanted a reason, if only to explain to Eileen, her human friend.

The lake would open in the morning, but for one more night it was hers. As she had before, she sought the water's edge, but crouched, listening, until long after sunset. The frogs began to sing, and deep in the trees the cicadas began, but when she opened her mouth to join, every other creature went silent. The sound that came from her was ancient, the kind of call scientists could only dream about knowing. It came from deep inside her, from a nameless organ—for her kind had never been discovered, dissected.

Her call rose from her body like a geyser, a building rush and then an exhale. A sound of isolation, of seeking. She had not called to others of her kind for longer than she could remember, and she did not want to do it now. She closed her eyes and called and called. Birds took nervous flight from nearby trees. The rest of the world did not move, did not breathe. Somewhere, she pictured a child sitting up in bed.

Dad, did you hear—what was it?

I don't know, honey—listen again.

She sank beneath the cool, dark water and opened her mouth to call again. The water changed the call—or the call changed the water, vibrations moving in every direction all at once. She became a focal point, the center from which all flowed—an antenna, tuning. *Come*, she said, *I am made ready.*

The youngling came because he was helpless to do otherwise. Her body was old, but she might mate yet again, and she gave every indication to the youngling that it was time. He approached her with mouth open, dragging in the scent of her. He leaned into her shoulder to smell her more deeply and that was when she smelled Sam on him. Eileen's offspring. Dead?

Her scent changed—from willing rut partner to hunter. She cursed herself as the youngling thrashed backward. She saw then the blood on him, the blood that had been trailed behind him. Human, crimson to her eyes even in the dark. The youngling fled. She followed.

He was not physically wounded, she thought, but something wasn't right—he'd been too long alone, had forgotten the ways of their world. He was still a cunning prey, eluding her easily because the scent of human blood masked him. She called to him again, but the lake grew still. The frogs and insects came back to their songs and she listened in defeat. Barefooted, she padded toward the blood trail, bent down and tasted it along with the dirt of the world. The world was old, the blood was new, and in this way she found him, Sam huddled inside a cave the youngling had been using. Sam startled at the sight of her, naked and smeared with mud, blood. He would know her as his mother's friend, but everything else about her would be unfamiliar. She stood unbowed before him. It was her lake.

"Your mother is at the lodge," she said.

"You're—" Sam broke off, shuddering.

What word would he have even chosen?

"Working," she said, and waited until he had gone before she searched the cave. Bones, scraps of fabric, nothing that made a life, only a layover. She rubbed her hands across the cave walls and pissed a line in the dirt before she left. Outside, under the clear summer sky, she lifted her voice in song once more. It was her lake.

The frogs went silent and the insects, too. In the near distance she heard him, panting and compelled to run toward her omnipresent call. He came faster and faster, on two feet and then four. At the sight of her he stumbled and fled anew. She followed after. There was an unhinged joy in the pursuit; the faster he ran, the louder she called. His knees buckled, body betrayed by instinct, and she rolled him into the long grasses she did not know the name of. His eyes would not focus and fever had made his skin clammy. His neck became fragile between her hands, his body easily limp, pinned beneath a log.

A bear, the papers said in the morning; the animal had been caught, tagged, and relocated. The lake flooded with tourists, with summer money. The chief assured everyone there was no cause to worry because bear attacks were rare, but here were the precautions they could take if they were concerned. Sam and Eileen stood nearby the chief, proof that the police had got their monster.

In the night, when the summer people had bedded down in lodge or boat, Annie lifted her voice to call once more and no bear came answering.

RETURN TO BEAR CREEK LODGE

TANANARIVE DUE

December 26, 1974

In Johnny's dream, he is running in white, snowy woods.

He hears music—distant, tinny-sounding trumpet fanfare from the Duke Ellington Orchestra—before he sees the light. The vague glow is brighter with every step, until darkness parts to reveal the wooden rail fence of his grandmother's lodge. One rotting rail has fallen out of place, leaving a breach he can easily run through.

But he doesn't. He stops short, staring at the lodge. And the back porch. And the woman sitting there.

In his dreams, Grandmother doesn't look the way she did the last time he actually saw her, when she was already emaciated and sharp-jawed from illness. This is Mazelle Washington the way she has immortalized herself on her photos framed all over her house: hair hanging long and loose (*straightened*, of course), in radiant makeup, shoulders nestled in the fur collar of her shiny silk bathrobe, the kind of garment only movie royalty would wear. She shines so brightly that the light seems to glow from her.

Something rustles just beneath her on the porch steps, snow flung aside by a long neck and then a head with a snout the size of a long weasel, white fur almost camouflaged by the snow. It rises between Grandmother's knees . . . as if she is giving birth.

Grandmother's face snaps into focus: but her eyes are the color of blue ice. She opens her mouth, and her jaw hinges beyond any human length, revealing rows of long, sharp teeth.

He screams as—

"Wake up, hon. We're here."

Johnny's mother's voice coaxed him to open his eyes, and his dream had come to life. Snow. The wooden fence rails. Grandmother's lodge. The back porch. He tried to rub it out of his eyes, but the nightmare was real this time. Mom had parked the rental car they'd picked up in Denver in Grandmother's snow-dusted driveway after driving up the mountain. He'd fallen asleep to static-filled AM radio, which was all the car offered. *Shit. We're actually here.*

Grandmother's lodge would seem like an ordinary two-story wood frame house if it weren't so secluded in the Rocky Mountains woods. Its isolation alone made it seem luxurious to have electricity lighting the windows, or a fence claiming five or six acres. Thirty yards from the main house, three small cabins stood in a perfect triangle as relics of a time when Bear Creek Lodge had provided dignity to Black celebrities lucky enough to get an invitation. In those days, fine hotels nationwide did not accept them, no matter who they were. Once, he'd been told, Grandmother had her own ski lift for her guests.

But all of that had been a long time ago.

"My stomach hurts," Johnny said. He had learned that his mother wrapped herself in silence like warm clothing, but he vowed he would never be like her. "This place already gives me nightmares, Mom. I want to leave."

"I know, baby. And I understand."

"But you don't care."

"Of course I do. If I could've left you somewhere else, I would have. I didn't want you here either. I don't want to be here my own self."

"Then why?" Johnny's voice hitched, but he would *not* cry.

"Because she owes us." *There. She finally said it.* "She owes *you.* She's got a college fund set aside for you. If I just . . . say goodbye this weekend. Two days. Her last Christmas. I haven't seen her at Christmastime since I wasn't much older than you."

Mom was thirty-one, although her face was still round and girlish. With a scarf wrapped around her Afro—probably hiding it from Grandmother—Mama reminded him of Aretha Franklin. Johnny had always assumed she ran away from home at seventeen because she was pregnant with him. Uncle Ricky's blue VW bug was already parked beside them in the lodge's driveway, a reminder that his uncle kept coming back although he had good reason never to speak to his mother again either, much less stay with her in the woods.

Based on his own short visit last year, Johnny could hardly imagine the horror of growing up in a house raised by Grandmother. His mother and uncle had lived in a mansion in Los Angeles, but Johnny would choose his two-bedroom apartment in Miami with Mom any time, even with the flying cockroaches that kept coming back no matter how much she sprayed.

"I don't care about her money," Johnny said. "She can keep it."

Mom blinked as if he'd struck her. If she'd convinced herself they were making this trip for his sake, he had just stolen that lie away. Good. Johnny wondered what other ways Mom had been lying to herself, or to him. He could never trust her again, not the way he had before. That idea, worse than his nightmare, cramped his stomach again.

"You'll be in one of the cabins, like I said," Mom said. "You won't even have to see her. She stays in bed in her room. Rick's been here looking after her, and a nurse comes in the mornings. This is our burden, not yours—okay?"

None of it was okay, and never would be. At fourteen, Johnny was already certain of this. His birthright was soiled to the core; not just Grandmother, but Mom and Uncle Ricky too.

But he nodded, a lie. Mom looked relieved, choosing to believe him. Or to pretend she did.

"All money ain't good money," Mom said, "but bad money can be put to good use."

When she got out of the car, she headed straight for the back porch that haunted him. And the small mounds of snow beside the three back steps.

"Can we go in through the front, please?" Johnny hated being afraid that a dream might come to life, but if he stared at the snow long enough, he thought he might see it move from something buried underneath. His mother cast him a confused look over her shoulder, but she changed course to walk around to the front double doors.

Inside, the smell of Grandmother's dying was everywhere. The smell froze him in the open doorway. Mom, behind him, patted his shoulder.

"You don't have to go in her room," Mom reminded him. Her whisper smelled like the peppermint candy she'd used to mask her cigarette smoke; she was still apparently afraid of what Grandmother might say if she caught her smoking. She cupped his chin in the way she used to when he was younger. "I'm still so mad at your Uncle Rick for not watching you like I told him to. And you heard me cuss Mama's ass out on the phone last year, didn't you? What she did to you is *not* okay, cancer or no cancer."

No one had said the word *cancer* before now. But Johnny swore he knew from the smell.

It was all in place: the white grand piano, the oversized fireplace with gleaming stones, grinning celebrity photos framed on the wood-plank walls, even the film projector where she'd caught him playing her old reels from the 1930s movies that filled her with shame. "You shouldn't have gone in Mother's things," Uncle Ricky had told him during the drive to the airport to go home last year, nudging blame back toward him after a night of consolation.

Nothing in the living room had changed in the year since Grandmother had burned leering teeth into his arm from her steel hot comb, scarring him with dark marks that would never go away.

◄•►

Uncle Ricky had gained at least ten pounds in the past year, his hair cut Marine short. He had trouble meeting Johnny's eyes—maybe because Uncle Ricky's eyes were so red from smoking grass every chance he got. The smell of grass baked from his uncle's clothes as he hugged him. Johnny saw his mother's lips tighten as she glared at Uncle Ricky. For an uneasy instant, Grandmother's rage was reborn in his mother's eyes.

"Good to see you, lil' man," Uncle Ricky said, speaking as quietly as he would in a hospital. "Front cabin's all yours. Star treatment all the way. Nothing but the best for—"

"Oh, hush," Mom said. "Nobody wants to hear all that."

Uncle Ricky was still in trouble with mom, so after saying hello, Johnny escaped to his cabin.

The cabin was decades past any elegance, but it was a good size, with a bunk bed, sofa, and a table near the front picture window. A too-large crack beneath the door couldn't keep out a bold breeze and traces of snow that melted in a pale ring on the floor. The air near the door felt ten degrees cooler, too. At least. The space heater's coils stank of roasting dust when he turned it on and they glowed bright orange.

Johnny pulled aside the fading curtains to stare out at the snow-covered woods beyond Grandmother's wood rail fence. He'd been excited to see flurries for the first time last year, but now snow was the backdrop to his nightmares. *You saw something in the snow,* his mind whispered, a reminder. *Or did you?*

All he knew for sure was that he kept having the same dream, when *something* popped up from the snow, its head appearing between Grandmother's knees. A pointy nose, so pink it was almost red. Long, active whiskers near its mouth. And white fur so tight across its frame that it seemed bony instead of soft. Not quite a reptile, not quite a mammal. In the year since, he had decided that maybe his waking mind had conjured a creature that mirrored Grandmother's true self—a vision for the casual monstrosity she hid from everyone except her own family.

The door to the back porch opened abruptly. He expected to see Grandmother glide outside in her fur-lined robe, staring straight at him. The thought raked the back of his neck with icy pinpricks. But Mom and Uncle Ricky came out instead, neither of them wearing a coat, and Mom was hugging herself tightly as she leaned close to her brother. They were trying to keep their voices down, their argument spilling outside from the kitchen.

Johnny knew they were talking about him.

". . . All I asked you to do was watch him in the goddamned cabin," Mom was saying to Uncle Ricky in the cold. "*Never* let him be alone with her. I haven't asked either of you for shit his whole life, and that's all I asked. *That's all*, Rick."

"Sadie, she said—"

"Damn what she said! You were supposed to stand up to her for once. You're a grown man! How's a sick old woman gonna' make you do shit? You want the Baldwin Hills house that bad? Is that what's got you so cowed that you couldn't do one simple thing? You *knew* better."

Uncle Ricky didn't have an answer for that, hanging his head. He listened in that childlike pose for some time, a big man made small. Mom's words knit his face until he finally said, "You acting like I'm the one who burned him! You know who you really need to be mad at. I wish I'd done more, but I ain't the one who did it."

At last, Mom had nothing else to say. She went back inside, slamming the door.

"What's all that noise?" he heard another voice call, perhaps through a cracked open window. Reed-thin, but he heard it. The dying woman was awake.

Johnny stepped away from his window. Even if the cabin was cold and only a short walk from the back door, at least he wasn't in the same house with her.

"Coming, Mother!" he heard his mom call as if she were a child again too. Johnny braved another peek through his window.

Uncle Ricky didn't go inside behind Mom. Instead, he sighed a cloud of breath and walked carefully down the stairs, nursing the knee his mother had hurt when he was young. He glanced up at Johnny's cabin as he passed on his way to his own and waved. But he didn't smile. Johnny did the same, running his fingertip across the raised bump of the dark keloid scar on his upper arm. His mother told him it would never go away unless he got plastic surgery–which meant they might as well find a doctor on Mars. A scar for life. More like a brand.

"How could she do that?" he'd asked his mother, tearful, when he came home with the fresh scar and its story.

Mom had met his tears with her own and said, "I don't know, baby. My grandmother told me she changed after she started working in pictures. Playing Lazy Mazy turned her into somebody else. I swear I used to think she sold her soul."

◄◦►

Mom insisted that he come inside to eat at the long dining table with her and Uncle Ricky, and that part wasn't bad. She served heated up leftover ham, macaroni and cheese, and greens from Christmas she'd carried in Tupperware on the plane from Miami. Then she lit a candle, explaining that she hadn't had room to bring the kinara from home, but she reminded him that the first principle of Kwanzaa was Umoja, which meant *Unity*. She squeezed his hand on one side and Uncle Ricky's on the other.

"So I'm glad we're all together," she said. She wanted to say more, but shook her head in a way that told Johnny she was trying not to cry.

Uncle Ricky said he had a surprise for Johnny and put the Jackson Five's "Dancing Machine" on Grandmother's console—oh so softly, if music could whisper—a peace offering like sage, since Grandmother had confiscated his cassettes and tape player last year. After venting at Uncle Ricky on the back porch, the anger had left Mom's eyes and she was already smiling and twisting to the music in her seat, especially after her second glass of wine. She and Uncle Ricky toasted "getting rid of that asshole Nixon," both of them tossing their heads back to drink. Mom's empty wine glass slipped from her grip, shattering on the wooden floor, and they both froze and waited to hear their mother call out, as they no doubt did as children, terrified of making her mad. When she didn't make a sound, Mom and Uncle Ricky smothered giggles. Johnny didn't like it when his mother drank, but it was good to hear her laugh.

Johnny was taking his empty plate to the kitchen, in the hallway just behind the kitchen doorway, when he saw, in a slant of shadow, Grandmother's partly-open door at the far end of the hall. His heart batted his throat at the sight of the space beyond her open door, a dim light shining out. Was she awake? Johnny ducked into the kitchen at the thought that she might be about to walk out of her room. He closed the swinging kitchen door behind him, breathing fast. He threw his plate into the sink so hard that dishwater splashed on the floor.

Why don't you go see if she's awake, chickenshit? Pussy. Mama's boy. Sissy. Lil' bitch.

Johnny thought of every name he'd been called at school, shouted across the P.E. field or whispered through his bathroom stall door. And didn't all those names fit? Wasn't he scared of a sick old woman, trapped under the same hex as Mom and Uncle Ricky?

Johnny's breath tickled the roof of his mouth as he walked closer to the sickroom, touching his feet down lightly until he was standing just beyond her doorway. Through the slit he saw a bed table and the side of her bed frame—not the fairy-tale princess bed with a canopy she'd slept in before, but a curving metal rail like a hospital bed.

A low *hisssss* floated from the room, the sound of a giant snake close enough to touch him. Johnny jumped back, startled. A mechanized click made him realize that the sound was coming from an oxygen machine somewhere near the bed. This time, he used the rhythmic *hisssss* to hide the sound of his movement as he cracked the door open wider to peek in. The sole tea lamp on the bed table offered the room's only light, patterns of green in panels of stained glass. Most of her furniture had been pushed aside, but he recognized the fur collar of her fancy bathrobe hanging on a hook beside the door.

Grandmother's bare brown arm lay straight at her side, the flesh at her elbow a mass of jellied wrinkles. She had lost weight, and her frame had been slight and bony in her clothes a year ago. Her face was hidden from him by the lamp. Her sheet rose up and down with her breathing; maybe she wasn't quite awake, not quite asleep.

"*I hate you,*" he whispered loudly enough to be heard over the hissing, but not loudly enough to escape the hallway. "I hope you die."

The words exploded inside of him, a shock to his own ears. His knees felt unsteady, so he leaned against the door frame with a small pant. Was she awake? Had she heard?

He waited three seconds, four, five, to hear any response except measured hissing. With each thin breath, his fear gave way to triumph. A celebration rose in him that he wished he could share with Mom and Uncle Ricky. *You'll never believe what I just said to that old—*

A chair across the room tipped so wildly that it almost fell over, rocking back and forth. A scrabbling shook the window above the chair, and for the first time he noticed it was open nearly six inches. (Had it always been open?) Something had bumped the chair and was crawling–snaking?—back outside through the narrow gap.

The creature from his nightmares with a long snout looked back at him, white whiskers sweeping back and forth across the pane like a dog's wagging tail. Two ice-blue eyes glittered at him. The creature's odd chittering filled the room.

It's real, he thought. *It's real and it's here.*

Johnny had not imagined how a demon might look until he saw the thing at the window. Maybe it had possessed Grandmother. Maybe that was what had brought out the meanness in her. But these thoughts didn't come to Johnny in the doorway: they would only come later. In that instant, all thought had vanished. His body was stone except for his savagely blinking eyes.

The thing at the window rattled the frame, and a mouth yawned open, revealing a row of top fangs so long and sharp that they gleamed in the moonlight. A white fox-worm from Hell.

"Johnny? That you?" *WAS IT TALKING TO HIM?*

The demon smacked against the window . . . and then it was gone. Outside, its slithering scattered the snow as it raced away in an erratic pattern, here and there almost simultaneously, moving *fast*. Impossibly fast.

"Johnny?" Grandmother's voice was louder, recognizable despite its deep hoarseness. Not the demon's voice, then. He was torn about which frightened him more—the demon in the window or Grandmother calling for him. She might have heard the terrible thing he'd said, the words he was certain had conjured that thing. What if she got up and staggered toward him . . . ?

"I'm sorry," Johnny whispered, just as he had as she burned him that night, senseless with surprise and pain. He closed her door and ran back to the kitchen, where he helped his mother and uncle dry the dishes, trying to hide his shaking hands.

He didn't tell them about the cracked-open window. Or the demon. He didn't say a word.

◄◦►

That night, Johnny didn't sleep as he sat sentry, fogging up his cabin's window, watching the back door and snowy patch of yard, reciting the Lord's Prayer like a record needle caught in a groove. He held a snow shovel in his hands, the only weapon he'd found in his cabin. Even with only the moonlight to guide his vision, he recognized the path the creature had left in its wake, a sinuous pattern of burrowed snow from Grandmother's window, between the cabins, toward the gate and the woods beyond. He might not have seen it if he didn't know it was there. All night he jumped at falling clumps of snow from the treetops, or rustling in the dried brush, believing the creature had come back for him. His fingers shivered, but not from the cold.

He only realized he'd fallen asleep by the window, slumped over the cabin's rude wooden table, when a knock at the door scared him so much that he fell to the floor.

"Hey, J!" Uncle Ricky's voice called. "You up? Said I'd take you rabbit hunting, right? Gotta' get 'em early if we're gonna' get 'em."

Johnny's head felt blurry. Then he remembered Grandmother's room, the thing at the window, and he leaped to his feet to unlock the flimsy pin and open his cabin door. He'd tried keeping the secret, but silence was burning a hole in him. He would have to confess, that was all. He would have to tell Uncle Ricky what he'd summoned from the snow. But how could he make Uncle Ricky believe him?

"You're already dressed, huh?" Uncle Ricky said. Johnny stared down and realized he was still wearing his jeans and aqua blue Miami Dolphins sweatshirt from dinner. He felt a strong certainty that he must be dreaming, that maybe he wasn't at Grandmother's property at Bear Creek at all. "Grab your coat and gloves. Cold as a witch's tits out here today."

Outside. He'd tell him while they were outside. He'd show Uncle Ricky the—

"Uh oh," Uncle Ricky said from the cabin doorway as he surveyed the snow, tipping back his suede black cowboy hat. He walked a few paces and squatted, staring down. Johnny ran outside, still pulling on his coat. Of course! As a hunter, Uncle Ricky had seen the creature's tracks right away. And Uncle Ricky had a gun! Now they could—

"Lookie here!" Uncle Ricky said, grinning up at him. He was squatting in the middle of the fox-thing's swishes in the snow, but he was pointing to much smaller tracks in an unthreatening, predictable pattern just beyond them. "The rabbits are out, see? Told you. You can always tell rabbit tracks 'cuz they land with their hind legs first, up front. They're bigger. And that's the front legs behind them, kinda' off center . . . see?"

Johnny didn't see, or want to see. He only saw the evidence the fox-thing had left behind, a trail like a broom pushed by a madman. He was agape that Uncle Ricky was missing what was right in front of him.

"They don't like to come out in the open, so I'm surprised to see tracks here," Uncle Ricky said. He leaned on his rifle stock to straighten to his full height and shook out his bad knee as if to wake it up, or quiet it down. "Let's go out in the woods where there's some brush. They like bushes, pine stands. Places they can hide."

Johnny swallowed back his disappointment that Uncle Ricky didn't know, that he must explain it all. And time was wasting. Who knew how far the thing had traveled overnight?

"This way," Johnny said, pointing toward the fence and the old growth forest of pine and spruce trees beyond it.

Following the fox-thing's trail.

-o-

They waded through snow so deep that Johnny wished he had cowboy boots like Uncle Ricky instead of the new Converse sneakers Mom had given him for Christmas. Fighting through a dreamlike feeling after so little sleep, he realized that he and Uncle Ricky hadn't talked about rabbit hunting at all on this trip; the proposed hunting lesson last year had been one more thing cut short by the burning.

Johnny never let his eyes veer from the wild flourishes of the fox-thing's path in the snow. Uncle Ricky seemed content to let Johnny lead, but he was studiously ignoring the creature's trail. Instead, Uncle Ricky pointed out places where he'd found rabbits.

Then . . . the trail was gone, as if the thing had burrowed more deeply underground and never resurfaced. Or vanished outright. Johnny stopped walking, panicked that the hidden beast might yank him by his feet and drag him away. He didn't know what he'd expected on the outing, but the lost possibility, once within reach, crushed him. They were beneath a towering old cottonwood tree with a dark gap, like a doorway. A mound of snow in front of the tree looked undisturbed, but who knew what it was hiding?

And were those blue eyes glowing from the folds of the dark? Instead of moving toward the shadowed hole, Johnny stepped away. He hadn't wanted to trade familiar terror for a worse one, sharpening the claws of his nightmares. With Uncle Ricky beside him, he hadn't felt scared until he lost the trail.

The morning woods were not quiet. Bear Creek was east of them, the babbling of water of its stony bed suddenly loud although most of the creek must be frozen. To the west, a coyote's far-off yipping startled him. He looked toward every noise . . . then back at the old tree.

"What's wrong, youngblood?" It might be the first time Uncle Ricky had looked him dead in the face since he knocked on his door. Uncle Ricky's eyes were an invitation to tell. And his eyes weren't red from grass, for a change. He had come to hunt with a clear head.

"I did something," Johnny whispered.

Uncle Ricky and his sober eyes waited.

"I . . . said something to your mom last night. Outside her door. But I didn't go in." He added the last part in case a respectful distance somehow made it better. He tried to bring the words he'd said to his mouth, but they seemed worse in daylight. "I said something bad."

"What'd you say?" Uncle Ricky's voice was only curious. No judgment.

Still, Johnny shook his head. He couldn't tell him. He would never tell anyone.

Uncle Ricky chuckled. "Listen—I'm sure you didn't say nothin' me and your mom didn't think up first. And she probably didn't even hear you. That what's got you all freaked out?"

"When I said it . . . " He wanted to say *A demon came.* That explained it best, but it would sound the worst. ". . . something climbed out of her window. It was in her room."

Now silence draped the woods. Uncle Ricky's eyes moved away, scanning the landscape. Beyond the cottonwood, they were at the base of a steep incline knotted with fir trees. Finally, Uncle Ricky stared toward the old cottonwood and its large gap before turning back to Johnny.

"Did you see it?"

Johnny nodded. "Kind of. It moved fast. But . . . I saw the teeth."

Uncle Ricky grabbed Johnny's shoulder, his fingers tight through his thick coat. "Did it hurt you?" For the first time, he sounded worried.

"No. It ran. It doesn't go straight, it goes like . . . "

Johnny scraped his shoe in the snow in a zigzag to show him. His toes were so cold inside of his sneakers that they burned. ". . . here . . . and then there. It doesn't go in a straight line. The tracks are right outside her house. They come out here . . . and then they stop."

Johnny pointed at the spot in the snow where the tracks ended a few yards in front of the cottonwood tree and the mass of snow that might be a perfect hiding place.

Johnny wanted Uncle Ricky to jack a cartridge into his rifle's chamber and say *Let's go see where it went.* Instead, a stormy uncertainty grew on Uncle Ricky's face. He tipped up his hat to run his hand across his forehead, fretting.

"What kinda' animal did it look like?" Uncle Ricky finally asked.

"Didn't look like *any* animal! It looked like a demon that crawled out of the ground."

There. He'd finally said it. He expected Uncle Ricky to laugh at him . . . but he didn't.

"Then you shouldn't try to go chasin' after things you don't understand." Uncle Ricky's voice was sharp with scolding. "Should you?"

The change in Uncle Ricky was troubling in an entirely different way. Johnny's ears rang as if his uncle had shouted at him.

"You already know about it. Don't you?"

"Don't ask me that." Uncle Ricky stared at the ground like when Mom told him off.

"Because it's a secret?"

Uncle Ricky's jaw flexed so tightly that he was afraid his uncle would slap him. "Hard headed, ain't you? What'd I just say? You listen to me good: we ain't gonna' talk about it. You're not gonna' say nothin' to your mama, neither. What you saw is just between me and you."

"But you believe me," Johnny said, testing him. His heart was pounding in his chest so hard that his lungs barely found room to breathe.

Uncle Ricky half-shrugged and half-nodded, the way he would if they were talking about when it might snow next. Or if Grandmother's private nurse might be late on the icy road.

"Say it," Johnny said. "Say you believe me."

Uncle Ricky nodded. Close enough. The pressure in Johnny's chest eased, but he was shivering despite his coat and gloves.

"I told you!" Johnny said. "I told you I saw something last year!"

"Yep, sorry." He didn't *sound* apologetic. "And you don't yell when you're hunting."

Despite his anger and a dizzy feeling from doubting everything he thought he knew about the world, Johnny obediently lowered his voice. "Well, why—"

"Come on," Uncle Ricky said, and walked toward less steep ground, away from the cottonwood tree and its yawning maw. "Let's get us a hare."

WHAT. THE. HELL. Johnny came as close as he ever had to cussing out an adult. He breathed in angry puffs, struggling to keep pace in the deep snow. The creek burbled ahead.

"You know what a nervous breakdown is?" Uncle Ricky said.

"I'm not crazy," Johnny said, still quiet. "I know what I saw."

"Not you—my mom. Remember I told you how she had to step away from Hollywood and spend some time by herself? They were forgetting her, or worse: calling her a coon. Oh, she hated that word. That grinnin' and foolishness she did to make all that money off white folks in those old movies came back on her after times changed. When I tried to visit to see after her, she just fussed and hollered and sent me away. Hell, she threatened to shoot me once. For five whole years, it was just her out here in these woods."

Johnny sensed that his uncle was winding to the point—*the creature?!*—so he tried to slow his breathing so he could hear past the pounding of his blood in his ears. Uncle Ricky held up his hand: *Stop.* Johnny stopped abruptly, nearly stumbling into him.

"Snow hares are brown in summer, but in winter their fur turns white," Uncle Ricky said. He nodded toward an arrangement of stones a few yards from them. Something moved, barely visible against the gray rocks—but it was small, not the creature in Grandmother's window. As Johnny stared, a form took shape: a white-haired rabbit was standing against the rocks, rubbing its face with its paws. Johnny couldn't help thinking of the hare from *Alice's Adventures in Wonderland,* as if it might pull out a pocket watch next. That wouldn't be any stranger than what he'd already seen.

To Johnny's surprise, Uncle Ricky slipped his hunting rifle into Johnny's hands, guiding him to raise it high with the stock beneath his chin. The gun didn't weigh as much as Johnny had expected, given its deadly power. Still, his arms trembled beneath its weight.

"So . . . " Uncle Ricky said, his voice low in Johnny's ear. ". . . one time I came out here, just like you, and I saw it's not just rabbits and ermines out here with white fur." He gently moved Johnny's arms to reposition the rifle slightly. "You see 'im?"

Johnny looked all around for the fox-demon, but Uncle Ricky was only pointing toward the hare. "Get 'im in your sight. You ain't even lookin'." Uncle Ricky pointed out the nub of the rifle's front sight and used his palm to push gently on the back of Johnny's head so he would lower it to a proper hunting stance.

The rabbit changed position only slightly, unaware that they were so close, favoring the other side of his face for cleaning.

"Where did you see it?" Johnny whispered.

Uncle Ricky chuckled. "I was sittin' outside in my old truck tryin' to figure how to talk sense into her . . . and that thing came runnin' out the back door."

"It opened the door?" Johnny remembered Grandmother's cracked open window.

"*She* opened it," Uncle Ricky said. "Let it out like it was her pet pooch. And then . . . boom. It was gone in a flash, just like you said. She saw me, too. That was the night she threatened to shoot me. She said to get the hell away from her and never come back."

A sound from closer to the creek made the hare stick its head up high, alert.

"Hurry," Uncle Ricky whispered. "Don't miss the shot."

But Johnny could barely remember who and where he was, imagining Grandmother feeding the fox-demon. It *hadn't* been a dream. He had seen with his own eyes and then in his dreams. His mind whirled with the dizzy feeling again.

By the time his wooziness passed, the hare was gone, only a pile of stones left behind.

"Dammit," Uncle Ricky said.

"What is it? I thought I made a demon come. Like . . . saying something so bad was praying to it."

Uncle Ricky didn't seem to hear him, staring with longing at the spot where the hare had been. "I got no goddamn idea, but it's no demon," he finally said. "All I know is, it's been out here with her, the two of them hiding from the world, I guess. She's been feeding it, and it's been here a long time. It was smaller when I saw it. Maybe it thinks she's its mama."

"So . . . what will happen when . . . ?"

For the first time, Johnny noticed that his uncle's eyes were red after all. And moist. "When the time comes . . . I suppose I'll have to come out here and take care of it. So it won't hurt nobody. Whatever it is . . . it ain't natural. Is it?"

Johnny shook his head. The cold hadn't been as bad when they were walking, but now that they were still the frigid breeze was slicing into his bare cheeks and ears.

"Don't feel bad about whatever you said to Mother . . . " Uncle Ricky said. "She brought it on herself. Besides, there's worse. Way worse. If I tell you something, will you keep it a secret? Never let your mama know I told you?"

Something screamed inside of Johnny that he should say *No*, that his mother would never want him to make that promise. It was bad enough he couldn't say anything to her about the odd creature—not that she would probably believe him. Maybe secrets, and silence, were a part of the key to becoming an adult, but they also took something away.

"Okay," Johnny said despite himself.

"It's hard, watching somebody dying," Uncle Ricky said. For a while, Johnny thought that was the end of the secret. "You know what bedsores are?"

Johnny shook his head.

"Believe me, you don't *want* to know. A body laying in bed a long time gets . . . holes in it. Big ones. *Sore* ain't even the right word. I could fit an orange in one. The nurse comes in and cleans her up, but . . . it hurts a lot. So anyway, last night your mama and I stayed up late talking about whether we should mash up some pills and . . . let her rest. Put a stop to her pain."

The world's axis tilted again, but this time Johnny fought the dizziness, staring into Uncle Ricky's eyes to make sure he understood: *They had talked about killing her.* A tear escaped the side of Uncle Ricky's eye, and he didn't wipe it away. "Only thing that stopped us? We couldn't be sure if we wanted to do it out of love. Your mama's mad as hell about that burn, and killing out of hate's a sin. Neither of us wants that demon on our backs. But it could be a worse sin to let her suffer. If she was a dog, we would've put her down a long time ago."

Uncle Ricky's confession sat heavy in the morning air, how he and mom had weighed whether or not they loved their mother enough to kill her. Or if they hated her so much that they must let her live. Johnny wished he could unhear all of it. The confession felt like a curse that would follow him. One day his mother would get old too, and she might get bedsores big enough to put his fist into.

"I'm cold," Johnny whispered.

Uncle Ricky nodded and took back the rifle Johnny had forgotten he was still holding. "Yeah. We better head back and make sure the nurse made it on that road. Always take your shot, Johnny. Now I gotta' drive to town or we're gonna' eat leftover ham for dinner. Again."

While Uncle Ricky walked ahead, Johnny noticed how his limp was worse in the cold; Grandmother's lasting gift to him in her moment of rage with a tire iron that had ruined his chance to play football when he was in high school, or anywhere. A year ago, Johnny thought it was the worst story he had ever heard. But not anymore.

Johnny landed his feet inside his uncle's deep footprints, hopping from one to the next, trying to keep the snow from burying his new shoes.

‹o›

The nurse, a white woman, jounced up the driveway in an old blue station wagon with snow chains, but Johnny never saw her except through his cabin window. He slept leaning in his cabin's hardback chair much of the day undisturbed, except when Mom brought him a ham sandwich for lunch. Her smile was so sweet that it made his stomach ache again. His secrets stewed inside of him while he mumbled his thank-you, trying to pretend he didn't know what he knew. This trip had ruined more than Christmas and Kwanzaa; he couldn't even reclaim joy from his mother's smile. Instead, his groggy mind kept flashing him the creature's sharp teeth.

He was nodding off at the table again when he heard the scream.

Johnny's hands tightened around the waiting snow shovel as he jumped up to stare out of his window. He saw the back door ripped away, the windows shattered, a bloody heap quivering in the driveway from a sudden attack—but all of that was his imagination, vanishing when he blinked. Uncle Ricky's VW bug was gone, leaving only the nurse's station wagon and Mom's rental car parked near the back door, but there were no new tracks. No blood. A bright light from Grandmother's bedroom shined through her window, which was now firmly closed. Last night's swishes from the retreating creature were unchanged because no new snow had fallen yet.

Another scream clawed through the stillness. He was sure it must be from Grandmother's room. Was Mom alone with her? Had the nurse gone on an errand with Uncle Ricky? A well of panic swallowed Johnny as he imagined his mother as a knife-wielding killer like in *Black Christmas*, which he had snuck into a theater to see while Mom was at work a week ago.

"Shhhh . . . it's all right . . . " Mom's muffled voice soothed, a plea nearly as sad as the screaming. "Emma's almost done . . . Please hold still. It's all right, Mother."

Mom wasn't alone! *The bedsores*, he remembered. That was why his grandmother was yelling: the nurse was doing her difficult work. Maybe Uncle Ricky hadn't left just to find something else for dinner; the suffering might have driven him away.

Another scream. Even muffled, the sound made him drop the shovel and mash his palms against his ears so hard that it hurt. He had never heard a person in so much pain. Sick people in movies and on TV didn't wail like wounded animals. Was *this* how people died? And last night he had heaped his horrible words on top of her suffering. Johnny could barely catch his breath.

Why had Mom brought him here for this morbid ritual? Why had Uncle Ricky told him a secret he would be forced to remember with every scream?

As he stared outside, Johnny glimpsed Uncle Ricky's hunting rifle leaning unattended against his cabin door on the other side of the yard. *Always take your shot, Johnny,* he had said.

As soon as Johnny saw the rifle, he rushed to put on his coat and sneakers, which he had dried in front of his space heater. Several facts fell into place: He had a gun. The creature's tracks were visible. He still had the chance to conquer his nightmares. He had missed his chance to fire at the hare, but he would not hesitate to pull the trigger again.

The tracks had ended right near that big old cottonwood tree, and the hollow in the trunk looked just like a doorway, didn't it? That thing in the woods was dangerous, or else Uncle Ricky's eyes wouldn't have widened so much when Johnny told him he'd seen its teeth.

Somebody needed to do what needed to be done, even if nothing could be done for Grandmother. Anything was better than waiting. Johnny grabbed the rifle, ducking under his grandmother's wood rail fence to run into the graying woods.

Farther behind him with every step, Grandmother was still screaming.

◄◦►

His feet, it seemed, remembered every dip and crevice as he followed the slashing, senseless trail between the firs and pines. This time, the creature's passage was accompanied by Uncle Ricky's boot tracks and Johnny's smaller ones beside his, sometimes intersecting, sometimes roughly parallel. Johnny panted with his mouth open as he ran, his breath charging in bursts from his lips. He held the rifle like a bayonet, ready to strike.

Fear made his legs heavy, but he pushed through until he was sweating despite the cold, until he could see the large tree ahead, dwarfing the surrounding conifers with a massive canopy of feathery branches made ominous without their leaves.

Yes, this was the place. He had no doubt. The tracks stopped abruptly, but the end of the creature's trail was a small heap, a sign of burrowing for sure. When he nudged the snow heap with his foot—(jumping quickly away, of course)—lumpy snow fell away into a hole as wide as a basketball. And the cottonwood stood only yards away from the creature's tunnel.

Upon his second visit, the mound of snow in front of the tree seemed like a wall, and the gap itself looked bigger; an archway of inky blackness against the snowdrift.

"Come out! *I'm not afraid of you!*"

In that moment, it didn't feel like a lie because his terror only felt like rage. He was enraged with his mother for bringing him on such a horrible trip. Enraged with Uncle Ricky for the secrets he kept, and the one he had shared. Enraged with himself for cursing Grandmother to die and then pitying her and for feeling anything for her after everything she had done. His rage poured out of him as tears, and his throat grew clotted, but he yelled again, "*Come on out!*"

He had never wanted to kill a thing, but he did now with a ferocity that felt primal. If he could turn back time, he would shoot that hare until his rifle clicked, empty. Maybe this creature had no more to do with poisoning his family than the hare, but he hoped that killing it would help him sleep without nightmares.

The silence infuriated him. Johnny picked up a stone and threw it at the dead cottonwood tree, missing the cavity by two inches. The second stone he threw flew inside and vanished in the blackness with a *THUNK*.

The chittering he had heard in Grandmother's room floated from the gap, but much louder than before. Agitated. Rising in pitch. A slithering sound echoed from inside the tree trunk, something moving fast, perhaps racing in a circle. Would it come outside?

Always take your shot, Johnny.

The rifle snapped into place beneath his chin, the perfect shooting stance. Johnny's sight was aimed directly into the dark crater, barely wavering despite his heaving breaths. Nothing else in the woods existed except the inky maw and his breathing.

Two ice-blue eyes emerged from the darkness. Moving toward daylight. Toward him.

Johnny's breathing stopped. The world stopped. For a moment, neither of them moved. The urge to kill, so consuming before, withered. *Might think she's its mama*, Uncle Ricky said.

"Don't come back!" Johnny said, although phlegm tried to strangle his voice. "You hear me? She's dying, so stay away!"

More chittering, but it seemed softer this time. Plaintive, even. Could it understand?

A large twig cracking from the creature's motion in the darkness sounded like a gunshot, snapping Johnny awake from his fugue state. Without realizing it, he dropped Uncle Ricky's gun when he turned and stumbled to run away.

His own scream was bottled in his throat, ringing between his ears.

◄o►

When Johnny made it back to the lodge, the nurse's car was gone.

Mom was bundled up in her coat and scarf on the back porch bent over with her head wrapped between her arms; the same spot where Grandmother was always sitting in his dream. He had never seen his mother look so weary and sad.

He thought Grandmother might be dead until he heard a soft moan through her window.

Mom sobbed so loudly that Johnny thought about sneaking back into his cabin unseen. But he decided to go to her instead.

Mom heard his feet crunching toward her and looked up with a smile she tried to paste in place to greet him. When she saw his face, her smile died unborn. Wildness was playing in his mother's eyes, and he suspected she saw the same wildness in his.

"This is no kind of Christmas for you, Johnny," she said. "I'm sorry."

"You neither. I'm sorry too."

He sat beside her, so she scooted to make room on the narrow stair. The part of him that wanted to tell her everything quieted, obsolete, when she hugged him close. And he hugged her, comforting, not merely comforted—different than when he'd been younger—something new.

Johnny knew then that he would never tell his mother about Grandmother's strange creature in the woods, perhaps the only one of her children she had not scarred for life.

◄◊►

Three weeks after their trip to Bear Creek, Grandmother died at a Denver hospital. Neither Mom nor Uncle Ricky gave her the pills to end her misery, although Johnny could never forget that only their fear of hating her had stopped them. Her lodge sat empty for a year, but then Uncle Ricky moved in. He and Mom split the proceeds from the sale of their childhood home, and Mom bought a three-bedroom house in North Miami with a yard full of mango and avocado trees. It was the best place Johnny had ever lived, but that didn't stop the bad dreams.

Five years after Grandmother died, Uncle Ricky vanished on a hunting trip near the lodge. His mother, of course, was devastated. By then, Johnny was in college in lily white Iowa on a full academic scholarship, never needing a cent from Grandmother's estate—and the story of his uncle's disappearance didn't sit right. Uncle Ricky had been a seasoned hunter, and he knew those woods well.

Johnny called the local sheriff's office to find out more, since a Black man missing in the woods surely wasn't their top priority. But the deputy who picked up the phone told him he drank beer with Uncle Ricky on Friday nights and had been a part of the search party. He didn't need to pull up a report to tell him the facts: a set of footprints they thought held promise had simply stopped cold in a clearing. The dogs sniffed Uncle Ricky to that spot and no farther.

"In front of an old tree?" Johnny said. Beyond his doorway, music blared from an impromptu dance party erupting in his dorm to celebrate the weekend. Metal rock. Johnny and his classmates were in two different worlds, yet again.

Come to think of it, a deputy said, there *had* been an old husk of a tree near where the tracks disappeared. The dogs had whined and circled, and one of them had started digging.

But all they found was snow.

THE ENFILADE

ANDREW HOOK

One

I first met Pryce on the grassy banks of the River Cam, although it was to be quite a different body of water that would signify his destiny. Pryce was a scraggy youth who stood with a dangled cigarette dropping ash into the water, as he gazed out towards Clare College Bridge with its three uniform arches. The structure was the oldest bridge remaining in Cambridge, and bore the oddity of a missing section of the globe second from the left on the south side. One story is that the builder of the bridge received what he considered to be insufficient payment, and in his anger removed a segment of the globe; another is that it was a method of tax avoidance, as bridges were subject to tax only once they were complete. Whatever the meaning, I was unaware of either back then. I was also unaware how the concept of *completeness* would be a major influence on Pryce's life, to the point of obsession.

It might be inferred that because we were in Cambridge that we attended the university, came from a monied background—or at the least, from opportunity—and were destined for high profile roles in either politics or business, where we might forever draw upon these formative years without ever understanding lives less fortunate than ours. In reality, little was further from the truth. I still lived with my parents in a terraced house in the Cambridge South area of the city, a location riddled with violence and anti-social behaviour, and whilst Pryce could be said to live opposite from me, in Cambridge North, the area was equally poor. A year older than me, Pryce had been renting a shared house with three students at the time we met, although they were barely on first name terms with each other. Pryce had become distanced from his parents, not that this was a matter he talked about, only something I inferred. He wasn't wholly destitute, and in fact had just started an apprenticeship as a mechanic. I was on the dole, uncertain as to a career path. We both were into music, recreational drugs, and—on rare opportunities—girls. I was also into photography, which was the second thing Pryce noticed when he turned his head to look at me.

"They're not quite right, are they," he said, watching as I balanced in a squat with the intention of taking a photo of the bridge. I put out a hand to the grass to steady myself, wondering what he meant. My own preference was for symmetry, and if you could somehow divide the bridge in two and fold it onto itself it would have been a perfect match.

"What do you mean?"

"Those arches. Ideally they should be behind each other, like a segmented tunnel. What do you think?"

"Like three single-arched bridges placed one after the other?"

Pryce grinned. "You got it." He nodded to my T-shirt. I had bought it at the Cud gig at the Junction the night before. It had been the last night of their *Robinson Crusoe* tour and the atmosphere had been—as all the best gig commentaries reported it—electric. "I was there too," he added.

He stepped to one side so I could take my photograph, then we sat on the bank and chatted about the gig. It was a warm October Sunday afternoon. An Indian Summer, as those unseasonably dry weather days are often referred to. Another reference which in hindsight could be seen as prophetic, even if the term had Native American origins rather than the Indian subcontinent which, in two short years, we would be travelling through.

Whenever I read about cult leaders their focus is always centred around a charismatic male, someone who exudes power or influence, an arch manipulator, or devilishly handsome to the extent that any commonsense considerations are thrown out of the window. Not so with Pryce. As he sat on the grass, picking dirt from under his fingernails, his jeans torn in places that even the later ripped-jean fashion wouldn't have considered, his face appearing gnawed whilst making a concerted effort on conversation, with post-teenage acne slow to make a disappearance despite us both having recently entered our twenties, I was more intent on wondering how quickly I might extricate myself than making a new friend. His lank black hair hadn't been washed that morning. In truth, we both smelt of the moshpit. When he asked if he could look at my camera, I half-wondered if he might run away with it.

The camera was nothing special, a Minolta Maxxum 7000 which had an autofocus feature that I'd always found useful. However it certainly looked more professional than the Kodak Ektralite that I'd owned before it. The equivalent of comparing a Morris Minor to a Jaguar. The Kodak Ektralite was a terrible camera if you cared about image quality, or features, or capabilities. If, on the other hand, all you wanted was to point and shoot, then it was a decent machine. The Minolta was more than a step up. It was an expensive birthday gift from my parents that I wasn't sure if they could afford, and seeing it in Pryce's hands brought me out in a sweat not entirely attributable to the heat of the day.

"Interesting," Pryce said, with the air of someone who knew nothing about cameras, but was nonchalant enough to pretend otherwise. "There's some countries where they believe taking your picture captures your soul, have you heard about that?"

I nodded, equally nonchalant, although this was the first I'd known about it. Many years later, I read an article where a Dr Venkataramananaan, Head of Paranormal Sciences at Arakab University, had postulated that this old belief might have some basis in truth. From the starting point which considered that the human mind and soul connect to create an *aura* sensitive to mood, Venkataramananaan suggested that cameras functioned not only by snatching all the available light within the frame but part of the aura too, speculating that people who are constantly photographed end up living empty and aimless lives. As examples, he referenced famous personalities such as Britney Spears, Lindsay Lohan, and Nicole Richie, in case studies which highlighted the drop in their personal and professional lives soon after they started getting photographed *more than the recommended average*, leading to dissatisfied and shallow behaviour. The article concluded by quoting the doctor as saying, 'The aura needs time to heal. If you continue to get photographed after completely losing your aura, the camera will take a toll on your soul next'. Whilst I took all this with the pinch of salt that it deserved, it certainly held more resonance than it would have had on the banks of the Cam in October 1990. Events were such that I wondered whether the University of Arakab ever designed their 'Gaia Refill Filter' that would reduce the effects of soul snatching cameras. No photo of Dr Venkataramananaan accompanied the article.

That day, Pryce had turned my camera over and again in his hands without any clear understanding. Then he handed it back to me and stood.

"Fancy a beer?"

-◇-

We embarked on a rough and tumble friendship where we drifted in and out of each other's social spheres as we discovered we had more in common than we had originally known. Pryce got his act together and in a couple of years had passed his apprenticeship and was earning what we called in the early nineties *good money*, parodying the *loadsamoney* of the late eighties. I'd found work in a secondhand camera shop, where I would eventually take over the business from the elderly Mr Coombes by the early two thousands. By 1992, however, we'd gone to numerous gigs together, even taken a holiday in Ibiza, and things were looking up. Pryce had a girl who draped herself around him on occasion, but usually stood at the back of the Junction or the Corn Exchange whilst we were throwing each other around in the pit. I'd also attracted attention once in a while, but couldn't latch onto anything serious. It wasn't for a lack of trying, but general shyness and uncertainty hampered those early efforts. In truth, it was only in the dark conformity of the moshpit where I felt confident and truly at home. Faces would blur in and out of focus, the occasional shared smile, the occasional brush of clothing or skin. Inevitably, these fragile existences would wink out when the lights came on, and I would search in vain for the individual I had cohabited with in a single moment of space and time only to not recognise them as the crowd filed out of the door.

This status of impermanence was at odds with Pryce's increasing permanence. Whilst I was still living with my parents, Pryce had been able to rent his own flat in a much more salubrious area, filling it with ostentatious items that I wondered if he needed other than as status symbols. His acne had gone, but he was in a permanent state of dishevelment, and the trappings of his work hung about him through the almost henna-like discolouration of engine oil and a lingering smell of metal.

Perhaps it was the journey along the seesaw of permanence/impermanence that tilted the balance, or simply a fear of stability associated with growing up, but it was Pryce who suggested we take time out for a 'life-changing' world trip which eventually was whittled down to two weeks in India, as the ambitious plans we pored over gradually gave way to common sense. Neither of us apparently wanted to leave our jobs.

We didn't choose India out of any burgeoning desire for spirituality, to temporarily remove ourselves from the rat race, or out of an appreciation of Indian architecture or culture. We chose it because we knew it would be cheap and we enjoyed a good curry. We were still unformed, malformed personalities treading familiar British templates of stereotypical behaviour. I stress this because there was nothing remarkable about either of us. Whilst Pryce might occasionally spout something that sounded vaguely metaphysical—*There's some countries where they believe taking your picture captures your soul*—these were thoughts soon forgotten within the humdrum of the everyday. He knew car parts and how to put them together. I knew cameras and how to take them apart. Whilst we wanted more than two weeks on a beach in Goa—we planned to make the *most* of our money, after all—we still chose an itinerary unintended to be off the beaten path.

"Matthew, mate," Pryce said, his hand slapping my back, "This is going to be lavish."

◂◦▸

We arrived in Delhi during the summer heat of 1993. The air humid, temperature nudging forty degrees centigrade. The plane doors opened onto an atmosphere so thick it felt that you could cut into it like cheese. There was no gradual assimilation; within moments of leaving the airport the cornucopia of life was thrust violently upon us. Innumerable people, vehicles, colours, sounds: we were bustled from one street to the next, accosted, propositioned, harassed. Doubtless there was a thrill to it, but my overriding reaction was to get back on the plane, or at the very least find our hotel room to catch a breath and a moment's peace. Pryce soaked it up, almost dancing from foot to foot as he navigated the streets and bartered for a taxi. I had heard of the term *culture shock* but had only the vaguest idea of the extent that a complete change of scene can induce it. For the first couple of days I felt benumbed, dissociative and even a little depressed. When on the third day I suggested remaining in the hotel to prepare ourselves for the next stage of the journey, Pryce regarded me as though I were insubstantial and spent the entire day on his own, only returning towards midnight with his face daubed in colours that accentuated the line of tears which had run down his cheeks.

"There's so much *here!*" he repeated, his expression manic, disconcerting. "What's up with you, Matthew, got a case of Delhi belly?"

I shook my head. It was so hot in the room I could imagine the whitewashed walls sweating emulsion. A fan turned desultory circles in the ceiling. A thin bedsheet covered my body as protection against insects, my contours clearly defined as though the sheet were a piece of muslin enclosing wet clay. I had spent the day running fantasies of returning home, eating Cornish pasties, unlocking the camera shop door and entering the cool darkness. I couldn't explain my reticence for the culture, which in itself was a further downer. Even Pryce's enthusiasm couldn't shake me. Eventually he collapsed on his bed, snatching a few hours before our scheduled train journey the following day. "I can't *wait* to get to Varanasi," he said, as I enviously watched him sink into an immediate sleep, as though his accumulated energies had tripped a switch and shut him down.

Yet there was no option other than to wait. The train journey was a thirteen-hour trip which took almost twenty due to an uncommunicated disruption at Kanpur. "Leaves on the line," chuckled Pryce. I stuck my head out of the window because it was marginally cooler with the vague suggestion of breeze.

When we were eventually disgorged at Varanasi train station, almost literally spewed onto the concourse as though ejected by a gigantic elongated beast, the benefit of a marginal drop in temperature from Delhi was offset by an immediate repugnant smell. The stench of urine, cow dung and uncollected rubbish jostled with that of spices, jasmine and incense. Once we had located a hotel, Pryce was eager to experience the River Ganges, so we picked our way as close as we were able, eventually surfacing from the everyday stink of the city to stand on the stone steps leading down to the water, where I discovered that decomposed bodies smell especially bad when they're set on fire. The scent was nauseating and sweet, putrid and steaky, something like leather being tanned over a flame. Pulling the edge of my T-shirt up and over my nose, I took in the admittedly fantastic and vibrant vista whilst being assailed through every sense known to man. Pryce handed me a cup of something which I later understood to be *bhang*, a concoction prepared with ground-up cannabis leaves and seeds that are mixed into a drink like a yogurt-based lassi. I tentatively lowered my T-shirt and took a sip from mine, whilst Pryce appeared to down his in one, before he flung his arms out to each side and appeared to embrace the entirety of everything before us. In retrospect, I wish I had been less narrow-minded and had taken the scene in with an equally unprejudiced gaze. Perhaps if I'd been more attentive then I might even have been able to prevent what happened next.

"Give me a minute," Pryce said, withdrawing into the crowd.

I wasn't to see him again for another four years.

◄◦►

Whilst there isn't an official psychological diagnosis, India syndrome has been documented as a condition whereby travellers to India—mostly those from the Northern Hemisphere—are adversely affected largely due to the culture shock experience. Upon researching it following Pryce's reappearance, I realised I had been affected in the opposite manner. Whereas I exhibited symptoms such as depression and isolation, stemming from a feeling of disorientation in an unfamiliar land and culture, Pryce had *found himself*. To the extent that acute psychosis, delirium and delusion could be described as *found*. I later learned that Pryce had burned his passport within days of arriving in Delhi, although his desire to disappear hadn't manifested itself until that afternoon in Varanasi. Studies suggested that India syndrome was more likely experienced by those who journey to the country with an expectation of spiritual enlightenment, but also—in Pryce's case—where as an ordinary tourist they unknowingly bring with them some emotional or psychological issue or trauma relating to family, relationships, or their past. The cultural changes forced a breakdown, an assimilation into an alternative way of living, which gripped Pryce like a cyclone and took him off into journeys unknown.

I spent two relatively quiet days at Varanasi, rarely leaving our hotel room, wondering at what point he might return. Initially I assumed he had become physically lost within the hubbub, not understanding he was psychologically unmoored. I oscillated between worry and anger, sick with concern that something bad had happened, whilst simultaneously annoyed that I'd been left to my own devices in a country that I had barely come to tolerate. I've since revisited India and have an entirely more favourable impression, but the headspace I inhabited then wasn't as informed as it is now, and every alien sound that filtered through the hotel walls was like fingernails down a blackboard. On the third day I ingested something ill-prepared which laid me out for a week. So decrepit did I become during that time that I was soiling myself in bed. If it wasn't for the fact that we had exceeded our paid for stay and the hotel owner had become curious, I wouldn't have received the medical attention which then—almost literally—brought me back to life. It was only at that point that I felt acclimatised enough to inform the authorities about Pryce's disappearance. As I queued for the plane a few days later I had a naïve hope that I might see him wave across the concourse, and join me on the return journey. But this was not to be.

It is easy to disappear amongst one billion people. Especially when you have no intention of being found. On my return to Cambridge I found the tranquillity almost equally as unbearable as the tumult. I returned to the camera shop which existed exactly as it had been, as exactly as I remembered it. There was no time for grief. Mr Coombes had his own holiday booked immediately after I returned from mine. Whilst Scarborough couldn't match the complexities of India, I'm sure he had a good time of it. I settled into the confines of the shop with the black camera boxes and their sightless lenses pointing towards me, but the familiarity of this shell was now at odds. I was a hermit crab seeking an abode that fit but which wasn't my own. It was hardly a busy store, there was too much time for reflection. And if I looked closely enough, there was plenty of *me* to be mirrored in those lenses.

What is a lens but a clear curved piece of glass or plastic used in eyeglasses, cameras, or telescopes to make things look clearer, smaller, or bigger?

In a recent article about India syndrome, the writer speculated that the new lens that the traveller begins to see through can distort even the surest of convictions, replacing hesitation with complete openness, scepticism with blind trust.

Pryce's whereabouts became apparent in the autumn of 1997. I caught a local news report which confirmed that a man who had gone missing in India four years previously had been discovered in the grounds of Mysore Palace, a magnificent structure in the Indian state of Karnataka, a distance over almost two thousand kilometres from Varanasi. The man wore traditional Indian clothing, sported several long necklaces, carried a walking stick, and wore red threads tied around his wrists denoting various blessings. Reports suggested that the man had adhered to a life so attuned to preaching asceticism that he had become confused as to his original identity. Whilst the authorities had considered there was no apparent harm if he were left to his own devices, a minor infraction at the Palace had led to his arrest, and the long-ago expiration of his visa coupled with the implication of India syndrome meant that he was to be deported to England within the next few days. The main risk, it was considered, was to himself. He didn't belong there.

Pryce had prostrated himself before the stunningly beautiful turquoise enfilade at Mysore Palace, blocking a tour party. He had remained immobile in the lotus position to the extent that four men had to forcibly remove him. One to each leg, one to each underarm. He had been carried as though a block of stone to one side whilst the police had been summoned. His beard reached down to his stomach.

At the conclusion of the BBC Cambridge report they confirmed the name of the miscreant as David Pryce, but I had identified him from much earlier in the broadcast. I had recognised him, because he had recognised me.

Two

When Pryce re-entered the camera shop in 1999 it was as though nothing had changed. His beard had gone, and his hands were once again oil-stained, the grit ingrained under his fingernails to that extent that you'd never accept a sandwich from him. I knew he'd found a job at a different garage, that he had reverted to himself once removed from the subcontinent. I'd heard through a couple of mutual friends that he'd also been *away for a bit*. The phrasing of which seemed completely inadequate.

This was the first time, however, that he'd reached out to me, and I certainly hadn't done so to him. In the aftermath of his return the newspapers had sought an interview from his *travelling companion*, in the same manner that they had done when he first went missing. I had held back from making any statement. My emotions were mixed. There was relief that he was still alive as I had shouldered a burden of guilt in the intervening years that his disappearance had somehow been my fault. But this was more than tempered by the anger I felt from him not having taken any attempts to contact me whilst he'd remained in India: psychologically deranged or not. It smacked of a selfishness that I couldn't put a handle on, which undermined the entirety of our friendship. And there was more to it than that, of course, there was the sensation of seeing his face on the news report that made me certain he had somehow *seen* me. That a connection existed completely unexplainable by anything other than the uncanny. That—whilst I had never actually taken a photograph of him—I had somehow taken his soul.

"Well Matthew," he said, leaning on the glass counter underneath which a variety of lenses blinked up at him, "it's been a while."

Mr Coombes had just left for his lunch break. I wondered whether Pryce had chosen this moment.

"You could say that."

"Doing OK for yourself."

"Not bad. You?"

He nodded. Then stood, shifted a bit, looked around the shop as if suddenly embarrassed at my presence.

"Look," he said, "about leaving you in India. It wasn't planned, you know. I would never have . . . "

His voice tailed off. It was hardly an act of contrition, but I felt embarrassed for him. Whilst we had both aged, I suddenly saw the face of the old Pryce behind the new one, as though an image were slowly developing in photographic fluid, his features gradually forming into his current appearance. In that moment, I understood the past was the past and the present the present. Acceptance flooded through me.

"When Coombes gets back," I said, "do you fancy a beer?"

-◦-

"You still into cameras then," Pryce said.

Coombes had given me the rest of the afternoon off under the circumstances, and we nudged a few jars in the Anchor on Silver Street with its glorious views of the river. There were a dozen or more questions I could ask Pryce, questions which I had previously run through an equal dozen times in my head, but which felt unimportant now we were down the pub with a beer in our hands, as though Pryce had simply stepped out for a moment during an ongoing conversation, perhaps returning from the toilet as though nothing had happened. The incident in India felt—and indeed, *was*—years ago. I was also mindful of Pryce's psychological state, not wanting to mention anything that might initiate a relapse. There was no indication of any outward difference, no matter how closely I watched him. No nervous twitches, no avoidance of my eye, as there had been initially when he'd entered the shop. Although I don't know what I was expecting: some religious diatribe or a mental breakdown. A recrimination. A challenge. There was none of that. He asked about my parents, my job, whether I had a girlfriend, as though he'd been out of town and we were old buddies catching up. Which I expect we were. So the conversation about the cameras seemed completely innocuous.

I sipped my beer. "The market is changing, but the interest is still there, yes." I explained that digital cameras were likely to take over from physical film, at least for common usage. I knew there were plans for such cameras to be incorporated into mobile phones, that from the following year onwards and into the two thousands it was highly likely they would proliferate. I didn't expect professionals to embrace the medium so readily, though, and mentioned this to Pryce.

He nodded thoughtfully. "That's what we said about CDs though, wasn't it, even when they were spreading jam on them during Blue Peter. But they've overtaken vinyl. The future is digital, man."

He said the last word with knowing emphasis, but I shrugged it off. "We'll see. Wasn't that Tomorrow's World anyway?"

"What?"

"The jam thing."

Pryce took a big gulp of beer. As though he were readying himself for something. "I suppose what I'm really asking," he said, "is if you can take my picture."

My mind flickered over photos and souls. Truth was, I'd always been more of a landscape photographer. It was rare that I'd photographed a person. Not because of the soul theory, simply I never saw a need to do so. Something I had begun to regret as my memories of people faded, particularly those of my parents. There was almost nothing of me from teenage upwards. Apart from one.

"But," Pryce leant forwards, "not just any kind of picture. I have something in mind. And I need someone I can trust."

I immediately thought *pornographic*. I shook my head, waving an unbidden image from my mind, which Pryce took as a rebuke.

He sat back. "Hear me out," he said. "We've some history and I just thought, Matthew, he'd do the job. You know what an enfilade is?"

I not only didn't know, I had to ask him to repeat and spell it.

"An enfilade is a suite of rooms formally aligned with each other, such that the doors entering each room are aligned with the doors of the connecting rooms along a single axis, which provides a vista through the entire suite of rooms. Look down from where we're sitting towards the toilets and you'll get the idea. Not particularly majestic, of course."

I glanced in that direction. The pub was broken into several spaces for privacy, each area with a connecting arch. From where we sat you could look through three of those spaces straight, until your eye alighted on the sign of the *Gents* at the end. I was suddenly reminded of Pryce's comment on the Clare College Bridge, that the arches would ideally be one after the other, rather than in a horizontal line.

"Where I was found," Pryce continued, his voice wavering almost imperceptibly on that last word, "at the Mysore Palace, there was a perfect example of an enfilade. Let me ask you something else, have you read Huxley's *The Doors of Perception*?"

This was something new from Pryce, who hitherto I never knew had read anything other than *Car Mechanics* magazine. "I'm aware of it," I answered, guardedly.

"Huxley took psychedelics as an experiment, and documented the results. I don't claim to understand any of it, but I gave it a flick through the other day and one quote stood out. Do you want to hear it?"

I had the distinct impression Pryce had more than *flicked* through it, and was certain Pryce was deliberating holding out, but I nodded and Pryce said: "The man who comes back through the door in the wall will never be quite the same as the man who went out."

I was about to say, 'Is this about India', when the waitress interrupted to ask if our empty glasses were finished with, before deftly collecting them between her fingers and returning them to the bar.

"What if there's more than one door?" Pryce said, leaning back in his chair, steepling his hands together as though he'd said something really profound.

"Are we talking physical, metaphorical or psychological?"

"Think on that," Pryce said, and whether deliberate or otherwise he walked through the enfilade to the *Gents*, returning five minutes later via the bar with two fresh pints.

"There's an enfilade in Wimpole Hall," he continued, supping from his new pint. "I want you to photograph me there, together with a few friends of mine. It's only ten miles out. We're going up there Saturday, what do you say?"

"Is it a public building?"

"It's National Trust. I just want someone who understands me and who looks professional with the equipment. I've asked them if we can have sole access for thirty minutes, Cambridge scholars that we are. It's agreed. I just need you to be part of it."

"Digital or film," I asked.

"Film. One shot on an extended exposure."

"How extended? I'll need a tripod."

"I dunno. Three, four, five minutes? I'll work it out beforehand." He drank again, a thin layer of beer adhering to his upper lip. I was reminded of the *bhang* for a fraction of a moment, and again, of a point of departure that I wasn't sure I wanted to take.

"Are you paying me?" It was a joke.

Pryce struck out his hand. "Ten quid. Deal done."

◂◦▸

The sky was burnished yellow. We were travelling in separate cars. Pryce's friends in one, Pryce driving me in the other. Trees glitched past the window, their autumnal leaves surrounded them on the floor as though they had stepped out of skirts. A Britpop compilation tape in the stereo. Fields of cows merged into one another, smears of white on black or black on white. Everything was a blur.

A canvas bag between my feet contained the Nikon F100, Nikkor 50mm f/1.8 AF-D that I'd borrowed from the shop. It had only been out a few months, but I'd already made good use of it. Sometimes on occasions that Mr Coombes knew about and sometimes when he didn't. A tripod lounged across the back seat like an anorexic model, but that wasn't what we were going to shoot. I had expected Pryce might have made more of an effort at his own appearance, but he was dressed as usual in T-shirt and jeans, the flesh on his forearms stippling in the cool air. I hadn't taken a good look at his friends; they were already in the car as Pryce pulled up outside my parents. My mother had waved to him hesitantly from the doorway as she wished us a good day.

"Don't," I said, upon entering the vehicle, "it's embarrassing."

"Not thought of looking for your own place?"

"Often. But, you know."

Truth was I didn't want to be alone. I occasionally had flashbacks to Varanasi. Not that you would class them as PTSD, but enough to remember that sweat-soaked bed linen and a feeling of utter alienation.

"These friends," I said, "a couple of miles out of Cambridge. Where did you meet them?"

Pryce kept his gaze to the road. "They sought me out. Read about me in the papers, didn't they? They call themselves acolytes, but I call them novices."

"Because they're under your tutelage?"

He laughed. "Because they're new and inexperienced."

I thought of saying more. Should have said more. But Pryce wanted to run through the specifications of the shoot.

"There's five separate connected rooms at Wimpole Hall. Each of us will stand behind the other underneath the respective doorways. You'll be in the dining room. Set up your equipment so that my body is obstructing the view of each of the others. Don't move from your position either. Keep the camera focused on me for the duration of the exposure. The camera's lens will be your lens, as it were. When the image is done, raise your hand. Only at that point can you move."

I could have asked why we needed his friends if they weren't going to be in the shot. I could have asked why the location mattered. I could have asked why he wanted the photograph taken in the first place. I *had* asked why he'd decided on a five minute timed exposure. It was a hell of a long while to maintain a fixed position.

"Don't worry," he'd answered, "we've practiced it."

The approach to Wimpole Hall was typically grandiose. It was a 17th century mansion set in extensive parks and gardens, once the home of Rudyard Kipling's daughter, Elsie. Although that was by-the-by, the Indian connection wasn't unknown to me. Whilst it was likely Pryce had chosen the location due to convenience of distance, I was beginning to realise that picking up from where we left off wasn't part of his agenda. That Pryce's experiences in India had made him an altogether different man on the inside, even if the outside was basically unchanged.

It was eight-thirty when we arrived. Permission had been granted to film before the Hall opened to the public an hour later. I was so preoccupied by the circumstances and the setting up of the equipment that I barely paid heed to Pryce's friends, a mixture of genders who kept in their group and who didn't approach me. Under the beady eye of a member of staff we were led to the enfilade and then left to our own devices. Everyone took their positions, and I squatted to screw my eye to the viewfinder.

I'm sure the enfilade at Wimpole Hall was far less impressive than that at Mysore Palace, but I understood the telescoping effect of the view. Pale green walls in each room were offset by pale pink carpets. Sculptured architraves bedecked each of the doorways. Pryce stood with his hands clasped in front of him, looking into the camera. Through my viewfinder the presence of his friends, lined up one after another to his rear, were invisible. When Pryce gave the nod, I depressed the shutter to take the picture. The timer would do the rest of the work. I was convinced the final image would be blurred, at least at the edges of Pryce's figure. It was virtually impossible to remain completely still for a few seconds, never mind five minutes. Even keeping my own position, as instructed by Pryce, knowing I wasn't being photographed, was almost impossible. I had initially intended to close my eyes, to place myself into a solipsistic reverie—for I was sure some kind of trance state was what Pryce was attempting to achieve—but as though I needed to remain true to the image I kept my eye to the viewfinder as patiently as I could. After a few moments, it felt that I couldn't move even if I wanted to, and I somehow perpetuated that state of mind until I heard the camera shutter click and I knew the shot was done.

I raised my hand as requested. Pryce relaxed. I looked behind him to the others and was mystified to discover they were no longer there. I certainly hadn't seen them step out of shot, but they must have entered the adjoining rooms during the process. It was the only explanation I had.

"Where are your friends?" I asked Pryce, but he didn't even look around. Instead, he tapped the side of his head. "In here."

⤙⚬⤚

Contrary to Pryce's strict instructions, I made two copies of the photograph. One copy I handed to him when he visited the shop, together with the negative. Mr Coombes had stood over me as I developed the image in the darkroom we had out the back. I had asked him to accompany me, as though I was afraid of what I might find. He had an interest in the long exposure, although I hadn't mentioned the disappearance—or even existence—of the friends.

"Something must have gone wrong with the timer," he said, as the image cleared into perfection. "There'd have to be some blur. No one can remain perfectly still for that long. It's a good photo, you've got the acumen for it, but that's a straightforward shot."

Examining the image I had to agree. Pryce was happy with it, though. He seemed full of himself when I handed it over. As if he couldn't believe how good it was. I remembered his comment about the man who comes back through the door in the wall never being quite the same as the man who went out. I realised that Pryce had been out far longer than he had been in. I wondered when that had happened. In India, or before? I wondered about his life before we had met. What trauma might have been suppressed there, if any. To be fair, Pryce seemed an open book, little different from as I had known him. I began to wonder if I was looking for something that didn't exist.

When we had left Wimpole Hall that morning his friends' car was still parked in the driveway where they had left it.

"Are they staying?" I'd asked. I wasn't particularly interested in stately homes and was eager to get going, myself.

"Temporarily," Pryce answered, his expression somewhat dreamy, "but then everything's temporary, isn't it?"

Once I'd handed Pryce the photograph I didn't see him for some years. I began to get curious about his friends, but not even knowing their names or their connection to Pryce I had nothing to go on. I dipped in and out of *The Doors of Perception*, but there was nothing for me in there. On some wild occasions, I wondered if Pryce had tricked me into a Satanic ritual. The disappearance of his friends troubled me, and whilst I didn't believe in such things, the everyday nature of the experience unnerved me more than a naked gathering and a sacrificial goat would have done. What might be more horrific than Pryce outwardly unchanged in an experience which had extinguished his friends? Then I reminded ourselves we were kids from council houses, not aristocrats dabbling in the arcane. Pryce had his own reasons for the photograph—for the *trickery*—that he didn't want to tell me. I was going to have to live with that.

Although there had been an instant when we were developing the photograph, using the enlarger to shine light through the negative to transfer the image onto photographic paper, where I fancied I saw a suggestion of movement, as if a figure were to the right of Pryce's head. Mr Coombes hadn't mentioned it and it didn't appear in the final print, even when I inspected it later with a magnifying glass. Nevertheless, I suspected what it was.

THREE

"Matthew?"

I grunted out of sleep. My hand held my mobile phone even though I couldn't remember picking it up.

"Who's this?"

"Pryce."

"Pryce?" The voice was so distant I wondered if he were calling from India. "Where did you get this number?"

"From Coombes. Listen, I don't want to be dramatic but I haven't a lot of time. I'll be outside yours in ten minutes."

He hung up.

I rubbed sleep from my eyes and took in the time. It was barely six o'clock. Tempting as it was to roll over and go back to sleep, I realised I wasn't in a position to argue. Pryce—sane or otherwise—would be knocking at my door shortly. I swung my legs out of bed, pulled on yesterday's underwear and clothing, and grabbed a warm jumper and my duffel coat before descending the stairs. I didn't need to be quiet. My parents had died two years previously, within months of each other. My father from a heart attack, and my mother from a different kind of broken heart. It had been five years since I'd last seen Pryce. I owned the camera shop now that Coombes had retired. I wondered how Pryce had talked him into giving him my number. Or how he had found him.

It wasn't that we had avoided each other since the photograph was taken, simply that our paths hadn't reconnected. I'd heard Pryce had moved out of the area. I had no clue to his whereabouts at all. In that time I had aged to my detriment, put on a few extra pounds. I had an occasional girlfriend, but couldn't seem to form anything serious. Just as with Pryce—I had assumed—there was always something missing.

Pryce was hopping from one foot to the other as I opened the front door. I was immediately shocked by his appearance. If I had aged eight years in five, then he had aged eighteen. His slack face was etched in lines and his hair was thinning. He'd even seemed to have lost a little height.

"Have you still got it?" he asked, quickly. "The camera. Have you still got it?"

I didn't need to ask which one he meant. I knew instinctively. I'd bought the Nikon off Coombes once I'd developed that photograph and hadn't used it since. It might sound strange, but it felt haunted to me. I didn't want anyone else to use it.

I nodded and returned indoors. When I came back out with the camera and tripod, Pryce was already in his car, gunning the engine.

"Get in, get in."

I got in.

"What's the emergency?"

"I don't know if I can tell you, Matthew. I don't think it makes sense to say it out loud."

He pulled sharply off the kerb and we headed west. Soon we were leaving the city and entering the countryside. It was a cold January morning, frost pixelating the foliage by the roadside.

"Where are we going?"

"The Gog Magog hills. I need you to photograph me again."

"There's an enfilade there, is there," I said, unable to hide the scorn underscoring my voice.

But Pryce didn't answer. For a moment, the only sound was the engine. Then he forced out some words alongside a laugh. "I've been a bit promiscuous, Matthew, when it comes to taking photographs. I should have stuck with you, someone I could trust, instead . . . well, I should have been more circumspect. I was protecting you, I think, but it's all gone tits up. That's why I need you again, to redo what I've undone. Or maybe to undo what's already done."

"You're not making any sense."

"None of it does!"

I placed one hand to steady the steering wheel as we took a corner so fast I thought we might skid off the road. "Careful!"

Pryce seemed to gain some control. I watched his eyes flicker to the dashboard clock. I wondered about the circumstances which had led to this moment. What journeys we had both taken to get here. Two old friends in a battered car out for a photo shoot. Our lives in the balance.

"The enfilade," Pryce said eventually, as we turned off the A11 onto the Babraham Road, a range of low chalk hills encroaching either side of us, "has two meanings, you see. Both the architectural definition, but also a military definition. In military terms, an enfilade is a formation where weapons fire can be directed along its longest axis. For instance, a trench is enfiladed if the opponent can fire down the length of it. A column of marching troops is enfiladed if fired on from the front or rear, such that projectiles will travel the length of the column. Do you see what I mean? The benefit of enfilading an enemy formation is that, by firing along the long axis, it becomes easier to hit targets within that formation."

"Can you put that in layman's terms?"

"When the doors are open, it's just as easy for me to gather others as it is for them to gather me."

"I can't see . . . "

Pryce pulled violently to the kerb. "We're here."

◄◦►

The Gog Magog hills didn't have a particularly high elevation, but they did afford a relatively unbroken vista across the Gog Magog Downs to Cambridge itself. We tramped up a slope. I noticed Pryce's shoes were already caked in mud in the way that mine were becoming. Any doubts that he knew where he was going and whether he had been here before were assuaged by the time we reached the top. Pryce was panting. I was too. It was a long while since I had traipsed across countryside in the sparse light and breathtaking cold of a January morning. It had been a long while since a moshpit, too.

"I've been here all night." Pryce was laughing. He didn't have much control over it.

From our current position, extending a good one hundred feet beyond, were rows and rows of roughly-built wooden structures, each one positioned behind the other, an approximation of an enfilade of door frames constructed by someone with poor carpentry skills in an obvious hurry and with inappropriate materials. Many of the doors listed, their dimensions inexact. Either way, it was an impressive sight. With barely a foot between them, there were at least one hundred doorways. As many as I could perceive until the early morning mist dulled them from my vision.

"What the hell."

Pryce leant on me, breathing heavily close to my ear. "Perhaps. Who knows. Now set up that camera and put a five-minute timer on it."

"Are you sure this is wise?"

"Was it wise leaving me in Varanasi?" he said, with a vehemence that made me question everything I knew. Then he calmed. "Do it, please. Just this once. A reset."

I thought of my warm bed. The safety of the camera shop confines. I thought of a bearded face watching me from a television screen. I thought of the River Cam and a Cud T-shirt. I thought of the connections that place ourselves where we are. I set up the tripod.

"I can't be held responsible . . . " I began. Then I said nothing. There was nothing more to be said.

Pryce stood before the first structure, his body positioned as it had been in Wimpole Hall. I put my eye to the lens. Behind him, the doors stretched to the horizon. I was reminded of a hotel at Heathrow, where I had been ensconced on my return from India and had been informally questioned by the police. One corridor was flanked by two large opposing mirrors. By standing at a certain angle the mirrors reflected each other over and again, their frames forming part of the reflection, as though they were doorways. I'd decided to take a photograph, but whichever way I positioned myself it was impossible to do so without being in the shot.

"I'm ready," said Pryce.

I depressed the shutter.

In the cold air, I could see Pryce shivering. I was too.

The effect was immediately obvious. Pryce wasn't fixed in place. Each time he shivered, he shimmered. Something shook out of him. With my eye fixed to the lens, I decided to accept this as part of the image capturing process, but the truth was I didn't want to look beyond the lens. After what seemed an indeterminable amount of time, the photograph was taken and the timer ceased its countdown.

I looked up from the camera. Before me, Pryce stood still. Whether it was the residue of my eye concentrating through the lens or a trick of the light, I wasn't entirely sure, but there seemed to be a hole directly in the middle of his forehead, through which I could see the beginning of the enfilade behind him.

"Did it work?" he asked.

But before I could answer 'Did what work?', his body fell forwards and he landed face first on the ground without any attempt to arrest his fall.

Behind him, beneath the first doorway, I recognised one of his Wimpole Hall friends.

"Did it work?" she asked.

I opened my mouth.

The girl fell forwards in domino fashion, her face centimetres from the soles of Pryce's shoes.

Behind her: "Did it work?"

Behind him: "Did it work?"

Behind him: "Did it work?"

"Did it work?" "Did it work?" "Did it work?"

Body after body fell through each respective enfilade onto the ground. Long before the last had fallen, I had fished Pryce's car keys out of his pocket and was skidding down the slope towards the parked car, the tripod tripping me up like a third leg, the camera slung around my neck like a third eye. I didn't stop the pace until I reached Cambridge, somehow navigating the beginning rush hour traffic. Leaving Pryce's car in an unlit alley, I walked briskly to the camera shop and let myself in. Images of bodies falling flickerbook fashion repeating over and over even with my eyes wide open. There was no turning them off. I sat in a corner, my head down, my body slumped.

◅◦▻

Before Pryce had handed me back my camera on the banks of the River Cam, he had quickly taken my picture. I hadn't realised it at the time, but when the photographs came back from the chemist—sandwiched between a not-quite-symmetrical shot of the Clare College Bridge, and a photograph of a Cud poster we had seen after our drink in the pub—there was an off-focus headshot of me. Blond hair cut in a circle, blue eyes, those lips that no one ever wanted to kiss, and the white edge of my T-shirt just in shot. It was a poor pic, taken in haste, taken without permission, but I'd always loved it because it was so candid. It caught a youth, out on a Sunday stroll, looking around at the world deciding whether it was willing or not to have him live in it.

LOVER'S LANE

STEPHEN GRAHAM JONES

Is there such a thing as an armchair folklorist?

I guess what I'm confessing to before I get started here is that I don't have the right degree for this. Or any degree. I was forty-nine last year when my youngest child, Greta, graduated college, and the previous three decades had been spent being either a new bride, a wife not sure she wanted to be a wife anymore, or a mother to two sons and one daughter, all of whom still come home for the holidays. But I can see in the way they hold their eyes and their shoulders that the old neighborhood is already growing small and quaint to them, will soon be a part of the past they're . . . not exactly embarrassed about—I raised them better than that—but that they maybe don't lead with?

I don't mean to grouse or kvetch, mind. This is as it should be. I remember going home with James on my hip when I was twenty years old and being surprised at how low the ceilings were in the house I'd grown up in. I even stumbled on the buckled floor of the living room and spilled my glass of lemonade down my front side, perhaps baptizing me into this next part of my life.

In that spill, though, I never dropped James. I might not always have been the best wife, but I know I was a good mother. That counts for something.

Also, it sort of counts against me, I think? In the fatigue department, I mean. For all three of my kids' childhoods, my life was so regimented into soccer practices and swim meets, PTA potlucks and booster club fundraisers, that the prospect of consigning myself to the rigorous schedule a degree in folklore would require was . . . daunting? It was daunting. I'm not ashamed to admit that.

This doesn't mean folklore isn't a passion for me. It is, and I think it always has been. I suppose it started with the fairy tales of my prekindergarten years, but on the playgrounds of elementary school and in the parking lots of high school, before I met and fell for Sam, I was always collecting the second- and thirdhand stories circulating over bags of gummy bears and, later, bottles of beer.

I think I always knew, at what I guess I would call an instinctual level, that these tall tales, while almost definitely false, were yet serving an important purpose. They were warning us away from this, they were urging us toward that.

Example: When I was growing up in South Texas, one of the urban legends whispered from kid to kid was the story of an eight-year-old who was down below the border with his parents for a day of shopping. I'm talking Old Mexico here. All's well and fine until these parents suddenly can't find their son. They run up this street, down this alley, back into this store, that restaurant, are in a complete, and completely understandable, panic.

When these parents can't find any Mexican police to report to, they go to the only law they know: the agents at the border. They run up to them, out of breath and crying, desperate for help, are trying to cross the language barrier with volume, really impress upon this disinterested officer the urgency of this missing child, when—*Is that him?*

A man is walking toward the bridge with their son! He's carrying him in his arms as if their son is sleeping, but that doesn't matter. Here he is! This kind man is returning him! Sometimes good *does* win the day!

The parents rush to this man, are shrieking their son's name the whole way, but when this man registers their approach, he takes a step back and then turns, dropping their son, and is gone, folding himself back into the anonymity of Mexico.

The parents slide to their knees for their little boy, they turn him over, and—

It's not good.

The boy's been killed, but not just killed. He's been killed and then his little body's been hollowed out, to be packed with bricks of drugs. He's been turned into a suitcase that won't get checked at the border.

Pretty terrible, I know.

And there's zero factual basis for it.

Yet?

What we all *got* from this thrilling little story was the simple truth that, in crowded places, we needed to stay close to our parents.

But that was years ago, Maddy, you might say. This is the *modern* world now, people wouldn't fall for that anymore.

Well.

Another urban legend going on in the here and now, then. In keeping with the times, which values bits and bytes, snatches and flashes, this one is less a scene, is more a lurid fact being passed around: "If you've cumulatively watched a total of more than four hours and forty-eight minutes of pornography online, then, statistically speaking, you've one *hundred* percent watched a 'performance' by someone who was kidnapped as a child."

The imperative there? Obvious, isn't it? Don't dial up pornography on your computer. At least not if you don't want your advertising pennies funding human trafficking. Not if you don't want to be complicit in children getting abducted, their futures ripped from them.

Effective, isn't it?

That's what I love about folklore. It's endlessly adaptive, and it's always apt. If the story develops a weakness, a hole in its plot, a crack of unbelievability, then . . . the next telling patches it. Or the next, or the next.

And of course that rule about three removes, as in *This didn't happen to me, but to a girl in my third cousin's Sunday school class*—that's one of folklore's more brilliant mutations. It puts these unlikely but compelling cautionary tales just out of arm's reach—just past verifiability, such that what serves as verification is the story's remote possibility and its internal, if tenuous, logic.

Elegant, isn't it?

The story's "truth" doesn't come from a police report, from a newspaper headline. It comes from the very story itself—a closed little ecosphere, dependent upon nothing but a willing audience. The axis the story's truth turns on is that this is too preposterous to have been made up, meaning it must have a kernel of the real nestled in the encrustations of this extended game of telephone.

And? I know that at my age, and with my perceived directionlessness at this point in my life—empty nester, preretirement, married mostly because being single's a bit unsettling—I should really join the rest of my cohort and give myself over to true crime, sifting through already-sifted forensic evidence and whatnot to try to solve cold cases. It's fun to play detective, right? And if you're just playing, are a dilettante, then the stakes are low, and you don't have to worry about politics in the bullpen, or making the grade at the shooting range, or taking the lieutenant's test to get that next pay bump, or what other cases working on this one is keeping you from.

Really, I don't know how more murders aren't committed by actual homicide detectives, finally fed up with all these amateur sleuths mucking around in their failures. Or maybe they are, right? Who would know how to get away with something like that better than the person who's called in to solve it?

But I never caught that true-crime bug. I don't even watch the shows—it never feels *proper*, looking at those photographs of dead people, even with those clean white sheets they spread over them. I mean, imagine you're sitting on the couch watching a show like that and the person on that couch with you is that dead person's spouse, right? Wouldn't you feel awkward, to say the least? And if you're any kind of good person, then . . . it shouldn't matter whether that widow or widower is sitting there or not, should it?

Or maybe I'm just squeamish, or sentimental. I'll admit to being both.

Anyway, I don't have to worry about carrying around the kind of guilt I see as resulting from being into all that true-crime stuff. Cold cases aren't my compulsion. What I *am* into, it's all the Little Red Riding Hood stories we can't seem to stop telling ourselves.

And, since I am—or *was*—just starting out on this new and stimulating venture, what better place to begin than with that most hoary of American urban legends?

Not Bigfoot, I know that's what you're thinking. Leave him to the crypto-zoologists, who have their own set of manias to live with. No, what caught my eye—and where I wish I'd never looked—was that story relayed by a woman who popularly went by the name Abby in 1960.

The hook-handed killer.

◂◦▸

By the time the hook-handed killer appeared in the advice column Dear Abby in 1960, it had already been circulating in America for . . . two years? Three? Five?

That's just it: nobody can really pin it down.

Similarly, they have no real idea where, geographically, this urban legend actually begins—probably due to how fast a good and scary story circulates among the younger set. In short, a couple is necking at a secluded spot when the not-uncommon postcoital excuse of a full bladder delivers the boy to the trees, leaving the girl alone in the car, only to be reduced to tears and shrieking when the boy shortly turns up dead—usually eviscerated and hung above the car. The Dear Abby version is tamer, of course, as her regular readers would only tolerate so much. In that version, a couple is making out at their local lover's lane when they get news that an escaped convict with a hook hand has been spotted nearby. They have a close call with . . . they're not sure what, probably just their own nerves, but when they get home later, they find a telltale hook in the door handle of their car, proving the closeness of this call, and, in the process, warning any would-be heavy petters away from *their* own lover's lanes.

One theory is that this story originates with the Texarkana Moonlight Murders, which seem to have spawned some movies, if not a whole genre of horror, but if you start there, you end up at the Zodiac Killer—someone killing couples parked in their cars—and, as that would land me in the true-crime territory I don't care for, I decided to try a different angle. My contribution to the legend wasn't going to be an interpretation or an analysis or an extended comparison or a possible identification of a regionally specific variant; it was going to be firsthand, feet-on-the-ground accounts.

By my math, if this killer at lover's lane was targeting teens in, say, 1957, then any survivors would now, two decades into the new century, be in their eighties, wouldn't they?

From my mother's long internment—"warehousing," she calls it—at a nursing home, I know that there are various apps and social networks specializing in reconnecting residents with one another after all the years.

To fast-forward past the part that the true-crime aficionados would probably salivate over—is this my "methodology"?—I generated "child-of" accounts with all the services that I could, using my mother's residency as an anchor, and essentially posted a listing in this twenty-first-century version of the personals: "Did you suffer, witness, or hear about a crime at a lover's lane in the '50s? If so, you can participate in this study. Meals will be provided." That last part was key. It was bait, plain and simple. From listening to my mother's and her friends' incessant complaints about the quality of the food at their facility, I knew that these residents were always looking for a meal that came from anywhere but the kitchen they had nothing but contempt for.

Still, it was two months before the first and only response trickled in.

It was from a woman I'll call Erma, for purposes of this write-up—I hesitate to call it an "article," as I'm not of the flock of academicians, and there's little chance of this showing up in a respectable journal. Rather, it'll be yet more publicly posted ravings from another madwoman locked in the attic of her life.

So be it.

Even we madwomen stumble onto something real every now and again. I know what I know, I mean, and it would be remiss of me not to at least attempt to pass it on.

Now let me get to Erma.

-◦-

Erma Lastname was from the Panhandle of Texas. I use the past tense as, shortly after our interview, she regrettably passed. Her husband predeceased her—that's such a remote way to dress something like that up—and she's survived by five sons, the eldest a decade ahead of me, each of the subsequent four a year behind the previous one.

Her reply to my posting was brief and, she would tell me later, had been typed by her assigned nurse: *I remember this, yes.*

By the time she responded, I had already, in my head at least, recommitted my folkloric efforts to what I thought would be more culturally relevant tidbits: *Did* police on detective shows always consult notepads because that's where they'd written their lines? *Do* hotels always leave the drains of sinks and bathtubs shut to stop insects and rodents from greeting guests? *Is* a not-insignificant supply of the earth's breathable air locked up in tennis balls and bubble wrap? *Do* space programs select crews to be heterogeneous, so that if there *is* alien contact, the aliens won't think all humans have the same skin tone, the same eyes, the same hair?

I was less interested in the veracity of these hard-to-disprove statements than with their various reasons for existing in the first place, but I should say I was also concerned with how folklore was shading away from narrative into plotless, characterless status updates meant to go viral. It seemed as if the truth valence of these statements was beginning to be based less on internal logic or the startle factor—that preposterousness I was talking about before—and more on whether they aligned with the audience's suspicions, and perhaps filled a crack in the edifice of their belief system, a crack they'd never even noticed before, but that, in light of this revelation, was now glaring.

But I dropped all that the moment Erma's reply came in. Her recounting was sure to be a *story*, and that's what the little girl in me still wanted to have read to her.

I remember this, yes, she said.

I booked my flight that afternoon.

⟨◦⟩

Erma was, with a four-footed cane, still ambulatory.

The afternoon meeting time I suggested happened to fall during her daily walk, so I shuffled along beside her, my hand automatically finding her elbow, which I think she appreciated.

Her nurse told me to have her back for her three o'clock meds, hear?

I heard.

We were in Oklahoma. It was where Erma had raised her family. It was where her husband was buried, and, she made a special point of telling me, pride glistening in her eyes, he had insisted on being buried on the *Indian* side of the cemetery.

"He was Native American?" I asked.

It's important to grease the gears of conversation.

Erma nodded, said her second-eldest was the first member of her husband's tribe to be elected to the House of Representatives—*twice*.

Her eldest ran a construction company and the other three were similarly accomplished in their respective fields.

"Do *you* have children?" she asked.

I lied that I didn't. Not because they hadn't risen to similar heights, but, I told myself, because a good folklore collector does just that: collects folklore.

Discovering the actual point of combustion for the hook-handed killer probably wouldn't earn me respect from the establishment, but it might at least get some of them to consider reevaluating *their* methodologies, I imagined. Just because you're unlettered doesn't mean you're incapable.

Too, I should confess, there was something especially thrilling about this. In cupping Erma's elbow in my palm, wasn't I, in a sense, touching the holiest grail of American folklore? If every urban legend does have the smallest dab of the real at its center, if you can ever peel away the countless layers the decades have folded over it, then, by dutifully soaking in Erma's version, I was inhabiting that prime layer, the one closest to the actual event. I was about to be taken by the hand to this lover's lane of sixty-odd years ago, when cars were heavier, skirts were longer, but teenagers were still, as ever, comporting themselves as teens are wont to do. As, yes, Sam and I were wont to do, once upon a magical summer, when I thought I was in love enough to last a lifetime.

But, Erma.

"Well, we weren't there to *study*, like we told our folks," she said with a mischievous grin. "But we also weren't intending to start a civil engineering firm, if you know what I mean."

I chuckled politely with my lips pursed, as you do.

Yes, yes, drive-ins and lover's lanes were, for a moment in American history, the conception beds for a whole generation. Which? Perhaps that explains that generation's turn to the countercultural: they were conceived with radioactive monsters coming through the windshield, or with the light from the dashboard glowing green on flashes of their parents' exposed skin.

That's just catty supposition, though. Not folklore.

Be better, Maddy. You're here to be professional.

"So you *both* survived, then," I led off, prompting Erma to continue.

"Lionel would never let me talk of it," she said, blinking perhaps a little more quickly, as if peering into the past.

"Lionel, your husband?"

Yes.

"Lionel Lastname," she filled in, grinning with a secret joke, I think.

I nodded, looked past her for a moment through a doorway we were passing, into the room of a woman in bed, either sleeping with her eyes open or . . . well. I don't want to put something like that out in the world. Again: What if that woman's son or daughter happens to read this?

"Because you were still arranging your skirts . . . ," I said confidentially, because we had an understanding here, didn't need to broach beyond euphemisms.

Erma brought her other hand around, patting the tops of my fingers on her arm.

"We'd heard about it on the radio," she added.

I mentally gulped, never imagining that *this* part of the story could be accurate.

"Someone had escaped from his chain gang," Erma went on. "There was a countywide manhunt underway, I believe. I only remember because Lionel was antsy. Had he not been on a date with me, I think he would have gone out with a lantern that night as well, to prove that he was an upstanding citizen."

"He felt he had to . . . *establish* that?" I heard myself asking, in wonder.

"People make assumptions, don't they?"

"Because of his—"

"Last name," she said. It was distinctly Native American.

I commiserated.

"Was there anything about . . . Did this escapee have a prosthetic of any kind?" I asked, very unprofessionally. Were I a hypnotist, I would probably provide breakthroughs to my patients at their most susceptible.

Like I said, I'm no professional, here.

Erma stopped walking, left her cane standing in front of her so she could turn, pin me in her watery eyes.

She neither confirmed nor denied this "prosthetic," but the mention of it had unsettled her, I could tell.

"What did the two of you hear?" I asked, redirecting her as best I could. If she ended this interview, all was lost.

"We thought it was junior high kids," Erma said, holding my eyes a moment longer, then turning back to her cane, and our walk. "They were always trying to catch a glimpse, you know."

I'd had two sons, yes.

"So he went to investigate this *sound*," I led off again.

"That was when I saw . . . saw—" Erma said, her non-cane hand coming up to the loose skin of her throat.

"Him?" I asked. "The convict?"

"It," Erma said, weakly.

Now it was my turn to stop walking.

Erma poled ahead, poled ahead, a Charon leading me across the dark waters—my middle child, Michael, had gone through a Greek mythology phase.

I coughed into my hand to explain my falling behind, caught up, took her elbow again.

"It?" I managed.

"His chest was—" Erma said, and instead of saying *heaving*, she mimed it, drawing in great breaths and expelling them.

"What was he—it—wearing?" I asked.

To be honest, my only conception of chain gangs in the '50s was from movies, and always involved two people shackled together, running from a posse.

Erma shook her head no at that, squinting now as if trying to see this escapee better.

"I think it was hurt," she said, finally. "That had to be it."

"Lionel hurt it?"

"It was . . . " Erma went on, heedless of my question, "I'm not sure how to explain it. It was tall like a horse is tall. Its eyes were that height, I mean. But it was all dark, too, like diesel smoke, and there was something oily dripping off one of its arms? It put me in mind of my—of my father coming back from the barn after birthing a calf."

"What color were the eyes?" I asked, when what I really meant was *Did those eyes reflect light?*

I was considering the distinct possibility that what Erma and her beau had encountered that night had been an actual *horse*, as she had almost said, broken free from its pen, a horse scared enough to rear up when approached, and terrify a couple of kids.

Urban legends have been started with less, I have to suspect.

"Yellow?" Erma answered, about the eyes, and this is when she stumbled. Physically, not conversationally. Distracted as I was—enthralled as I was—I didn't catch her, instead fell to my own knees in trying to soften her fall.

Because this was the kind of facility it was, there were cable-pulls above the handrails in the hall to announce an incident like this. Dutifully, even though it would be the eject lever on this interview, I pulled that cable.

"It was dripping off its wrist," Erma went on, clutching my forearm with her fingers now, as if desperate to finally get this across to someone, unburden herself of it. "It was dripping where its hand *had* been, see? I would find Lionel in the bushes later, unconscious, and some of that . . . some of it would be on him."

"Blood?"

"It was oily."

"What happened to the hand?" I asked.

Feet were scuffling our way. We were almost out of time.

"The reason it was breathing so hard was that its . . . it was pushing the bone out from its arm, I think. The new bone. And it was—the end of that bone, it was curled at first, like it wanted to go back up, like the night air hurt it."

Erma mimed this, forming her own hand into that iconic hook for me.

I was trembling at the base of my jaw. In my chest.

"And then what?" I managed to ask.

"That's when I started screaming," Erma said, with a self-deprecating chuckle. The fall had been slow enough that she had suffered no injury.

Though my posting had intimated a meal for participation in this study, Erma's main nurse informed me she was on a limited diet, and probably wouldn't remember my obligation to feed her, anyway.

I sat in the parking lot for two hours afterward, my hands shaking, trying to write down every last detail of this: lover's lane; tall as a horse; chest heaving; no hand; blood or oil; boyfriend unconscious; the screaming.

Urban legend indeed.

⟶

The autumn after that summer was when that nurse from Erma's facility notified me of her passing, as I'd requested. I imagined her five sons standing graveside, their cheekbones sharp as tomahawks, their eyes flinty sharp, their suits perfectly tailored, none of them knowing of the horror their mother had lived through, or of the folkloric cycle she had once been involved in.

Because I had to know, I petitioned for her husband's death certificate. It was leukemia, when I would have bet on diabetes or high blood pressure, but not the stereotypical alcoholism or suicide—give me some credit, please.

Idly, very circuitously, I asked Sam if, had we had some unexplainable event during our short courtship, would *he* have asked me not to speak about it?

"Unexplainable how?" he asked back, his engineer brain already scoffing at the possibility of something existing beyond explanation, his index finger hovering over the remote to un-pause the airplane documentary I'd just forced him to look up from.

I told him to never mind, never mind, and went about my day.

That night it was grilled-cheese halves and tomato soup from the can. The sandwiches were browned darker than he preferred, but, perhaps sensing the glare waiting for him, he didn't say anything.

Such is marriage.

When he went on his annual golfing tour with his old pals from the military, I went to Texas.

Erma's hometown wasn't difficult to find.

As near as I could tell, not only had it not grown in the years since she'd been a girl there, but it had actually contracted. What this meant to me was that, cell phones and internet be damned, the teenagers around these parts were probably still sneaking out to more or less the same places as their parents and grandparents had.

I wanted to stand in the place Erma and Lionel had parked, once upon a frolicsome Saturday night.

Would the moon look different? Would the pull tabs stratified into the dirt have changed designs as technology got better and better, the closer they were to the surface? Would I still be able to hear the insincere protestations of Erma, and the regrettably sincere protestations of less fortunate dates? Would the muttered promises of all the boys still be whispering on the night breeze? Would there be a single headstone planted there for all the lost virginity?

More important, would there someday, after my discovery surfaced and caught the world by storm, be that least likely memorial ever—a historical plaque to commemorate the actual, physical, geographical starting point for our most widely disseminated piece of folklore in, as *Reader's Digest* would have it, "these United States"?

I was hopeful, I'm saying.

But I was also completely unprepared.

⬩

Erma's hometown was a grain elevator, a drive-up hamburger stand, a feed store, a sprawling gas station, and one-story homes gridded out from that for a few blocks, with everything huddled around the train tracks, which I'm sure once upon a time had chugged economy and possibility to these dusty plains. I am from Texas, yet this was unfamiliar to me. South Texas towns, perhaps due to different geography and different industries, are completely different, might as well be in a different state altogether.

In my head I was now calling myself Abby. As if, to research the column I was planning in 1960, I'd done my due diligence and come to confirm this story. It doesn't matter what goes on in your head, so long as you don't let it percolate out to your face. Like I said, I've been married for thirty years now.

Since I was woman alone in strange environs, the first place I went was the gas station. It wouldn't do to strand myself on some farm-to-market road.

The clerk informed me that there was a motel, but it had been shut down for ten years. After delivering this, he just watched me.

"You grew up here," I said, as if informing him.

He nodded, rolled his toothpick from one corner of his mouth to the other.

"Can you tell me where—" I said, leaving a pause like that so he could suspect I was gathering my words. Actually, I'd been considering them for the whole flight out. "Can you tell me where the high schoolers go on the weekends, to . . . be *alone*?"

He extracted his toothpick, studied its wet-broomstick end, then flipped it, inserted the dry end into his mouth.

"You mean Black Man's Bluff?" he said, the most beautiful dimples creasing his stubbly cheeks.

This caught me off guard. There's every chance I gasped the slightest bit, big-city woman that I guess I am now. I'd been expecting something more along the lines of *Babymaker Bluff* or even something as crude as *Park 'n' Ride*—I hadn't allowed that anything *racist* would come into these proceedings.

The clerk chuckled at my reaction, then upped his chin to a burly man suddenly behind me, wishing to purchase a loud bag of chips and a precariously tall soda. After this transaction, I stepped back into the clerk's judgment radius.

"What?" he said with a grin. "*You're* not Black."

He was right. But still.

This brazen clerk shrugged like the jig was up, or not worth maintaining, said, "It's not what you think. My dad's science teacher tried to get the college down toward Closest City to come do a study, but they said it wasn't in the style of the Indians of the region, so had to be contemporary, a prank or something."

"It?" I had to ask.

This urban legend was spilling over with that pronoun.

"The Black Man," the clerk said with a shrug. "You'll see."

"I will?"

"Why do you want to go out there?"

"Curiosity," I told him. It wasn't the full story, but it wasn't a lie, either. When he just stared at me, I added, "My aunt told me about it, and she just passed."

Mentioning dead relatives usually stops more questions from coming. But there was also the fact that to someone hovering around twenty, I couldn't have been interesting to this boy. Had I been his definition of young and pert, he might have offered to chaperone me out to this Black Man's Bluff.

Instead, he drew directions in smudgy blue ink on the back of a napkin.

And, yes, if you're wondering, this is a significantly reduced and edited account of how I found my way out to Black Man's Bluff. If only investigations were as coin-drop as my rendering, yes? But you don't want to follow me all around town for two hours, asking this and that person, then cobbling together a location and history from these grumbled tidbits. Rather, I'll just agglomerate them all into the clerk, the gas station.

All that really matters are the directions, right?

I was forging out into the wasteland to see this town's lovers' lane.

If I'd thought Sam would pick up, I might have informed him of this, for safety, but he never answers his phone when he's "on the links," as he says.

I was on my own.

-◦►-

The name *Black Man's Bluff*, instead of being racist, was in fact strictly descriptive: there was a ridge of sandstone thirty feet high cresting out of the dryness like a submarine prow, gradually surfacing for maybe forty yards, tonsured in brush, and on its pale face, just like the clerk at the gas station had intimated, there was the eponymous Black Man. I couldn't miss him. He had been outlined in bright yellow spray paint, and had been given those yellow eyes Erma had remembered, which didn't exactly give me confidence in her story. Alongside him on that rock face were other outlines—blue, red, green—around a diminishing line of smoky black men, and on every other reachable surface there were names and years, hearts and stars, and more than a few rude cartoons.

At one time, this bluff—a generous term for the formation—could perhaps have held petroglyphs. Kids had found it decades and decades ago, though, and made it their own. To be honest, I wasn't even sure which "black man" was the one that had given this lover's lane its name, but I knew one of these gentlemen must have been there first, before his scissor-angel siblings lined up to either side of him.

What it looked like more than anything was that a regiment or unit of soldiers—Sam would know the proper term—had marched up from the earth's molten interior, and, still hot from their march, sizzled out through the rock, leaving their ashy silhouettes behind.

The name of the place and that name's origins weren't why I was there, though.

Driving carefully, I crept my rental car up the backside of the bluff to park near the sharp drop-off, as senior class after senior class must have done. At nighttime, my headlights would have been two discs glowing on the clouds like alien saucers, and the view, which already went for miles, as flat as this landscape was, stretched even farther now, from this higher vantage point.

I stepped out, soaked this magical place in.

"You found it, Abby," I said out loud, proud of myself.

The brush immediately to the left could be where Erma had first seen "it," and the brush a little farther out was probably where she had found Lionel curled up, and sat with his head in her lap until he opened his eyes, saw this angel smoothing his hair.

I wanted there to be footprints I could run my fingertips over, or ichor still balled up in the dirt, immune to the decades. Instead, not unexpectedly, there were beer bottles and beer cans scattered about. Standing on the precipitous edge of the bluff, I could see an old couch rotting in the brush below—surely it had been delivered out here to stargaze from, to make out on, to drink beer on, but then later visitors had tumbled it off just to see it fall.

"Erma," I said into all the nothing. "Lionel."

That's not his real name either, mind.

I turned back quickly to my car as if to surprise the two teens behind the windshield, who could have been Sam and me during our whirlwind courtship, but of course my rental car was empty.

And, I wish I could make this more exciting by detailing how I lost my balance, had to pinwheel my arms to keep from falling off the bluff myself, but I'm hardly so careless.

I did, however, imagine Erma's hook-handed killer from that night sixty years ago. He wasn't a convict trying to make his—*its*—escape, he was a being who had smoldered up through the rock itself to climb the bluff, investigate the mating rituals of these high schoolers.

And I would be remiss if I didn't offer the parallel you can probably already see, obvious as anything: These lurkers at lover's lanes, they're grim reapers, aren't they? They're a relationship's expiration date, personified.

What I'm saying is, had I, in my girlhood, looked past Sam's shoulder, over the dashboard, then surely I would have seen a similar figure menacing us. No: waiting us out.

But, as happens, the windows were too steamy, and life was already getting started anyway, never mind my palm slapping the fogged glass, nor the yelp I tried to swallow, which of course coincides with my eldest, James.

I say this just so you can trust that I'm being honest here.

You'll need that trust for what comes next.

◄◦►

The lie I told Erma's youngest son's wife from my home in California, with Sam right in the other room, was that I was looking for information on her erstwhile father-in-law's graduation class, as it had also been my grandfather's graduating class.

I was an amateur genealogist, see?

"Are you a twin, then?" she asked back.

"Excuse me?"

"You're from That Town, aren't you?"

"We moved before I started school," I informed her, praying for no more questions like this, please.

"Oh, wait, you must not be old enough," she said, perhaps switching her phone to the other ear, by the sound. "How old are you?"

I told her.

"Yeah, you just missed it, then," she said. "But Glen says they held the record for a while, for the most twins per capita. Wild, right?"

I didn't know what to say to this.

"That was only for a few years, though. Someplace in India has that crown now."

"India," I said, just to be participating.

"Who are you, again?"

"Abby Indian Name," I lied, on the spur of the moment.

"Oh, you're Indigenous," she said.

"Native American," I corrected, but not forcefully. Wasn't that what I was supposed to do in this imaginary headdress, these invisible but beautifully beaded moccasins?

"We might be related, then, right?" she said with a nearly palpable titter.

I laughed along with her.

And, yes, I'm setting this up like she was my first call. She wasn't. Members of Congress aren't easy to get hold of, and CEOs can be tricky as well. I'd learned, through much trial and more error, to call these five sons' homes during working hours. The men were perpetually unavailable, their wives even less so.

"We might be, yes!" I said, about the two of us being related.

"You're not a five like Glen, either," she said.

"A five?" I asked back, standing to walk and talk, in hopes of working some of my nerves out. It's not often that I impersonate another culture, I mean, and I knew from previous interactions that these wives weren't supposed to be giving information out.

My genealogical mission was surely harmless enough, though.

And? With Erma, as near as I could tell, possibly being the only one from her graduating class to have still been recently living, these Lastname descendants were my only hope for more information.

Lionel might not have wanted his *wife* talking about their premarital escapades, but . . . fathers will, in the sordid ways of men, pass on certain tips and tricks to their sons, yes? At least they might if they want grandchildren?

The so-called moves Sam had used on me, anyway—I was pretty sure, even at the time, that they'd been drawn from a well of lore passed down from his older brother, who had to have gotten it from their father.

For all I know, James and Michael deployed those same moves in *their* adolescent escapades, about which I knew never to ask.

"You know, like Glen and his brothers," this wife said.

"I don't follow," I told her.

"That's right, you left," she said. "I mean, but it's no secret. Before all the twins, five of the football players—Glen's granddad was a linebacker—each had, if you can believe it, five sons themselves."

"In the same years?"

"Weird, isn't it? Why five? And why all boys? Can you imagine how those houses must have smelled?"

I could, yes.

"That's . . . statistically unlikely, isn't it?" I said.

"And on top of that?" she said, whispering now, perhaps because Glen was coming in the front door. "They're all like Glen, like Angus, like Mark . . . "

When she left that open-ended, I filled in, "Successful?"

Yes.

"Do you know if these other four fathers of five"—it was the only term I had—"do you know if they had an experience out at Black Man's Bluff, by chance? That's the lover's lane in Erma's hometown."

"I know what it is," this wife said. "Glen took me there, showed me the . . . *it*. It was like going to church for him or something."

This confirmed it, then: Lionel *had* told his sons about that night.

"What was that out there that night, with your—your mother-in-law?" I asked, trying and failing to keep the urgency from my voice. "It wasn't that man from the chain gang, I know."

"*Chain gang?*" this wife asked, louder now, as if announcing our call to whoever was in the room with her. "What does this have to do with—with ancestry? What did you say your name was?"

"Dear Abby," I said in farewell, and gently re-cradled the phone, held my hand over the receiver as if to keep Glen Lastname from working his way up from it to continue the conversation.

Maddy, Maddy, Maddy, I said to myself. What *have* you stepped in?

-‹o›-

In researching this statistical anomaly of five sons per father for all five fathers, who are *brothers*, I found the names of the other four football players from Lionel's class.

Each son had made something of his life as well, just like the Lastname boys. These men now held public office, chaired boards, were television evangelists, news anchors, celebrity actors, and, just as statistically unlikely, none of them had passed on yet, or divorced, or fallen into any kind of ruin.

I could confirm the cause of death only of two of their fathers—cancer, leukemia again—but . . . I scrambled to add all this together: five boys take their soon-to-be wives out to lover's lane, each fathers five *sons*, and then two of them die from either leukemia or cancer. But, possibly, the other three did as well?

The real question, though, is: Did they each also have an experience out at Black Man's Bluff? With an "*it*," not a "him"?

This isn't how folklore is supposed to work. Again, I don't have the proper training, but I do have a library, and the internet, and I know that these urban legends and regional or era-specific fairy tales aren't meant to hide a truth, they're meant to deliver a warning: *Don't do this like the people in the story did, lest you share their fate.*

Yes, I had gone looking for the origin point, but it was supposed to have just been a Peeping Tom amputee or some such—a curious anecdote at best, and, if I was lucky, something that could really make my case, a footnote in some conference proceedings. One with my name attached.

When you go through life as this one's wife and those ones' mother, there's a certain rush in finally getting to be yourself, isn't there? And if it's in print, then no one can take that away.

"What is this?" Sam asked me, though. He was standing in his customary space: the doorway between the kitchen and the living room, one shoulder cocked against the door frame.

He was holding the credit card bill from last month.

"When you were golfing," I informed him, "I had to go home, to see to Mother."

He read the bill again, as if unwilling to believe what his eyes were telling him, and he just looked up at me, the question in his eyes migrating to his lips, when the phone ringing startled the cup of coffee from my hands.

I grabbed the closest dishcloth to sop this mess up. Sam crossed to the phone, squinched his nose up about it, was about to hang up when I knee-walked over, took the receiver, and pressed it between my ear and shoulder.

"Maddy here!" I said, my customary greeting.

On the other end was just silence.

But it had a quality, I think. A presence.

"Yes?" I prompted, my eyes flicking away from Sam, who wasn't looking away.

The sense I got from the receiver was . . . emptiness. This great yawning void, like I was back at Black Man's Bluff, only it was darkest night now, and I was alone.

Well.

Up there on the bluff, I *had* been alone.

I could now hear the deep breathing behind me, though. The—and I have no other word for it—*distasteful* breathing? As if this presence either didn't approve of me or didn't like the quality or the taste of this Texas air.

Paranoically, I looked down to my own hand, sure it was going to be gone, that my radius and ulna were going to be spiraling out in a helix to confirm the baseness of this air before trying to curl back up into my forearm.

"Nice, Maddy," Sam said from the sky of my reverie.

It brought me back to the living room of my home.

I lowered the phone to see what he was scoffing at.

I'd cut myself, cleaning my shattered coffee mug up, and my blood was slathering the receiver.

"*Texas?*" Sam said then.

I closed my eyes.

⁃o⁃

Be aware that this isn't a confession. It is my fault, I'll own that, but there's what happened, and then there's what's *happening*. Of the two of them, my complicity hardly matters at all.

But for you to believe what's happening, I do need to first take you through what happened.

The calls persisted for four days, but they never again came when Sam was home. What this told me was that the caller must have eyes on the house. What other explanation could there be?

I kept the curtains drawn, the doors locked.

In the darkness of my living room, I watched the news report about Glen Lastname's wife's tragic accident. Even in death, she was still a "wife," not a person with a name.

"Oh," I said, bringing the side of my fist to my mouth.

This prompted me to call the home phone number of Erma's main nurse. She'd given it to me, she said, because the facility's phone banks were a labyrinth.

This nurse wasn't with the facility anymore. Evidently, Erma hadn't passed of natural causes, but rather had aspirated her dinner, which had turned into pneumonia, which at her age had been a death sentence. This nurse, whose duty it had been to proctor each of Erma's meals, had been let go for neglect, even though, she insisted, she had spooned each bite of Erma's dinner in with no issues whatsoever.

I told her I was sorry, I was sorry, but the whole time I was picturing a tall form of swirling darkness at Erma's bedside deep in the morning, pouring cold chicken noodle soup down her throat.

Two people I'd spoken with were dead.

Could this be coincidence?

Worse, it being election season, the second eldest Lastname son was in the news, and on commercials.

He was tall, handsome, reliable, and had, according to his party, a certain higher office targeted.

This was when I stopped watching the television.

"Mail?" Sam asked one evening after dinner.

For our whole married life, I had always been the one to trek to the mailbox, then sort the mail between us: junk mail to me, bills to him.

I nodded that, yes, I'd forgotten to get it, but didn't explain to him that it was because I didn't want to be outside.

People always talk about the Texas sky? How big and empty it is?

I felt like it had expanded. I felt it was out there waiting for me.

"Maddy?" Sam said, when I wasn't replying.

"Okay, okay," I said, and battened my robe down, checked my hair to be sure I didn't have curlers in—this wasn't 1988, but still—and shuffled out the front door.

How, in the movies, certain directors have their thumb on that ZOOM button that makes an object's or a person's background stretch away? I was experiencing this with the mailbox: it was both the only thing in the world and the thing the farthest away from me.

Step by reluctant step, I crossed that impossible distance, my back crawling with what felt like the weight of hungry eyes, and when the Dickersons' garage door across the street suddenly sprang to life, grinding up, I actually gasped, my heart hammering under my palm.

Karl Dickerson's headlights swept across me, stranded there on the sidewalk, and I shielded my eyes as best I could, which he must have taken for a wave. He stopped, his passenger window lowering so he could say, "Maddy! Been too long!"

"I know, I know!" I called back to him, so grateful for this tether back to the world.

"Cards and drinks Friday?" he asked.

It's been our neighborly ritual once a month for years.

"Tell Cindy to bring those sausages?" I said back.

"You know it!" Karl said, and swung his car into their garage, leaving me alone again.

Struggling ahead to the mailbox, I noted that my right hand was extended as if holding a precious egg—no, I realized: as if cupping a fragile elbow.

In my folklore studies, which is what I called the library books I checked out, the internet searches I ran, there are always stories of someone going for firewood on a winter night and then not coming back. All that's left of them are their abbreviated footprints in the snow.

It doesn't snow in my part of California, but this was no assurance.

All I seemed able to think of was that dark form at Black Man's Bluff, its chest heaving. It was—in my susceptible state, I could now see that that smoky form hadn't been drawn on the bluff at all, but rather it had been left behind when this thing emerged.

To do . . . what?

But I knew, of course.

The reason it wasn't killing these football players was that it *needed* them. It was doing something to them, or implanting something in them, or infecting them with something.

Something that they, returned to the front seats of their cars, were passing on to their wives. To their sons.

I think, standing out there, my mailbox receding and receding, that what I was certain was about to happen was that a black SUV was going to ease past. And even though a member of Congress isn't the president, it was going to have little American flags at the front corners of its hood.

It was going to stop, I knew, and a rear door would open for me, to swallow me.

All because I like fairy tales.

I stumbled ahead, the fingers of my hand spread for this fall, but instead of concrete, they found the mailbox.

I clattered it open, pulled the mail out, held it against me, and when I looked back to the house to see if Sam was watching, if he was documenting this continuing indignity—

This is the part where I need you to trust me. To believe me.

These aren't just the rantings of a woman who spends too much time alone with herself. I have read too much folklore, and read too much into it, I know, I admit to that, it's got to be a documented danger of the profession, but that doesn't mean I didn't see what I saw.

Standing on the roof of my house was a tall form, its chest heaving.

It was here.

Just like Erma had said, too, its left hand—of course the left—wasn't a hand at all, but something else. A weapon? An ovipositor? Something dripping, that black whatever running down our composite shingles to pool into sludge in the gutter.

"Go away!" I screamed to it, the mail fluttering away from me.

I had fallen to my knees but had not felt the impact.

Russ and Caroline's porch light next door came on and I looked to it, grateful for witnesses, but I immediately knew this to be a mistake.

I shouldn't have looked away.

By the time I settled my eyes back on the roof of the house I'd raised my family in, there was nothing standing there.

Caroline rushed out, held me by the shoulders, and Russ stumbled out a moment later, his long-retired service revolver by his leg.

"There, there," was all I could get out, pointing to my house.

Russ and Caroline, with just their eyes, confirmed their respective roles here: she stayed with me while he crossed the lawn, stepped onto our porch.

Sam met him, drink in hand.

"Russell?" he said, looking past the revolver to me, on my knees at the mailbox.

And so I became the crazy woman that night. The one whose own terrors get the better of her. The one who flinched away when her husband extended a hand to touch her shoulder. The one whose daughter was called in to talk to her.

I didn't tell Greta any of this, though, and she's my flesh and blood.

I'm only telling you, dear reader.

Only you.

◄◦►

You might ask why I'm posting this in this forum.

First, it's that I don't have permission to place this anywhere respectable. I mean no offense, but the internet version of a tabloid is the only outlet available to me.

Second, if you're seeing this, then please, copy it out, paste it forward? What I mean is that instead of attaining political office, Glen Lastname pioneered a social media company. One with its fingers in every last cookie that makes up our digital souls.

I have to think that my efforts to publicize this—to alert the world—will be swarmed with bots, or however things are disappeared in today's online world.

Third, the dynamic of this forum seems to privilege inexperience and ineptitude. Again, I mean no offense, but it seems that, here, the less well an account is written, the more it comes off as a transcription of something real and actual. Each missing comma is another mark in the account's favor, yes?

Though I don't have the stomach for the various spelling and grammar gaffes that are a badge of honor at a place such as this, please don't hold that against me. I am *roiling* with ineptitude, here, I hope that's obvious. I looked where I shouldn't have, without the training one needs for an expedition like this. My errors may not be mechanical, but, believe me, they're there all the same.

Just, instead of being in ink, as it were, they're in blood. The blood of a woman content in her nursing home. Of another woman, who never should have answered the phone one afternoon.

And of someone else, yes.

When my paranoia became more than Sam could deal with while sticking to his golfing schedule, and when I refused the various dementia tests my neighbors were whispering to him—fifty isn't too young—he bundled me into the car to deliver me to James, who was supposed to talk some sense into me.

Whereas Greta was the child I would confide in, James had always been the one I would *listen* to. His rationality and calm demeanor—I was proud to have produced a son like that, and I trusted his judgment.

Because his practice is in Salt Lake City, however, this was to be an all-day drive.

Sam dialed his sports statistics in on the radio, and we drove into the heart of America.

Being funneled through a construction zone, I recalled that the first Lastname son had won building contract after building contract—his company was responsible for this bridge, that dam.

Of course.

Let the heavy equipment come, then, I said inside.

Let it flatten this car, and all in it.

The second-youngest Lastname son was, of all things, a novelist, capturing the imaginations of millions of readers across the world.

The youngest was, if you can believe it, the president of the largest folklore society in America. Because? Because it's important, in an effort like he and his brothers are involved in, to keep your finger on the pulse of urban legend. So you can control it. So you can shunt it into the academy, for the stodgy scholars to digest and analyze, explaining how this story is told for this or that or whatever reason—of course it's not real. Is Little Red Riding Hood real?

And, no, I don't know the true nature of this folklorist and his brothers, or of the four *other* sets of five brothers. Aliens, demons? The Antichrist? Something ancient that's been shadowing humanity for eons? If so, then the cryptozoologists, of course, are doing their good work to delegitimize them.

It's all so perfect, so well designed, this invasion, this infestation.

We vote for them, we drive on their roads, we tap our lives into their search bars, we invite them into our heads for four hundred pages at a time. And all because the place where their grandfather—surely that's who Erma saw in the dark that night—all because the place where that tall dark figure with one hand happened to step out of the rock was where the local kids liked to make out.

Dusk fell when we were two hours shy of Salt Lake City.

I wrapped my cardigan tighter around myself and looked over at Sam, intent on the road, right hand at the top of the steering wheel.

Up ahead was an underpass.

Running alongside us in the darkness, five dark forms.

"There, please," I told him, pointing ahead, my whole life tunneling down to this moment, this decision, this—as I saw it—last option.

"What?" he said incredulously, letting his foot off the gas.

"I just need to—to stop for a moment, please," I said, patting the top of his right thigh with my hand.

Scowling at the delay, Sam eased us under the bridge, alongside the concrete abutment.

My plan was ill formed and embarrassing, but—

Fifty isn't *that* far gone from nineteen, is it?

I was going to leave my hand on his thigh in that way he knew, and I was going to hold his eyes and then fold myself across the console, straddle him, the two of us kids again, starting over. After, he would step out to give me a moment, or to feel the wind on his face, glory in his victory, in how good and real and *vital* the air felt coursing through him, and . . . and—

This would be my proof, wouldn't it? If he clambered back behind the wheel in a minute or two, satisfied with himself, then it would have been only my tenuous grasp on reality that had momentarily slipped. It would have been just my nerves getting the better of me. And maybe it would be best, all things considered, if I submitted to those tests, as much as they disconcerted me. Ignoring them, or dismissing the remote possibility of the early onset of dementia—that wouldn't stop its progress, would it? I'm not so irrational as to be able to resist facts.

If Sam didn't climb back in, though. Well.

I honestly hoped he would. I would rather live in that world. Even with him.

But to do this right, I couldn't think about him as he'd become. I had to dial him back in my head to how he'd been on those first dates, eager and sure of himself, full of potential, brimming with hope. In turn, I could feel myself becoming again the girl I'd been thirty years ago, about to embark on a whole new journey, about to have to become aware of a completely different aspect of myself.

I could do this. I *was* doing this.

"Maddy?" Sam said, though, when I started moving across the console—I'm embarrassed to say—he cringed away from my advance, he actually curled away from my monstrousness, pressing himself against the door, a big rig blasting past, perhaps warning him to be careful.

No, I wanted to tell him, *no no no, this is part of it, we have to do this part, it's the invitation, it's the first step, it's how you call them—*

But he was already holding his index finger up to me, though, instructing me to wait while he checked the mirror. When it was clear, he stepped out, holding his phone to the side of his head.

Of course. It wasn't me he was shrinking away from, it was his precious schedule, and his reputation. For our whole marriage, he had always gotten us to our various destinations precisely on time. It was a point of pride with him, not being late. He was calling James. To explain that this wasn't his fault, that "your mother, your mother."

Because he didn't want me to hear, he stepped away, into the darkness.

He was Lionel Lastname, walking far enough out into the night that his date wouldn't have to watch him pee.

"Sam!" I—I finally *didn't* call to him, my fingertips reaching across the dashboard, touching the cool glass of the windshield, the amateur folklorist in me dialing back to Dear Abby, and how that couple hadn't actually rounded any bases, had they? That didn't stop their hook-handed killer from making his approach, though, did it?

I held my cardigan even tighter to my throat, my breath coming in hitches.

When the shadow rushed past my door like smoke, I flinched away, even gave an involuntary yelp, and I was still sitting there when the bushes and abutment and road around the car pulsed red and blue, hours later.

It wasn't a flying saucer; it was the highway patrol.

"Ma'am?" the officer said, leaning down to my window.

I was crying, I admit. Crying and shivering.

We were hours late for James.

"You all right?" the trooper said, and then stepped away, looked at whatever he'd pressed his hand into, leaning down on the car.

I'd been hearing it drip for half the night already.

The trooper, confused, shone his powerful light onto the top of the car, which got his right hand to the handle of his pistol.

And then he trained his light up, and up, and then he was falling away, trying to get his pistol up from his holster, and—

You know the rest.

What you've never heard on the playground, though, probably because you didn't grow up in South Texas, is a certain story about a boy whose insides were scooped out, so he could smuggle illicit material across the border. What you haven't heard, because it's been tamped down and hidden so well, is this series of football players from the '50s, whose insides were similarly scooped out, so that what was being placed inside them could cross the border, into our world.

Once upon a Saturday night, a boy led a girl out to a place where they could have a little privacy.

What's important are the girls left behind in the passenger seat to pat their hair down, and straighten their skirts, and raise these ravagers, set them loose upon the unsuspecting world.

My name is Maddy Greenwold.

I'm the girl who finally stood from the car, her husband covered in a white sheet right there on the road for all the world to see. I'm the girl who, late in life, drifted over to the abutment, to almost but not quite touch that smooth concrete holding thousands of tons over her head.

There was an ashy residue coating the concrete, the rough human form tall and looming.

I expect that over the next few decades there will be a rash of similar, um, "graffiti."

Watch those passages, though, won't you?

I heard from someone in my Thursday yoga group that her former roommate's boyfriend once saw a pair of striated yellow eyes opening in the face of one of these shapes.

Behind them, he says, was the cold pull of eternity.

HARE MOON

H. V. PATTERSON

Mom's ragged scream woke me. I turned over in bed and locked eyes with my twin sister, Lia, as the scream became a wail. And then I heard Dad's voice, a rumbling baritone, comforting her.

"Jana?" Lia whispered, voice taut with fear.

"It'll be okay," I said, getting out of bed. "Come on."

Lia, ever my shadow, followed me to the front door. It was slightly ajar, and our parents huddled just inside, clinging to each other. They didn't stop us when we stepped onto the porch. We'd turned twenty last week; we were old enough to see.

The headless hare hung from the door, a nail through each paw. Its blood was dry already, hours old. A jagged line ran down its belly, and its eviscerated guts and organs lay coiled in a stinking spiral on the welcome mat. Flies and ants feasted on the hare. Their quiet buzzing jarred my ears.

Two guards stood at the foot of the porch. They nodded at me, rifles respectfully lowered. I pulled Lia back inside, shutting the door behind us.

"No!" she said. "Why us? Why our family?"

"It's Ostara's will," said Dad. He and Mom reached for her, but she turned to me.

"You said it would be okay!" Lia said, starting to cry. "You lied!"

"I'm sorry," I said.

I held out my arms, and she collapsed into me. I held tightly while she wept, her tears dampening my nightshirt. Mom and Dad closed in around us, and the four of us huddled together, mourning.

Eventually, the shock wore off. Lia was the first to break from our huddle.

"I want to bury Harvey," she said.

I hadn't recognised Harvey without his head, but I'd never cared for the hares like Lia did. Lia had raised Harvey when his mother rejected him, and he'd been her special pet. I thought it was a mistake to name the hares, to grow so attached to something you knew would die to feed you. Besides, the hares unnerved me. When they stretched, they were longer than seemed decent, and when they stared at you, they saw too much.

"Sweetheart, are you sure?" Dad said. "You don't have to."

"I have to do something," Lia muttered, sniffling.

Lia wore her heart on her sleeve for the whole world to see. I felt things as deeply as she did; I just hid my emotions better. It was hard to be strong all the time. But I was the oldest sister, even if only by a handful of minutes, and it was my responsibility to make the tough choices.

"I'll help," I said. Unlike me, Lia wasn't used to handling dead bodies.

"I want to do it myself," she said.

"Fine," I said, a little shortly.

Our hands were the only thing about us not identical: Lia's were soft, her palms smooth; mine were calloused and rough from my lessons with Dr. Fetch and working in the fields. Digging would hurt Lia's delicate hands. She'd regret not accepting my help.

While Lia dug Harvey's grave, I helped Mom make pancakes with huckleberry syrup and fatty strips of salty bacon. I savoured the tastes of smoke, salt, sugar on my tongue.

We ate no hare. No one ate hare on the sacred day of Hare Moon.

After breakfast, we spent the day together, playing board games and downing endless cups of coffee, tea, and cocoa. We didn't say much, but our eyes spoke volumes, every glance a declaration of love. Instead of lunch, we wandered in and out of the kitchen, nibbling on cheese and crusty bread with butter. Somehow, I'd never realised before how lovely salted butter was, the blessing of it spread on soft bread. I licked my fingers, savouring the sensation.

In the afternoon, I made cookies, desperate for something to do with my nervous hands. Baking wasn't as satisfying as practicing stitches under Dr. Fetch's astute eye or grinding up plants for medicine. Dr. Fetch taught me anatomy as part of my training. She'd shown me skeletons of hares, humans, cats, and dogs, pointing out the similarities in structure all mammals share. Harvey's paws and my hands both possess carpals, metacarpals, and phalanges. I loved watching the miracle of my fingers, my flexor tendons beneath my skin, all fifty-four bones and forty joints in my hands and wrists working together as one, just as every member of our community did.

As God in his Heaven and Ostara in the Earth willed it. Amen.

The hours bled through my fingers more quickly than I thought possible. Soon, the sun was a searing ball of orange fire setting the tops of the Hawthorne trees alight. We dressed in our finest clothes and headed for Church, flanked by our guards.

I couldn't help looking back over my shoulder. The moon was rising behind our house, painting it silver. Lia squeezed my left hand, and Mom took my right as Dad pressed gently against my shoulders, urging me onward. We were all thinking the same thing as our home vanished from sight: one of us would never see it again.

⟵○⟶

We walked into our Church's cool vestibule, down the centre aisle to the very front of the congregation. As I settled into my seat, I held myself straight and tall, my thoracic vertebrae pressing against the hard, juniper pew. My mind turned over what would come, what Dr. Fetch had whispered would happen if our family was selected. What I needed to do to survive. I wasn't sure if I could make the choice if the moment came. My heart beat quickly, in time to my racing thoughts, and I was grateful no one could see the fear and grief lurking beneath my composure.

A stranger, a young man about my age, pulled me from my thoughts. He smiled widely as he seated himself in the pew beside me. Outsiders were rare, but we received them graciously when they arrived in our community, guided by the hand of Ostara.

"Hello! I'm Isaac," he said.

"Hello," I replied. He waited, but I didn't give him my name.

"I'm really excited to be here today, on the Feast of Ostara! I'm writing an article about it," he said, gazing around the Church. "This is a gorgeous building. It's so similar to my grandparents' Church!"

I smiled politely. I don't interact with many outsiders, but Dr. Fetch said they're always surprised that our Church looks so familiar. I don't know why. Our ancestors were Christian, and we still honour God the Father who created the world and Christ the Son who died that our souls might be redeemed. We sing the same hymns and read the same Bible our forefathers brought ashore after The Second Flood.

Dr. Fetch arrived, clothed in dark grey, and sat on Isaac's other side. Her silver-white hair was swept into an elegant bun at the nape of her neck, and her worn but vital hands were folded devoutly in her lap. Isaac introduced himself and started asking her questions about the Church and the significance of 'Saint Ostara.' Dr. Fetch answered politely and neither of us corrected him, though it was hard to sit there hearing the Holy Mother stripped of Her divinity. Rendered a mere saint.

"The Crucifix is . . . interesting," he said, gesturing to where it hung above the pulpit. "Do you know how old it is? Who carved it? It's very . . . expressive."

"It's been with us since the founding," Dr. Fetch said.

During my lessons, Dr. Fetch often spoke to me about suffering. She'd told me that many outsiders shy away from Christ's suffering. They minimise the holiness of pain, rendering Christ's body without the stigmata or even displaying a bare cross without a body. Our Christ doesn't hide the truth, the holy agony of his death. His face is contorted, and his crown of thorns drips painted blood. The wound at his side gapes wide, a loop of intestine trailing from it, slithering down his left leg, like the serpent twisting round the Tree of Knowledge.

Reverend entered, cutting short Isaac's impertinent questions. The congregation hushed. Reverend wasn't a harsh man, but his very presence demanded respect. He'd led us through many trials and tribulations, as had his father before him, and his father's father, and his father's father's father, all the way back to the second drowning of the world. His brown eyes were kind but firm. The rustling of his black vestments was the only sound as he ascended to the pulpit and began to speak.

"Brethren, we are gathered here on this most Holy Day of Hare Moon, when we give thanks not only to God in his Heaven and Christ the Redeemer, but to Ostara, the Hare Mother, the Earth Mother, the Warren Mother, whose bounty nurtures us in this life, on this earth."

"Hail Ostara, the merciful," we chanted as one.

"Ostara feeds us—"

"—and we feed Ostara," the words slipped from my lips. Beside me, Isaac scribbled furiously in a notebook, and I tried to ignore the disrespect, the blasphemy. He would be punished soon enough.

After Hare Moon service, everyone filed out of the nave and into the community hall in the basement where the feast lay waiting. Despite my trepidation, the hall was still a cozy, protected space, filled with the delectable scents of food. Great platters dripping with every kind of meat but hare. Bottles of wine, cheeses, nuts, loaves of fresh bread. Salads heaped with all the bounty of the earth, great steaming plates of roasted vegetables. Eggs in every form. The dessert table groaned beneath a wealth of cakes, cookies, brownies, and even specially imported chocolates.

But I couldn't enjoy myself because this year wasn't like other years. My family walked to the raised dais at the front of the hall and sat at the table of honour with Reverend, Dr. Fetch, and Isaac. The guards brought us platters of food that I didn't feel like eating. No one at our table had much of an appetite. Except Isaac, who sat between Lia and me and wouldn't stop stuffing food and wine into his mouth, smiling between bites.

"I haven't eaten a meal this good in years," he said, grease dripping down his chin.

"I'm glad you're enjoying it," Lia said, looking down at her plate.

He probably thought her shy, but I could see the tears shimmering at the corners of her eyes. My heart twisted. How could I bear to lose Lia today, to lose any of them? I silently prayed to Ostara to make Her will known without my intercession, to take the choice from me.

Our guards returned with dessert: piles of cakes, cookies, chocolates, and sweet wine. I bit into a chocolate. It was chalky and bitter on my tongue.

There was no clock in the community hall, but I felt the press of time, of minutes passing. Some people danced, unable to control their exuberance. The young children started to fuss, their faces and fine clothes stained with chocolate. A couple argued, faces flushed with wine. A chair clattered to the floor. Grease and crumbs and icing smeared the walls, the ground, the very air. From the dais, above and apart from it all, the scene grew increasingly nauseating to behold.

I was relieved when the bell rang, silencing the hall. A thousand pairs of anxious, curious eyes turned to us, wondering who wouldn't return. Reverend stood and made a short speech I didn't pay attention to. Finally, the hall drained, leaving us alone on the dais.

"Isaac, we're having a special afterparty celebration," Reverend said. "Would you be so kind as to join us?" His benign smile didn't reach his eyes.

"Sure," Isaac said, swaying a little as he stood. "I think I'm a little drunk."

"It won't take long," Reverend said, holding out his hand.

Isaac beamed back at Reverend with all the trust a boy has for his father. He took Reverend's hand, sealing his fate.

Reverend led Isaac to a small door half-hidden by shadows. Dr. Fetch and my family followed, and the guards trailed behind. It was an ancient door hewn from white oak and secured with a padlock. An image of three hares running in a circle was burned into the door. Their sightless, ancient eyes watched us approach. I'd seen this door dozens of times, but I'd never seen it opened before.

"Remove your shoes, everyone," said Reverend, letting go of Isaac's hand. We obeyed. Isaac fumbled with his laces and needed help.

When all were barefoot, Reverend pulled out a brass key and forced it into the battered lock. The door creaked on rusted hinges. Lia grasped my hand and squeezed. I squeezed back. We saw a dark, narrow tunnel sloping downwards into the earth. Dad wrapped his arm around Mom, and she sagged against him. They looked as if they'd aged ten years in a single day. I gazed into Lia's haunted eyes, identical to my own. My future grief looked back at me.

Ostara, please, I thought. *Please spare her.*

"Single-file," Reverend announced, lighting a lantern. Behind us, the guards and Dr. Fetch lit lanterns as well.

I dropped Lia's hand as Reverend started down the tunnel first, followed by Isaac. I took a deep breath and followed.

Reverend's lantern flickered, casting fantastic shadows on the walls as we descended. The tunnel wound in a tight spiral, like a serpent coiling deeper and deeper into the earth. It smelled strange, not like dirt or musty air, but like dew-drenched clover on an early spring morning.

Finally, we entered a small, roughly oval room. At the far end stood two wooden thrones and a small table. The thrones were tilted back, like lawn chairs. On the table were four small boxes wrapped in green and silver paper, a tray of Dr. Fetch's surgical equipment, freshly sterilised and gleaming, and a large, golden wine glass. Reverend led Isaac to one of the thrones. Isaac blinked and opened his mouth to speak, but Dr. Fetch stepped forward smoothly and pressed a small, liquid-filled vial between his slack lips. Startled, he coughed, then swallowed.

"What—" He tried to rise, but Dr. Fetch pushed him and he slumped onto the throne. Dr. Fetch's tinctures worked quickly. Her scalpels gleamed in the lantern light. I knew Isaac would not rise again.

Reverend set his lantern on the table and gestured for us to stand before it. The guards stood behind us, illuminating the room. I could see a half-dozen tunnels, none of them more than three feet high, branching out around us. I wondered where they led. I hoped we wouldn't have to crawl through them; the very thought made my skin prickle.

"We are gathered here beneath to give thanks to Ostara, the Hare Mother, Queen of the Earth," Reverend said. "Blessed be God in Heaven, and Blessed be Ostara in the Earth."

"Blessed be Ostara," we said.

"We honour and love you, Ostara. We obey your Word and eat of your Flesh. For you, the flowers grow. For you, the Earth is fruitful. You are the nourishing of our bodies."

"Blessed be Ostara."

"We remember your mercy, Ostara. We were cold and adrift on the sea, and you rescued us. We have fed from your bounty, and now we will feed you."

He nodded to Dr. Fetch, who began threading a suturing needle.

"We sew shut the mouth of the Outsider," proclaimed Reverend. "We sew shut his eyes and his ears, for these secrets are not his to speak, his to behold, his to hear."

Isaac's eyes widened, but he couldn't move. Dr. Fetch started with his mouth. I admired her skill, the precision of her stitching. I'd practiced on leather, cuts of meat, and the occasional injured animal. It wasn't easy work. But her weathered hands were clever and sure, never missing a stitch. She only stopped occasionally to dab blood from her fingers. Blood is slippery. I'd dropped more than one blood-coated suturing needle during my training.

She sewed up his pretty eyes next, and I wasn't sorry. He kept staring beseechingly at Lia, and though she stood steadily beside me, I could hear the uneven catch in her breath. It was hard for her, hard for all of us. But that was the nature of sacrifice: it wasn't supposed to be easy.

A few quick stitches closed his ears.

"We now sanctify this offering," said Reverend. Dr. Fetch picked up her scissors and cut away Isaac's shirt. His chest was startlingly white and hairless, like a boy's. Dr. Fetch grasped her scalpel and began the incisions.

I admired her work as she made a long, smooth cut from navel to groin. She cut through epidermis, dermis, subcutaneous fat, and muscle, then made a few vertical slits and carefully pulled the skin and abdominal muscle back in two flaps. Isaac's exposed viscera glistened, untouched by the scalpel. Only the angle of the throne kept everything from spilling out onto the floor. Isaac was still living when Dr. Fetch dipped her hand into his abdomen and carefully examined the intestines. After a few minutes, she turned and smiled approvingly to Reverend, who nodded back. Whatever she'd seen augured well. Someday, I too would gaze into the hidden, secret places of a living, breathing body and discern what lay ahead: a good year, or a hard one.

Carefully, she slid Isaac's intestines from his body and arranged them in a spiraling coil on his lap. The smell of dying overwhelmed the room. My parents winced, and Lia covered her nose and mouth. I didn't move; I was accustomed to the stench of death.

"Have you sanctified this offering?" Reverend asked.

"I have, praise Ostara," Dr. Fetch said.

"Then proceed."

She picked up the knife, and Reverend picked up the cup. She stepped to Isaac's side and drew the knife across his carotid artery. As his life's blood poured out, Reverend caught it in the cup, filling it almost to the brim. Isaac died sightless, unhearing, and in great agony.

"Blessed be Ostara," Reverend said.

"Blessed be Ostara," we repeated.

Reverend turned to us next.

"Martha Abraham, Mathias Abraham, Jana Abraham, Lia Abraham. Do you come here, to the sacred Warren of the Hare Mother, of your own free will?"

"We do."

"Do you accept the fate Ostara decrees for you?"

"We do."

"Then step forward, Martha, and choose."

He gestured to the four boxes on the table behind him. Mom walked forward with her head held high, but I saw her hands trembling as she chose a box and returned to her original position.

"Step forward, Mathias, and choose."

I swallowed as Dad stepped forward, steeling myself. In my chest, my heart raced like a hunted hare, but I kept my face composed and my breathing even. I was the eldest daughter. Only by a handful of minutes, but the eldest still. I was next.

Please, merciful Ostara. Take the choice from me.

"Step forward, Jana, and choose."

I walked to the two remaining boxes. They were covered in a pattern of green leaves and grass intertwined with leaping, silver hares. I stared hard at the boxes, praying that they were identical. At first, they seemed to be, and I felt something loosen in my chest. But then, I saw the left-hand one had a single speck of dark red on its lid.

My hands clenched and unclenched. The red drop of blood watched me unblinkingly, waiting to see what I'd do. I could feel Dr. Fetch's eyes burning into me, could hear her whispered instructions. The marked box held death; the other held life. This ritual was supposed to be a game of chance, fate directed by Ostara's will, but Dr. Fetch had interceded for me. And now, despite my prayers, I was being punished by Ostara: mine was the hand which held my sister's fate.

I wanted to stop time, to reveal the deception, to demand we start over. But I knew better. We'd begun the ritual, and we must see it through. My heart thudded painfully in my chest, a snared hare. It broke something inside me to make the choice, to know that Lia stood behind me, waiting her turn. I reached for the marked box, hesitated, then picked the unmarked box instead. I stepped back, avoiding Lia's eyes.

"Step forward, Lia, and accept what remains."

Lia took the last box and walked, trembling, back to her place.

Reverend nodded to Mom, and she opened her box and pulled out a bright, red apple. Next, Dad opened his box. It held a loaf of bread.

Reverend turned to me. I reached into my box and pulled out two large, white eggs.

Lia looked at me, understanding and anger in her face. She knew that I'd cheated, somehow. She opened her mouth as if to speak, but hesitated. Her face became still and resolved. Guilt, fear, and sadness rushed through me. But someone had to die, and it couldn't be me. Lia had to understand that, didn't she? The community needed me to replace Dr. Fetch when Ostara called her body to the earth, and God took her spirit heavenward. Would Lia understand, or would she halt the offering?

Lia pressed her lips firmly together and looked away from me. She reached inside the box. Slowly, hands shaking, she pulled the hare's head out by one ear. His eyes were half-closed, his mouth open in surprise. Through blood-clotted fur, I could see the pink-white edges of cervical vertebrae.

When Harvey was born, he'd been the runt of the litter. Lia had bottle-fed and tended him before he'd even opened his eyes. Now, she held his severed head.

Tears ran down her face, down Mom's and Dad's faces. My own cheeks were dry, though I knew the tears would come later. Behind my ribcage, my heart shuddered. Bile flooded me, and I hated myself, hated that Dr. Fetch's cheating and my desire to live had sealed my sister's fate. But even as my heart broke, I curled my fingers tightly around my box and did not regret my choice.

Reverend and Dr. Fetch moved towards Lia. She trembled but didn't flee. Reverend offered the cup to Dr. Fetch, and she added a medicine I recognised, one I'd helped make. It removed pain from the body and made the mind go calm and far away.

"Do you, Lia Abraham, of your own free will, take this cup?" Reverend held the cup filled with Isaac's blood and Dr. Fetch's medicine to her lips. "Do you, of your own free will, accept the death within it?"

"I do," Lia said, voice barely a whisper.

"Then take it and drink."

Hands shaking, she reached out. Her nose wrinkled at the taste and smell, but she drank.

Reverend offered the cup to Mom, Dad, and then me. His eyes were firm, but kindness softened the firmness.

"Do you Jana Abraham, of your own free will, take this cup? Will you bear witness to the death of Lia Abraham?"

"I will," I said.

"Then take it and drink."

Despite all the times I'd assisted Dr. Fetch while she set a bone or pulled a child from a screaming mother's womb, I'd never tasted blood before. The blood was warm and thicker than I'd expected, thicker than water. The ancient saying was true. Salt coated my tongue and throat. I pushed down my nausea as I swallowed. A wave of calm washed over me. Reverend walked past me and offered the cup to the guards. Only he and Dr. Fetch didn't drink.

"Lia, please step forward," he said, gesturing to the empty throne opposite Isaac's remains.

Lia looked at me again. Love, anger, and resentment burned in her gaze. Then she turned away. Reverend took the box and Harvey's head from her and set them carefully on the table. Lia stood, gaze unfocused, as Dr. Fetch picked up her scissors and carefully slit her dress open from hem to collar. Barefoot and wearing only her undergarments, she must've been cold, but Lia didn't shiver. Dr. Fetch guided her onto the unoccupied throne.

"The Hare Mother honours your sacrifice, daughter," Reverend said. "She does not wish you to suffer unnecessary pain."

He held the cup to her lips again, and Lia drank deeply until her eyes went soft and unfocused, and she sank against the back of the throne.

Dr. Fetch stepped to the table and picked up a clean scalpel. Reverend bowed his head, hands folded in front of him. Lia stared straight ahead as Dr. Fetch's practiced hands moved down her stomach, and the scalpel slid through her skin like it was butter. Blood trickled out in red rivulets. Dr. Fetch made three precise cuts, forming a rectangular window around her belly button, much smaller and neater than the hole she'd made in Isaac.

When she eased the skin and muscle away, I could see Lia's stomach. Dr. Fetch gently pushed it aside, leaving a bloody cavity. Reverend stepped forward and handed her Harvey's head.

The head fit into the cavity like a child curled inside its mother's womb. Dr. Fetch took up a new suturing needle and stitched Lia closed with care. My own fingers twitched at my sides, my hands mirroring her movements. Someday my hands would be that skilled and precise.

The entire time, Lia didn't look at Dr. Fetch or at any of us. Her breathing quickened as her body slid into shock, probably from blood loss, but her face was blank, serene. I'd never noticed before how large and dark our eyes were, the colour of earth after a summer storm.

Dr. Fetch finished the stitches and took up her sharpest knife. The light gleamed off its unsullied edge. Her arm moved in a single, decisive slash across Lia's throat. Lia convulsed once, twice—then went still.

Seeing my twin dead before me, her sightless eyes still gazing serenely at the dirt ceiling, should have throbbed like an open wound. I knew that tomorrow I'd mourn her, that I'd despise myself, that I wouldn't be able to look Dr. Fetch in the eye. Tomorrow, the whole community would honour and mourn Lia. Her funeral would be beautiful, though the casket would be empty.

But now Dr. Fetch's medicine filled me, leaving room for nothing but the taste of salt and the smell of blood. It was done; there was no turning back time. We had done what was best for all. Praise Ostara.

Reverend began a familiar scripture, one I'd heard so many times my lips moved in tandem as he spoke.

"In the beginning was the world, and the world was wicked," he said. "And so, God sent a flood, and humankind was humbled. But we forgot the lesson, and so God sent a second flood, humbling us further. If not for the mercy of the Hare Mother, our ancestors would have perished."

"Hail Ostara, the merciful," we recited automatically.

"Ostara sent us to this rich and fecund land."

"Hail Ostara of the Fields."

"She sent us braces of hares to eat."

"Hail Ostara, Hare Mother."

"As the hares have fed us, so too do we feed the hares."

"Accept our sacrifice, Dread Ostara."

"Amen."

Reverend fell silent. My gaze drifted from Lia's body to the dark corners of the room. To the tunnels, spiraling off into darkness. I wondered how far they went: how far out, and how far down.

The sounds were faint at first, so faint I thought I was imagining them. The scuffle of small bodies moving steadily across the dirt floor. Then I saw eyes gleaming in the lantern light, one pair, two, a dozen, a multitude. Hares poured into the room, hares of every colour. They surrounded Lia and Isaac, concentric circles of hares, spiraling unending lines of hares. Hundreds of gleaming eyes studied us. And more kept coming, pouring from the tunnels.

Reverend bowed low to the hares. I found myself folding too, my spine curling against my will. And then Reverend was retreating, and we fell into step behind him, heading back the way we'd come.

As she headed past me, Dr. Fetch paused to whisper in my ear.

"I know it's hard, Jana, but you made the right decision. The community needs a doctor, and I am too weary to train another. Ostara understands and honours your sacrifice." She squeezed my wrist then turned and followed the others out of the room.

I was the last to leave, and though I knew I shouldn't, like Lot's wife I looked back. Lia was covered in an undulating sea of twitching fur. I could hear the hares gnawing at her, see the blood staining their paws and twitching noses. From the tunnels, thousands of bright eyes approached, waiting for their turn at communion. I turned and followed the others, my mouth dry and coated with salt.

BUILD YOUR HOUSES WITH THEIR BACKS TO THE SEA

CAITLÍN R. KIERNAN

1.

Sure, I took the assignment, because the rent has to be paid somehow, and somehow I have to keep the lights on, and so what if I was hardly the right person for the job, if the subject in question lies outside both my expertise and interest. I took the assignment because it was offered, and I because I learned a long time ago that if I wanted to get enough work that I don't have to resort to some or another day job, beggars can't be choosers. I take what I'm offered, from whichever print magazine or website, and so tonight I've driven all the way up from Providence to Cape Ann, looking for a gallery in this downpour, the windshield wipers of my POS Honda losing their battle with the cold rain blowing in off the Atlantic. I've had to pull over twice now and wait until it slackened off enough that I could creep along at fifteen or twenty miles an hour. And by the time I reach Gloucester, I'm pretty sure the whole damn thing will be over and done with long before I even *find* the place.

I didn't set out to become an art journalist, or any sort of journalist at all. Thirty, thirty-five years ago, I was going to be a painter. I was almost dead certain I was going to be one of those vanishingly rare exceptions who make a name for themselves, who make a living, who have something to say and say it and, in so doing, leave a mark on the world. That didn't happen. This other thing happened, instead. Doesn't make me special, and I try to keep that in mind. But writing about *other* people's art, that wasn't even Plan B. I was too sure of myself and my talent and entirely too naive to be bothered with a Plan B. And yes, it's made me bitter. It's worn me down. And it's why, this night, I'm on this road on Cape Ann, squinting through the rain-slicked windshield. It's the edge in my voice. And maybe it has left me more vulnerable than some others to what's coming.

"Oh, trust me, you'll know it when you see it," Case said during our very brief phone call the afternoon before. Case Mitchell, the Boston Ave. trust-fund brat whom I suspect wouldn't know a Monet from a Manet, but why should that matter, so long as she pays me on time. Case is the sort of editor who calls her writers *content providers*, who talks about *curating* whichever month's issue, and seems to preface every other word with *super*. But, well, that thing about beggars and choosers, remember?

"Really," she said, "I don't think there's even anything else on that stretch of road for five or ten miles in either direction."

"So, you've been there?"

"Not lately," she said, and I could hear her lighting a cigarette. "Look, if you don't want the job, I can find someone else."

"No, I want the job," I lied.

"Then just show up for the opening, try to talk to the artist, get a feel for the work. We'll be happy with a couple thousand words. Thirty-five if you can manage it." And I told her sure, I could manage it. I am nothing if not a prince among those who pad their articles and squeeze even the driest subject until the very last noun and verb and adjective has been wrung from the thing.

She asked if I still had the same PayPal address, and I told her I did.

"If I don't get lost," I said.

"You'll know it when you see it," she said again, and then she hung up before I could say goodbye or thanks for nothing. And now here I am, picking my way through a nor'easter (or near enough) along the narrow, winding Thatcher Road. On my left there's a fieldstone wall, trees stunted by the incessant wind, underbrush; on my right, there's a wide salt marsh, revealed by the frequent and all-but-blinding flashes of lightning, a strip of mudflats and cordgrass dividing the road from a narrow beach and the granite promontory of Cape Hedge.

I come to a stretch where the road makes a very wide curve, prudently skirting the salt marsh, and *voila*—there it is, so lucky fucking me. The place, this ersatz *gallery*, it truly isn't much more than a shack propped up on a stingy patch of sand and gravel, surrounded on three sides by the marsh. It's hard not to believe the place didn't once upon a time sell live bait or freshly dug quahogs, back before some idiot inherited it from their great uncle Wilbur and decided it could ever pass for anything else. I pull into the tiny, unpaved parking lot, the gravel crunching beneath my tires, cut the engine, and sit staring through the rain at the blinking neon sign above the door, glowing some or another garish shade of bluish green or greenish blue. The glass tubing and rarefied incandescent gas trapped inside spell out JENNY HANIVER, so yeah, this is the place. X marks the spot, as advertised. There are maybe half a dozen other cars out front, all Massachusetts tags (I notice this sort of thing). There's light coming from the windows of the shack, so I know someone's in there. So much for my half-hearted fantasies of "called on account of frog-strangler" and me getting a bottle and some skeezy motel room and watching pay-per-view porn until I fall asleep and dream of more rain.

"Fuck it," I mutter. "Get it over with," and I can hardly hear my voice above the rain on the car's roof. "Get it over with."

Stop stalling, buck up, and yank off the damn Band-Aid. It can't be that bad, and hey, if it is, that just makes the story easier to write. The lousier the art, the easier the copy.

I reach for the black umbrella tucked behind the passenger-side seat, wondering briefly whether it has even the ghost of a chance against this storm. And then I glance back at the windshield and that blue (or green) neon sign. It's not hard to imagine what my father would say right now, my dad who wanted me to go to URI and study something practical, anything I could actually hope to make a living from, at least *enough* of a living to keep up with the damn student loan payments. Sitting there with the rain hammering on the roof, it isn't hard to imagine his gloating "I told you so" scowl, accompanied by one or another incarnation of the jabs that always, inevitably come down to my BFA from the Rhode Island School of Design and fifty cents being maybe worth a cup of coffee. Yeah, fifty cents. No, Dad's never darkened the doors of a Starbuck's. I doubt he's even seen the inside of a diner since 1980, so . . . fifty cents.

I steel myself for the rain and whatever's inside passing itself off as art, and I think about what Joe Gillis says in *Sunset Boulevard,* about how sometimes it's interesting to see just how bad bad writing can be. Or bad painting. Or sculpture. Name your poison.

Then again, I might be surprised. It's happened before.

But I've learned not to hold my breath.

The umbrella does its best. Tattered or not, it's a trooper. I only get a little bit soaked running the twenty or thirty feet from my car to the front door of the place. Splashing through potholes that have become small lakes, and the rain is almost blowing sideways off the marsh. There's no porch, by the way. Not even a bit of an overhang from the roof, so it's a miracle that neon sign hasn't fallen prey to the weather a long time ago. Then again, maybe they only put it out during events, and from what Case told me, those are fairly infrequent. I open the door and step inside, the wind pulling the knob from my hand and banging the door closed behind me. There's a little foyer or anteroom of a sort, a claustrophobic cracker-box affair, and there are metal hooks on the walls for coats. There's also another sign, this one on plywood painted white with bold black lettering: NO SHOES INSIDE. Beneath it, there's a shelf with little cubbyholes; there are shoes tucked inside some of the cubbyholes.

Whatever. My feet are soaked anyway, and I've seen weirder shit at galleries. I take off my shoes and socks, find an empty cubbyhole—not hard, only about half are in use—and stow them inside, laying the socks out flat in the vain hope they might dry out at least a little while I'm inside seeing whatever it is I've been sent to see.

I should say, for what little it's worth, I'm not walking into this bait shack *cum* gallery entirely ignorant. I did take the time to look at what little I could find online about the artist, which truly wasn't much, some scanty reviews. Mostly on West Coast websites, one short write-up in the *Seattle Weekly*. And I also talked to an acquaintance in San Francisco—sort of an ex, a lazy on-again, off-again fuck-buddy thing before I moved back East. He had a taste for twinks and threeways, and I didn't. Anyway, he'd actually been to one of the artist's shows down in Monterey, at a gallery on Cannery Row—Green Chalk Contemporary. No idea what the name signifies, why *green* chalk; maybe it's some obscure reference to the death of the "Sardine Capital of the World." I didn't ask. I tried to get some details out of him about the show, some specifics that might help me prepare, but found him annoyingly reticent to talk about the show. He kept trying to change the subject, asking me when I was moving back to the Left Coast, whether I was sick of New England yet, and so on and so forth. But he did tell me that he'd found the whole thing in rather bad taste, crime-scene type photographs of drowning victims, a couple from a shark attack. He said there'd also been some sort of film, but he didn't elaborate. Then, right at the end of the call, he said something odd, and maybe if I were a little less desperate for work, and a little easier to spook, what he said might have made more of an impression. Maybe I'd have told Case I'd pass on this one, thanks, but call me next time. "It's a rabbit hole," he said. "A real goddamn rabbit hole."

I left my soggy shoes and socks behind, hung my raincoat on one of the hooks, and opened the screen door that led into the gallery proper. I'd already been able to hear the music through the walls—This Mortal Coil's version of Jeff Buckley's "Song to the Siren." But once I got inside, I realized the song was mixed with an assortment of sound effects—a constant sloshing, not the crashing of waves, but more like the slap of water against the hull of a boat tied up to a dock. And gulls. And buoy bells. That sort of shit. It all seemed a little heavy handed, truth be told. But then I saw the masks and forgot all about, well, anything else.

There were maybe twenty people in attendance, more than I'd have expected from the handful of cars parked out front, and every one of them was wearing a mask. I'm not talking domino masks like you'd see at Mardi Gras or Carnival or a masquerade ball. These fully covered the head, so there were only holes to see through. And I'll admit, they were works of art themselves, wearable sculptures cast in what looked to be latex or even silicone, and some of them even had these lights—wait, I'm getting ahead of myself. The masks were meant to represent various sorts of fish, various very particular sorts of fish, the sort that live at the bottom of the deepest parts of the sea and have to make their own light, if they want any. Gaping jaws and needle teeth. Or no eyes at all, just little slits that allowed the wearer to see, but didn't spoil the effect that I was being shown something that was *meant* to be blind. Anglerfish, pelican eels, viperfish, something albino and eyeless—I found a book on deep-sea fish afterwards and looked them up. The sculptor had done their homework. The things were plenty enough lifelike. Grotesque is putting it mildly. And yeah, a few of them—like the anglerfish—had dim lights built in, to simulate bioluminescence, and after they'd been painted some sort of varnish had been used to make them look wet, slimy. For a moment, I thought there must be more of these somewhere, and I was going to be asked by whoever was running the event to put one on. But it didn't happen. That was one of the evening's few mercies. At least I wasn't expected to don one of those godawful masks.

I shifted tense, didn't I? If I actually intended to hand this in, to hit send (so to speak), I'd backtrack and fix it. But I don't.

I'll stick to first-person present. There's something more honest about it.

At least I'm prepared for the photographs. They're pretty much what was described for me from the show in Monterey. Drowned men and women, one child, and all the photographs in black and white. Bloated bodies, faces and fingers that the crabs and other things had gotten to before the corpses had been recovered, those were pearls that were his eyes, and so forth. They're bad enough I almost forget about the masks. I'm standing there looking at them, when I realize no one's saying a word. Not even a peep. Nothing. There's none of the usual indecipherable chatter, hushed voices, everyone talking over everyone else so you can't catch a word of what's being said. There's only the music, "Song to the Siren" on an endless loop, and the accompanying sound effects. I get the Moleskine and a pencil from my jacket pocket, because I should be taking notes. That's what I'm here for, after all, to scrounge enough material for a couple thousand, thirty-five hundred words, just enough to satisfy Case Mitchell and maybe make rent. On the other hand, tonight notes seem like overkill. It's not like I'm going to forget any of this weird-ass shit.

I'm starting to get a pretty good idea what the ex meant by *rabbit hole.*

And I haven't mentioned this yet, but the place smells very strongly of the marshes. You know that saltmarsh, mudflat smell. Part sewage, part sex, salty and slightly fishy. That smell. It shouldn't come as a surprise, but it does.

2.

I want to skip ahead for a moment. Sorta skip to the end, past the end, actually. Someone else might tack this on as a postscript to that night. A final dramatic, eerie beat. For whatever reason, I feel like it belongs here.

It's been almost a week now since the drive up to Cape Ann, and the longer drive back, a week since the show at Jenny Haniver. I blew the deadline, so all that and then there's not even a paycheck waiting at the other end. Just me making excuses when Case Mitchell called, after she'd emailed. After I ignored the email. I don't think there will be any more work coming my way from her. Anyway, it's been almost a week, six days, and last night I get a call from the on-again-off-again ex in San Francisco. Right off, I think he sounds odd, not like himself, but . . . honestly, everything's seemed a little off since Cape Ann. Everything has seemed at least very slightly skewed since that night. Like—I know, like going to see a movie in the middle of the day, a long summer day, and coming out of three hours of darkness back into bright daylight. Your eyes hurt, and sometimes it's hard to shake the feeling that the make-believe world of the movie you've just exited was more real than real life—

Or it's like waking up, after an especially vivid nightmare.

Point is, he calls out of the blue, and he sounds—worried, I think—but I figure that's just me projecting, just my anxiety that's been sitting around drinking and smoking and waiting the past six days for *something* to jump out of the bushes and shout boo. This wasn't that, the call. At most, it was a loud whisper.

But sit alone in a dark room long enough, that's all it takes, right?

"How'd it go?" he says, and I know what he means.

"You weren't kidding," I reply. Not that he'd actually *said* very much at all about that show at Green Chalk Contemporary on Cannery Row.

"Were they wearing the masks?" he asks.

"You could have warned me about that, you know."

"I could have," he says, and maybe he sounds a little sheepish, or maybe it's just that I'm pissed and I want him to. "Frankly, it freaked me out a little when you called like that. I hadn't heard from you for—what?—two years?"

"Just about that," I say.

"You caught me off guard, and then you ask about just the very last thing in the world I would have expected. That godawful show. It freaked me out a little."

"You said that already," I tell him, and he apologizes. "Don't," I say. And when he asks don't what, I say don't fucking apologize. I tell him yeah, it was weird. It was a lot worse than weird, it was some sort of goddamn sideshow, mad Captain Ahab's take on Le Théâtre du Grand-Guignol.

"Then it wasn't just me."

"No," I assure him. "It wasn't just you."

"Well, look," he says, "I came across something, and I thought you might, you know, I thought you might be interested, that maybe it was something you could use in your story." And I tell him there won't be any story, and he apologizes for that, too.

"Fuck it," I say. "I was fed up with that woman, anyway." I'm sure she has a whole stable of Gen Z brats fresh from the Ivy League, armed with newly minted liberal arts and gender studies diplomas, just waiting to do her bidding. And she never has to tell them we're no longer permitted to use words like *Oriental* and *spooky* and *crippled*. "It was a long time coming," I tell him. "So, fuck it. What did you want to tell me."

"But you're not writing the article."

"No, but you called, and this book I'm pretending to read is boring, and I don't feel like TV, so you may as well spit it out, whatever it is."

He's quiet for a moment, a long enough moment that I'm starting to think he's not going to tell me after all, that he's about to apologize for the third time and wish me a good life and vanish back into my past. In retrospect, that wouldn't have been so bad.

"You said Cape Hedge, right? That the gallery was out on Thatcher Road, just before Cape Hedge."

"If you can even *call* it a gallery. You should have seen this shithole," and I start to say more when he interrupts to tell me that he has seen it, that after

I called, and after he found whatever it is he found that's the reason we're talking, he got on Google Earth and had a look at Jenny Haniver for himself.

"It's just a shack," he says.

"That's being generous."

"Something happened there, back in the nineties. Well, not *in* the shack. I don't know if the building was there at the time. It happened in the marsh behind the shack. There's that tidal estuary that winds along parallel to the road, then empties out at the beach, right at Cape Hedge."

"I've been there," I say.

"Right, well . . . back in the nineties, and I want to say it was '94, a girl died there, in the estuary. A Harvard biology student who was up there doing field work, monitoring water quality, salinity levels, plankton, something like that. She wasn't alone. There was another girl with her, another student, and what happened, well, I mean there was a witness, someone who saw what happened."

"Okay, so what the hell happened?"

"A shark attack," he says. "Or an attack by something. It was reported in the papers as a shark attack. The tide was in, so I suppose the water was deep enough it *could* have been a shark. But the other girl, the other student, she said it wasn't a shark. And I can't imagine she wouldn't have *known* a shark if she'd seen one up close like that. They were marine biology grad students—"

This time I'm the one who does the interrupting.

"What did she say it was instead?" I ask.

"Well, she wouldn't. Or couldn't. The two articles I found, they were vague about that. They just said she kept insisting it *wasn't* a shark. But someone from Fisheries and Wildlife who examined the body, *he* said it had been a shark, no doubt about it, probably a bull shark or a great white. A pretty big one. And they took his word for it."

"She would have known what a shark attack victim looks like," I say, and there's this sick feeling in the pit of my stomach, and I'm wishing he hadn't called.

"Well, sure, but she was right up on the thing, trying to save her friend."

"That's it?" I ask. "A girl was killed by a shark off Thatcher Road?"

"Essentially," he says. "I saw that show in Monterey, so I have a pretty good idea what you saw, and I just thought it might be something you'd want to use. But if you're not writing the article . . . "

And there's more to the call, but I change the subject, start in asking him how his job is going, if he's seeing anyone, I don't know. The most mundane questions I can come up with. We talk for another ten or fifteen minutes, maybe. He says if I'm ever back in town I should look him up, for drinks or coffee or dinner or whatever, and I say sure, of course, and then he says he should go. That he has a meeting with a client the next morning, and he hasn't been getting enough sleep. I don't try to keep him on the line. We say our goodbyes. And then I sit there in my kitchen, a cup of coffee going cold, and I stare at my iPhone lying on the table where I set it down. I sit there and I think about the gallery, and I think about the salt marsh behind the gallery, and the river winding out to the sea.

3.

So here I am, barefoot in the shack on Thatcher Road. Here I am in the gallery named after counterfeit mermaids, with this odd mix of "Song to the Siren" and sloshing ocean sounds leaking from unseen speakers, and there are all those awful photographs of dead people, and there are the living in their abyssal masks. It can't be more than seven or eight minutes since I walked in the front doors. The air smells like low tide, and no one has said a single, solitary word to anyone else.

I haven't mentioned the chairs. Towards the rear of the shack there are wooden folding chairs set out, and beyond them is a portable movie screen. There's an aisle dividing the chairs, and just before the aisle begins, there's a film projector set up on a sort of rolling wooden table that looks as if it's been nailed together from driftwood, then given the mismatched wheels of four different office chairs. The projector is an old Bell and Howell. I recognize it because I was in AV club in high school, and there was a time I could break one of those things down and put it back together again. This is a chunky old battleship grey 285 16mm. And at some (I assume) predetermined moment, all those people in fish masks stop milling about and move to the back of the shack, taking their seats in front of the screen.

I say *taking their seats,* because that's the way it feels, as if each of them knew ahead of time which chair was meant for them. It's that precise, that orderly. And when they're all seated, there is exactly one chair left.

The music stops.

The lights dim.

And I almost leave then, just turn around and walk out. I'd done my due diligence. Surely I'd seen enough to scribble down the requisite few paragraphs that would satisfy Case Mitchell. I could tack on a mention that there'd been a bit of film at the end, noting that element of the show without actually divulging the contents of the film. Who gives a wet fart anyway, right? And that's what I'm thinking, standing there, when someone in black—black sweater, black slacks, barefoot like the rest—emerges from—honestly, I have no fucking idea where they came from. They weren't there, then they were, so maybe there was some sort of trapdoor in the floor or something. I don't know. It's a woman, with close-cropped hair that looks as black as her clothing, and she goes to the projector and switches it on.

And I take that last seat.

Call it curiosity. I don't know. I want to leave, as much as I've ever wanted anything. I want to put my wet socks and muddy shoes on, and go back out into the storm, get in my shitty little Honda and drive away from this place as quickly as the speed limit and slick roads would permit. Instead, I sit down.

There's the familiar, nostalgic click-click-clicking from the projector, and 16 SOUND START, then PICTURE START flashes across the screen and the SMPTE Universal Leader counts down, eight to two inside black-and-white rotating clock arms before the jarring sync beep, the 2-pop, and I'm assuming this was tacked on for effect, for a sense of authenticity, maybe; whatever I'm about to see, it seems unlikely it's ever played in any theater or on television. The film begins, a wide shot of a rough sea crashing against a rocky shore, and I'm sitting there half surprised that there's a soundtrack and thinking how that monochrome ocean, captured in a thousand shades of grey, how that could be anywhere at all, the Atlantic or the Pacific, New England or California or . . . anywhere . . . when the waves and the rocks are replaced by a marsh, a cordgrass saltmarsh exactly like the one dividing this shack from the sea, and the camera pans slowly right to left across the grass and mud and settles on the winding course of a shallow estuary channel snaking its way towards the ocean.

The crashing of the waves has been replaced by the soft rustling of the wind blowing over and through the grass, whistling across that grey world.

I don't want to be sitting here. I want never to have sat down. I want to leave, but I keep my seat.

The camera pulls in, only a little, as a naked woman emerges from the grass, the mud halfway up to her knees, and she moves towards the stream, slogging, slow-motion steps. Her blonde hair is long, down past her shoulders, and the wind whips it same as it whips the cordgrass. Her skin seems pale as chalk. The sky above her is overcast, with only a bright smudge to mark the sun, not so high above the horizon. I think it must be morning in the film. Somehow, it *feels* like morning, and if it is, then the eye of the camera has to be looking east, if the sun's that low. And if it's looking east, that's probably the Atlantic, after all. The camera follows her, pulling in close enough that we can see the strain on her face, the effort required of each footstep in that deep, sucking mud. She isn't particularly pretty; I think it would have ruined something if she were. Tiny crabs scatter before her, waving their claws, skittering out of her path.

She pauses and looks back the way she's come.

I don't know where this is headed, and I don't want to find out. I know that something's coming. Something dreadful, and I don't want to see it. I'm free to leave, but I sit very still, like all those others in their masks, and I watch, as if helpless to do otherwise.

Teach me to live, that I may dread the grave as little as my bed. Teach me to die so that I might rise glorious at the Judgment Day.

Who said that? Thomas Hardy? George Eliot? Someone else? Is it a line from a poem or a hymn, and why does it come to me now?

The woman has stopped only a few feet from the water, and for a moment she stands there getting her breath and staring at the stream. It's just possible to hear it flowing past above the ceaseless sounds of the wind. She looks up, just for an instant, as if maybe she's heard something, a gull or a crow or some other bird or another sound entirely, and then she leans forward and plunges her right arm into the mud. She grits her teeth, and she strains, all the muscles in her back and shoulders and forearm going taut as she drags something up from the marsh, up and out—a hand, a mud-slicked arm, and now she has to crouch low and use both arms to get a better grip. I sit there and I watch as she pulls a body from the mire. I can tell that it's the nude body of another woman, but the clinging mud obscures her features entirely. I assume—at first, remembering the photographs of drowning victims—that it must be a corpse, but then it opens its mouth wide and draws a breath, gasping loudly, gasping again and again. Deep, whooping breaths, breaths that hurt to hear, and the blonde woman—almost as muddy now as the body she's rescued from the muck—is murmuring comforting words. I can't actually make them out. The wind's too loud. But her tone is clear enough.

. . . *and with sleep my eyelids close, sleep that may me more vigorous make to serve God when I wake.*

The blonde woman is wiping the thick mud from the other's face, from her nostrils and her eyes, and now I do make out just six words—*It's over. You can rest now.*

And at that, as though these words were a spell or a prayer, the briefest of invocations to Poseidon or Neptune or Proteus or to some other ancient deity of the sea, the mud all around the two begins to seethe and roil. In hardly more than an instant, it has begun to spit up fish that wriggle and flop about them, cod and mackerel and fuck only knows what else. The camera pulls in tighter, and I can see that it isn't only fish, but lobsters and crabs and the writhing tentacles of little octopuses and squids, tangled lumps of starfish. And the woman from the mud screams—

I don't shut my eyes.

I don't look away.

I see very clearly what happens next.

—the woman from the mud screams, and it is the most terrible scream I think that I've ever heard or ever could hear. A scream of pain, of fear, of loss, a scream that seems not the least bit rehearsed, because no one could fake that sort of terror and agony, and it goes on. And on. And on, until I'm about to tell the projectionist to turn the goddamn thing off. To please make it stop, because surely we've all seen and heard enough by now, myself and all those silent people in their masks. I'm about to say *something* when the screaming finally ends—because the body in the arms of the blonde woman has suddenly come apart, collapsed in on itself, dissolved into the same viscous mud that she's only just pulled it from. And all those wriggling creatures from the mud burrow out of sight, and she's left standing there alone beneath the grey morning sky and that dim smudge of a sun, surrounded by the tall, restless cordgrass. She gazes blankly down at the mud and at her hands and—

It ends. The film. Right here it simply ends. The reel runs out, and the tail's allowed to flap for a few seconds, until the lights come up again. No one claps, and they don't say anything, nothing at all. Whatever they're thinking behind those awful masks, whatever the film may have meant to them, they keep it to themselves. They merely stand, only *almost* in unison, and move away from the folding chairs, leaving me sitting there alone and breathless, sweating and my heart racing, and I can hear myself whispering over and over *What the fuck was that. What the fuck was that . . .*

4.

This is the last of it. The very last. At least, this is the last of it so far. Before, when I said that I was skipping ahead to the end, *past* the end, I was either lying to myself or it was wishful thinking. Or maybe there's no difference between the two. Maybe I am simply an unreliable narrator.

I went to Cape Ann on Saturday night, and now it's Saturday night again, one week later. Last night, I spoke with the ex in San Francisco. This morning I woke from a long nightmare about the gallery, and I lay in bed as the sun rose over Federal Hill, thinking how much less odd the whole thing would have been if any of the people in those masks had spoken, and how their silence had to have been something mutually agreed upon ahead of time. And I also wondered *what* exactly was on display that night. Was it really only those photographs and the piece of film? Were the masks part of it?

I've thought a lot about the film. I've thought more about the film than anything else. Until the very end, nothing about it couldn't have been done on a shoestring budget, nothing until those final, horrible moments. But even that—I don't know much about making movies. For all I know CGI has rendered such elaborate special effects cheap as dirt. Or, for all I know, the film actually cost quite a lot of money to make.

I lay there in bed thinking how it only occurred to me days later that Case Mitchell never gave me the name of the *artist* or *artists* represented at the gallery. For that matter, the name didn't come up in my call to San Francisco. And, stranger still, it simply never occurred to me to *ask* for it. And, finally, nothing at the gallery offered any clue. So, that mystery added to the rest, and lying there as the sky turned from grey-violet to a murky blue, I was utterly at a loss as to why it took so long for me to even realize there's never been a name. Or names. If I had written the article, or at least tried to write the article, would it have occurred to me then? And if I had gone looking for it, could I have discovered anything at all about who chose those photos, who made that film, who handed out the anglerfish and black gulper masks to everyone but me?

I got up. I showered and had breakfast. I thought about how maybe it was time for a day job again, at least for a little while. I decided to spend the day in a library, and crossing the Point Street Bridge on my way to the Athenaeum, I looked out towards Narragansett Bay, past the open gates of the hurricane barrier, and there was something about the sun shimmering off the water that almost made me turn around and go back home. But it's not exactly practical, living in Rhode Island and trying to avoid the sea, and I told myself I was being ridiculous, and that seemed to do the trick. I made it to the library. I stayed until closing, and on the way home I got slices from a place on Wickenden Street and ate them in the car. And then I went home to my apartment. I locked the doors and turned on the television. I had a beer, and then another beer, and then the phone rang.

I'm almost to end the end of it. For real this time.

At least, the end of it so far.

The phone rang.

The phone *rings*. Not my iPhone, but the landline. It was here when I moved in, and I decided to keep it, pay the extra $44 a month (as if I can actually afford such luxuries) for a little bit of nostalgia. Anyway, the landline rings. I look at the caller ID, but the number's blocked. I answer it anyway. And for almost a minute, no one says anything at all. There's a very faint sound, and I'm still not certain what it was. A cracking of white noise. Or wind. Or the muffled sound of waves.

I've said hello for the third time, and I'm about to hang up.

And finally someone speaks.

Someone. I can't tell if the voice was male or female. It could be either.

"Not everyone accepts the invitation," the caller says. "You'd be surprised how many have the opportunity, but never show. And then it's all such a waste."

The sexless voice is very, very calm. Very smooth. The voice is like vanilla ice cream or black ice on asphalt.

"It was a job," I reply, and it doesn't even occur to me to ask who the hell I'm talking to or how they got my unlisted number. "I needed the work. I still do."

"We were pleased you came," the caller says. "We all were very pleased that you came." I think there might be a hint of a Portuguese accent (my mother was Portuguese), but I might be wrong. "Still, it's a shame you didn't write the story. It would have been better if you had."

"If I wanted to see it again—" and I stop myself, wondering why I'm asking *this* question, when I don't even want to have seen it the first time.

"It's better if you don't," the voice replies. "You saw enough. You saw all you needed to see."

"What does that mean?" I ask.

"You saw enough," the voice says again.

"Yeah, but what does that *mean?*" And I don't know if I'm getting angry or impatient or frightened or . . .

The voice sighs. It's an exasperated sort of sigh.

"You almost drowned when you were fifteen," it says. "You were a good swimmer, but the sea was rough that day, and you swam out very far. You were a good swimmer, a *strong* swimmer. It never even occurred to you that you could get into trouble. But the water was rough and very cold, and there was a rip current."

"How do you know about that?"

"You didn't panic. But you didn't think you'd make it back to the beach. You were a long way out. But you were a strong swimmer, and you knew not to fight it. You knew to swim parallel to the shoreline until you were free of the current. You knew to swim at a right angle to the current when you did start back towards the beach."

"I've never told anyone that." Which is true, so far as I can recall.

"Maybe you did. Maybe you did, then forgot. It was a long time ago."

"What did you mean, I saw all I needed to see?"

"On the way back to shore, it felt like something was following you, and you were afraid it was a shark. There were seals at that beach, grey seals and harbor seals who came for the cod and the flounder, and so there were sharks."

"How do you *know* that?"

"Regardless," the voice says, "we are pleased you came. It would have been better if you'd written the article, but we're pleased you showed up, all the same. You might be surprised how many don't. And then it's all such a waste."

"I'm going to hang up now," I say.

"That's fine," the voice tells me. "We're finished. It's over. You can rest now."

There's a second voice then, a woman's voice, in the background, but I can't tell what she's saying. I only hear her for a moment, and then there's a click, and then only the dial tone. I sit and listen to it for what seems like a long time before returning the handset to its cradle. And then I sit and stare at the television and finish my second beer. It's gotten warm, but I finish it anyway.

The day I almost drowned.

I've never told anyone. I'm sure of that.

I've never told anyone about the shark, either.

Sure, there are questions I could ask. And there are people I could talk to about this. I've considered driving back up to the shack by the salt marsh at Cape Hedge. I've wondered what I would find there if I did. But. I think it's best if I try and let this be the last of it. The *very* last. If I'm lucky, and if the caller was true to their word, it will be.

THE SCARE GROOM

PATRICK BARB

Helen sits on the edge of the bed, waiting for her scare groom to be brought upstairs and placed in their marriage bed. Freshly bathed and left alone for the first time in more than a day, she doesn't cry over what's about to happen.

She's decided tears are for the past.

The antebellum plantation's floorboards bow and whine as the procession nears her closed door. It's the one room on the hallway locked from the outside. After her first few days in town, Helen's learned to keep her head down, to ignore the "signs and portents"—to borrow a phrase uttered by the drunken Reverend in his rambling homily at the wedding ceremony—suggesting trouble to come.

After all, there's nothing I can do to stop it.

But the scratching of straw and dried corn husks against the floor and along baseboards makes her lean forward, turning an ear to the door.

The pearl doorknob rattles once, then twice, signaling it's time for the ritual's next stage. The bride picks her feet up off the floor and tucks her toes behind the hem of the long white nightgown they've insisted she wear. She wiggles them, the way she'd do when she and her brother Stephen were younger, staying up late at their grandmother's house, telling stories about the shadows on the walls, the black smudges covering old wallpaper depicting columns of meticulously illustrated pieces of fruit.

A thick iron key turns in the lock and old tumblers move into position all matter-of-fact. As though the old house itself is a willing participant. A salty droplet splashes onto Helen's bottom lip and her tongue darts out to intercept it. For a moment, she worries her tears came despite her protests to the contrary. But a hand to her forehead reveals a steady stream of sweat from her hairline.

The door opens. Flickering candlelight illumination from the hallway sconces throws new shadows across the room. The enlarged shade of the scare groom covers the floor, the bed, Helen's body, and the wall behind her. With her hands folded across her lap, the way they taught her, she keeps her chin up and eyes staring straight ahead.

At first, it appears the scare groom came alone. The dented, rain-ruined broad-brimmed hat covering a potato sack face with features painted on in tar-black and blood-red on top followed by an oversized flannel shirt and overalls stuffed with straw and corn husks below, all appear to float above the threshold when viewed from Helen's vantage.

The scare groom says nothing because his mouth's painted on, an artisan's flick of the wrist casting a curved line across the aged burlap. Helen counts in her head, figuring how long it'll take before her next breath. Then, the Ladies' Council pushes through the entrance and the illusion of the floating scare groom is shattered. Instead, four women, the same ones who bathed Helen, preparing her for the evening, carry the scarecrow inside.

"Stand, girl."

The voice comes from behind the scare groom and his bearers. At the pronouncement, Helen rises, pulling her toes from the hem of her gown and planting them on the floor. In doing so, she thinks she notices the scare groom's straw-stuffed sack head turn and tilt, as though he's noticing her for the first time and making an evaluation from behind dark, two-dimensional eyes.

Then again, it could be the way they're carrying him.

"Place him on the bed," Sonya commands the others with thunderous certainty. Helen's not surprised. She's come to understand the vital role played by the librarian and other members of the Ladies' Council. If the bombastic Reverend's a mouthpiece, then Sonya, with her dusty old bookmobile parked forever on the outskirts of town, is the unfiltered voice of God itself.

After last observing her from the meeting-hall floor, where she and the other members of the Ladies' Council sat on the raised dais for the wedding ceremony and subsequent feast, Helen's forgotten how small of stature the librarian is. As the other women arrange the scare groom on her bed, Sonya stands on tip-toes to make her inspection of the straw-man's newest bride.

The librarian's fingertips are warm, enriched by the earthy aroma of the fields surrounding the town, and Helen trembles at the older woman's touch. It's not meant as a comforting gesture. Sonya turns the young woman's head from side to side, pulling her lips apart to check her teeth.

"The last girl, the one we'd *wanted* for Harvest Bride, got her hands on a sewing needle. The poor dear must've snuck it in her mouth. We found her bloodless and cold on that very bed come morning. Poked and scratched herself all over. The blood soaked through the sheets and mattress. Dribbled onto the floor. Can you imagine?"

Helen nodded yes. She *could* imagine. After all, she'd witnessed far worse since her brother's car broke down outside Crowfly. The town so small it didn't show on GPS or maps. The town where the bones of her brother and his two college suitemates now lay buried under their fertile fields ready for reaping.

Completing her inspection, Sonya turns her attention to the other women of the Council and the scare groom on the bed. "We changed the sheets, as you'll note . . . Deirdre, Peggy Ann, move him over. You know we've gotta leave room for both on that bed."

Running through the remaining ritual with a skilled taskmaster's efficiency, Sonya returns to Helen's side. "All right, young lady, arms up. Laurel, Sage, help Miss Helen undress."

Helen keeps her arms up as she's told but does manage to find her voice. "Are . . . are you all staying? But you said . . . "

Sonya flashes a vulture's grin which ages her as it breaks the otherwise placid, unmoving features of her face. "Of course, dear. Of course. This is how it's always done, you understand? You must go to your groom pure, unadulterated."

Helen waits until the nightgown's off her head and the attending women have run their fingers through the wild strands of her hair to settle them against her scalp. Then, she nods. Her shoulders, knees, and wrists ache with the pain exacerbated by the chill prickling up and down her exposed form.

The bramble bush scratches across her breasts have nearly healed thanks to the ointments the women rubbed into her skin. Raised pink swirls surround her nipples, like branding on her soft, sensitive flesh. The four attendants keep their eyes low, studying the ground. They mumble *thanks* and well-wishes to the bride and groom. Then, one by one, they're swallowed by the flickering lights in the hallway, reduced to creaking floorboards and breathless, excited whispers.

Helen finds Sonya's hand encircling her wrist, drawing her the short distance to the bed. The others placed the scare groom flat on his back, clothes still on in contrast to Helen's nudity. His piecemeal body's a jagged, lumpy mass beneath layers of hand-me-downs. Sprigs of golden-brown straw sneak through the fabric of his face-covering. Their color reminds Helen of times she spent cutting up old issues of *National Geographic* for elementary school art projects, finding spreads of tribespeople so matter-of-fact in their nakedness with piercings through noses, ears, chins, and foreheads. Except the scare groom's dressed like her grandfather, with his too-large shirts and wild hair, adding to the unease she experiences in *his* presence.

The scare groom studies the ceiling. For the first time since they placed her in the room, Helen does the same. The entire expanse is painted a deep maroon, dark red like the wounds on her brother's body after the sickle-bearing executioners descended, ignoring his pleas for mercy.

"There we are, dear," Sonya says, moving Helen into position. "Lay down right here. Right like . . . yes. Perfect."

Once the back of her head touches the pillow, Helen closes her eyes.

She won't open them again until Sonya's footsteps recede into the hallway, the doorknob turns, and the tumblers in the locks move back into place. When she opens her eyes, a trembling travels from low in her stomach up to her shoulders. She turns her head, expecting to find the scare groom on his side, regarding her as well. In the eternal moment between having her eyelids over her eyes and opening them, she imagines his stuffing turned flesh and bone and blood like a fairy-tale prince when the curse is lifted.

She pictures dark eyes made whole, regarding her with a curious, yet lustful consideration. Her waking dream features lips curled back into a semi-smile, showing teeth.

But it's not what she finds.

Musty straw, ancient clothes, hat splattered white with crow droppings, the scare groom remains as he was.

"He'll come to you when the time is right."

Sonya's words from the feast echo in Helen's mind as she lays beside her groom. They're too close together in the confines of the bed, making it impossible to avoid contact. Helen's too afraid to move besides. She follows the lead of her betrothed and regards the blood-red ceiling again. She holds her eyes open for as long as she's able, so if the tears come she'll blame them on dust and dirt caught in the fleshy pink behind her blue-green orbs.

She squeezes the bedsheet in her hands, twisting the stiff white material over and over until it surrenders to her ministrations. Until something tickles the sunburnt skin of her arm and she gasps, producing a tiny-mouthed coo. Like a bird in a cage.

Her scare groom's ready.

Helen's grateful for the long hours spent sick before they locked her in the bed chambers, the desperate moments spent expelling the rare sweetmeats they'd forced her to consume at the post-wedding feast. Emptied, left hollow in mind, body, and spirit, she's prepared to let herself be filled.

She doesn't find a storybook ending. No stars in her eyes or butterflies vibrating with delicate wings and inquisitive antennae inside her stomach. She still wants to believe her scare groom will change. Feeling him bare inside her, she wishes for a gentle, human touch. Not because she believes she deserves it, but because she's left one final scrap of hope clinging, digging its nails in deep.

But there's no guarantee for dreamers. Not of safety or security. When he fills her, his straw scratches her inside and out.

She presses her lips thin but keeps her eyes open. She wishes harder, screaming inside. A penitent asking for reprieve. If there's a chance he'll change, the rustling, thrusting movements between her thighs becoming a gentle caress followed by a firm, ecstatic connection, then she'll resist despair.

Lifting her hands off the bed, she caresses a burlap cheek. An act of pity. He rubs hempen-bound ligatures against her blistering skin.

Then, Helen wraps her legs around his loose workman's pants and pulls him tight, holding her scare groom closer.

"I'm sorry," she whispers.

Unclear who the apology's meant for, Helen's surprised when his wheat-sprout fingers caress her cheek, then open her mouth. They leave a gritty coating across teeth and gums and tongue.

He makes her want to scratch the flesh from her bones until she's truly bare. When she glimpsed him across the fields, one trembling hand shielding her eyes from the unbearable mid-day sun with its last vestiges of fading summer, she sensed this would happen.

Even then, I knew.

She holds him down, lowers herself back onto him, and whispers into the ears he doesn't have.

◄◊►

The next morning, the scare groom leans against the door, as though preparing to leave, set to return to the fields and resume his post. The thin, early morning light trickling in through the barred window above their marriage bed forces Helen to sit up so she'll get a better look at her partner. Viewed in this dimness, there's no way to be sure: is he standing there, waiting, hesitating, or is he no more than straw, stuffing, and rags, propped up to frighten birds?

The wide spherical pearl twists and the door's hinges draw in a screeching breath. Letting the bedsheets fall from her body, Helen crosses to the door and loops her arm around the scare groom's bulging midsection. She presses a warm cheek to his feed-sack visage. "Come back to bed," she says, pulling him from the door and leaving the knob tilted at an angle from the other side.

Helen turns her back to the steady, patient exhalations in the hallway. As though the breather's mouth sits not far from the keyhole.

The scare groom moves with his bride. Swept off feet he lacks. If his naked escort, returning him to the confines of a bed perfumed in sweat and sex and straw, remains as frightened as she was before the consummation, then she's managed to press it down until her eyes become the becalmed surfaces of twin ponds and her smile's a flat, impoverished assembly of lines and shadows.

When the door opens, they leave together—bride and groom. The Ladies' Council stands in the hallway, heads down, hiding rosy cheeks and eyes tilted to the heavens, exalting their new Harvest Bride for fulfilling her sacred duties. Someone hands Helen a long blue farm dress, the hem traveling to her ankles and buttons extending up to her chest. Another reaches for the scare groom's hand, prepared to take him away. *The way it's always done.*

But Helen won't relinquish her groom. "He stays with me," she says.

There's no argument to counter. Her words have an icy sharpness, setting the Council back on their heels. She's dark storm clouds and heavy rain on an otherwise warm and pleasant day.

Sonya stands apart from the others, waiting by the stairs. She nods, letting her fellow council members know it's okay. If Helen wants to hold the old scarecrow's hand and keep him by her side, then who're they to tell a young bride no.

⟶⟨⟩⟵

"No, no, no!" Helen's pleas fell on indifferent ears as they dragged her from under the bookmobile parked sideways across the lone road out of town. The Crowfly men—a huddled mass of tree-trunk arms and legs, barrel chests, and square, dimpled faces darkened from working in the fields so they resembled the covers of Gideon's Bibles—moved as one, holding her and pulling her from the vehicle. She broke her nails scraping silver and brown paint off the service truck lined from floor to ceiling with books for every age.

When she twisted and turned, trying to break free, two of the men pulled her arms back, pinioning them against her and wrenching them to her shoulders. She wanted to scream. It took a minute before she realized the ringing in her head came from her doing that exact thing. Her shriek was long, loud, and animalistic. Like she'd become a creature caught in the ravenous, unquenchable jaws of a hunter's steel trap.

Her brother remained where they'd let his lifeless body fall, with wounds open all over, resembling thin lips whispering secrets on a wind-blown day. His blood stopped flowing at some point while she'd hidden, holding balled-up fists under her eyes to stop the downpour of tears. She spied some of the ladies regarding Stephen's body. One old spinster pinched the fat on his back like she was considering a prized hog to gauge how much meat they'd get from the slaughter.

Helen fought all the harder, biting through her bottom lip to endure the pain.

"Wait."

The men stopped, and the crowd parted. Bleary-eyed and bloody-chinned, Helen lifted her head to find a little girl standing before her, tipping a cup of water against her Kool-Aid-red slick lips.

"Drink, my dear."

The voice wasn't a child's. Helen recognized it, as she choked and sputtered, spilling pink-tinged water onto the grey earth below.

The librarian.

What'd she tell us when we walked into town down the old road that's not there anymore?

"Everyone's got a part to play in Crowfly."

Helen spit, a wad of bloody phlegm striking Sonya's forehead. The sting of a palm against Helen's cheek made for swift retribution.

"Why don't you kill me?" she asked, each word pained, stretched like a body on the rack.

She didn't acknowledge the surrounding crowd. She focused on her brother, calling to their Mom, saying he was afraid to die—because they'd reached a point where those words had become necessary.

She watched her brother's friends. *No friends of mine, though.* First, Dean—with the plow-horse's hoofs awash in blood and brain matter, face peeling back from skull like a Halloween mask slipping off a sweaty child's face. Then Robbie, whose own face turned black and purple, yellow at the edges from the rope pulled tight around his neck.

Eyes bulging from sockets, the stench of his final release made everyone's eyes water.

"Kill you?" Sonya said. "Killing you's not why you're here. You're for the scare groom."

◦

They've moved Helen from the main house to a tiny apartment on the far edge of downtown. Every morning, Helen wakes and pulls the curtains back to reveal the lush fields of Crowfly. She opens the window, fingertips resting on the screen, and breathes in the small-town scents—all cut grass, burnt leaf piles, and apple pie crusts. It's quiet, even with the steady hum of life proceeding in the streets and fields below.

On this day, there's a knock at the door. Two quick, successive raps. Helen tightens her robe against her body. The fabric's soft, gentle on her tanned flesh. She opens the door and finds the boys waiting.

"Hello, Gabriel, Matthew, Ezekiel, and . . . "

"Paul, uh, ma'am," the new one answers. He's stouter than the others. Eyebrows sit heavy on a Cro-Magnon brow hooding bloodshot eyes. He coughs, covering his mouth, trying to keep out the peppermint scent of schnapps mixed with the flat tannins of stolen communion wine.

Helen doesn't like him.

The others she knows. The others she's tolerated.

But this one . . .

Her fear's not something she's willing to share. So, she steps aside to reveal the scare groom, waiting in a chair beside their bed. Dressed for his work in the fields. Always dressed the same day after day.

The boys enter, getting their arms under the scare groom and lifting him from his seat. They make their way back across the room. When they get close to Helen, she holds a hand up. "Wait," she says.

She leans toward her husband of straw and sticks, plants a dry kiss on his cheek. *It's about the one thing planted here that hasn't grown, hasn't flourished. Yet.*

When she pulls back, she finds the new boy—*boy-man, man-boy*—Paul watching from the door, holding it open for the others to lead the scare groom out for his *work* in the fields, scaring away crows and other invaders. Paul's tongue runs across his bottom lip. Despite her months of practice at keeping her emotions in check, Helen still shudders at the sight.

When she's finished, there's no one left in the apartment and the door's clicking shut. She steps closer like she's going to grab the knob and pull the door open wide. But she stops short and listens instead.

"You shouldn't disturb the Harvest Bride," one of the smaller boys says.

A mean, nasty laugh follows. She knows in her heart who it comes from.

"Soon enough it'll be time for this old straw-boy to get a new bride and the missus in there'll need a new man. Reckon it'll be me."

Paul speaks too loudly, as though he's trying to convince himself as much as the others. Helen moves closer to the door and presses her ear against it. She does her damnedest to will a new sound from out in the hallway. She wishes for the rustle of straw, her mate turning, reaching, grabbing . . . punishing those who'd speak ill of his bride.

Like we practiced.

But there's nothing, except the sound of footsteps receding. The alarm clock on Helen's side of the bed rings, a long, loud shrieking bell. Like a fire alarm in an old building.

"getout, getout, getout, getout . . . "

She dresses in the clothes provided and leaves the apartment to begin her own day's work.

◄◊►

Helen finishes her thirtieth reorganization of the Children's Book section of the old bookmobile that month when Sonya stands and stretches, signaling the end of their work day. Everyone in town plays their part and Helen's chosen to help maintain the library. She'd prepared a whole argument about Sonya getting older and someone needing to take the reins. But the Council went right along with it. No resistance whatsoever.

"Come on, dear," the older woman says, tidying a stack of cards to go into the backs of books when they're returned by the few Crowfly readers.

Helen slides the last bound square of thick board pages onto the nearest shelf and stands as if yanked to waking from a dream. "What's that?" she asks.

Sonya laughs. Her chuckle's like the cry of a bird of prey circling above its next victim. "Oh, surely you haven't forgotten dear. We've got a Council meeting this evening."

Helen registers her protests, even as she follows Sonya out of the back of the bookmobile and down the small set of steps leading to level ground. "But my scare groom . . . " she starts.

A hand in her face, coming close to striking her across the bridge of her nose and squishing the plumpness of her lips, quiets her arguments. "He'll be fine. The boys will put him where he belongs."

After almost a year, Helen knows when to stop digging. She hangs her head, adding a simple "Yes, Sonya" to make it clear she'll obey.

Crowfly's small enough—a two-traffic-light town, if they ever bothered with such technology—so it's not long before they reach the meeting hall. Helen's always slow to enter, swallowing hard before crossing the threshold. She's watched the other women—Sonya and her followers, searching for a similar reaction on *their* faces.

Do they gag on the sense-memory of feeding on the meat of whatever loved ones they were captured with when their turn came to serve as Harvest Bride and wed the scare groom?

Of course, she's yet to work up the courage to ask anyone something so personal. Her concern for raising suspicion is too great an obstacle.

While the menfolk and a small percentage of the younger women born in town go about their lives, preparing dinners, and settling in for the evening, Helen, Sonya, and the other members of the Ladies' Council file into the hall. Soon, the chairs in the first couple of rows on the floor are filled. The raised dais remains from Helen's ceremony. Sonya sits there, along with the key members of the Council. The blessed number of those most recent former brides who'd wed the scare groom before Helen. Deirdre, Peggy Ann, Laurel, and Sage.

Each woman inside the meeting hall once served as Harvest Bride and married the scare groom. The ritual's kept the town's crops bountiful and hid its residents from outsiders' prying eyes.

"Those who wouldn't understand," as Sonya put it.

Helen knows she's meant to sit on the dais next year. The new Harvest Bride's meant for her current seat, down among the older brides. Each one's remarried, paired with one of the menfolk from town. She's dropped casual inquiries about how the menfolk learn about Crowfly and the answers she's received trend toward vague, incomplete, and unsatisfactory.

"They come because we're here."

"There's no ceremony needed. We reach out to potential citizens and they come when ready."

"Never you mind, dear . . . "

At the center of the dais, Sonya clears her throat. Silence follows. Helen notes how everyone takes to the librarian's commands, whether spoken or merely suggested.

She's the real mother of us all.

In their quiet labors, sorting through the catalog of books, Helen's learned much from being in the older woman's presence. There's a reserved confidence in the librarian's working methods. She shares when she's ready and never before.

Despite spending the most time around her, Helen's gained the least solid information from their interactions. It's a shame as far as she's concerned because it's obvious to anyone—Sonya's the one with the answers. *The real answers.*

As quiet settles through the building, Sonya nods to two of the others on the dais. The pair, Laurel and Sage, rise from their seats and pull down an old film screen that's centered on the stage. Helen tenses in her seat, as this is the most modern convenience she's encountered since getting trapped in Crowfly.

Except for the bookmobile, of course.

"Reverend . . . "

Sonya signals to the back of the hall.

While the other women remain locked in place, rictus half-grins on their faces, staring straight ahead, Helen plays Lot's wife, turning back because she's got to see for herself.

No Sodoms or Gomorrahs are found, only the Reverend flipping on an overhead projector to shine a single photograph onto the screen on-stage. He nods to Sonya and the other women at the front. Then, catching Helen's gaze, he winks. So many of the menfolk (and the boyfolk and now the men-of-Godfolk) have eyed Helen over the last few days. Like they're sharing a secret—on a one-way street where Helen's standing frozen with headlights bearing down on her. The Reverend nods, then motions for the young woman to turn around, before he shuffles into the shadows.

The girl projected onto the screen is pale, with high cheekbones and ears too large for her teardrop head. *Like a fairy princess.* She stands beside a beat-up old station wagon, a carrier case strapped to the top with multi-colored bands. Her ears hold so many piercings that Helen first mistakes them for rolls of quarters taped in place on either side. The girl's t-shirt is dirty, stained brown around the neck, but her black skirt customized with tulle trim is a clear work of art.

Helen imagines the girl sewing up ragged holes in flannel shirts and patching weather-washed jeans bleached white under the unforgiving sun. She pictures the scare groom's painted-on grin and envisions its half-smirk rising an inch or two. A black line spreading like ants on the march.

"Our people on the outside tell us the girl and her father—an old man, weak, bit of a lech but harmless—are about a day away. They'll get the sign placed . . . with the shortcut . . . "

Helen remembers the sign. She remembers jerking the steering wheel and barreling down the one-way road, all hard-packed dirt with clumps of grass as mile-markers. Tears drying fast on her face because it was so damn hot. And she can't forget Stephen, grabbing her arm, not hard, not pinching her, but strong enough. She hears the eternal echo of his last words before Crowfly. "Helly, look, listen. I don't know what you *think* happened back at the rest stop. But I'm sure the guys, they . . . "

"Her name's Monica," Sonya says, breaking up Helen's journey through unwelcome memories and also making the new girl real by giving her a name.

The hairs on the back of Helen's neck rise. Everyone's watching her. Waiting, expectant. "Well?" The librarian speaks as though she's addressed Helen and Helen alone for the majority of the meeting. "Are you ready to leave the scare groom? Ready to enter the next phase of your life in Crowfly?"

Helen lifts her head, chin out, eyes proud but not defiant. "Everyone plays a part," she says.

The women wait until Sonya nods to do the same. Then, they add their voices to the chorus.

"Everyone plays a part."

◄◦►

At night, Helen lies with her scare groom.

She might be the only bride who's continued to do so after the initial wedding night consummation. When she tried to bring it up at a luncheon, the women at her table went red in their faces, tittering like cartoon chipmunks. Like girls playing tea-party dress-up before finding nudie magazines in the forests behind their homes. The dissonance was striking.

Helen remembers the day because she figured out it was her nineteenth birthday. Instead of a cake, she'd eaten corn mash and collard greens. Then, she'd learned songs in praise of the harvest and its eternal bounty.

It didn't hurt anymore. The scratches, scabbed and scarred over, left smooth lines in her folds like frost patterns on windshields. When he touched them, she shivered and considered it close enough to love. She didn't even care too much if it wasn't. After all, the love she knew before Crowfly expired before the scythes had cut her brother down.

It died when her brother told her, "I love you, Helly. But I'm not sure I believe you."

It passed when he witnessed her shoving open the heavy door of the rest area bathroom, come stumbling out with a bloody nose and her shirt pulled half down on one shoulder but also bunched up around her midsection with his two shit-faced friends stumbling behind, and then decided he *wasn't sure what to believe.*

If that's love, then I'll take this instead. Give me this. Give me this . . .

"Give me!"

Helen reaches up to her scare groom and pulls him deeper inside. Her fingers tear away the buttons on his shirt. She squeezes him, letting the straw and twigs rub her blistered palms raw. Until she bleeds on him, into him. She pulls more and more of his insides out, all stuffing, dry and fragile like old kindling.

Until *he* stops her. Pulling himself away with strength like something from a ghost story where a formless void's capable of opening windows and slamming doors shut. He collapses beside her, nothing more than a lifeless, rag-garbed husk.

Helen lets her scare groom sleep or whatever it is he does. She moves to the corner of their bedroom and works until sunrise. She takes corn husks pulled from her lover's body and twists them, tying them together with bark stripped slowly, carefully from his twigs.

Before the boys come to take the scare groom to the field, where she knows the new bride will connect with him, experiencing the same uncanny jolt that traveled through her all those months before, Helen wakes *her* scare groom from his slumber. She shows him what she's made. His body, her blood. Their baby.

When they pass by the window, she's sure her scare groom looks back. And she makes certain he witnesses her nursing, letting their corn-husk child suckle.

◂◦▸

There's chaos in Crowfly. First, the boys—the ones who came almost every day to fetch the scare groom and set him up in the fields—went missing. They've kept the search secret as the new bride and her father already made the turn down the one-way road into town and ran over the spikes laid across the path—front tires popping, one, two.

The parents of a boy named Paul interrupted the would-be slaughter of the old man as he begged and pleaded for his daughter to be spared. The distraught parents sought answers from the Reverend and Sonya the librarian and any other member of the Ladies' Council they could get their hands on. The rumor-mill engines churned and a story emerged concerning a single body part left on a front porch, straw sticking to the bloody end of the appendage. No one specified *which* appendage—only saying it was something his mama would recognize.

Helen played her part. She pulled hard on the new bride's arm and whispered alleluias in the girl's trembling ear while the remaining menfolk landed rabbit punches to her father's kidneys until the old man's skin turned yellow and the front of his pants was stained with sticky red wetness.

Helen made sure Sonya caught everything.

She'd never signed up for plays or the closed-circuit TV morning announcements in high school, but she damn sure believed she'd given the performance of a lifetime. Good enough to land her an unsupervised trip to bring the new bride water and crackers before her father's scheduled execution and the new bride's naked run through the brambles. Like Helen had done a year before.

Helen opens the door to the utility closet at the back of the meeting hall. She checks behind her, making sure the surrounding hallway's empty. Then, she steps inside. Monica, *"the girl who would be bride,"* rubs her wrists and ankles. She's free of the handcuffs. All thanks to the keys Helen slipped the girl earlier.

"Are you ready?" Helen asks the girl and her father, who's a collection of bruises more than he's anything close to a human being.

"My Daddy," Monica answers. "I'm not sure if he can . . . "

But Helen doesn't need to counter. The beaten, bloodied man stinks of rot and festering, tainted blood, but he finds the strength to rise.

"You don't have much time," Helen says. She holds the door open, letting them shuffle past on whisper-soft, shoeless tiptoes.

Helen points to the backdoor. The watchman and the watchwoman wait on either side of the exit. Except, they're already dead, eyes lacerated with twig finger scratches, throats torn open and splinter-filled in the same manner. "Once you're out," she continues, "head for the fields. Don't stop until you reach the other side."

The girl, *who won't be a bride, after all*, turns to Helen. One last time she seeks answers that won't come. "How can we thank you?" the girl, who's no more than a year younger than Helen, asks.

"Don't."

Then, they're gone. Running into fields already standing smaller than before, with the forthcoming harvest made of less vibrant greens and diminished dulled golds.

Helen doesn't know if the girl and her father are destined to find a way out or if they'll wander forever amid rows and rows of cornstalks that once appeared as though they'd stretch to the sky. But she knows staying behind offers no chance at all, so at least she's given them that.

It's more than she got.

◂◦▸

Someone rings a town crier's bell up and down the streets, long, loud, and persistent. But devoid of rhythm. The atonal clanging serves as a disjointed soundtrack to the panic consuming Crowfly. Bodies show up on doorsteps, in the haylofts of the barns, and some are even drowned in ditch water. All of them marred by straw, twigs, mud, dirt, and rocks. As though the land itself fights back against the people it once held fast to its bosom.

Sonya waits by the bookmobile, refusing to be swept up in this hysteria.

Helen doesn't disappoint her. She steps toward the vehicle. Sonya crosses her arms over her chest, her gaze rising no further than the Harvest Bride's mid-section. "Did you assume you'd sneak away without me knowing?"

The young woman shakes her head. "Of course not. I've listened. I've learned."

As Helen moves closer on her longer legs, Sonya backs herself against the bookmobile. "Stay back," she says.

Helen obliges, letting her words do the work. "You talk a lot when you're lost in the books, finding homes for them. I know you're the one who found Crowfly, taking a wrong turn in your vehicle there. Makes sense you're the one traveling at night when we're all asleep. Bringing people out, bringing people in. You mark the other cars, don't you? Leaving a book in the backseat or the trunk . . . "

The silence is confirmation. There's no need for Sonya to say more.

But she doesn't know that.

"He's nothing more than straw and sticks and rags. You've fooled yourself like all the others. You want him to be something more, but he's not. He's a scarecrow. It's all he ever was, all he ever will be."

Helen pulls down the front of her dress, letting Sonya lean closer for a better look. The corn husk child pulls its tattered lips and toothless gums from its mother's breast. Green and brown skin flushed a yellow-white from the milk scrunches up as barely discernible facial features dimple the squalling visage.

The color drains from Sonya's face. She presses against the vehicle, trying to become one with it. Too late, she realizes the door's already open. Stick hands wrap around her shoulders. The scare groom leans close to his first bride's ear. There's so much he wants to say.

Helen wishes she stood closer, near enough to make out the words of her beloved. But she's far too busy comforting their child.

⊰⊹⊱

The key pulled from Sonya's pocket works as Helen suspected. With a turn in the ignition, the bookmobile engine roars to life. Those Crowfly survivors left behind, prisoners in a land where no crops will grow, bear witness to the new family's departure. They stare in heartbroken reverence at their town's librarian, stuffed full of straw, tied against the hood of the bookmobile with brambles sticking through her skin, exiting Crowfly for the last time.

The vehicle lurches forward, unsteady at first but hitting an even clip once they've passed the border into the next county.

The last Crowfly Harvest Bride and her scare groom take their corn husk child further west, navigating lost, forgotten roads. They let the rotting corpse of the librarian serve as a warning to any who'd try to stop them—*stay away, this beautiful bounty is not for your consumption.*

THE TEETH

BRIAN EVENSON

The first time he had gone over to Brother Monson's, Jens had known something was wrong with the man. His teeth were *not right*.

"What do you mean, *not right?*" asked his friend David later.

"Like they weren't really teeth," said Jens. "Or more like they were the ghosts of teeth."

"How can teeth have ghosts?" asked David, confused.

Jens, puzzled, just shook his head. It wasn't something he could explain well, but he was sure he was right. He had gone there with his father, who had been sent over by their church to check on Brother Monson, to make sure he was, more or less, okay. They had knocked on the door and had stood there for what seemed to Jens a very long time. If it had been just him, he would have left. But his dad just continued to wait, unperturbed, as if this were normal.

"I don't think he's there," said Jens.

"Where else would he be?" asked Jens' dad, and ruffled Jens' hair.

And indeed, a moment later, the door opened.

"Yah?" said Brother Monson, "Who dere?"

He wore an olive work shirt with a buttoned pocket over each breast. The shirt still showed creases from where it had been folded. He stood uncomfortably straight, as if he had no ability to bend or otherwise shift the vertebrae in his back. He wore thick glasses that were smeary with fingerprints and his mouth hung partway open. Jens could see right inside of it. Brother Monson's teeth were ground down: they looked hollow inside, like empty casings. They didn't strike him as functional teeth at all.

"It's me, Brother Monson," said Jens' father. "Just checking to make sure all is well for you."

"All well," said Brother Monson, though he made the "w" sound like a "v". And then, stiffly, he waved one hand at them and closed the door.

Jens' father turned to him, face still creased with concern, and then, slowly, he shrugged. "There's only so much you can do," he claimed. And then they both left.

◄◦►

He had not said to his father: "Something is very wrong with Brother Monson's teeth." He wasn't sure why he hadn't said this. He just hadn't. For one thing, his father hadn't seemed to notice, but he wasn't sure if that was the main reason. For another, he felt it was a mistake to talk about such teeth out loud.

When he had seen the teeth, Brother Monson's teeth, the thing he had thought was that Brother Monson was not completely alive. Both his teeth and the way he held himself stiff had made him think this.

What a terrible thing, he couldn't help but think, walking beside his father as they reached the top of the street and then cut left and walked to their house. *What terrible teeth.*

◄◦►

It was of course, he quickly convinced himself, all nonsense. He'd let the strangeness of an old man get the better of him. He had bad teeth—so what? He was old. That someone that old still had teeth at all was a sort of minor miracle. No, it was nothing to be concerned about.

And yet, when his friend David came over, he couldn't help talking about the teeth. Or, at least, trying to: he didn't know how to describe them. He didn't know what to say.

⟨o⟩

That had been the first time, a little over a week ago. This was this time.

School had let out for the day, and Jens was playing Chinese checkers with David, talking about nothing, when he heard the phone ring upstairs.

"Do you need to get that?" David asked.

Jens shook his head. "My mom will."

The phone rang another four times, though, before they heard through the ceiling the sound of his mother's heels tapping their way across the floor above. The ringing stopped. A moment later, his mother called down: "Jens, it's for you."

Jens sighed and stood. He climbed the stairs and took the receiver from his mom where she proffered it, cord stretched taut, from the head of the stairs.

"Hello?" he said.

"Jens?" It was his father's voice. He wanted Jens to go over to Brother Monson's and mow his lawn.

"The church asked me to do it a few days ago," said his father, "but I have too much on my plate. I need you to help out."

"David's over," said Jens.

"You're doing homework?"

"No. Just hanging out."

"Take him along, then," said his father. "He can help haul the push mower over there."

"Brother Monson is kind of weird," said Jens. He didn't feel he could say no outright, but he didn't want to see the old man again.

"He's just old," said his father.

He held out a little longer, but in the end gave in. He went back downstairs and told David.

"The teeth guy you were telling me about?"

He nodded. "You don't have to come," Jens said. "You can go home if you want, or just hang out here until I'm done."

David shrugged. "I don't mind," he said. "I'm curious. Let's go."

⟨o⟩

And so they went, taking turns pushing the lawnmower along the sidewalk and across the street, bumping it over the curb. It was warm outside, the air muggy, and even though it wasn't far, by the time they arrived they were sweaty and short of breath.

They pulled the lawnmower onto the parking strip in front of Brother Monson's house, wrestled it into Brother Monson's yard. The grass there was high and ragged enough that it was going to seed. They abandoned the mower there and climbed the steps to the porch.

Jens rang the doorbell. He and David waited.

"Maybe he didn't hear it," David finally said.

"He just takes a long time to come."

But when, after a minute or two, Brother Monson still hadn't come, Jens rang the doorbell again.

Again, they waited.

"He's not here," said David.

"He's old. He never goes anywhere."

"Maybe this time he did."

Jens shrugged.

"We can just mow his lawn," said David. "We don't have to get permission in advance, do we?"

"Sure," said Jens. But just as they were turning to go back down the steps, the door opened.

It was Brother Monson. He was wearing the same shirt he had been wearing when Jens had last seen him, or at least one very much like it, but now it was dark and stiff all along one side, as if that side had soaked in a thick, dark liquid and then dried without being cleaned off. He smelled strange, as if something inside his body had curdled. His posture was just as stiff as before, perhaps stiffer: in addition to his back he didn't seem able to rotate his neck at all. His eyes behind his lenses had gone milky and opaque.

Brother Monson mumbled something incomprehensible.

"Brother Monson?" said Jens. "We're here to mow your lawn. The church sent us."

The old man turned his body slightly, directing his head vaguely in the direction of Jens' voice. He gave no impression of having understood Jens' words. Beside him, Jens felt David take a step back. Brother Monson just stood there, mouth drooping open, hollow teeth on display. *How can he even chew with those?* Jens wondered. And then the old man shuffled slowly around until he was pointed back into the house and tottered back into the darkness, not bothering to close the door.

"What's wrong with him?" asked David.

"He's just old," said Jens, just as his father had said to him.

"Those teeth . . . " said David. "Are they even teeth?"

"I told you."

"I just remembered," said David quickly. He looked panicked. "My mother wanted . . . I've got to go."

"David," said Jens, "I need your help." And to David's credit, that appeal to friendship was enough to keep him from leaving.

◄○►

They mowed quickly and sloppily. If his dad was there, Jens knew, he would have taken his time with the edging, made sure to sweep away the clippings that scattered onto the sidewalk. But Jens hadn't brought a rake or a broom and he wasn't about to go into Brother Monson's house and ask to borrow them. He pushed the mower until he was tired, then David spelled him. At the end, there were places where there were still tufts of grass that hadn't been fully cut, though not all that many. It was, it felt like, good enough. After all, Brother Monson wasn't likely to spend much time in the yard.

When they were done, Jens climbed up onto the porch again. David, behind him, muscled the push mower out onto the sidewalk, ready to leave. Jens moved his finger toward the bell, but hesitated before pushing it.

He stared into the open doorway, into the darkness beyond. The air coming out through the doorway was warm, a faint awful smell still threaded through it even without Brother Monson's presence at the door.

"Come on," said David from the sidewalk. "Let's get out of here."

Jens stepped closer to the doorframe but couldn't bring himself to enter.

"Brother Monson?" he called out.

He listened. He didn't hear any noise from inside.

"We finished the lawn!" he called.

He waited. Nothing.

"We're going now!"

And then he reached inside just far enough to grab the doorknob and pull the door shut.

◄◦►

"You did Brother Monson's lawn?" his father asked a few hours later, once he was home from work. Jens nodded. "You talked to him?" Jens nodded again.

"How's he doing?"

Jens opened his mouth, then closed it again. "There's . . . something wrong with him," he finally said.

"He's old, Jens," said his father tiredly. "We talked about that already."

"Sure," said Jens. "That, too. But he was trying to speak but wasn't making any words."

For a moment his father stared at him, then, without a word, he slipped his shoes back on and left the house.

◄◦►

At first Jens felt relief: Brother Monson was no longer his problem. This was his father's problem now. His father would go and check on Brother Monson, help with whatever was wrong with him and then return and reassure Jens that everything was okay. How long could that possibly take? Fifteen minutes? Thirty?

Forty-five? he eventually thought, once both fifteen and thirty had passed. But as forty-five minutes stretched into an hour and one hour stretched into two, Jens began to be concerned.

"Where's your father?" his mother eventually asked.

"He went over to Brother Monson's," said Jens.

"He probably got talking and lost track of time. Can you walk over and tell him dinner's waiting?"

And so Jens put on his shoes and socks and walked over.

When he turned onto Brother Monson's street he saw the flashing lights. *They don't necessarily have to be at Brother Monson's,* he told himself. *They might be at another house.* But he knew that at Brother Monson's was exactly where they were.

When he reached the ambulance, he saw his father standing on the sidewalk, arms crossed, beside several of Brother Monson's neighbors, waiting. He gave Jens a quizzical look as he approached.

"What happened?" asked Jens.

"Brother Monson passed away," said his father. "Why are you here?"

"Mom sent me. Dinner's ready."

His father nodded but made no move to leave. Together they watched two EMTs carry a stretcher with a body bag on it down the steps. They were both wearing oxygen masks.

"Why are they wearing masks?" asked Jens.

"The state of the body," said his father. "For safety."

They slid the body into the ambulance and shut the doors. A moment later, they drove away. At the front door of Brother Monson's house, a uniformed officer was busy affixing a lockout device around the doorknob. They watched him struggle with it. When he was finally done, he made an X across the door with police tape. *Crime scene*, the tape said over and over, *do not cross*.

"It was a crime scene?" Jens asked.

"No," his father said. "But nobody should go in there. It's awful."

They watched the officer leave the door and make his way to his vehicle. Then Jens felt his father's hand come to rest lightly on his shoulder. "Let's go home," he said.

⟶

They walked most of the way in silence. They were just a few houses away from home when his father cleared his throat.

"You didn't have to lie," his father said.

"What?" asked Jens, startled.

"About talking to Brother Monson. In fact, I'm glad you didn't try to talk to him."

"But I wasn't lying!"

His father stopped, turned to face him. "Jens," he said, voice level, "the man's been dead nearly a week."

"But—" Jens started to say, and then stopped. He'd just seen Brother Monson standing at the door, he was sure of it. He'd seen into the man's mouth, seen those teeth. Jens opened his mouth to speak again, and then hesitated, remembering how the old man had smelled, what his eyes had looked like. Yes, the old man had been there, at the door, moving, walking, mumbling—his friend David had seen Brother Monson too, hadn't he?—but despite that Jens wasn't entirely certain that he had been alive.

"I'm not mad at you," his father was saying. "You're not in trouble."

"I'm sorry," Jens said, almost reflexively. But he could not bring himself to say directly that he had lied, because he hadn't. He had talked to Brother Monson. He really had.

"He must have died right after we saw him last," said his father.

Or maybe right before, Jens thought, remembering how his teeth had looked even that first time.

His father squeezed his shoulder again and they continued walking. They were nearly home. But they were, Jens knew, in two different worlds now. In his father's world, things still made sense, the dead stayed dead, everything acted as it should. In Jens' world, however, anything could happen. In Jens' world, even if someone was dead, if you rang twice they still answered the door.

NÁBRÓK

HELEN GRANT

There are very few Icelanders living in Britain; I doubt most people know one. Well, I've always liked to be the exception who proves the rule.

Ólafur Gunnarsson was originally a friend of my parents'—a near neighbour, in fact. After their demises at the relatively early ages of sixty-three and sixty-eight, I kept in touch with Ólafur. Every December I used to travel up from Edinburgh to the bleak stretch of coastland where my brother still lived, to spend a distinctly joyless Christmas with him and his wife. Visiting Ólafur a few houses down represented the only means of escape from this low-grade Purgatory.

He was perhaps seventy or seventy-five years of age, below the middle height and full-bellied, with startlingly blue eyes and a kindly, bearded face. He looked like nothing so much as an Icelandic Father Christmas, and indeed most of the festive cheer I ever got from visiting my home village came from him. Ólafur could always be relied upon to produce a bottle of something interesting, although he didn't have a lot of cash to spare. I sometimes wondered how he ended up living in a remote part of the Highlands, or indeed why he had left Iceland, although we never discussed it. I suppose he could still stare out to sea, over the turbulent grey waves, and think about his former homeland far away on the other side.

This particular Christmas was exceptionally grisly. My brother was in a permanently foul mood thanks to some dispute going on within the village which was too dull and parochial to care about, and his wife was as pursed-lipped as ever. I arrived on Christmas Eve, half an hour later than I'd said I would, and seemingly this had laid waste to all their dinner plans. I did my best to smooth it all over, but eventually I'd had enough, so I made up some flimsy excuse and went over to Ólafur's.

When I got to Ólafur's bungalow it was looking as jolly as I've ever seen it, with coloured lights strung up outside and draped around the little fir tree in the front garden. I went up the front steps and knocked on the door, glancing down with amusement at a rotund little ceramic Santa guarding the threshold. I was just about to knock again when it opened and there was Ólafur, in an unashamedly tasteless Christmas sweater.

"Stephen!" he said, with obvious delight. "Come in."

I followed him down the little hallway and into the sitting room, pulling a bottle of malt from the inside pocket of my coat.

"Merry Christmas," I said, handing it to him. I glanced around me.

The place really was looking amazingly festive, and cosy too. There was a brightly-lit Christmas tree in the corner by the television, tinsel around all the picture frames, and two long stockings hanging from the mantelpiece. There was also an impressive selection of bottles on the sideboard. It looked as though Ólafur had splashed out this year.

"This looks very good," I said. "You don't usually run to all this."

Ólafur beamed. "Yes," he said. "I am coming into money."

"Really? That's splendid."

"From a friend," said Ólafur. "Very soon." He held up the bottle of malt. "One of these?"

"Yes please," I said.

Ólafur fetched two crystal tumblers, poured us each a generous measure of whisky, and handed one to me.

"Sláinte," I said, raising my glass. I knew my brother would disapprove when I came home smelling of Scotch, but I didn't care. He'd have disapproved even without the smell of whisky, after all.

"Cheers," said Ólafur.

We sat down in the two ancient armchairs, and I had opened my mouth to make some commonplace remark when I noticed there was a suitcase standing against the wall. I gestured at it.

"Are you going somewhere, Ólafur?"

He shook his head. "No. It's from a visitor."

I looked around. I couldn't see any sign of anyone else. "You have a visitor? I'm sorry. Did I interrupt?"

"No, no. He's not here anymore."

"He's left his suitcase."

"He doesn't need it now." Ólafur sounded quite cheerful. "He's dead," he added.

I spluttered into my malt. "He is? My God, Ólafur. I'm so sorry."

He shrugged. "No need to be sorry. It was time. He knew he would die."

"All the same . . . "

Ólafur reached for the malt, poured himself another one, and then offered the bottle to me. "He was an old friend, from Iceland. Aron Jónsson, that is his name. We agreed long ago—if one of us is dying, we will go to the other one. Aron is dying first."

I didn't know what to say to this.

"He is the friend," Ólafur continued. "The one I am getting the money from."

"He is?" For one bizarre moment I wondered whether Aron Jónsson had brought the cash over in the suitcase. Perhaps it was stuffed with notes.

Ólafur nodded. "Yes. One or two things to do first. But it is nearly finished."

I supposed he meant legal matters. I wondered, though, how the whole thing had worked. I didn't think a citizen of Iceland could travel to Scotland with the express purpose of dying in a hospital here—could they? Not without running up an unpredictably large bill, the settling of which would cause endless administrative complications.

"That must have been difficult," I ventured, sympathetically. My second very generous serving of malt was burning a pleasant trail down my throat.

"Very difficult," agreed Ólafur.

We sat for a while in comfortable companionship, chatting of this and that. Then Ólafur went and fetched nuts and little spicy crackers. I tucked into those with enthusiasm because dinner had been quite frankly unappetising, and eventually he went off and produced something more substantial: slices of rye bread with pickled herring. The level of Scotch in the bottle I had brought was going down at an alarming speed.

I suppose the alcohol made me loose-jawed, because otherwise I would have left the topic alone.

"So when did your friend die then, Ólafur?"

"Yesterday," he said.

I winced. "Right before Christmas. I bet the undertakers didn't like that."

"I don't know," he replied.

"Well, I guess they can't complain to the customers' faces." I took another generous mouthful of the malt.

"It's a lucky time," said Ólafur.

"To die? Is that an Icelandic thing?"

He shook his head. "No, but it's a good time for me. I can go to church tomorrow. Christmas Day."

"I didn't know you were religious, Ólafur."

"I am not. I am going to get a coin."

I began to feel that the whisky had fuddled me. I wasn't keeping up with this at all.

"What coin?"

I think Ólafur was probably in the same state, because he swayed a little as he leaned towards me, and some of his Scotch slopped onto the carpet.

"Widow's coin. Most difficult thing to get."

"Why? What are you on about?"

"I will take it between the Letter and . . . " He looked puzzled for a moment. "Fagnaðarerindið."

"What's *that*?"

"Words of Matteus, Markús, Lúkas, and Jóhannes."

"Oh, the gospel."

"Yes, gospel." Ólafur hauled himself to his feet and stumbled across the room to the dresser. He came back with a piece of paper in his hand. "Also needing this," he informed me, slurring slightly.

"What's this?"

With some effort I focussed on the paper. There was something inked on it, but I couldn't tell what it was: a lot of loops and curves and little lines.

"Nábrókarstafur."

"Náb . . . I don't know what that is."

"Sign for making Nábrók," said Ólafur. He gave me a huge grin, his lips shining wetly through his beard. "Way to make money."

Unwisely, I picked up the whisky bottle and poured us each another one.

"I'll drink to that," I said, and I did. "So," I said. "How does it make money?" I gestured vaguely. "That piece of paper."

"Not just the paper," said Ólafur. There were crumbs and little bits of pickled herring in his beard, I saw, and also on the Christmas sweater which strained across his not insubstantial belly. "Three things. Paper, with Nábrókarstafur on it. Coin from widow. And Nábrók."

"Alright," I said. "But what's Nábrók?"

Ólafur appeared to think about this. "I don't remember the English word."

This struck me as somehow amusing, and I laughed. "Can't you explain it?"

"Like trousers," said Ólafur seriously. "Only from skin."

"You mean leather?"

"No, skin. Skin from a man. From the legs."

I stared at him, and then I began to laugh again. Icelandic humour is legendarily dark, but this was something else.

"Come on," I said.

"No, truly."

He said this absolutely deadpan, and that just made it funnier.

"How would they stay up?" I said. "Are they like legwarmers?"

"No," said Ólafur. "The butt is attached, and the front."

"The front? You mean like the . . . ? And the . . . ?"

Ólafur nodded. "That part is important. Nábrókarstafur and the coin go in that part. You put them on, and then there is always money in there. Not just the coin you put in. Lots."

"Ólafur," I said, wiping my eyes, "That is hilarious and also truly disgusting. You have a wild imagination."

He wasn't listening. "I remember the English name," he told me. "Necropants. Nábrók is Necropants."

Well, that was the end. I laughed until I was very nearly sick. Eventually, through the fog of single malt, I became uncomfortably aware of a pressure in my bladder, worsened by the spasms of laughter racking my body. So I stood up, holding onto the back of the armchair for support.

"I have to use your bathroom, Ólafur," I said, swaying slightly on my feet. "Be right back. And honestly, that was the best thing I've heard in ages. Absolute genius."

He waved in the general direction of the bathroom, but I knew where it was from previous visits. I lurched my way down the hall, still chuckling to myself, and went in.

It was a dowdy sort of bathroom, though perfectly functional. I don't think it had been redone since the 1970s; there were tiles with some kind of white-and-orange kaleidoscopic design on them, and a seedy-looking orange cover on the toilet seat. There was a very large tub which also served as the shower; it had a rail around the top with a plastic shower curtain hanging from it. The curtain was currently drawn all the way around the bath, which only registered because it brought the room in a bit; it wasn't a huge bathroom to begin with. I was more interested in relieving the pressure in my bladder.

I raised the shaggy orange toilet seat, unzipped and started to pee. As I stood there, I also found myself sniffing. There was an odd smell in the air that was hard to miss even in my current state. Blocked drain, I wondered? But it wasn't exactly like that. There was a kind of mineral quality to it. It was persistent, and unpleasant, and it made me feel I'd like to finish my business and get out of the room.

I turned, zipping up, and now I noticed something else. The bath was not, in fact, empty; through the opaque white curtain there was a bulky item dimly visible. The lower third of the curtain wasn't entirely white, either. A casual glance might have suggested a decorative pattern in toning shades of brown, but a closer look revealed uneven blotches and smears, and at the bottom, a solid dark stain.

It was absolutely not my business to investigate what Ólafur kept in his bathtub. It could have been . . . Well, I couldn't think of anything it might reasonably be, not with that pervasive odour and that ominously suggestive colour. I'm not sure it's possible to sober up instantaneously from that much malt whisky but it's fair to say the clouds parted. I put out a hand, grasped the curtain and pulled it back. It caught a little, because the end of it was tucked under whatever was in the tub, but then it came free.

There was a dead body in the bath. It was a man—an older man, about the same age as Ólafur, but thinner, hollow-cheeked as if he'd been unwell before he died. His eyes were not quite closed and his mouth yawned open. There was a faint blue-grey tint to his skin, a lot of which was on display, as he appeared to be naked. I say *appeared*, because there was a dark brown towel covering the lower part of the body.

I knew what the smell was now, and I had my free hand over my mouth and nose. Even so, I was gagging. I let go of the curtain and grasped the very corner of the towel, trying not to touch anything else. It was stiff with dried fluid. Underneath it was something that looked very much like meat. It *was* meat. I let the corner of the towel fall, turned very swiftly and threw up in the sink. The aroma of partly-digested herring and Scotch whisky did not improve the malodorous atmosphere in the bathroom, and I vomited again several times before I was done.

Eventually I recovered myself enough to leave the bathroom, though I took care not to glance into the tub again. I closed the door behind me, and staggered back down the hall.

The contrast between what I had just seen in the bathroom, and the festive cheer on display in the living room was distinctly surreal. Ólafur was sitting just where I'd left him, with his merry Christmas sweater on and a glass of malt in his hand. Everywhere, fairy lights gleamed in rainbow colours. In the corner stood the Christmas tree, decorated with baubles and tinsel, and there was also tinsel around all the picture frames. And from the mantelpiece there hung two Christmas stockings. Two very long, almost transparent stockings, tinged with brown and red. I looked at those stockings. In fact, I couldn't *stop* looking at them.

"Ólafur—" I said.

THE SALTED BONES

NEIL WILLIAMSON

he last stretch of the long road to Selston was a single-tracker badly in need of human attention. The surface, crumbling and caried like old teeth, the sides hedged in by silver birches and vigorous thrusts of bramble and fern that shouldered the sides of the car like contemptuous street thugs. Patrick, unused to traveling any sort of distance these days, felt increasingly remote with every tick of the mileometer but he chewed down his misgivings. According to the satnav app on his phone, he was almost there, albeit even now the road seemed determined to snake interminably on.

The thing was, he needed to know. Needed to understand what he'd seen inscribed on the girls' bones.

The flat envelope he'd brought from the unit lay on the seat next to him. It contained printouts of the x-rays he'd taken. The left forearms of the Masson twins, who'd arrived at the hospital with near identical ulnar fractures and an unlikely, mumbled story about a farm gate. With those unsplinted arms, however the teenagers had managed their southerly journey along this rotten road, it must have been a prolonged agony. Especially alone, as he believed since no one had come into the hospital with them. Just the two sixteen-year-olds with their haystack hair and wind-slapped faces, keeping their business to themselves. A single woman presenting with such an injury, similarly tight lipped, would have been a potential DV flag. Two sisters even more so, and Patrick's first thought *had* been to raise it with the doctor. It really had, but there'd been something about those girls. Not the usual home violence vibe, something else he couldn't identify. A hunch that they were a problem, and it would be better if they were someone else's. So, in the end, he'd just taken the shots and sent them back out to wait for the doctor to pass them down the chain for surgery or, more likely with such clean and stable breaks, to simply have their arms cast.

Which was when the pair—Deirdre and Karyn, they were called—had finally opened up enough to demand printouts of their shots. Patrick had turned them down flat. He was far too busy. There was a drunk with a skull fracture kicking up a stooshie out in the corridor, the latest in an already long line of Saturday lates horrors, for a start. When they'd started to beg, their soft accents souring into gull-like keening, Patrick had huckled them out with the old boilerplate promise that they could request their personal medical data via the Trust website if they really wanted it that badly. He'd felt like shit for about a minute, but then there was that concussed drunk to be dealt with and so the night had rolled on.

Asking for printouts of an x-ray was actually a fairly common request, but it stuck in his mind this time, snagged like wool on a thorn. It hadn't been the injuries themselves but the obvious desperation to examine them that had caused the girls' impassivity to crack. That was what had made him go back at the end of his shift and look again.

He'd had to compare several different projections, zooming right in, before he spotted what was odd about the two otherwise healthy-looking bones. The letters were so thin, so faint, he didn't blame himself for missing them on first inspection. The doctor had too; well, their attention was primarily on the fracture sites, wasn't it? Any other indicators of pathology that'd come up during the examination would have been noted, of course, but . . . it wasn't exactly *pathology*, was it? That fine, curling script viewed on the volar aspect, ghosting along the bones' surfaces like the most delicate scrimshaw. Carved by the tip of something hard—or so he'd have surmised if the twins' notes had indicated they'd ever been in hospital in their lives before that night.

Even disregarding the official records, amateur surgery would certainly have left scars, and the skin of their arms was flawless.

The writing, then, was impossible and, like everything else about these girls, identical. No, not *quite* identical.

The words themselves were different.

One said, *Warden*. The other, *Witness*.

Instantly consumed by the mystery, Patrick had tried to catch up with the twins only to find that they'd left the hospital and were already on their way home. Recalling his earlier wariness, he'd resolved to take that as a sign and put them from his mind, but over the days and weeks that followed, the desire to understand this inconceivable phenomenon had grown into a need so overwhelming it had become all Patrick could think about. A private mission. A very private one, in fact, as he discovered himself surprisingly reticent about revealing the details of his quest to anyone else. When he'd consulted colleagues, it was in the vaguest terms. When he stayed up at night scouring the medical literature for mention of anything similar, only making himself stop when he'd exhausted everything but the ultra whackjob end of the internet, he was careful to delete his search history. At first, he thought it was because he feared people wouldn't believe him, think him crazy even, but instinctively he knew that the reason went deeper than that. It felt like he was looking for something forbidden. But still he *needed* to know, and all his inquiries had proved fruitless anyway. So, here he was now, crawling along the farm roads of Argyllshire in search of a village that wasn't even a dot on an all but featureless area of the map and, given the nature of his quest this far, he half-suspected did not actually itself exist.

The satnav, which had given up providing vocal directions some time ago, pinged to tell him he was going the wrong way.

The fuck? How? This was the only road.

Pulling over, Patrick examined the map on his phone. Sure enough, there was a slender offshoot, like a thin, creeping root, a hundred yards back along the road. He must have missed it among the overgrowth. Cursing aloud, he considered reversing, but the snaking bends were tight and it'd be just his luck to back into a farm truck coming up behind him. *Fuck.* He eased the car forward again, hoping that it wouldn't be too long until he found a place wide enough to turn around and trying not to think about the extra petrol the diversion might consume. He'd budgeted on being able to do this whole trip on a single tank and it had been a while since he'd last passed a filling station. The sun was high now, the inside of the car starting to bake. Feeling a trickle down his back, Patrick opened the vents, but he didn't dare chance the fuel-hungry aircon.

His need to know was increasingly battling against the resurging conviction that this was, after all, a very bad idea.

His phone chimed again. No, it was ringing now. It took him three swipes to answer.

"What?"

"Charming!"

"Sorry, love," he told Vee. "Bit frustrated right now."

"Well, that answers my first question of *how's it going*," his wife said with a little laugh. Trying to keep it light because they'd argued about this. The *whys* of it all that he'd tied himself in ridiculous knots trying to articulate, because as far as she was concerned there was no real, good reason for him to drive all the way out here. No medical or social care emergency that ought to involve Patrick personally, anyway. His professional duty of care had ended when the sisters had walked out of the hospital. *But he'd just had this feeling, see, and no one else was doing anything. He didn't want them to slip through the net . . .* It had been a rambling and embarrassingly thin fiction, but he hadn't been able to tell Vee about the writing any more than he had anyone else.

"Must be nice to be out in the countryside at least." She said this breezily enough, but he felt the intended barb. Because, if he was determined to waste north of a hundred quid on a jaunt up the West Coast, couldn't they at least have made a family outing out of it? The kind of trip Dad had taken Patrick on regularly—*C'mon, son, mum needs a break today*—when he was a kid and thought nothing of it. It was a fair question, and one Patrick had no answer for. Just another loose thread that Vee would be unable to help herself tugging at. Hadn't she, right off the bat, asked about the girls' mother? Straight in there, first question, regardless of the fact the woman had played no part in the tale. Because there always had to be a reason for Vee. A reason why Patrick had to work longer and longer hours. A reason why, despite that, the money had got so tight. A reason why everything once sure was crumbling these days.

None of that invalidated the fact that it *was* nice being out here away from the city, in a landscape so barely tended it seemed on the brink of turning to wild. The verges were glorious with verdant nettles and explosions of frothy hogweed. The weeds used to be taken care of by the Council during the summer months. Patrick remembered the old trundling tractors hacking their way through the vegetation, and his Dad's fretful muttering whenever they were caught in tailback behind one of them as if his desire to get away had been foiled. Hobbled. But those were bygone days, before the decades of local authority cuts and the fuel crisis and the government's eternally compromised attempts at implementing some sort of environmental policy worth a damn.

"Yeah, it's nice," he said, and did not add *being away from the city*, because that really meant *away from you* which even the emotionally clueless Patrick had finally understood had been his Dad's true motive for their frequent jaunts the mornings after the furiously silent nights before. He told himself that he wasn't like his Dad. More and more frequently as he got older.

He wasn't even sure if *nice* was the right word, though. Hard to appreciate all the beauty around him with a mind constantly full of competing anxieties.

"I've not really time to enjoy it, though," he said. "I'm just focussing on trying to find this place, you know? Check up on those lassies and then back down the road by bedtime."

"Right," Vee said. "Well, it's your turn to read tonight, so . . . "

"Yeah, I know. I'll do my best. Promise."

But then it was Jackie's voice. "Daddy, where are you?"

"Hiya, Champ!" Their kid was seven now but sometimes he still sounded like a baby, tiny and fragile and prone to night terrors, even as he was growing physically into a proper, rangy little boy. "I'm visiting some patients from the hospital right now, but I'll be back later on. What story do you want to read tonight?"

"Hmm." Patrick pictured the index finger tapping the chin, the kid's new affectation that demonstrated that he was giving the question proper consideration. "We'll see. When the time comes," he said, suddenly sounding absurdly grown up.

Patrick couldn't help laughing. "Aye, I guess we will, Champ." The car nosed around the next corner and there at last was a farm gate with just about enough space to pull a three-pointer.

"Okay, Jackie, I've got to go now. I'll see you later on, okay?" Bringing the car to a stop, Patrick reached to disconnect the call.

"Daddy?" His son's voice suddenly thinned to a whisper, fracturing into surf as the phone's reception dropped to the lowest bar. What Jackie said next was indistinct, but it sounded like: "How do we know when it's too late?"

Patrick pulled on the handbrake. The engine idled unevenly. "What, Champ?" he said. "What did you say?"

"At school," the signal gained a notch, "we learned about No Planet B because of global warming. And Mrs Gillies said we have to save the Earth before it's too late."

"Oh, mate," Patrick said. "Well, we are doing stuff to save the planet, aren't we? That's why we walk to school and compost our vegetable waste and do our clean-up volunteering along the riverbanks." Although, not nearly as often as they meant to, if truth be told. "If everyone does those things then it won't be too late, will it? The planet will be just fine." Patrick felt the dishonesty leaking around his words like sump oil, but what else was a parent supposed to say? "Listen, we can talk about it when I get home. Maybe make a special effort this week. How does that sound, eh?"

There was no reply because the reception had died completely.

Patrick puffed his cheeks. He could have handled that better. Should have. He tried not to feel annoyed at the school. Environmental responsibility lessons were vital, of course they were. More now than ever. It was just that Patrick had been hearing the same well-intentioned shite most of his own life and . . . Honestly? What good had any of it ever actually done? Here they were at thirty-four degrees on the dash thermometer and rising. In northwest Scotland, for fuck's sake. They couldn't even call it *rare* anymore.

How do we know when it's too late? Fucked if I know, son.

Cracking open the windows, Patrick tried and failed not to think about the exhaust fumes trailing out behind the old car. They'd been waiting for the right time jump to electric, and waiting, and waiting. Patrick's Dad, who for years had run an old twin tank XJS, would've split his sides. But he'd been a manager at the Grangemouth refinery, hadn't he? In a different age.

The road, when Patrick found it, was little more than a farm track, tuffets of long grass sweeping the underside of the car as it jostled down the gradient. At least he finally had a view of the sea, and with that he felt his heart settle a little. He'd forgotten how clear the water was up in this part of the country, how white the beaches. Looking at it now, the bay calm and glittering under the sun, the natural beauty trapped his breath like a trembling bird between cupped hands. Even the grey houses down there, clustered around a short slipway and then strung out along the bay's gentle curve like oyster shells, didn't spoil it. He counted three flaking boats up on the wildflower-strewn machair too. High and dry, less sea-worthy vessels than just another feature of the landscape.

This'd be Selston, then.

Patrick pulled up near the first of the houses, grabbed the folder, and got out of the car. It was so still, so quiet. No gull chatter, no wave rush, not even the whisper of a breeze. The warm air tingled his nose as he breathed it in. The unpaved . . . street, he supposed you'd call it, was choked with tall spears of purple loosestrife and hemmed by bushes, heavy with swollen red rosehips, though no blackbird or thrush bustled within. The only other vehicle in evidence was a once-yellow Toyota, parked flush against the first building's gable end, slumped on soft tyres and clamped by yellow dandelions. Patrick wondered if he was in the right place after all until he saw in a window a sun-faded Royal Mail sticker with a sliding panel that said: *Open*.

Tentatively, he pushed at the weathered red door and found himself in the local shop. The counter was just large enough to hold the till. Next to it hummed a glass-fronted fridge containing a few cartons of dairy milk and a packet of bacon. The rest of the room was shelved, with corner shop staples—stationery, tinned vegetables, and soup—crammed alongside more esoteric produce like pimento stuffed olives and potted stilton. Most of the food was only just in-date, but the shop was at least tidy and that gave Patrick the confidence to call out.

"Hello?" The flat echo made him feel like an intruder. It had taken three weeks for his curiosity to overcome what remained of his professionalism. For him to look up the Masson twins' medical records to find out firstly the landline number they'd given that went continually unanswered, and then their address. In that time, he'd almost convinced himself with his self-justifications, but now he was here . . . *Jesus*. How would he react if someone turned up at his house with a story about words written on his Jackie's bones? This was stalker behaviour. *Wrong*. He had to leave.

Backing away, Patrick's hip jostled the magazine rack. He caught it before it toppled but couldn't prevent it knocking against the shelves with a ringing clang.

"What do you want?"

In the dimness, he'd not noticed the door at the back. But he did recognise the person who had appeared through it as one of the twins, though which he couldn't tell. Taller than he remembered, she was wearing jean shorts and a loose, tie-dyed cheesecloth shirt that made her look like a refugee from Woodstock.

"Uh, hi," Patrick said stupidly. "I—"

"You what?" The girl shut him down, displaying scant evidence of her previous reticence. Instead, this bordered on aggression.

"Sorry," he said. "I'll start again. My name is Patrick Morgan. I don't know if you remember me from the hospital?"

"I remember you fine. Much use you were. What do you want?"

"I came to see you," he said. "You and your sister. Sorry, is it—are you—Karyn or Deirdre?" The girl didn't reply. Patrick tried again. "Or perhaps I should talk to your parents?"

"Mum's dead," the girl said bluntly, but with those words something changed. Like her anger was suddenly revealed as a glassy veneer beneath which another emotion boiled to be expressed. "That's why we went down to the hospital in the first place," she said with a little less venom, now more like the teenager he'd first met.

"To see these?" Patrick held up the folder. "You went through all of that just to get x-rayed?"

"You want to know, do you?" she said bitterly. "You *really* want to know?"

For several long seconds, Patrick couldn't answer. He did want to know. He needed to know. It was his duty, he still insisted on telling himself, as a health care professional, as a parent, as a member of a civilized fucking society. But he utterly dreaded it too. Again, he asked himself: *what if it was Jackie?* And made himself nod.

The girl retreated into the room she'd emerged from. Following, he discovered a cluttered domestic kitchen that appeared to have last been modernised sometime around the millennium. There were dirty dishes heaped up around the sink and what looked like stockpiles of bottled water, tinned beans, and boxes of crisps stacked up along the wall behind a drop-leaf kitchen table Patrick remembered from the days he and Vee had also furnished their own house from Ikea.

"We never had twins in the family before," the girl said. She was standing by the sink, her face striated with light filtered through the loosestrife that crowded the kitchen window. She was plucking nervously at her sleeve, and he realised that she wasn't wearing her cast. Instead, he caught a glimpse of a dressing. It had a rust-coloured fringe. "We didn't know who it would be," she finished.

"Who what would be?" Patrick said quietly, unable to look away from the evidence of what the girls must have done when their request to see their x-rays had been denied. They'd have scars now, for sure.

That was on him, but there was little time for self-recrimination because the next words he heard her say were, "The new Warden." And it was a shock hearing that word spoken aloud, the secret he'd felt compelled to keep all these weeks, although he was still unable to say why. But it made sense. They must have known about the words all along. They'd been looking for confirmation.

"What does that mean?" Patrick said hoarsely. The stillness of this place was a weight now, slowly crushing him.

The girl rolled her eyes contemptuously. As her head moved in the barred light, Patrick noticed a flushed glisten to her skin. Just the day's heat, he hoped, instinctively shutting down thoughts of sepsis brought on by their self-mutilating misadventure. Then he chastened himself. He'd come here on the pretext of caring about these kids, hadn't he? He was no doctor, but he could check her out, make sure they were both okay before he left. He just needed to understand first.

"Please?" he said.

She looked like it'd kill her to tell him any more, but then she pointed to something on the kitchen counter. It was propped up against the wall between a cheap plastic kettle and a roll-front bread bin. A wooden frame which he initially took to be a spice rack but, as he approached, he realised lacked the expected jars filled with once pungent dust and dry leaves.

Instead, the narrow shelves held bones.

Each was slender and around nine inches long, give or take. The ones at the bottom were dark brown with age, but they got lighter, yellower and then whiter, the higher you went up the ladder. The one on the highest rung was all but luminous in the wedge of window light. It was easy to see the writing. The same word that Patrick knew he would find on them all if he were to examine them.

"We've always had a Warden here," the girl murmured as both of them gazed down at the homemade rack. There was something else about it, he realised. Something that wouldn't have shown on the x-rays. A gentle scintillation in the half-light that made the bones beautiful, not grisly, as they ought to be by rights. "The Warden is an accord between the people, the land and the sea," the lass went on. "Passed down, mother to daughter."

And was that it, he thought. The source of her anger? There's always a warden—whatever that *actually* might be—and it wasn't her. She'd been heads and she was pissed off that the coin had come down tails. He knew which of the twins she must be now.

"Where is Deirdre, Karyn?" he said. "Where's your sister?"

"She's out on the wall." Karyn's voice was thin as thread now and she was crying hot, hateful tears.

"What's she doing out there?"

"She's doing her best."

"Karyn," he said. "What's going to . . . " He couldn't finish the sentence. He knew the words. *Happen. What's going to happen?* But they were too large to squeeze out into the thickening air.

The terror and anger in her young face. "You already know," she said. "*All of you know.* You've known for years."

Patrick blundered away, bumping and stumbling. Back through the shop, and then yanking open the door and recoiling because the sun was so bright now it hurt to look at anything for more than a few seconds. Red and black spots swam in his vision, and there was a brutal aridity to the air too. The razor-sharp tang of salt. Looking beyond the blinding white beach he saw that the tide had gone out in the time he'd been inside. It was just glittering sand as far as he could see now. Featureless, except for a long lump a hundred yards or so out. Too far to identify what it was, only that it was absolutely still. Maybe a dead seal, he thought. Yeah, probably that.

Then he thought of the newest, whitest bone on the rack. *Mum's dead.* Could be that as well.

Dragging his gaze back to the shoreline, Patrick made out at the far end of the low wall that delineated the machair from the road, a slight figure standing, facing out to the Atlantic. One that at least was very much alive, although it had to be the heat haze that made Deirdre look as thin as if she'd be remoulded by Giacometti himself.

Patrick cast his eyes to the ground and followed the track along the curve of the wall. It was still so oppressively quiet that he was startled by the scuff his steps made on the shell-strewn road and he found himself treading carefully, as if not to disturb . . . he didn't know who. The houses he passed had the same shuttered air as the one with the shop, but who could say if there was anyone in residence observing him from behind the shimmering squares of liquid light the sun made of their windows? And as soon as he'd thought that, he began to imagine that he heard a faint, but unmistakably human sound coming from within each building he passed. That of inconsolable sobbing. "Come home," he heard between whooping hitches. "Please, just come home." He didn't pause. He didn't look. He walked on. The air was so dry, it was getting hard to breathe. He could feel his skin drying out, the salt burning his throat and the inside of his nose. But still he needed to know, and there was no going back now, was there?

It was several minutes before he realised that he'd stopped getting closer to Deirdre. Her disturbingly etiolated figure remained a stubborn fifty feet away, up on the wall and now taut as a kite in a full-on westerly. Though Patrick still felt not a puff of wind, the girl was bowed, almost bent double but, somehow, she prevailed. Her hair whipped around her head and her mouth was shout-wide.

"Deirdre!" he yelled, though it hurt like fuck to do so, and his voice came out muffled anyway, like shouting inside a closet surrounded by winter coats. He'd known before he even tried that she wouldn't hear him. Nevertheless, he yelled again. "Deirdre!"

Heedless, the girl began gesticulating. Waving her arms in the face of the invisible force, plainly trying to placate it. Pleading. Such a tiny figure. Jesus, she wasn't that much older than Jackie. Someone ought to be doing something to help. The authorities, the adults. Patrick tried again to reach her. There was no force preventing him, no invisible wind beating him back. He just couldn't.

Then Deirdre sagged, dropping her arms and turned back landwards. Towards *him*. The look on her face was not the hate of her sister, but one of utter defeat. And of betrayal.

In the next moment, she buckled and flipped, and was whiplashed up into the air. And was gone.

For a second there was perfect stillness. Then Patrick heard it, far off. A simple, soft white noise, at first; a shush, a hiss, then taking on more complex textures, like the relaxation playlist Vee played in Jackie's bedroom to ward off his night terrors. Except there was nothing soothing about this sound. In seconds it was the rumble and rush of angry seas, the bellow of vicious winds. Out in the bay, he saw fury on the horizon. The wave was coming at last, and it was coming fast.

Patrick ran back towards the car. Past the crying houses. Past the shop. He didn't stop. He couldn't. Not with the wave building at his back. Now its thunder contained the screaming of sea birds, the bellowing of seals, the ghostly rage of whale song.

He couldn't see the car. Just an old wreck that someone had abandoned next to one of the houses. A cancerous pile of junk all but lost amid the loosestrife. But of course, it *was* his car.

The wave was coming. Hissing, roaring up the shore behind him. He fumbled his key into the lock. Yanked open the stiff door and got inside. Jabbed it into the ignition.

But what was the use of turning it?

He knew it was too late.

He knew it was too late.

Karyn Masson was right. He'd known for years.

◄◦►

Afterwards.

An hour later, or maybe a day. After he sat in the car and dry sobbed out of shame, he turned the ignition key—*come home*, well, what else was there to do now?—and was astounded when the car's filthy engine spluttered to life. He bumped the vehicle out onto the road and cajoled it up the hill and stole guiltily away from Selston. His lungs burned and his hands bled from the sharp silicate deposits that stubbornly encrusted the steering wheel and gear stick and sparkled throughout the car, inside and out, but he paid the pain little mind. Neither did he really notice the shrivelled, blackened, salt-poisoned hedgerows and trees, crops and weeds in the verges and the fields as he limped past. The carpet of already dead fur and feathers beneath his wheels. The glittering road.

All he could think of was what was written on Jackie's bones. His and those of his entire generation. And whose obdurate, careless ignorance had inscribed it there.

Witness. Witness, witness, witness.

Blameless, powerless witnesses, every last one.

TELL ME WHEN I DISAPPEAR

GLEN HIRSHBERG

"**A**ll right, tents zipped, lights *out!*" Kerber shouts, and just like that, they're gone. All of them. Not the kids, obviously, the kids are still staggering out of the chemical toilets and making exaggerated vomiting sounds, spitting toothpaste any old where as they stroll through camp pitching sand or whipping frisbees at each other. But the rest of the adults—our colleagues—vanish in the dark like desert foxes, hole up in their own tents, wake their phones if they still have charge and can get signal, or just burrow into their sleeping bags on their air mattresses.

Leave us to it. Me and CFK. Which is only fair. We chose this duty.

I pop a watermelon mint in my mouth, watch the lights in the faculty tents bloom like night flowers. They won't stay on long. It's exhausting, chaperoning teens on anxiety-therapy trips to the desert. We're teachers, not naturalists. Didn't sign up for this, we like to complain. But of course we did. It's right there in the contract. Once a year. Every damn fall. I've never been sure these weeks do much for the children. But their parents sure love it.

Beneath my feet, the Earth rumbles. The flash comes a split second later, out of order, from the base of the mountains way off across the sandy emptiness—the Nothing With Teeth, as Steph used to call this whole place, or maybe the whole Mojave. The Marines at Twentynine Palms have been especially restive this week, dropping practice bombs pretty much every night, sometimes all night. Hardly surprising, I guess. So many possible wars to look forward to, now.

"Hey, Amelia," CFK stage-whispers. "Want to Blair Witch 'em?" He's standing astride the campground's two stone picnic tables, one foot on each, hands extended over the circular grill/firepit as if there's a fire there. Some years we do have fires there, every night, no matter who's on get-them-to-sleep duty, and all the adults stay out and huddle together and stargaze and talk. Share gum, shiver, complain, gossip. Remind one another to turn off roaming so our phone charges last longer. Get the baseball score from Amy or CFK, because we're usually out here World Series week. It's not fun, exactly. But there's fun in it. A teaching life novelty, being at work but with adults and not at some mandatory meeting about dress code standards or lunch supervision guidelines or roleplaying SAFE (our district's latest behavior management acronym, for Steps to Avoid Flashpoint Episodes).

But the nights have been freezing this week, and the rangers don't want us or anyone lighting fires, anyway—too dry, too dangerous—and most of us are tired of talking. To anyone. Sick of each other, and the monster in the White House, and the murders of Black men climbing our feeds, and the constant smoke from the fires burning yet again upstate or out by the coast. Sun broiling all day, every day. This year, instead of just complaining nonstop about the chemical toilets at this campsite, the kids have been sneaking across the road and shitting in the cacti. Not even cleaning it up, then lying about it to our faces.

Not typical. Not in my experience. Not to *my* face. They know I like them too much.

I think I still do. But there's no doubt, something has shifted in me, too. In the country, and the Earth. Some nights, I swear I can smell it. Something even worse coming. Already loose in the air.

"Want a mint?" I say.

CFK jumps down and pads around the fire circle. I offer him my tin, and he scrabbles around in it with filthy fingers. His gym-rat shoulders ripple under the short-sleeved polo he insists on sporting no matter how cold it gets, even though I can see goosebumps atop goosebumps all over his skin.

He's got his black wool beanie in his hands, and so I get a good look at just how bad his latest buzzcut is. As though the clippers kept slipping, skimming over patches. Possibly, he did it himself. Or else he ordered precisely this look at the super high-end male beauty salon I am confident he frequents. Both equally possible. Not even mutually exclusive, in his case.

C.F.K. I used to know what the C and F actually—no, *originally*—stood for. Saw it on some official looking reprimand notice from the district he left on the Faculty Center desk we share. But these days, to everyone who knows him (and to himself, I'm pretty sure), he's Crazy Fucking Kerber. As I watch, he bounces up and down beside me, either because he's cold or he's really itching to go terrify kids for fun.

His? Theirs?

He flexes his arms at nothing and no one. Certainly not at me. Sometimes, I still think he's a big, bouncy Labrador. Lots of bark, no bite. Sometimes, I think I know better. His Dartmouth PhD dissertation is on proto pan-sexualism in Edna St. Vincent Millay. I've read it.

"Now do you want to Blair Witch 'em?" he says.

Laughing, I lean back and catch some starlight in the burls of my fleece sweater-jacket. I imagine it pooling in the crags and ridges of my cheeks. Backs of my hands. My old lady hands. Not too many more of these trips for me. Gently—the way it mostly comes on me now, almost kindly, like a cat—the longing for Joe stirs. I wish he were the one here beside me, maybe even holding my old-lady hands. Or that he would be home when I got there. Or anywhere in this world.

On the other side of the little stand of mesquite bushes where the baby rattler was when we arrived this morning, as far back into this bowl of rock and away from chaperones as they can get, the kids are still circulating among their tents. They're flirting in their fluffy hats and pjs, or bent over cellphones, or clustering for safety with their friends, toothbrushes dangling from their lips like Joules. The ones actually sneaking vapes are back farther still, probably up *on* the rocks where they're not supposed to go, around behind boulders, feet brushing the mouths of snake burrows they'll hopefully never realize were there.

I sigh. "If we scare them, we're just going to rile them up."

"So?"

I shrug. "Okay with me. I've got nowhere to be."

As usual—though not always—he's all bark. He nods. "Should we put 'em down, then?"

The choice of words is artful. Intentional. Probably. He's doing it partly for my amusement. Definitely for his own. But that doesn't quite mean he doesn't mean it. Unless it does. CFK.

"If we try to get them settled now, you know we're just going to have to do it again in ten minutes."

"Half the fun."

"Let's give them their unaccosted minutes. These kids don't get many."

He takes another mint I didn't offer. Then he leaps back to the tabletop. "*IN YOUR FUCKING TENTS!*" he roars, and glances back my way, practically wagging his tail.

I don't reprimand. Don't say anything. My best and hardest-learned teacher trick. Human trick, really. I just lean into the starlight. He hops down again. For a lot more than ten minutes, we stand silent together and watch the night come out. The deer mice and kangaroo rats are already stealing into the mess area, hunting scraps. Dessert, actually. They've no doubt had their primary meals during the day, in the tents, rooting out the snacks the students are forbidden to have from unzipped backpacks and duffels while we were out scrambling or climbing. At our feet, the sand stirs, and two stink bugs and a scorpion surface like impossible alien submarines and lurch off about their moonlit business. Up on the nearest rocks, eyes glint here and there. Ground squirrels, probably. Ringtails. Even a desert fox or bobcat, maybe. Every now and then, in luckier years, we see one of those.

The Nothing with Eyes and Claws. Nothing with Spines. Nothing Camouflaged as Nothing. All ways Steph referred to the Mojave during the one week I knew her. I've never forgotten.

"Shit," says CFK, stepping forward, raising his right sneaker.

"Leave it be," I say, because I know him. Know this about him, anyway.

He lets it be, and I see it. Fat black tarantula bobbing along, almost floating over the sand like a jellyfish. This really has been the strangest year. Strangest trip.

The hiss jerks me ramrod straight. CFK hears it, too, whirls to stare with me into the mesquite stand.

"Didn't they catch it?" I say. Careful and calm, though I'll admit I don't love rattlesnakes. "I thought they caught it."

"They said they caught it." He sounds remarkably like a regular person for a second. Someone with healthy fears and appropriate responses to stimuli.

"The mom, too. Right?"

We'd had to call the rangers five minutes after our arrival this morning. Keep the kids on the sweltering bus, with the pissed-off driver glowering at them and growling at us that his vehicle was not a mobile home, he had places to be, and at the very least we better fucking silence our students. I got some of them playing heads-up for a while. That didn't calm the bus driver much, and in fairness it didn't lower the volume any, but at least it provided a distraction.

The rangers took over an hour to roust the snake. Not kill it, though I didn't see what they did with it. Move it, supposedly. Then its mom showed up. That was another, scarier hour.

Maybe that's why I keep thinking of Steph right now. She was the junior ranger enlisted to guide our hikes and boulder scrambles on my very first trip here. Maybe five years older than the students. She wore a floppy green sunhat and smiled all the time. The two key components of her disguise. I saw that right away. She saw that I saw. "Always remember," she'd told me at the end of our first campfire, after a good night, when all the other adults had turned in. "Everything here is trying to kill you."

She haunts me, sometimes. Steph. For years afterward, I'd asked other rangers who joined us if they'd heard from her. Knew where she was now, or what she was doing. Whether she'd made it, though I never quite asked that. Most of them had no idea who she was. One guy shrugged and said, "Oh, yeah, her. She just vanished."

Another hiss, now. Except . . . not exactly a hiss. Maybe. It also seems farther away, the sound echoing from somewhere over by the rocks. CFK just stands next to me with his hands on his hips like he thinks he's Gary Cooper, mid-showdown. A split second from drawing. From this angle, I can still see the shadow of the black eye he came to campus with a month or so ago. He stomped past the open door of my room, already ten minutes late for his sunrise class, tie twisted sideways like a noose he'd slackened but not ripped free of, silk shirt buttoned wrong.

I didn't ask. Teacher trick.

As he went by, he scowled at me. But all he said was, "Amelia." And then, "Barfight."

Possible? Yes. But also possibly imagined. Or invented. That's *his* trick, of course. I've taught in the room adjacent to that man for fifteen years. I teach AP Psychology. I still have no idea. Whatever his mystique is, he's committed to it.

Gary Cooper or no, he's not moving to check around in the rocks. I move to stand shoulder to shoulder with him. Maybe one of us is reassuring the other. Wind kicks up, rips straight through my jacket and alpaca hat. My thin skin. Thinning hair. I mostly haven't minded getting old. Arthritis, stiffening of the spine, whitening hair, faces dragging along in my memory like cans on a newlywed's car—*Just Lived!*—mostly that has all seemed appropriate to me. In rhythm, part of the harmony.

But I'm definitely colder, now.

CFK digs an elbow into my ribs. "Okay, Mealie. Blair Witch time."

"Sure you don't want to roleplay some SAFE?"

"That's not even funny. Why would you even say that?"

"Because you called me 'Mealie'."

"You don't like it?"

"No."

"How's this for SAFE?"

Then he's off, clapping and shouting, pouring through the kids like a fox in a chicken yard. He barges right into a barrel cactus, roars louder, never even slows down. Shrieking, laughing—some of them are laughing—the kids dive for their tents. Hands in my pockets, I make my way carefully around the mesquite stand where the snakes were, across the sand toward the flags we've put up to divide the girls' and boys' sleeping zones.

At the flag line, I gently funnel the stream of girls tentward. Most of the ones still out don't even want to leave their tents during the day for fear of sand-scuffing their shoes. These girls are all pretty sure CFK's crazy is a threat for the boys, but flirting for them. If we were talking about any other teacher but him, I'd worry they were right.

Other years—every other year—even these girls tend to gather around me by this point in the evening. Ask me to tell them one of my stories, or do my night magic, or just sit and look at the stars with them. I'm the island they wash up on. A lot of them love it. I still love that they do.

But like I said: strange year. Most of these kids just stream past. One or two say "Good night, Ms. Joseph."

"Sleep well," I say back.

It's possible I hear the next thing wrong. I'm almost sure it comes from the group of three in the tent pitched nearest the flag line, all in matching pink pussycat hats, none of them in my classes. It's whispered, but not quietly.

"Cool your catheter, Granny."

I keep my hands in my pockets, my shoulders un-shrugged. Watch another twenty or so girls I'll never really know, or only know briefly on their way to becoming women I'll never meet, as they disappear into tents, switch on camping lanterns or ridiculously bright mag-lights that are going to lure any beetle or stinging thing in the vicinity. Another ten minutes, and I'll make the lights-out rounds.

"Ooh!" says another girl, just to my left. Jayna, from my class. "*Shit!*"

I whip around, scanning for snakes. But she's just standing with one foot in her tent, one out. I move toward her, but not as quickly as I should. *If she's got a rattler in her sleeping bag . . .*

"Did you see it, Ms. J?"

She has her arm up, finger jabbed at the horizon, and I abruptly realize I might have. A streak of light, way off in the far corner of my eye.

"Perseids," I say.

"Those come in summer." ˙

Good kid, Jayna. On the spectrum somewhere. Nervous all the time, chattery but distant from her peers. Interested in things. "The rangers say you can still see them out here some autumns, on clear nights."

Nothing with Lights. Did Steph coin that one?

"I wish the sky were like this in L.A."

"Me, too, Kiddo."

We scan the heavens together. Automatic, after a shooting star. One of those experiences that instantly triggers longing for more. Like lots of experiences, I have learned. But with shooting stars, that longing is the very core of the thing. Almost the whole thing.

"I wish my sister were here," Jayna murmurs after a while, in a tone that suggests her sister isn't home, either. Is elsewhere.

I wish Joseph were here, I don't answer back. *And* my *sister. And my mom and dad.* I wish any of them were anywhere.

"Thanks, Ms. J," says Jayna, and I blink.

"For the shooting star?"

She laughs. Not even dutifully. "'Night." She ducks into her tent, and abruptly, I have to clamp my mouth shut and my elbows to my sides. To keep from shouting, *Snakes! Wait!*

At my feet, the sand stirs, slides over my shoes. Not like snakes. But like my feet aren't even there. Which is and always has been the way of the desert and everything in it. Another memory surfaces, from a long time ago. Fifteen years, at least. Possibly twenty. Somewhat younger me—on the outside, anyway, inside I feel the same, or think I do—with that year's Jayna, a whole trail group full of Jaynas, crouching around me in the dusk, all of us holding each other still as we watched a desert tortoise amble slowly, slowly past. One leg at a time rising as if cranked on some rusted winch under that beaten, sand-colored shell. One by one, in no order I remember making, we all crept forward for a closer look, loomed directly over the tortoise. Which took no notice.

The only desert tortoise I've seen in all these trips here.

"Oh my God," one of the pussycat girls says, laughing nasty. When I look that way, she's pointing *at me*, and oh, it's still so powerful, that tone and that gesture; it works on everything *not* a tortoise. I find myself wanting to check my sweatpants on my hips, straighten my glasses or what's left of my hair (as if that would do any good).

Except she's not actually pointing at but past me. With her fingerless glove. Pink pussycat paw.

"CFK!" she shouts.

Then all the girls are shrieking and giggling. Leaving me a tortoise once more, ambling quietly out of their lives. Out of life.

I turn and look.

He's by the trouble tent. Of course he is. Those boys have pitched their camp way closer to the rocks than they've been told they can go. The scatter of dirty socks and journals they will never write in and headlamps they refuse to wear and high-end thermoses their parents bought them encircles their area like a moat.

Not deep or wide enough, boys, I think, watching as CFK advances. Herds them before him. He's got his back to me, but I can hear him from here. The whole camp can. Trick of the rocks. Also of his. He's not even yelling.

"Want to stay up late? Is that what you're saying? Want to stay up late with me? I've got some fun we can have. Want to meet at the toilets? With your toothbrushes?"

"CFK!!!" calls another pussycat, but too loud, I know it even before CFK spins around.

He is good. He's easily fifty yards away. But the girl doesn't just go quiet; she ducks. He glances once around the whole camp, a prison searchlight on legs. "Anyone else want to meet me at the toilets?"

It's the contempt, I realize, that's so devastating. It might or might not be real. But it's all-encompassing, aimed at this whole experience and every kid here and every adult, too. Including me, probably. Himself, definitely.

Two minutes later, the boys are in their tents.

That next stretch of time can be magical, most trips. Almost as electrifying as slipping out of my own tent to brave the bathroom at 2:30 in the morning, the whole camp asleep, the moon gone and the stars everywhere, lining the sky in whirls and furrows. Seeded light.

Ironic, really. Those moments when I most doubt the importance we place on being "alive"—meaning, witnessing the universe at the expense of feeling part of it—are the ones I've been surest I was living.

Certainly since Joe died. Almost a decade ago, now.

Tonight, though, I can't get that pussycat girl's sneer out of my ears. I'm also finding CFK's act predictable. A tired show in its ten thousandth performance, there to be captured on cellphones and memed. How much did I ever really like it, anyway?

Also . . .

Everything here is trying to kill you.

All around me, I'm sensing if not quite seeing tiny faces peeking out of burrows. Overhead, just occasionally, I can hear the hunters that prey on them skimming by. The cacti scattered everywhere seem to twitch in the barely-there breeze as though signaling each other. From the base of the one nearest me, another scorpion scuttles out. I've gone whole years without seeing one, but this trip, they're everywhere. My least favorite desert animal, the creature I've been most sure would hurt me sooner or later. "Always check your sleeping bags," Steph warned our whole group, with that same smiling not-smile. As if checking sleeping bags is a thing you can do well by flashlight in the dark in a too-small tent. "Also your shoes when you put 'em back on. Scorpions like it warm."

CFK is sauntering my way, snarling warnings as he goes. Stomping out chatter, crawling things, whatever else he thinks needs stomping. Up on the rocks, the night shadows are creeping down. They always do, and I always wonder what, exactly, is up there to cast them. But tonight . . . I don't know. They look wrong. Meaning, I think, that they look more like shadows of actual things. Long and spiny, causing little waterfalls of pebbles as they slide down. As if the sky has sprouted fingers. Gone hunting in the crags.

"Mealie!" CFK calls when he's close. Practically skipping. Labrador-CFK. He comes right up beside me. "Do the thing."

As though I'm a character in his show, I find myself starting to ask what he means. Pretending I don't know. Saying my line. Instead, I make myself smile.

"Hold still," I say.

He really does have wild eyes, dark yellow by starlight, like a bear's.

"Look at me." I don't really need to tell him that. Just part of the script. "Keep looking."

The key, Steph taught me, *is the wait. You have to wait. Let all the pathetic, insufficient tools we have for adjusting to the dark do what they can.*

"Okay," I say. When it's time. "Tell me when I disappear."

Very, very slowly, I slide right.

If I really thought back, I could probably remember her exact explanation. Rods, cones. The way our eyes sense movement or change as opposed to actual light in darkness. Or the other way around? But as with stars, tortoises, the miracle of sparked kids' interest, the discovery of stillness inside myself as my husband withered, I am more about the thing than the explanation of the thing. Though in the moment, I can love the explanation, too.

"*Rad*!" CFK whispers suddenly. "You're . . . " He starts to reach out, but stops. I am less than two feet from him, maybe fifteen degrees to his left. And, if we both hold still, completely invisible to him.

The scream ricochets around the campground like gunfire, sets off an avalanche of tent zippers coming down, heads popping out like tumbling boulders as I startle and CFK glares everywhere, hands flying up into guard position, as though whatever's happening, he's going to box it. At first, I don't know where to look. But then I spot the streak of pink, the glary pussycat girl stumbling back across the flag line with both hands at the tie of her purple sweatpants. Her cheeks glisten with tears. Or maybe sweat.

"*He fucking grabbed me.*"

"Never even left my tent!" calls one of the asshole boys. Fletcher. The worst of them. He's all the way out, standing barefoot in the sand with his flashlight on himself. Bare gym-pumped chest, bare legs. Black boxers.

"You appear to have left it now," I say. Not yelling. I move toward the girl, leaving Fletcher to CFK.

He's already on his way. But not before yelling to the pussycat. "Course, if you'd stayed where you belonged . . ."

I flash a glare. Make sure he sees. I almost say it, because I'm really not sure he gets it, and I want the kids clear on what has happened. Even in the midst of the era we're in, CFK apparently still needs this explained to him.

But if he does, it's too late for him. And he's not my primary concern.

I reach the pussycat tent at the same time as the girl, put my hand out to touch her shoulder. "Come here, Hon. Are you all ri—"

"Get away from me, Grandma."

Which shouldn't bother me. Doesn't. I stay right where I am as she rips open the rainfly and her so-called friends gather her in. Leaving me to stand right where I am. Where I'll be if she needs me. Or doesn't. A wall they can bang on. Forget was there. Sleep near.

One last role I've realized I've come to like, or at least believe in.

CFK has a different approach. "*Out!*" I hear him snarl from all the way across the camp. "Get out. All of you!"

Inside the pussycat tent, flashlights switch off and whispers drop low. Mostly, that's so they can listen to CFK, but they also know I'm still here. They're waiting for me to walk away. They won't know when I do.

I allow myself a small smile, by myself in the dark. My husband gone. My long-ago regional theater life, such as it was, even more gone. The few faculty friends I've made in a quarter century of my second career retired, one by one. The hundreds of students I've loved and laughed with scattered into their lives, never looking back, and why should they?

"Nope," I hear CFK snap. "Did I say you could get dressed? Put it back."

Meaning everything, I realize. Pants. Shoes. He's got all four asshole boys out of their tents, standing barefoot at attention in the desert cold in their underwear. Laughter flickers across a few of their faces but dies fast. A fire that won't catch. Behind them, the night shadows have reached the base of the rock wall. Started across the sand.

I dig my hands into my pockets. It's his show. But those boys should be in their tents. Us, too. It bothers me that I can no longer hear him, and I lean forward. Consider going over there, but for all kinds of reasons, I stay put. Stand sentinel over this tent, and keep these girls inside it. This night needs no additional accelerant.

I'm not even sure CFK is talking anymore, and he doesn't seem to be moving, either. He, too, knows how to stand still, though he uses stillness differently. Teaching strategies, I have learned, are like martial arts disciplines, and we all pretty much subscribe to one form or another. Some are primarily about defense. Some—like mine, I hope— are for centering, locating qi. Some are for control, which can look and feel an awful lot like attack. Sometimes, it is.

Under our feet, the ground shudders again, the flash on the horizon beating the muffled *boom* to our senses as the bomb drops and the mountains twitch like images on an old antenna tv. Settle again, or don't, quite.

CFK has released the boys. Which is a relief. He's not coming back, yet, though. Is lurking outside tents, absolutely still, same as I am (except not quite. I hope. Guarding vs. stalking. Different disciplines).

Abruptly, I whirl, gaze flashing over flat sand toward the rocks. Shadows seem to slide off them, go still the split second before I catch them at it. Then I'm staring at my feet, thinking *snake, scorpion*.

What I see is my feet in sneakers in sand in moonlight. As though I'm standing on a beach at the lip of an ocean of shadow. Ghost of an ocean. Of the ooze we all crawled out of, evaporating now as our climate shifts and our age ends.

That first year—the Steph year—we had campfires every night, and the kids wanted ghost stories. We had a woman, then, an art teacher, young and

Indian and beautiful and strange. Subscriber to the mesmerize-them teaching discipline. Hardest to maintain, at least once you're out of your twenties. She told a long, truly unsettling tale about hiking the perimeter of the Bloody Lake on the Northern Ridge in New Delhi, and dead children following her. It kept us all spellbound for a good fifteen minutes, and the adults for another ten. Then our students just wanted s'mores, and to throw graham crackers at each other. We let them wander back to their tents piecemeal. At the end—heat on my face, cold on my back, living children everywhere around me and the empty, black desert beyond—I asked Steph if there were any good Joshua Tree ghost stories. To my surprise, she smiled, looked young. Younger even than our art teacher. Barely older than my students. She probably was.

"Not that I've heard, believe it or not. No good ones. There's just not that much alive out here. Or that ever was alive. And the things that do die here die quietly. Or . . . "

That was the end of the smile. And the looking young. Instead of a ghost story, she told us about a tent full of dead migrant laborers the rangers had found a few months back. And then about a girl she'd known in Twentynine Palms whose mother had been gang-raped by Marines and left out here. The Marines got caught, confessed, tried to show police where they'd dumped her body. But she'd never been found.

That was also the night Steph showed me the disappearing trick. Stood up, shook herself hard as though exorcizing her own thoughts, motioned me to stand, and pulled me away from the firelight into the shadows. She told me to look right at her. Held still. Slid right.

The pussycat girls, I realize, have gone silent. Not only quiet but still. Possibly, they're sleeping. *How long have I been standing here?*

Too long. The cold isn't just creeping up my sleeves or under my scarf and hat; it's gotten inside. I'm about to yell to CFK to let the damn boys back in their sleeping bags when I realize he already has. He's just standing, too, ankle-deep in shadows, still and prickly as a barrel cactus. I'm tired. I don't want to be out here anymore. I want my tent and my air mattress—I got it to discourage scorpion climbing, not for glampy comfort, though that's not a distinction any real desert adventurer would recognize—and my little hooded camping lantern and my book. My earplugs so I won't hear my colleagues snoring, though I hate wearing those because then I can't hear the wind, either. Or the desert quiet.

I almost leave CFK to finish up. But he waves and trots back over. We meet at the flag line.

"All clear," I say, a little more firmly than I believe, and CFK holds up a finger.

We wait. Cold vibrates inside me, as though I'm a cave and *it* the living thing. I can almost hear it calling to itself in there. Sounding echoes. I'm watching the shadows all around the camp, which is why I actually see the shooting star this time, less a single streak than a scatter, like a thrown sparkler that flashes surprisingly low over the ridge to our east and then winks out all at once.

Sucking in a breath, I make myself *be here*. Remind myself to be. Cold, dark, kids, sand, crawling things, flying things, *no* things. Emptiness. Joe memories. That stupid song we danced to at his father's third wedding. *Uh-huh uh-huh uh-huh.* Only words I remember or need to remember.

"Okay," says CFK. "All clear."

We get maybe five steps from each other toward our own tents before the shrieking erupts.

It's right on top of us, and even as I'm ducking, hands flying to my head to ward off talons, I realize what it is. CFK does, too, or should; he had to have been here when we heard it last. But of course his first thought is that it's students, and he's whirling all over himself like that cartoon Tasmanian devil, eyes everywhere, legs crouched for the lurch. He figures it out a few seconds after I do. Straightens, and I straighten, get my hands back down by my sides. I shrug. Smile at him. What else is there to do?

"Goddamn it," he mutters, right as the kids start sticking heads out again. "Get back in!" he yells, but it's whack-a-mole, hopeless, and will be until the concert is over. So I just listen.

Another shriek, then a long moan. A breath. Six or seven staccato shrieks, not quite in a pattern, but then another bomb rumbles the earth, and for a few seconds, it really is like music, some contemporary Morton Feldman-type thing, little blips or bursts of sound, long silences. The sounds nearly falling into rhythms, falling apart. Drifting out of phase.

"Do you remember this story?" I say to CFK. Even I don't know if I'm calming or provoking him. Either way, it's a sort of fun. A way not to be annoyed or bored or even cold.

"I remember this *guy*."

I glance sidelong at him. "You actually saw him? I thought even the rangers didn't know who it was."

"I know who it was. That fucking beard. You need a beard that long to hide a smirk that deep."

Amazingly, I know who he means. Of all the bearded park service personnel we've spent time with out here, that guy liked himself most. And the kids least. Tom, I think.

But Tom was not the Naked Flautist. Was way too resentful of the imposition work placed on his time to want to entertain teenagers, or wow them, or even scare them.

The Naked Flautist. Who crawls up the rocks some starlit nights, flings off his clothes, screws together his instrument, and lets fly. Not a ghost story, exactly. Not even a story. But effective for keeping certain kinds of kids *off* the rocks. Or luring others on. Or making a whole camp groan and laugh. Or, just sometimes, triggering awe all over again in the middle of the Nothing in the middle of the night.

It's already over, I realize. A shooting star of a Naked Flautist show. There and gone.

The hooting starts. On the girls' side, for once, the pussycat tent, and I sigh as hoots break out all over our camp, from every corner. Like freaked out chimps, I'm thinking, except less wild than that. Stupider. Its only intention communal disruption, not warning.

"*God*damn it," says CFK, and he hurtles straight through the boys' area toward the asshole tent.

With a sigh, I pocket my hands, start toward the pussycats. But I stop when I see Jayna poking out of her tent, staring up at the rocks. Her blunt-cut, dyed-red hair all over the place, like kicked embers. Tears in her eyes. Tears.

"You okay, sweetie?" I say. I consider crouching, but don't want to draw other kids' attention to her. She's alone in there, I remember. Parental request. She still gets too nervous to sleep near others.

I try following her gaze, but all that's up there is ridge and shadow. From the boys' side, I hear Fletcher or one of his cronies shouting, "We didn't even do anything!"

Followed by CFK's snarl. "Well, you're not going to, now."

Like rams rutting. For whom, and to what end?

The stars go out.

Have been out? How long has it been this dark? Is that what Jayna's looking at? Of course it is.

"Ms. J," she whispers, and I want to shush her, slip her a tissue, remind her that she has classmates all around and pussycat predators ten feet away and laughing, though probably not at her. At least not yet. "It's so deep."

I'm half into my crouch, hand reaching to wipe her cheek, the obvious question on my lips when Fletcher screams, "OW! *You fucking bit me!*"

Just like that, I'm sprinting across the sand in precisely the way twenty years of instructions from rangers have warned not to. All around me, kids are out of their tents, blinking in the lack of light. They look grayed, two-dimensional. *Vulnerable.* No prickers or stingers or stink-glands to keep them safe.

Everything here is trying to kill you.

"Kerber, get away from that tent," I'm shouting, but even as I do, I see, and in my panic, I pull up too fast, almost tumbling into the cactus that's twitching like a Venus fly trap right next to me. It has blooms on it. In the gloom the blooms look gray, like stars this thing has caught and webbed.

From the place *he* stopped—a good ten feet from Fletcher's tent, nowhere near biting distance—CFK hunches by a mesquite bush, hands up in a sort of wrestler's crouch. He's swaying slightly, which has the effect of making him look rooted. Part of the plant. Like a yucca stalk.

Like the rangers around the rattlesnake bush this morning, after they realized Mama had come home.

"Okay, guys," he's saying. "Slowly, okay? One at a time. Move away from there. Away from the tent. Toward me."

And the kids, the asshole boys—who are just boys, for at least a little longer—they're doing exactly what he says. One at a time.

"Look at me!" CFK snaps. "At *me*."

One by one, they come, almost tiptoeing. But fast. As though evacuating a crashed plane. As they reach CFK, every single one glances back. Only when the last reaches him do I realize Fletcher isn't with them.

That his tent is rippling.

That there are noises coming from it.

For one moment, CFK swings around. His eyes grab mine. His face is half-obscured by shadow. By *these* shadows. Even so, I finally see what I should have years ago. Have always seen but never recognized.

Crazy Fucking Kerber is afraid. He is always afraid.

"Stay there," I call. "Kerber, wait. I'm . . . " But the rest dies in my mouth.

Beyond him, Fletcher's tent has swelled. It's not billowing, not even ballooning. Just . . . shoving outward. Like the neck of an anaconda with a rat in it.

I stumble forward, but way too slow. CFK has already spun back that way, and he's seen. Then he's diving headlong for the tent. He rips at its still-zipped front, tearing it open, and there's a *wetness* to that sound, like tendons being severed, and then he's through. Inside.

Gone.

Instinctively, I dart sideways, not toward the tent mouth, which *stinks* even from here like the chemical toilet, except minus chemicals. Like the raw, rotting insides of us. "Help me," I'm shouting to the boys. To any kids who will listen.

A shocking, marvelous number of them do. Immediately, without hesitation. Three of them right there with me, hurtling across the sand. "The tent," I'm shouting, not making sense even to myself, but somehow the kids understand. They always understand, so much more than we think or is good for them.

Even as the canvas bells out to meet them, two start ripping at the rain fly, peeling it free. The rest drop to their knees around me, digging at the stone-hard sand in all four corners. Grabbing the metal spikes, which should be freezing but instead are warm. Not in and of themselves, I realize. More *bathed* in warmth. Bones in blood.

"*Pull!*" I'm shouting as the tent flaps, leans way over sideways (in wind, just wind), snaps straight, and there are voices in there, just the two, "Get off, get it off!" and "CFK, FUCK!" Hands over mine, seemingly becoming mine, and we're yanking, straining. The peg pops free of the ground. Seconds later, they're all out, and for one horrific second, the tent seems to lift off the desert floor like a magic carpet. Or a bloated dragonfly.

Then it sags to the ground and lets Fletcher and CFK go.

Spits them out.

That's what it looks like. That's what it was. I know, already, that I will always think so.

We're staring at each other. All of us. The pussycat girls, so many girls over here where they're not allowed. Fletcher's tentmates and their peers who hate them and their peers who are just other kids who happened to be in their class on this trip on this night on this day when the snakes and shadows came to camp. When the desert finally noticed us.

In a surprisingly short time—less than an hour, I don't even remember anyone breaking off to use the toilet—we are all back in our tents. Even CFK and me. I do ask, one time, what he thinks happened.

For answer, he looks at me. The look I now recognize. But he gives the CFK shrug. "When?"

We don't realize, of course, until the next morning. No one does. Not even the kids in the tents around her. That's the worst part. It doesn't even seem possible unless you've been out there. When I ask the rest of them later, after every single tent is down and packed except hers, whether it occurred to anyone to check on her, or to come ask one of us, the other girls just say they figured she'd gotten up early, gone for a dawn walk. Seemed like something she would do.

Which is true enough. I'd seen her do it earlier in the trip. We'd seen each other out there, walking the dawn. Waved but left one another alone.

Jayna.

I don't cry while I'm still with the kids. There isn't time. First, we have to do the frantic search, all day, in heat that suddenly roars in from the open Mojave and envelops the rangers, police, everyone. Then there are calls to the school to make, the helpless attempts at explanation which sound pathetic even to us. Because what do we even know?

That they came in a pack? Whatever they were? One group distracting us at Fletcher's tent while the other . . .

Is that even what I think? Because like Steph said. Every single thing out there . . .

Finally, in the end, there's nothing left but the drive home to my empty house, to sit on my porch and stare helplessly over the tops of the city lights, through the silhouettes of the San Gabriels toward the nothingness beyond. The Nothing that Lives. And Preys. And, like any proper predator, takes the ones from the back. The weakest and smallest. The ones who are alone.

THE MOTLEY

CHARLIE HUGHES

Who told the Motley,
You kissed that girl?
Who told the Motley,
You stole that pearl?
It wasn't Tammy Jenkins,
It wasn't Mistress Drew,
So, nobody knows how the Motley knew.

She remembered her father as a huge man, towering above his friends, bulky and muscular. Now, the weight had dropped away and he stooped, even as he sat in his wheelchair. His hands, holding the knife and fork, shook like leaves in a gentle wind.

Eloise raised herself and wiped away stray flecks of cod caught in his moustache.

"Tell me, Eloise," he said, "What did the Motley show?" His eyes were bright and wide.

He had moments like this when he asked questions and talked politely. Once, she'd taken these interludes as a sign of hope, even recovery. But over the years, it became clear they were nothing of the sort, just cruel reminders of a father she'd already lost.

"I haven't been to the meeting yet, Dad. My first one is tonight."

"Oh."

Eloise rubbed the bridge of her nose, then took his hand in hers. "Dad, can I ask you something?"

"Of course." He smiled with fatherly indulgence.

"At the meeting, will it tell us what happened to Rachael?"

"Will who tell you?"

"The Motley," she replied.

He spoke in stages, constructing the sentence out of each individual thought. "You want the Motley, to tell you what happened, to the little girl, your friend?"

"Rachael. Her name was Rachael. You remember."

"She went missing. Poor little girl."

A lump rose in Eloise's throat.

His eyes shifted from side to side, then he smirked, as if Eloise had said something amusing.

"Wonder if you'll get some fun at the meeting. I always liked the funny ones."

"Fun?"

"The sex ones are good," he said.

Eloise grimaced and prayed he would stop. He'd forgotten who he was talking to.

"Someone screwing someone they shouldn't or stealing or fraud. They think the Motley won't know. They stick their fingers in the till or cook the books. I remember Ronny Jenkins getting caught . . . " He trailed off, losing the thread of his thoughts.

His eyes went wide, then fell, the look he always gave just before she lost him. In these moments, she was convinced the horror of it all settled on him: his impotence, his dependence, the bonfire of dignity.

He looked dully at the blank TV screen in the corner of the room.

Eloise stood and wheeled him around in front, then switched it on. A programme about wildlife in South America. "Is that okay, Dad?"

He stared, silent.

She kissed him on the forehead then whispered in his ear, "I love you, Dad."
He looked up at her. She wanted him to say it back, just like he always had.
"Cunt." he said. There was no anger in his voice. He could have been commenting on the weather. "Dumb cunt."

◂◦▸

Eloise pushed through the door of the town hall and found herself reciting an old nursery rhyme under her breath, one the children still chanted in the playground.

Who told the Motley,
You kissed a girl?

She removed her coat and hung it on a peg in the reception room.

Roland Peebles sat on a chair outside the assembly room. He wore a blue tunic which strained to cover his bulk, the crest of the town council sewn to the pocket. Roland got paid for a few hours each month as assistant to the town clerk, checking off the councillors as they arrived among other menial tasks. Eloise suspected this was his only income. She approached and stopped beside him.

He whispered, not looking at her, almost without moving his lips, "Don't say anything," he said. "Just nod."

She shuffled on the spot, wondering if she should move on.

"You're still going to try?" he said.

She nodded.

"Do it quickly, as soon as you have the chance."

"Okay," she said.

"Be quick, they'll drag you away as soon as they twig."

Eloise walked into the council chamber.

Inside, fifteen or twenty councillors were taking their seats or talking in small groups. The chairs were set out in a broad U-shape, five lines deep, all facing toward a grand bench raised on a stage.

"Three from the left, two rows from the front." Her father had reminded her many times. Eloise found the appointed place and sat.

She offered a tiny smile to Oliver Hemsworthy, seated next to her.

"Aha! The new girl," he said.

"New, yes," she replied. "Girl, no."

"Quite right, quite right." He grinned. "Looking forward to it?"

"Oh yes, good to get going."

"That's the spirit!"

She noticed his shirt cuff had ridden up, exposing his forearm. Two- and three-inch scars striped his skin, the same as her father. Hemsworthy saw her looking and shifted his shirt down to the proper place.

Eloise looked up to the public gallery where several groups were settled, including wide-eyed children staring down on them.

On the stroke of the hour, a loud knocking from behind the stage and the room fell silent.

A snaking line of suited men emerged from behind the stage, winding up the steps and into their seats. In the grandest chair, chains of office draped around his neck and chest, the town clerk peered down at them.

His name was Oliver Maynard, a rotund, po-faced man who owned a land drainage firm on the town's industrial estate. Maynard had once been close to her father but hadn't visited once since his illness became evident.

"Be seated." he said, "We have plenty to cover this evening and I will begin by noting apologies . . . " And so, he proceeded with the public meeting: A tree preservation order, a licensing application, and a new contract for mowing the grass verges.

The mundanity of it allowed Eloise to relax. How could she be nervous when grown men spoke gravely of dog fouling on the rugby fields?

Some of the councillors engaged with these items, raising points and asking questions, but Eloise got the impression the majority viewed these interventions as poor form. Oliver Hemsworthy huffed and puffed each time someone raised their hand to speak, as did several others.

When the town clerk moved onto the final item, the room came to life. The councillors shifted in their chairs, shuffled papers and stretched limbs.

"That concludes our formal business. Thank you one and all for attending." The town clerk nodded to the officers sitting beside him. They stood and walked out of the hall. Maynard remained in place. He motioned to the public gallery.

Slowly, reluctantly, they began filing out. One boy, no more than eight or nine years old, stayed rooted to his seat.

His mother turned back and raised her voice to him. "Come along then!"

When he continued to gawp down on the assembly, motionless, she went back, grabbed him by the collar and dragged him after her.

"But I want to see," he screeched. "I want to see it, Mum."

"You're not allowed," she replied. "Only the councillors are allowed."

◄०►

They were not sisters. Her mother would remind Eloise of this whenever Rachael could not sleep over or stay for tea.

"It's nice that you have a friend, Eloise, but Rachel has her own family."

Inseparable since nursery school, they spent every possible moment together, playing, taking long bike rides, building dens in the woods behind Eloise's home.

Rachael's parents were not wealthy like her own, they lived in a tiny cottage on the other side of town. Her father fixed cookers and washing machines for a living. Her mother cleaned other people's homes. Neither would ever sit on the Town Council, like Eloise's father.

If Eloise ever noticed these differences, it was only as obstacles to her time playing and adventuring with her friend.

The day Rachael disappeared, they were supposed to go fishing in the Stour. It was a pastime her parents hated, her mother describing the sport as "common" every time it was mentioned.

Rachael Peebles had learned to fish from her own father and proved a patient teacher to Eloise, even gifting her an old rod and a box for tackle.

That day, Eloise had rushed home from Sunday school to collect her equipment from the shed, pausing only briefly to tell her father where she was going.

Eloise waited on the riverside in their favourite spot, soaking in the sun, watching the heavy brown water of the Stour flow past, reluctant to cast her line until her friend arrived. When she thought back to those moments, the reflection of the sun on the river and the sound of the water sloshing past always came back in vivid detail. Her world was changing irrevocably and she knew nothing of it. She waited and waited. Minutes passed, then hours and the sun began to fade. Eventually, downhearted, Eloise trudged toward home.

On her way over the fields, a figure appeared bobbing up and down in the distance. For a few paces, she was sure Rachael had finally come, complete with smiles and excuses for her tardiness. Then she noticed the short hair and heavy gait of the figure coming towards her and realised it was not Rachael, but her brother, Roland.

He was a year older, but the kids at school teased him because he was an inch or two shorter than his sister. He was strange, insular. Always telling stories about the Motley which nobody wanted to hear.

When their paths met, he said, "Mum sent me to get her."

"Get who, from where?" Eloise already knew the answer, of course, but the narrowing of Roland's eyes was enough to catch a breath in her throat.

"She's still fishing? Mum wants her home for tea."

Eloise felt a sudden sinking sensation in her chest. "She didn't come."

"Where is she?" Roland said. "Where's my sister?"

·◦·

Only the councillors were left in the room now.

The town clerk looked up from his desk and gestured to two councillors seated in front. "Gentlemen."

They stood and went behind the stage. The room fell silent.

A minute later, the despatched councillors reappeared, moving slowly, clumsily. The structure they carried resembled a miniature sedan or litter. Instead of an emperor or ark riding between them, they carried an object encircled by drapes. Its outline reminded Eloise of a bird cage.

She'd heard rumours of the cage, the stories told by children in the playground, tales the adults of the town soon learned to avoid.

From the back of the hall, Roland Peebles appeared, carrying a silver tray. A huge slab of meat, grey-green in colour, rested on top. Even from metres away, she smelled rancid flesh. He placed it on a table and walked out of the hall. Only the closest of observers would have noticed the look he gave to Eloise as he went by.

The town clerk came down from his platform, stood beside the tray, then picked an object from beside the meat. He twisted it at eye level, the steel glinting in the light.

A dagger.

Maynard turned and looked towards the councillors. "The Letting." he said, his low, stern voice filled the chamber. "Approach."

From the nearest line of seats, they rose and filed towards him, a congregation rising for communion.

The first to reach the town clerk was Frederick Costard, a tall, thin-faced man, who looked as if he were sucking a boiled sweet. He stood proudly before Maynard, pulled up his sleeve and presented a milky forearm.

Maynard presented the blade and slid the tip across Costard's wrist in a short, sharp motion. A crescent of blood bloomed against his white skin. Quickly, Costard held his arm over the meat and let his blood run onto it.

From beneath its covering, the cage rattled. It was a small sound, a minor shift of mass from within, but all eyes turned toward it.

Eloise stood and followed the flow of councillors into the aisle, joining the queue.

The town clerk cut, and they bled onto the meat. Cut and bleed, cut and bleed. After each new supply, the cage shuddered.

She reached the front. Maynard gave a sly wink before beckoning for her arm. She hesitated, then complied. Eloise gasped at the jolt of pain, but kept her expression neutral, her stance steady.

She leaned towards the meat.

The smell here was thick and rich with decay. She covered her nose and mouth with her free hand. Red, red, red dripped onto the mouldering flesh.

The cage rattled again, more violently this time. And there was a sound, a voice. Throaty, sickening. "Yes."

She was supposed to scurry back to her seat now, but she had a promise to keep.

"Where is Rachael? Who took her?" she whispered.

A cry of "No!" came out from behind, but Eloise ignored it. She had reduced her universe to the curtain and the cage and whatever lay on the other side. Nothing else existed.

"Rachael Peebles," she said.

There was another shifting movement from inside. It was about to say something, she was sure of it. "I tell . . . "

But before she could hear more, two sets of arms were pulling her away, dragging her back to her seat.

◅o▻

By the time the last of the councillors had passed by, the meat was immersed in a soupy claret mixture.

The town clerk turned to address them and began with a deep sigh. "Before the Sharing, I must remind all town councillors of their solemn and sacred responsibility to follow custom and protocol in this chamber at all times." These last three words were given such emphasis that the town clerk's voice descended to a primeval growl. "We must never use the access granted to us to pursue personal obsessions or vendettas . . . " and so it went on, his eyes and those of her fellow councillors boring into Eloise whilst she sat among them, isolated and shamefaced.

Maynard shook his head as if to rid himself of a terrible memory. "Now for the Sharing." He turned and addressed the cage, "Motley, are you ready?"

A voice from inside came, "Yes," then a pause. "I'm awake. I'm ready, sir."

To Eloise's ear, the voice sounded adult and childish, simultaneously mocking and desperate.

"Please give, sir," it said.

Maynard picked up the platter and placed it on the table in front of the cage. Carefully, deliberately, he reached up to the curtain and pulled a cord. The drapes moved back and the thing inside was revealed.

Eloise leaned forward. She had known, deep down, that one day she would see it. And she had known that it must be something fantastical to hold a town in its hand for so many years. But all that knowledge, all those stories, every hint and rumour, every nursery rhyme and poem could not have prepared her for this.

It moved.

It writhed and moved and breathed. She could see its little chest rising and falling. And yet, it should not have moved or breathed, most definitely should not have made sounds or spoken. Every instinct told her it should be inanimate, unliving.

And yet, there it was, a hideous amalgam come to life. She prayed it would stop moving, but it kept on.

"I am hungry," it said.

The central column of this abomination, the part that they called its "body", was covered in a leathery layer of skins, stitched together with thick black twine. Some said the skin had been human once, taken from the bodies of children back when the passing of an infant was a common occurrence. Inside, they also said, it was stuffed with grass or straw. Small stems poked out of its exterior, here and there.

On its oversized head, where eyes might have been, were two simple cross stitches. The Motley was blind, in the conventional sense of the word.

Its arms and legs were made of sticks. Small, but thick and robust, broken tree limbs which bent in places where a human arm might also join.

The Motley sat with its legs out in front, the same way a baby might sit when it learns to hold its head upright. "Can I have the food, sir?"

"You can have the food if you share your secret," the town clerk replied.

"I have a good one," it said.

"Then you will feast." Maynard leaned forward and unhooked the latch on the cage.

Eloise wished with all her heart that it would stop being alive.

It shifted its weight to one side, then hopped up onto its stick legs, and walked out of the cage, onto the table, scuttling like a spider.

"Sir ready for secret?"

The town clerk nodded.

The Motley reached out both hands and Maynard took them in his. His entire body jolted, as if subjected to a shock of electricity. He continued to judder and flail, somehow staying on his feet and keeping his hands clasped to the doll's. This went on for almost a minute, the other councillors watching, enthralled.

It ended suddenly, Maynard suddenly rigid, still, then releasing its hands. He turned to the councillors, "I have the secret," he said.

There was a murmur of approval from his audience.

"Can I eat, man?" the Motley asked.

With a wave of his hand, Maynard gave his permission.

It descended onto the meat, its face plunging into the blood and flesh. The head bobbed up and down, side to side, and tiny pieces of meat sprayed around its head.

Eloise cast her eyes down. She could not look, did not want to think about its sharp little teeth or why it wanted the rotten meat drenched in the blood of the town councillors.

Hemsworthy spoke to her out of the corner of his mouth. "Eloise, you must watch. It is your duty to bear witness."

She looked back to the thing and saw it had taken the meat down to the bone, was near finished, had devoured its meal with incredible speed. The Motley pulled back from the platter, blood smeared around the hole that was its mouth.

The words danced from her lips again, whispered before she could stop herself.

. . . It wasn't Tammy Jenkins, It wasn't Mistress Drew,
So, nobody knows how the Motley knew.

When it was finished feasting, the Motley shuffled back into its cage. The same councillors carried it back to its room behind the stage. Meanwhile, Maynard prepared his speaking notes, readying himself to share the Motley's secret.

◄◦►

Eloise entered the market square an hour before the Giving of the Truth. She pretended to look at shop windows and chat with acquaintances. Her eyes kept drifting to the corner of the square, where a curious wooden structure squatted, hunched over like an ogre.

The occasional outsider who saw the stocks would assume they were a whimsical hangover from a bygone age, or perhaps a prop for some harmless tradition. Unsuspecting tourists posed for photos, pretending to be locked in, pulling pained faces for likes and shares on social media.

Shipstonians did not like to see this, and local shopkeepers and others would shoo them along if they stayed too long.

"Not for playing on," Bobby Mayo, the butcher, would say, "They're not toys."

The sharp-eyed newcomer might, as they reluctantly shuffled away, notice the rouge tint to the stocks and the paving around it.

On days like this one, the third Tuesday of the month, the square was sealed off from prying eyes and a ritual was observed.

The Giving of the Truth.

Right on time, June Chandos was marched around the corner, held by three men, two holding her arms and another, the town clerk, gripping the scruff of her coat. She looked grey-skinned, petrified.

Eloise knew her well. She'd served on the parent-teacher committee of the primary school with her mother. June Chandos was near sixty years old, but that morning Eloise would have guessed nearer eighty.

There was no mob, no fire and brimstone, not yet. They took her to the stocks in silence and the town clerk's minders locked her in. When her head and hands were held firmly in place, the town clerk stood next to her and rolled out a piece of paper. He read aloud.

"Our people know the soil and know our ways. We are better for it. Here, we look out for our own, and punish the misdemeanours of our brethren. It is the only way."

As Maynard spoke, more and more of the people in the square moved across to the area around the stocks. A group of larger, younger, more physically imposing men edged themselves to the front. There were some in the town who enjoyed participating in the Giving of the Truth, more than they would admit.

The town clerk continued, "We do right by each other and allow no thievery, nor fornication nor cruelty to our fellow man. We listen to the Motley. It shows us the error of our ways and allows us to correct them."

He went on: "Ms. Chandos and her neighbour Ms. Dillis Cooper have for many years quarrelled over petty things. They grew to hate one another. On the sixteenth of September this year, June Chandos decided to take vengeance on Dillis Cooper. She tempted her neighbour's dog over to her back garden and fed it poison . . . "

"I did not! I did no such thing."

"Quiet!" Maynard snapped.

"Shut up," came the shout from one man at the front. There was a murmur of assent from the others, who had grown in number, perhaps thirty or forty now.

"The poor dog died a horrible death. Ms Dillis Cooper is most aggrieved. June Chandos, this is a good town because the Motley knows our secrets, the truth of our actions."

"No," the old woman whimpered.

From behind the crowd, a wheelbarrow emerged, pushed by one of the town clerk's assistants. He struggled to keep it steady, such was the weight of its contents. The barrow was full to brim with rocks and stones.

June Chandos saw and wailed again, frantic this time, the sound of utter desperation.

Eloise had seen the Giving of the Truth before, many times, but this was different. This time, she had raised her hand, along with all the other Councillors, and agreed to the proposal for her punishment. Her father had always reassured her that the system was just, that the Motley kept the town pure, disciplined.

She tried to turn and walk away, when large hands gripped her by the shoulder, long fingers digging into her collarbone. Oliver Hemsworthy's face was smiling down at her. "Going somewhere, Eloise?" he asked, his voice was low, conspiratorial. He leaned in toward her, "You're on the Town Council now. You must bear witness."

June Chandos called out again, "Please, no!"

Her entreaties were joined by the sound of rocks and heavy stones clicking against each other as hands took them from the barrow.

Eloise closed her eyes.

◄◦►

Her father's head lolled to one side; his mouth half-open as he snored. Eloise turned off the TV and tried to summon the energy to get him onto the stairlift, then into bed.

Ever since the meeting and June Chandos, this was how it had been. She went through the motions—shopping, cleaning, cooking, and caring for her father—but it was harder now. Eloise was tired, weighed down by her participation in the town's unforgiving traditions.

Before she could dwell any longer, the doorbell rang.

Eloise opened to find Roland Peebles standing in the rain, his thin hair stuck to his head in clumps, leaving ugly islands of white baldness. She was about to chastise him for being out without a coat or umbrella when she caught the look on his face. Eloise had seen sadness before, many times—the town was a breeding place for it—but this was something else, something much worse. Desolation? Something had broken Roland Peebles.

His skin was pale, almost blue.

"Please . . . " he managed, a raw edge in his voice.

"Will you come in, Roland?" she said, gently.

But he was too far gone. The words tumbled out, "Her name was Rachael. A little girl called Rachael . . . "

"Roland?"

He was shaking uncontrollably.

"Please help me, Eloise. You're the only one. I see her in my dreams every night, I see her in the street even when I know it's not her. I can never reach her, never tell her I'm sorry."

Instinctively, she held out a hand, touched his cold arm. It was like flicking a switch. He fell to his knees, and folded into the foetal position, sobbing right there on her doorstep.

She hovered over him, unsure what to do. Slowly, the shaking calmed and the sobbing subsided. She coaxed him into the house. After a time, she had him sat in front of the fire, wrapped in blankets, a hot cup of tea beside him.

Eloise checked that her father was still sleeping in his chair, then sat opposite Roland. Eventually, without prompting, he told her, in a distant voice, as if speaking from the other side of a thick dark cloud, what had happened.

Roland had been feeling unwell, depressed for a long time, and it got much worse after the Town Hall meeting, he said. That night, to take his mind off things, he'd gone to the rugby club to watch an evening game. Over the sound of shouting spectators, he heard the chatter of kids playing on the playground. A parent walked over to them and shouted for their child to come.

Roland held his hands in front of himself and spoke to them, as if the secret of his disintegration could be found in his palms.

"He called the name of the child, over and over. 'Rachael! Rachael, Come here darling.' The girl rushed to her father. It was her, Eloise. Just like *our* Rachael. Bright and so alive."

"You've had a breakdown, Roland. There's no other way to put it."

"Have I?" He seemed bemused by the thought.

"Yes, I think so," she said.

"Oh."

"You need to rest, and then you need to see a doctor."

"Why"

"To help you get better."

"So, I can do it all over again next year? Or the year after?"

"This isn't the first time, is it?"

"No." he looked at his hands again.

"You must take better care of yourself."

"I need to know, Eloise. I need to know what happened to her." His voice was soft, but resolute.

"But I tried," she said. "It didn't work."

"We could try something else."

"Careful, Roland. Remember . . . " she spun her finger in the air, as if the Motley were hiding, waiting for them to make a mistake so it could pounce.

"It's my sister I remember, and you should, too. Or is that seat on the Town Council a little too comfortable already?"

It cut deep. Eloise rocked back in her seat. They had spoken about Rachael many times over the years, but he had never blamed her, never lashed out like this.

Her voice cracked as she spoke. "That's unfair, Roland."

"We should try something else . . . "

She brought her finger to her lips. "Don't say another word."

"We could take the Motley," he said. "Kidnap it. Make it tell us."

"Shut up, Roland!"

"We could find out what happened to Rachael, once and for all."

She stared at him, unable to believe he'd been so reckless as to say it aloud. Silence filled the room, closing in on them.

She said, "They keep it in the Town Hall. They guard it." The words were out before she could think to stop them.

"Then we need to find a way of getting past them."

"Like how?"

Roland cast his eyes to the floor.

"How?" She kept on. "You're going to beat them up?"

"I haven't thought it through. I don't know."

"You want to be a hero now?"

He held his head in his hands, and Eloise regretted speaking so harshly.

"You could get in by the attic." The voice was hoarse and sleepy. Eloise's father turned in his wheelchair and grinned at them. "That's what we used to do."

Eloise gawped, open-mouthed.

He went on. "That's what we used to do in my younger days. Me and Ronny Maynard would get up into the rafters from the stage ladder. Then up into the attic. Every room in the Town Hall is linked by the attic. There are no walls up there, you just have to get up and find the right hatch, and you're in."

Roland looked at Eloise, amazed, then back to the old man. "Mr. Phillips, you used to sneak in to see the Motley?"

"Oh yes, all the time. We liked to talk to it. Find out some extra secrets."

"And you got in from an attic?"

Eloise's father didn't respond.

She saw it, that look again, when he understood what he'd become.

"Find the girl," he said. "Find her." And then they lost him again to the clouds in his mind.

⟨⟩

She could've crawled across the dusty, cobwebbed boards in a minute or so, but she had to wait for Roland. He wheezed, heaving his body over the top of the ladder and into the loft.

She shuffled along on her hands and knees until she reached the hatch for the room behind the stage. When Roland arrived, Eloise twisted and pulled the handle. A haze of dust flew up around them. Below, through the opening, there was only darkness. She wondered if they'd made a mistake, but then picked up a gentle metallic rattling sound coming from below.

Roland tied his end of the rope around his waist. Eloise lowered the rest down into the room below. She clambered through the hatch, Roland took up her weight and she began the descent.

Eloise suddenly thought of its hutch as a delicate, breachable thing, and remembered the council meeting and how the Motley returned to it after feeding, peaceably and without coercion. It stayed in the cage because it chose to, not because it couldn't escape.

The descent took an age, the ridges of the thick rope rubbed her hands sore. As her feet touched the floor she whispered to Roland. "I'm down."

She released the rope and stepped back. In the dark, something pulled on the back pocket of her jeans. She lost her balance and stumbled, banging her hip into something hard. There was a loud crash, so shocking that Eloise dropped flat on the floor, as if cowering from an explosion.

"Jesus, Eloise! You okay?" Roland's voice was shrill, panicked.

"Yes. Shut up."

Slowly, her eyes adjusted. Outlines emerged against the lighter colours of the walls. There was a table next to her and, now fallen to the floor, the cage. Toppled on its side, the cage rolled back and forth, creating a metallic, jangling sound. The little door on the side flapped from side to side, wide open. Eloise scanned the room for the Motley but saw nothing. She took out her phone and switched on the torch.

Scratchy steps.

She swung around, the crystalline beam from the phone flaring against grubby cream walls.

"Hello?"

More steps and she turned again, back towards the cage.

"Mr. Motley, hello." She cringed. Did it even know its own name?

Without warning, without sound, it was on her.

There was the physical sensation of its weight arriving on her back, like someone hitting her with an old lumpy pillow. Next, and much worse, its bizarre twig arms wrapped around her neck. The suddenness of the invasion stunned her to silent, rigid stillness.

It spoke into her ear. "Lady have treats!"

Every instinct she possessed told her to reach back, rip it off and fling the freakish doll across the room. Somehow, she held the impulse at bay and answered.

"Yes, I have treats for you. If you let go, I can get the treat."

"You don't like close, do you, lady?" Its mouth was beside her ear, but no breath escaped, just the faint whiff of something carrion. The Motley shuddered against her when it spoke, like a clockwork toy wound up too tight. "Lady doesn't like Motley close."

"Oh, that's not true," she said. "I just want to get the treat."

"Sure?" Its tone was babyish, mocking.

"Oh yes. Real sure."

She felt its scratchy arms loosen their hold and its body slid down her back. Eloise turned to find it settled on the floor, sitting, its awkward large head swaying like a waning metronome.

"They won't like. Visits not allowed," the Motley said.

The voice retained its strange mixture of innocence and sarcasm, but in the lightless confines of the room, there was menace too—hatred, even. Eloise felt a momentary sense of gratitude for the darkness. She could see the outline and position of its black cross-stitch eyes, but not the detail of its hideous movement.

Slowly, never taking her eyes from the Motley, she took the meat from the bag.

"I want you to tell me a secret," she said. "And I'll give you this."

"Does it have blood? Right kind?"

"It does. My own."

The Motley paused, like a patron considering which wine to order. "Yes. You on council. You asked about girl."

It remembered her. She hadn't expected that. "Yes, I did."

"You want know 'bout little Rachael."

She bit her lower lip. "Yes, yes. Will you tell me?" Eloise held up the meat again.

"You promise to give me?" Its stick hand pointed to the meat.

Eloise pulled the package back into the crook of her arm. "If you tell. Only if you tell."

"Bad question, lady." The Motley's twig arm tapped its cheek. "Hurt my head."

"Why?"

"Why! Why, she says," It laughed, and the sound was awful, like sandpaper rubbing on coarse stone. "'Cos I told. Secrets, secrets, secrets, they want. Never listen. Motley secrets should be used, not forgotten."

"What do you mean, 'you told'?"

It yawned and then grinned at her. "I got sharp teeth," it said, ignoring her question. "Motley take meat. Tell no more secrets."

She had hated the idea of being near the Motley but hadn't considered being in actual physical danger. Did it do that? Would it bite her? All it wanted was the blood from the town's people, the councillors' blood.

Panic rose through her chest and throat. Her breathing quickened, but unevenly, without rhythm. "Why would you want to hurt me? I don't know what happened to Rachael. Nobody does. That's why I'm here."

It smiled and even in the dark, she could see the points of its teeth jutting out at bizarre angles. Eloise glanced up towards the hatch and wondered if she could climb the rope quickly enough to get away.

"Big boy up there," it said, chuckling now, "he's a greedy boy."

She whimpered. Her body was shaking now, riven with fear.

The Motley's head tilted to one side. "You ask. At meeting. And I show him, the man. Just like I did before."

"You didn't tell."

The doll shook its head.

"You told us about a dog. A fucking dog. A woman died, horribly, because of a dog." All the years of anger and frustration and pain welled up inside her and poured out. "Children go missing, but the Motley tells about dogs."

"Lies, lies, lies," it screeched.

The Motley leapt up onto the tabletop and then dived, full length, at Eloise. For a fraction of a second, she saw only teeth coming toward her. In that moment, she knew everything was over, that her life would now end in terrible suffering, without ever knowing what happened to her friend.

The teeth stopped in mid-air, the Motley's gnashing incisors reaching for her face, but somehow suspended before her. Eloise stepped aside and saw Roland in the dusky light, still holding the rope, reaching down and gripping the monster on its back. He wheeled away and slammed it down on the table, pinning it in place.

"Tell us! Tell us what happened to my sister."

The thing gagged and spat and a substance flashed past Roland's head.

"I'll tear you apart, rip you to shreds. Tell us," Roland said.

Roland dug his fingers into its soft body and began to pull apart. The Motley squealed in agony.

"Stooop! Stoooop!"

Roland relaxed his hold, just a little.

"I see Rachael," it said, wheezing, in a weaker voice than before. "I always tell. Every time. I tell for the meat."

"Who? Who do you tell?" Roland had bent down, his face pressed down towards the Motley.

"At the big meeting. The man with the chain. Many years now, I tell. I show."

Eloise experienced the dizzying sensation of sudden and unexpected understanding. Tiny interlocking fragments of truth began to click together in her mind. The way Maynard always returned the Motley to its room before the Sharing, the look he gave her when the Motley released his hand.

"He knows?" she asked.

"He knows. Motley secrets should be used, not forgotten," it said.

Roland wept as he spoke, still pushing down on the Motley. "They didn't tell us. We didn't know."

"You're her brother?" the Motley said.

"Yes."

"Let go. Give me my feed. I show you."

"He's lying. Keep him there," Eloise said, but there was the unmistakable lilt of doubt in her voice.

"I need to know." Roland was trembling.

"Don't, Roland."

He released the Motley.

Slowly, it raised itself up and stood on the table, its face directly in front of Roland's.

It proffered a mangled limb of twigs and sticks. "Take hand, boy. I show you sister."

‹◊›

Three from the left, two from the front, Eloise sat in her chair, doing everything in her power not to draw attention. She nodded and smiled and frowned in all the appropriate places. The casual observer would not have noticed the insistent twitch flickering beneath her left eye, nor the way she pressed her hands together on her lap, as if holding herself in place.

At the end of the public meeting, the gallery was cleared of everyone, except for her father. There were raised eyebrows from those who'd spotted him but, as a former councillor and Alderman of the town, he was permitted to stay. Roland had wheeled him up to the gallery several hours before. There'd been no outbursts or reasons to attend to him. The familiar rhythms and rituals of the gathering seemed to soothe his temper. Despite everything, he was still a man in his element.

Eloise forced a smile and waved. He returned the gesture, looking for all the world the proud and loving father.

They carried the Motley out from his room and placed his cage on the table next to the town clerk, just as always. Maynard said his piece and the councillors were brought forward to give their blood to the meat. Eloise followed obediently, never taking her eyes from Maynard as he cut her arm.

For its part, the Motley gave nothing away. It rattled and snarled and pretended this meeting was the same as all the thousands which had gone before.

Eloise and the rest of the councillors returned to their seats. Maynard and the Motley spoke the words of ritual.

"May I have food, sir?"

"You will have the food if you share your secret," the town clerk replied.

"I have a good one," it said.

"Then you will feast." Maynard leaned forward and unhooked the latch on the cage.

Eloise glanced up to the gallery and saw Roland had taken a seat next to her father. He was not supposed to be there, but if anyone had spotted him, they gave no indication. Roland caught her look and raised a finger to his lips. She nodded back.

At the front, the Motley held out its hand for Maynard to take. They touched, but the town clerk did not jolt or spasm as he had last time. A look of confusion spread across his face.

"You come closer, mister man." the Motley said.

And he did. Maynard leaned his head down towards the doll, as if it were about to whisper its secret to him.

The Motley raised itself up, so that its head was above the town clerk's. Maynard had no way of seeing its teeth emerge from behind those strange, mangled lips. A fraction of a second before it struck, some of the councillors understood. Shouts went up, but it was too late for Maynard. The Motley's fangs came down on the side of his face, and a red haze sprayed up onto its patchwork skin.

There was pandemonium in the room. Some screamed, some leapt to their feet toppling chairs around them. Next to Eloise, Oliver Hemsworthy backed away, wide-eyed, transfixed by the butchery ahead of him, but knowing he needed to move away, fast.

Eloise had expected councillors to rush to Maynard's aid. Several approached, and the Motley raised its head and hissed viciously at them, spitting Maynard's blood in their direction. Timidly, they retreated. None were prepared, it seemed, to risk personal harm to protect their leader.

Maynard lay on his side and the Motley berserked its way from the face to the neck and the chest. The spray and splash of Maynard's insides followed its mouth like little red fountains, each snap of its jaw producing another burst of blood.

There was a crush at the exit to the assembly room as councillors fled.

Eloise sat in place, watching the Motley eat, occasionally glancing up to the gallery to see her father's reaction. The old man was almost impassive, only furrowing his brow at the scene below, as if sensing a misplaced note in a symphony.

The sounds of human flight and fright dissipated, almost as quickly as they arose. With the councillors gone, only Eloise and the Motley were left in the expansive hall. The doll slowed its feasting, as if sensing urgency was no longer required. What remained of the cadaver rocked to the rhythm of its inquisitive teeth. The front of Maynard's body now resembled a soft fruit, peeled and opened.

Eloise felt nothing for him. The Motley had shown Maynard Rachael's fate many times over, but the old man had chosen to conceal the truth. They couldn't have members of the town council, his own friend no less, being thrown into the stocks, could they? Instead, he used the situation to his advantage and sought to settle old scores.

There was a clatter from behind, and Eloise turned to see Roland manoeuvering her father's wheelchair through the broken doors.

She got up and met them in the aisle. Roland stopped and Eloise bent to be at eye level with her father. She took his hand in hers and patted it. "Rachael arrived early, didn't she Dad?"

"Silly, silly girl." It wasn't clear if he was referring to Rachael or his own daughter.

"She arrived early, so she came to the house to see if I was there." Eloise continued, "and you told her to come in and wait. She didn't want to. She'd sensed something wrong in you long before. Rachael was smart like that. I was blind to your demons, but she could see them, even if she wasn't able to put them into words."

"I'm thirsty. Get me a drink, girl."

She ignored him. "Rachael came into the house and you did terrible things. Unspeakable things. She never came out again, did she, Father?" She spat out the final word at him, as if to expel their relationship, to deny it had ever been part of her.

"I said, get me a drink!" He was shouting now, fury coursing through his every word.

"We know, Dad. The Motley showed Roland. And Roland told me."

"You're a disgrace, girl. Get me . . . "

"I found her. Buried in the garden. You put the fishing rod in her hand, didn't you? That was your little joke, wasn't it? Did that make you laugh, Dad?"

He began to pant, short shallow gulps of air taken through clenched teeth, "Take me home."

"No more laughing. Rachael deserves that, at the very least."

She stood, took one wheelchair handle, and Roland took the other.

The Motley had stopped eating Maynard and now stared down the aisle through cross-stitched eyes.

"Bad man," it said. "I can smell."

A few metres away from the doll, both Roland and Eloise gave the chair a firm push, and it rolled to the Motley.

"Bad man," it said again, grinning, hissing, baring its bloodstained teeth.

HONORABLE MENTIONS

Broaddus, Maurice "The Norwood Trouble," *Out There Screaming*.

Collins, Nancy A. "The Drive Invasion: A Short Feature," *The Drive-In: Multiplex*.

Coney, S. L. "Wild Spaces," novella chapbook.

Dries, Aaron "We Called It Graffitiville," (novella) *Vandal: Stories of Damage*.

Evenson, Brian "It Does Not Do What You Think It Does," *Mooncalves*.

Ford, Jeffrey "Pretty Good Neighbor," Reactor, May 24.

Hirshberg, Glen "Dry and Ready" *Christmas and Other Horrors*.

Hughes, Charlie "Fell Mill," *Horror Library Volume 8*.

Jones, Stephen Graham "The Night We Made it to the Horror Show," *The Drive-In: Multiplex*.

Kadrey, Richard "The Ghost of Christmases Past." *Christmas and Other Horrors*.

Khaw, Cassandra "The Salt Grows Heavy," novella chapbook.

King-Cargile, Gillian "Chainsaw: As Is," Pseudopod May 26.

Koch, Joe "By Their Bones Ye Shall Know Them," *Aseptic and Faintly Sadistic*.

Little Badger, Darcie "The Scientist's Horror Story," *Never Whistle at Night*.

Manusos, Lyndsie "The Sound of Reindeer," Tor.com December 13.

Miller, Sam J. "If Someone You Love Becomes a Vurdalak," The Dark, July #98.

Mohamed, Premee "Preservation of an Intact Specimen," *Wilted Pages*.

Mohr, Jacob Steven "Empty Shells on a Cold Shore," CHM #38 August.

Murray, Lee "Despatches," novella chapbook.

Oates, Joyce Carol "The Return," *Harper's Magazine*, August.

Ogundiran, Tobi "Jackal, Jackal," *Jackal, Jackal*.

Partridge, Norman "An Ill Wind Knows Your Name," *The Drive-In: Multiplex*.

Patten, Steve Van "Dead Man Country," *Blackened Roots*.

Pelayo, Cynthia "It's Only a Movie," *The Drive-In: Multiplex*.

Piper, Hailey "There is No Cult, This is No Classic," *What Draws Us Near*.

Read, Sarah "Good Bones," *Darkness Beckons*.

Rickert, M. "The Lord of Misrule," *Christmas and Other Horrors*.

Rucker, Lynda E. "Knots," *Now It's Dark*.

Slatter, Angela "The Tissot Family Circus," *Twice Cursed*.

Strantzas, Simon "Clay Pigeons," (novella) *Only the Living Are Lost*.

Tremblay, Paul "If Dillon Believed in Any Kind of Ghosts," *Unspeakable Horror 3*.

Triantafyllou, Eugenia "Six Versions of My Brother Found Under the Bridge," Uncanny 54.

Turnbull, Cadwell "Wandering Devil," *Out There Screaming*.

Williamson, Chet "Blood Harmony," *The Drive-In: Multiplex*.

Wise, A. C. "Carcossa! The Musical," *What Draws Us Near*.

Wise, A. C. "The Dark House," Tor.com May 24.

York, Jessie Ann "Dimorphism," *Seasons of Severance*.

Young Wolf, Royce K. "Human Eater," *Never Whistle at Night*.

ABOUT THE AUTHORS

Patrick Barb is an author of weird, dark, and horrifying tales, currently living (and trying not to freeze to death) in Saint Paul, Minnesota. His published works include the dark fiction collections *The Children's Horror* and *Pre-Approved for Haunting*, the novellas *Gargantuana's Ghost*, and *Turn*, as well as the novelette *Helicopter Parenting in the Age of Drone Warfare* (Spooky House Press). Visit him at patrickbarb.com.

The *Oxford Companion to English Literature* describes Ramsey Campbell as "Britain's most respected living horror writer," and the *Washington Post* sums up his work as "one of the monumental accomplishments of modern popular fiction." In 2015 he was made an Honorary Fellow of Liverpool John Moores University for outstanding services to literature. His latest novels are *Somebody's Voice, Fellstones, The Lonely Lands,* and *The Incubations.* His Brichester Mythos trilogy consists of *The Searching Dead, Born to the Dark,* and *The Way of the Worm.* His most recent collections are *Fearful Implications,* a two-volume retrospective roundup (*Phantasmagorical Stories*) and *The Village Killings and Other Novellas.* His non-fiction is collected as *Ramsey Campbell, Probably* and *Ramsey Campbell, Certainly,* while *Ramsey's Rambles* collects his video reviews, and *Six Stooges and Counting* is an appreciation of the Three Stooges. *Limericks of the Alarming and Phantasmal* is a history of horror fiction in fifty limericks.

Ray Cluley's work has appeared in various magazines and anthologies and has been reprinted several times, such as in Ellen Datlow's *Best Horror of the Year* series, Steve Berman's *The Year's Best Gay Speculative Fiction*, and *Benoît Domis's Ténèbres* series. He has won the British Fantasy Award for Best Short Story ("Shark! Shark!") and has since been nominated for Best Novella (*Water for Drowning*) and Best Collection (*Probably Monsters*). His second collection, *All That's Lost*, is now available from Black Shuck Books. He lives in Wales with his partner and two troublesome but adorable cats.

Tananarive Due is an award-winning author who teaches Black Horror and Afrofuturism at UCLA. A leading voice in Black speculative fiction for more than twenty years, Due has won a Bram Stoker Award, a World Fantasy Award, a Shirley Jackson Award, an American Book Award, an NAACP Image Award, and a British Fantasy Award. Her books include *The Reformatory, The Wishing Pool and Other Stories, Ghost Summer: Stories, My Soul to Keep,* and *The Good House.* She and her late mother, civil rights activist Patricia Stephens Due, co-authored *Freedom in the Family: A Mother-Daughter Memoir of the Fight for Civil Rights.*

She was an executive producer on Shudder's groundbreaking documentary *Horror Noire: A History of Black Horror.* She and her husband/collaborator, Steven Barnes, wrote one episode for Jordan Peele's "The Twilight Zone", and two segments of Shudder's anthology film *Horror Noire.* They also co-wrote the graphic novel *The Keeper*, illustrated by Marco Finnegan. Due and Barnes co-host a podcast, "Lifewriting: Write for Your Life!"

Brian Evenson is the author of a dozen and a half books of fiction, most recently the collection *None of You Shall Be Spared* from Weird House and the microcollection *Black Bark* from Black Shuck Press. His collection *Song for the Unraveling of the World* won the Shirley Jackson Award and the World Fantasy Award and was a finalist for the *Los Angeles Times'* Ray Bradbury Prize. Other recent books include *The Glassy, Burning Floor of Hell* and *A Collapse of Horses. Last Days* won the American Library Association's RUSA award for Best Horror Novel of 2009. *The Wavering Knife* won the International Horror Guild Award for best collection. He is also the recipient of three O. Henry Prizes, an NEA fellowship, and a Guggenheim Award. A new collection, *Good Night, Sleep Tight* will be published by Coffee House Press in 2024. He lives in Los Angeles and teaches in the Critical Studies Program at CalArts.

Christopher Golden is the *New York Times* bestselling author of such novels as *Road of Bones, All Hallows, Ararat,* and *The House of Last Resort.* With Mike Mignola, he is the co-creator of the *Outerverse* comic book universe, including such series as *Baltimore* and *Joe Golem: Occult Detective.* He has also written for film, television, video games, and animation, and he co-wrote and co-directed the Audible original series *Slayers: A Buffyverse Story.* He was born and raised in Massachusetts. His work has been nominated for the British Fantasy Award, the Eisner Award, and multiple Shirley Jackson Awards. Golden has been nominated for the Bram Stoker Award ten times in eight different categories, and won twice.

Scotland-based author Helen Grant writes Gothic novels and short supernatural stories. Her most recent novels are the Dracula Society's Children of the Night Award-winning *Too Near The Dead* and *Jump Cut,* about a notorious lost movie, *The Simulacrum.* Some of her recent short fiction includes "A Curse is a Curse" and "The Professor of Ontography", both of which appeared in Titan anthologies in 2023. The latter title is, of course, a tribute to M. R. James.

Glen Hirshberg's novels include *The Snowman's Children, Infinity Dreams, The Book of Bunk,* and the *Motherless Children* trilogy. He is also the author of five widely praised story collections: *The Two Sams, American Morons, The Janus Tree, The Ones Who Are Waving,* and *Tell Me When I Disappear.* Hirshberg is a three-time International Horror Guild Award Winner, five-time World Fantasy Award finalist, and he won the Shirley Jackson Award for the novelette, "The Janus Tree." Check out his Substack at https://glenhirshberg. substack.com/. He lives with his family and cats in the Pacific Northwest.

Carly Holmes lives and writes in a small village on the banks of the river Teifi in west Wales, UK. Her debut novel *The Scrapbook* was shortlisted for the International Rubery Book Award, and her debut story collection

Figurehead was published in limited edition hardback by Tartarus Press in 2018. The paperback edition was published by Parthian Books in 2022. Her second novel *Crow Face, Doll Face*, an uncanny tale of flawed mothers, unfulfilled dreams, and dysfunctional families, was published in 2023. Her prize-winning short prose has appeared in journals and anthologies such as *Ambit*, *The Ghastling*, *Shadows & Tall Trees*, and *Black Static* and has previously been selected for Ellen Datlow's *Best Horror of the Year Volume 11* and *14*.

Andrew Hook has had over a hundred and eighty short stories published, with several novels, novellas, and collections also in print. Recent books include a collection of literary short stories, *Candescent Blooms* (Salt Publishing), and *Commercial Book* (Psychofon Records): a collection of forty stories of exactly one thousand words in length inspired by the songs from the 1980 record "Commercial Album" by The Residents. The novel *Secondhand Daylight*, written in collaboration with Eugen Bacon, was published in 2023 by Cosmic Egg Publishing. Andrew can be found at www.andrew-hook.com

Charlie Hughes writes dark suspense and horror stories. He lives in South London with his wife and two children. Since taking up writing in 2016, his work has appeared in *Ellery Queen Mystery Magazine*, *The Magazine of Fantasy & Science Fiction*, *Cosmic Horror Monthly*, and Mark Morris's anthology *Close to Midnight*, among other venues.

Several of Hughes's stories, including "The Motley," are inspired by his hometown of Shipston-on-Stour, Warwickshire, England. He hopes the locals forgive him.

You can find Hughes on Twitter/X at @charliesuspense, and a full list of publications at charliehugheswriting.blogspot.com.

Stephen Graham Jones is the *New York Times* bestselling author of some thirty-five novels and collections, novellas, and comic books. Most recent are *Earthdivers* and *The Angel of Indian Lake* and *I Was a Teenage Slasher* and *True Believers*. Stephen lives and teaches in Boulder, Colorado.

Paleontologist and fantasist Caitlín R. Kiernan is a two-time recipient of both the World Fantasy and Bram Stoker awards. Their novels include *The Red Tree* and *The Drowning Girl: A Memoir,* and their short fiction has been collected in more than twenty volumes, including *The Ape's Wife and Others* and *The Dinosaur Tourist.*

Adam L. G. Nevill was born in Birmingham, England, in 1969 and grew up in England and New Zealand. His novels *The Ritual, Last Days, No One Gets Out Alive,* and *The Reddening* were all winners of The August Derleth Award for Best Horror Novel. He has also published three collections of short stories, with *Some Will Not Sleep* winning the British Fantasy Award for Best Collection, 2017.

Imaginarium adapted *The Ritual* and *No One Gets Out Alive* into feature films and more of his work is currently in development for the screen.

Nevill lives in Devon, England. More information about him and his books is available at: www.adamlgnevill.com.

H. V. Patterson lives in Oklahoma and writes speculative fiction and poetry. She has work published or upcoming in *Etherea Magazine, Star*Line, Haven Speculative,* and *Wyldblood Press,* as well as several anthologies. Her poem, "Mother; Microbes," was selected for the inaugural volume of *Brave New Weird* from Tenebrous Press. She's a cofounder of Horns and Rattles Press, and you can find her on X @ScaryShelley and on Instagram @hvpattersonwriter.

Priya Sharma writes short stories and novellas. She is the recipient of several British Fantasy Awards and Shirley Jackson Awards, and a World Fantasy Award. Her work has appeared in venues such as Tor.com (now Reactormag. com), *Interzone, Black Static,* and *Weird Tales*. She lives in the UK where she works as a medical doctor. More information can be found at www. priyasharmafiction.wordpress.com.

Steve Rasnic Tem's writing career spans over forty-five years, including more than 500 published short stories, seventeen collections, eight novels, miscellaneous poetry, and plays. His collaborative novella with his late wife,

Melanie, *The Man On The Ceiling*, won the World Fantasy, Bram Stoker, and International Horror Guild awards in 2001. He has also won the Bram Stoker, International Horror Guild, and British Fantasy Awards for his solo work, including *Blood Kin*, winner of 2014's Bram Stoker for novel. In 2024 he received the Horror Writers Association Lifetime Achievement Award.

E. Catherine Tobler's short fiction has appeared in *Clarkesworld*, *The Magazine of Fantasy and Science Fiction*, *Beneath Ceaseless Skies*, *Apex Magazine*, and others. Her novella, *The Necessity of Stars,* was a finalist for the Nebula, Utopia, and Sturgeon Awards. She currently edits *The Deadlands*.

Neil Williamson lives in Glasgow, Scotland. His work has been shortlisted for British Science Fiction Association, British Fantasy and World Fantasy awards, and his most recent offering is an urban folk horror novella, *Charlie Says* (Black Shuck Books). "The Salted Bones" is part of a sequence of tales featuring weird bequests and inheritances. Some of these have been published in magazines such as *Black Static, The Dark, Weird Horror,* and *Interzone Digital*, and there are more forthcoming in 2024.

ACKNOWLEDGMENTS OF COPYRIGHT

ABOUT THE EDITOR

Ellen Datlow has been editing science fiction, fantasy, and horror short fiction for forty years as fiction editor of OMNI Magazine and editor of *Event Horizon* and SCIFICTION. She currently acquires short stories for Reactor and novellas for Tor.com. In addition, she has edited about one hundred science fiction, fantasy, and horror anthologies, including the annual *The Best Horror of the Year* series, and most recently *Body Shocks: Extreme Tales of Body Horror, When Things Get Dark: Stories Inspired by Shirley Jackson, Christmas and Other Horrors,* and *Fears: An Anthology of Psychological Horror.*

She's won multiple World Fantasy Awards, Locus Awards, Hugo Awards, Bram Stoker Awards, International Horror Guild Awards, Shirley Jackson Awards, the Splatterpunk Award, and the 2012 Il Posto Nero Black Spot Award for Excellence as Best Foreign Editor. Datlow was named recipient of the 2007 Karl Edward Wagner Award, given at the British Fantasy Convention for "outstanding contribution to the genre," was honored with the Life Achievement Award by the Horror Writers Association, in acknowledgment of superior achievement over an entire career, and honored with the World Fantasy Life Achievement Award at the 2014 World Fantasy Convention.

She lives in New York and co-hosts the monthly Fantastic Fiction Reading Series at KGB Bar. More information can be found at www.datlow.com, on Facebook, and on twitter as @EllenDatlow. She's owned by two cats.